Praise for
An Affair with Mr. Kennedy

"An intriguing debut. . . . A satisfying romance featuring a genuinely original pair of lovers and sparkling supporting characters against an unusual social and political background." —*Publishers Weekly*

"The sexy, smart characters will appeal to modern readers as much as the suspense. Their repartee and sensuality heat up the pages, promising a treat for readers." —*RT Book Reviews*

"A romance in every sense of that word. . . . Perfectly balanced between pace and plot but always and without a doubt character driven to a point that a reader is living the emotions of the characters and feeling the danger around them." —*Bookworm2bookworm*

"A brilliant historical romance that is totally different from the type you may be used to. . . . A totally delightful and provocative story. . . . Will grab your attention and keep you enthralled all the way to the end. This one's a keeper!" —*Romance Reviews Today*

"Sizzling hot. . . . An exciting, mysterious historical romance suspense that will steal your heart." —*Romance Junkies*

"Intriguingly suspenseful with unique dilemmas and a number of dangerous risks. . . . Stone has created a noteworthy setting for the series, one that is continuously attention-grabbing. Part romance and part mystery with a hefty dose of suspense, where each moment of the novel is imaginatively captivating." —*Single Titles*

ALSO BY JILLIAN STONE

An Affair with Mr. Kennedy

Available from Pocket Books

A DANGEROUS LIAISON

with

DETECTIVE LEWIS

JILLIAN STONE

Pocket Books

New York   London   Toronto   Sydney   New Delhi

Pocket Books
A Division of Simon & Schuster, Inc.
1230 Avenue of the Americas
New York, NY 10020

This book is a work of fiction. Names, characters, places, and incidents either are products of the author's imagination or are used fictitiously. Any resemblance to actual events or locales or persons, living or dead, is entirely coincidental.

First Pocket Books paperback edition September 2012

POCKET and colophon are registered trademarks of Simon & Schuster, Inc.

For information about special discounts for bulk purchases, please contact Simon & Schuster Special Sales at 1-866-506-1949 or business@simonandschuster.com.

The Simon & Schuster Speakers Bureau can bring authors to your live event. For more information or to book an event, contact the Simon & Schuster Speakers Bureau at 1-866-248-3049 or visit our website at www.simonspeakers.com.

Manufactured in the United States of America

10 9 8 7 6 5 4 3 2 1

ISBN 978-1-4516-2905-7
ISBN 978-1-4516-2908-8 (ebook)

For Joy!
A most wonderful sister who deserves
an exclamation point.

Acknowledgments

Writing a novel is often a lonely business, but the process has been made into a pleasure with my encouraging and brilliant new editor, Kate Dresser. I am so grateful to have her. And to everyone in marketing and publicity, you all did such an amazing job on my debut release. I can't let this acknowledgment go to print without a word about my agent, Richard Curtis, who mentors when I require mentoring and who makes me laugh when I very much need to laugh.

I am also grateful to a talented group of writers who also happen to be my friends. A special thank-you to Cheryl O'Donovan for your writer's eye and kind encouragement. To the wonderful Brenna Aubrey, Kristen Koster, and Tessa Dare, who made my debut a memorable one. And my lovely Chimes ladies: Mary Ambra, Margaret Taylor, Pamela Scheibe, and Stephanee Ryle. Lastly, a nod to the awesome writers and bloggers at Get Lost in a Story: Angi Morgan, Cat Schield, Heather

Snow, Maureen McGowan, and Simone St. James. What a year we're having, ladies!

As is the case with some of the more *historically advanced elements* in The Gentlemen of Scotland Yard series, I have taken off into occasional flights of historical fantasy. What can I say? These intrepid detectives need their gadgets.

∽ Chapter One

"You've got bollocks the size of St. Paul's dome to work this lane."

Raphael Lewis leaned against the lamppost and struck a match. "Kiss my arse, Flynn." He lit the posh kind of cigarette fancied by male prostitutes.

"Nah, not me, but one of the mollies wouldn't mind." Flynn Rhys stepped out of the shadows.

If there was a seamier side to working for Scotland Yard, this was it. Rafe blew out the match. "Bloody entrapment if you ask me." The stink of sulfur hung in the air. He and Flynn had taken up a post yards from 35 Cleveland Street, the most exclusive molly-house in town. There had been an embarrassing spate of blackmail of late, all of it involving men posted to high-level government work.

Their assignment was to apprehend a few top-level peers or Whitehall officials. Randy toffs with a taste for younger men. Simple enough. Arrest the molly chasers, toss them in the lockup, put a scare in them. Word would soon get out.

He opened a small paper sack, popped a butterscotch in his mouth, and passed the sweets over. "Care for a taste, Mr. Rhys?"

Flynn chewed on a toffee. "Don't tempt me to bugger you, Mr. Lewis."

Rafe exhaled a trail of smoke into the night. The summer heat lingered in the tepid darkness. "Spiffing job, by the way. You cuffed that last bloke smooth as silk."

A well-appointed carriage, a clarence, rounded the corner and slowed. "Shall we try for another?" Flynn gave a wink and moved off into the alley known to familiars as Shag Row.

The driver pulled beyond the streetlamp and stopped. Rafe stuffed the sweets in his pocket, pushed off the post, and sauntered over. Some frequenters preferred a boff in the close confines of their coach. Rafe approached the door, catching a glimpse of a wraith in motion as Flynn quietly rounded the rear of the vehicle.

The carriage window slid open. *"Such manly grace, is this strange flower for rent?"*

Rafe recognized his cue. *"Welcome to my arms, thou best of men."* He squinted at the dark silhouette of a man wearing a bowler. The genteel nobs often used the homoerotic verse of the poets to identify one another.

A slow curve edged a generous mouth—all he could see of what appeared to be a handsome enough gent. The man's whispered breath smelled of good tobacco and aged whiskey. *"Such prodigious beauty is—"*

Rafe tipped his chin to feign a smile while he racked his brain for a line of sonnet. "—*the very heart of vice and sweet sins. But not for free.*"

"Pay you two and eight, and not a farthing more." The gentlemen leaned into the light from the coach lantern.

Rafe placed an elbow on the open window. "If I had a beauty like yours at home, friend, I'd let the wifey polish the knob."

"Get in, Rafe."

He squeezed into the seat beside the number two Yard man himself, Chief Detective Inspector Zeno Kennedy. The man had recently made quite a name for himself, breaking up a dangerous ring of Fenian dynamiters.

The senior detective grinned. "How goes the sweep?"

Rafe shrugged. "Caught a very big fish."

"How big?"

"Prince Eddy's friend. Had to cut him loose."

Zeno sucked air between his teeth. "Melville will hear about that one. Where's Flynn?"

"Evening, sir." His partner in trickery appeared at the door.

"Pop inside, then." Flynn climbed in and pulled down the folding seat. Zeno rapped on the roof and they lurched off.

Zeno shook his head. "So you two jollied up to Lord Somerset. Not bad for a couple of Night Jacks."

"I prefer Agent Provocateur." Rafe studied Zeno. He understood the enigmatic Yard man better than anyone else with a desk at 4 Whitehall Place, with the possible exception of William Melville, director of Special Branch.

A shaft of pale gaslight illuminated Zeno's jawline, enough for Rafe to make out a twitch. Never one for small talk, Zeno got straight to it. "Quite a grisly scene in the House of Commons. Tried to hold the press off." Kennedy handed over a folded news sheet. "Unsuccessfully."

Rafe opened up the *Manchester Guardian* and squinted at the headline.

MURDERED MP FOUND IN
COMMONS CHAMBER

He skimmed the article. "Our victim's name is William Patterson Hudson. A caretaker found the poor bloke around teatime," he summarized. "Seems the perpetrator placed the remains, neat as you please, on his regular bench in the House of Commons chamber."

"In broad daylight?" Flynn snorted. "Bloody bold for a murderer."

Rafe dipped his head as the carriage turned onto Millbank. Westminster Palace loomed straight ahead. "So what do we know about Hudson personally?"

Zeno grimaced. "Cursory at the moment. Made his fortune in banking and railway investments." The carriage slowed and the senior-ranked detective released the latch. Exiting the coach, he led them through the imposing limestone facade of the Members' Entrance of Parliament. "Hudson won his seat in government four years ago. There's a residence in town and an estate in Canterbury."

Inside the palace, Zeno ushered them past guards at the rubble arch and up the stairs to a bench seat in the third tier of the chamber. Lab technicians, some with magnifying glasses, combed the aisles for evidence.

Rafe scanned rows of green leather benches. Nothing but empty seats. "Where's the body?"

Zeno stepped to one side so both detectives could get a good look. As a matter of course, corpses were an integral part of the job, but this one set both Rafe and Flynn back on their heels.

On a seat midway down the aisle, a disembodied head had been placed neatly atop two feet soaked in blood. The sight was at once comical and disturbing, as if the head grew directly out of a pair of fashionable, narrow-toed shoes.

Rafe swept his jacket back, placing his hands on his hips. "Nicely ghoulish."

Flynn nodded. "Any idea who might want him done for?"

Zeno shook his head. "A man of his wealth and power is bound to have enemies." He settled onto a step just above Rafe and Flynn.

The lab man in charge held up an evidence case. "All right if we move the remains, Mr. Kennedy?"

Zeno raised a brow and turned to Rafe and Flynn. "Seen enough?"

Rafe settled onto his haunches. "Let's have a look at the cuts." The evidence collector lifted the bloodless head.

Rafe removed a pencil stub from his inside pocket to pull back the gentleman's hose. The wounds on both the ankles and the neck were clean, pressed together, as if they were done by a heavy blade or machinery. "Do we know if Hudson was a large man—tall in stature?" After receiving a shrug and a few blank looks, Rafe turned to the lab man. "Is there some way to estimate the victim's height?"

The technician placed the head into a plain sackcloth evidence bag, then unfolded a metal pocket ruler. He measured one of the shoes. "Tall, sir. My guess would be something over six feet."

Rafe nodded. "And the gauge of the railway tracks in Kent?"

Zeno stared at Rafe, a glint in his eye. "Does anyone here know railroad gauges?"

Another lab assistant poked his head up from the aisle below. "Different rail lines have different track gauges, no standard as yet, Mr. Kennedy." The young man took off his cap and scratched his head. "Something between four feet nine inches and a bit over five feet, if I remember right."

Rafe did not check the upward tug at the ends of his mouth. "So it would be possible to lay a tall man across a narrow-gauge track . . . train comes along . . ."

"Off with his head." Flynn flourished a macabre grin of his own. "And feet."

Even Zeno's mouth twitched. "I've conscripted our lab director into field service. He's in Kent interviewing the dead man's family. I received a wire from Archie earlier this evening. It seems Hudson may have gone missing in the middle of the night."

Rafe leaned against a bench. "Abducted from his bedchamber?"

The chief inspector scanned the surroundings and exhaled. "Appears so." His gaze landed on Flynn. "Archie's a good man, but he's a scientist. He doesn't have your instincts. I need you to meet Archie in Canterbury." Zeno removed a packet from an inside breast pocket and passed it over to Flynn. "There's some per diem in there as well as contact information.

"And take Alfred with you." Zeno nodded to the lumbering bloodhound snuffling along the aisle of bench seats below them. "I'd say a walk down the rails between Hudson's estate and Canterbury station should turn up the missing torso."

"Saves a muck about the countryside." Rafe winked at his partner. "At least you're off Cleveland Street."

Zeno angled toward Rafe. "You don't enjoy trifling with the light-foot lads?"

"Poking about in a man's bedroom affairs?" Rafe scoffed. "Not much glory enforcing the Criminal Law Amendment Act."

Zeno offered a grunt of agreement. "Damned blackmailer's charter is what it is."

They left the House of Parliament stringing the hound behind them. Zeno dropped Flynn and the Yard dog off at the detective's flat in Soho. "I expect twice-daily reports, Mr. Rhys."

Rafe barely caught the tip of Flynn's cap as the carriage lurched off. "Where to now?" he asked.

"Charing Cross station." Zeno's gaze hardened. "Flynn and I will work the case from here. You're off to Edinburgh."

Edinburgh? Good God. Rafe squirmed uncomfortably at the thought. "Working a case in my home territory? Who—?" Call it a flash of intuition or insight, whatever it might be, but he thought he might know the reason why, and it sent a chill down his spine. "Ambrose Greyville-Nugent."

"You're on your game tonight, Rafe."

Ambrose was arguably an important inventor and without a doubt the richest industrialist in all of Scotland. The man had made his fortune in steam-powered farm and mining equipment. Days ago, Rafe had been stunned to read of the prominent mogul's horrific accidental death. "My family became somewhat friendly with the Greyville-Nugents over the years."

Zeno lifted a brow. "Is that so?"

"The Greyville-Nugent property borders ours in Queensferry, West Lothian. I was just a lad when Ambrose purchased the neighboring estate."

"Didn't you tell me you grew up in a castle?"

Rafe grinned. "No more than fifty rooms. A croft cottage by English standards."

Absently, Kennedy scanned the passing street scene and nodded. Clearly distracted, his mind was on more pressing matters. "One can never be sure, this early in an investigation, but a pattern may be developing. Two captains of industry dead in less than a week. Rather peculiar." A ray of light passed through the cabin, enough for Rafe to notice the sunrise over a block of terrace homes. Zeno's mouth formed a thin, grim line. "Melville doesn't believe in coincidence when it comes to murder."

Never one to disagree with the head of Scotland Yard's Special Branch, Rafe swallowed. "Can't say as I blame him." A painful knot formed in the pit of his belly. He didn't like where this assignment was headed. "I take it you surmise Greyville-Nugent's most unfortunate death by threshing machine was not accidental?"

"Taken together, these two murders may indicate a macabre scheme at work. One with a touch of grotesque wit—some sort of mad poetic justice." Zeno leaned forward. "Greyville-Nugent leaves behind an heiress, one who has made it publicly clear she intends to carry on her father's legacy. At this juncture, we are prepared to offer her protection."

"Francine Greyville-Nugent." Rafe grimaced. "Just like Fanny to carry on—business as usual."

"The young lady is unaware of our conjecture as yet. Until we have an inkling as to what is going on here, Melville and I thought it best to send up an agent. Do a bit of poking about, see if you can—"

"You realize I have a history with this girl—young lady?"

Zeno's stare bored into him. "What kind of history?"

Rafe steeled himself. "Rather awkward, I'm afraid."

Zeno's gaze narrowed further. "*How* awkward?"

He glanced outside the carriage. The pale dawn

illuminated a few shop-fronts as they traversed St. Giles Circus. Rafe shook his head. "Going to have to beg off on this one, Zeno."

"I might have switched you with Flynn, but it's too late. I haven't another man to spare. You're just going to have make the best of it." One side of Zeno's mouth twitched upward. "Catch up with relatives and friends. For now, all that is required of you is to guard Miss Greyville-Nugent with your life."

Rafe slumped in his seat. Dear God, fraternize with old chums and relations. Friends who had long ago turned away and a family who nearly disowned him. In fact, he wasn't exactly sure who he was on speaking terms with anymore. Rafe tallied up the number of relations who would be overjoyed to see him in Edinburgh and counted one. Aunt Vertiline.

Sensing his trepidation, Zeno shoved a packet into his hands. Absently, Rafe untied the string and flipped through a number of large banknotes. He opened a folded message written in code. "Contact names and safe houses."

"Greyville-Nugent's funeral is set for this afternoon. I understand rail travel to Edinburgh is down to seven and a half hours. If there are no delays en route, you should be able to attend the wake."

"How delightful." Rafe frowned.

Zeno's jaw twitched. "Closed casket if I understand right. The police report indicated Greyville-Nugent was up in a barn loft pitching sheaves into the feeder—demonstration of some sort—took a misstep and fell headlong into the machine. Struck the cylinder running full speed. He was instantly—" Kennedy halted midsentence. "You all right?"

Even in the dusky bleak light of early morning, he supposed he appeared a bit green around the gills. "Knew the man since childhood is all."

Zeno hesitated before plunging on. "He was instantly drawn into the teeth of the cylinder. His head and the upper portion of his body were reduced to a shapeless mass of crushed bone and flesh."

Rafe recalled a large, gregarious sort of fellow with a heavy moustache and a ready smile. A decent enough man who had treated him as a son after the earl died. Ambrose had always been kind to him, until Rafe spurned his daughter. "So, you want me to keep an eye on the young heiress, as well as poke about the accident scene—"

The carriage slowed as they reached the train station and Rafe jumped out. Kennedy's driver handed down a leather satchel. Zeno spoke from inside the carriage. "Had your man Harland pack a bag. Rather a surly chap."

"Ah, you noticed." Rafe gripped the satchel. "Keeps me in clean shirts and undergarments. I dare not ask for more."

The number two Yard man leaned forward to close the door. "These crimes, if they are indeed homicides, are rather like executions, wouldn't you say? Hate to think what kind of fiend might be out there, picking off wealthy industrialists."

Rafe studied his supervisor. "Fanny could very well find herself in grave danger," he said.

"The gravest." Kennedy rapped on the cabin roof.

∽ Chapter Two

"Simple, really." Fanny closed her eyes. "I shall just ignore him." Barely more than a whispered breath, her words were not quite soft enough to avoid the sharp ears of Vertiline Lewis.

"I cannot think why my nephew has decided to make an appearance on this mournful occasion, though I must admit I am rather glad to see him." Vertiline squinted, straining to read Fanny's expression through her mourning veil. "Please don't hold that against me, dear."

Fanny shivered, though she wasn't cold in the least. In the late afternoon, there was often a chill wind off the firth. But not this summer. "No, of course not, Vertiline." Her lower lip slipped out from under her bite. "I suppose someone in his family has to speak with him."

After cultivating a lingering disdain for the man, Fanny had finally given up on Raphael Lewis. For years she suffered untold indignities for the humiliation he had wrought in her life. But her sentiments for and about him had finally toppled to the correct level of contempt.

She hated him. Only that wasn't exactly true, even if she fancied it so. Truth be told, Fanny couldn't bring herself to hate anyone. Not even Rafe. She could, however, greatly dislike him.

Fanny followed the elderly woman's gaze as she turned to study her nephew, who stood on a rise above the ceremony grounds. Fanny gulped air and released her breath slowly. He had always been striking, even princely, but he had grown into a most imposing man indeed. Fanny peered out beyond the veil, vaguely aware of Vertiline's chatter. A wave of outright mortification crashed up against a horrid force of attraction for the arrogant St. Aldwyn, who was certainly no gentleman.

"Of course we all know he can be the devil's own son. You, more than most, my dear. How long has it been, since the . . . ?" Vertiline's eyes darted about as if she might find the proper word hiding in the trees or shrubbery of Greyfriars Kirkyard.

"Five years." Fanny took hold of the elder woman's arm and set off for the queue of vehicles parked along the road. They followed a path that cut neatly through lush green lawns dotted with slabs of stone. Reaching the drive, she helped Vertiline into her carriage and turned toward her own.

"Good afternoon, Fanny."

He stood a few feet away, hat in hand. She had almost obliterated his face from memory. But not quite. The offshore breeze pushed a thick shock of dark chestnut hair across his forehead. She took in a sharp breath. Five years had chiseled out the cheekbones and deepened the cleft in his chin, but otherwise he was the same as she remembered. Perfectly handsome.

From under a slash of dark brow, penetrating green eyes flecked with brown and gold watched her closely. The laughing eyes that had teased her so often during childhood appeared a good deal more chastened now, under the circumstances.

"Please accept my condolences—"

She pivoted on her heel and walked off toward her carriage. She would accept nothing from him. Neither his condolences nor his apology. Ever. She bit down hard on her lower lip and cringed inside. She could not still her racing heart, nor quell the nauseating sense of panic that fluttered through her body.

Safely tucked inside her own vehicle, Fanny let the rock and sway of the family carriage lull her deeper into a reverie of distraction. Her father's only living brother, Edward, and his ridiculous wife, Ophelia, rode with her.

"How you could bear to speak to the scoundrel, I have no—"

"I did not speak to him, Ophelia."

Vaguely, in the background, her uncle's voice filled the air space between them. "Mind you don't upset Fanny any further."

Her aunt barely paused long enough for a breath. Ophelia's chatter drifted in and out of her own confused and conflicted thoughts, to the point that she could not be sure which was more unnerving: her aunt's incessant blather, or a sudden disturbing recollection of Raphael Lewis the night of their engagement announcement.

She had received an urgent note to meet in Father's study, and had found him out on the small veranda. She remembered quite willfully stepping out onto the balcony alone in the most daring gown she had ever worn in her entire young life. She would never forget the look on his face as he turned toward her.

Raphael stared as though he had come across a creature in a wood. That startling moment when a person is confronted by something ephemeral and wild. No man had ever looked at her like that. Her rapid pulse flushed a trail of heat after each of his unabashed admirations. His gaze slipped from her lips, down her throat to the plunging décolleté of her gown. "My God, you are ravishing."

She blushed at the compliment, but somehow managed to keep her wits about her. "Indeed, look what goes on without you when you go away to school. If you had graced us with even one brief visit—"

"But I did return home." His eyes shimmered in the darkness. "You were off summering in Rome and Florence, if I remember correctly."

She tilted her chin. "If I recall *correctly*, you were to come abroad with us and were sorely missed. You can't imagine what Florence was like with Aunt Ophelia and Cousin Claire."

"Solamen miseris socios habuisse doloris." He held up a glass of spirit. "Misery loves company." He tossed back the rest of his drink and set the empty on the balustrade. "I'm sure you got on perfectly without me. Just as well—all those nude frescos and giant statues? Magnifi-

cent carved phalluses at every turn? A beautiful, over-stimulated female by my side?" His eyes sparkled and his grin stirred a tingle of excitement. "Why, you might have taken advantage of me."

The mistake she made was not laughing at the ribald remark, but answering truthfully. "I certainly would have tried, sir."

He took one long stride and caught her in his arms. "A kiss, *la mia belleza*?"

Boldly, she covered his mouth with hers and he returned her ardor. He held her against the wall and his tongue plunged deep as her body softened against him. He eased up enough to brush husky, whispered words over her mouth. "You would have had your way with me after our first tour of the Uffizi." He teased her lips farther apart with his thumb.

"A brief tryst between the Botticelli and the Raphael?" She opened again to his fervent intrusion, and quickly discovered how lovely it was to tangle with that velvet tongue of his.

Raphael nuzzled her cheek and temple. His fingers plunged into her hair. "I would have insisted on returning to the *pensione* for a long afternoon." His warm breath traveled over her cheek to her ear. "In my bed." She experienced an uncontrollable tremble through her body. He smiled, ever so slightly, before trailing soft caresses from the tip of her earlobe down the length of her neck.

He touched her in places he ought not touch. She did not protest as his fingers worked their way under the neckline of her dress. She inhaled so deeply the bodice loosed itself, or had he nudged the garment down? Her knees trembled as his fingers explored her flesh intimately, brushing over each curve.

"Fanny, much more of this and I will not be able to stop myself," His voice was gruff with desire. "I made a very grave mistake not accompanying you to Italy. Whatever happens, after tonight—" He lifted a breast and lowered his gaze. She felt like the statue of a half-clothed Sabine in the Loggia della Signoria, all falling folds of gown and wickedly exposed flesh. Her body shuddered as his warm breath wafted over sensitive skin. He dipped lower and used his mouth and tongue to tease up a rose-tinted nipple. A bolt of desire shot through her body, and like a foolish wanton, she had moaned her consent for more.

Even now, thinking back, her cheeks burned as she recalled the creak of a door as it opened and softly closed. A stifled giggle had come from inside the study and a muffled harrumph. Rafe lifted his mouth from her breast, caught her eye and slowly turned his head. She had followed the direction of his gaze through the small square panes of glass and met the stern disapproving glare of her father, standing with his current *maîtresse*.

Fanny jerked herself back to the present. Externally her body swayed gently with the roll of the carriage, while inside she quaked from such heated memories. She swallowed. Her departed father was barely covered with earth and she had spun herself off into a whirlwind of licentious, humiliating recollections.

During her lapse, Ophelia's vitriolic twaddle had risen

to a fever pitch. "The effrontery of the man, to make such an appearance. Shocking, really. How wretched you must be feeling. Poor dear."

She did not temper a pointed glare. "Ophelia, it would take every scrap of imagination you possess to fully realize my unsettled frame of mind."

There was a sharp inhale and a desperate searching about of watery eyes. The very sort of manipulation her aunt was so accomplished at. "Oh, Francine." She tsked. "Edward is right. I have agitated you. I have made you cross with me."

With each simpering apologia Fanny sunk deeper into the squabs of the upholstered bench. "Not cross, exactly, but you do go on so."

Ophelia tried a reproachful pout. "St. Aldwyn or no, he had no business turning up like he did and spoiling your dear father's burial service."

She sighed. "Mercifully, I did not see him until well after the Benedictus, so he didn't entirely ruin the ceremony." She made no eye contact across the cabin, preferring to gaze out over the blur of rooftops and chimney stacks visible from North Bridge. The stultifying air inside the coach had become insufferable. Fanny snapped open her fan, but found it impossible—no, ridiculous—to maneuver beneath the veil. A drop of perspiration trickled down between her breasts.

She unlatched the window and inhaled several deep breaths. The wind off the Firth of Forth might almost be called tropical, but she was grateful for a breeze. Until this afternoon, the weather had been unusually cool for summer. Now everything seemed balmy and unbearably . . . sultry.

Her aunt uttered something between a snicker and a snort. "I rather hope he tries to attend the wake, so we can turn him away at the door."

The suggestion brought Fanny upright in her seat. "We will do no such thing."

Her aunt's eyes widened in confusion. "We will not?"

She met the startled woman's gaze and considered the veritable garden of revenge fantasies she had tended over the years. "I believe the time has come to confront the Honorable Raphael Lewis St. Aldwyn." She quirked up the edges of her mouth. "He shall be brought to confession, but never fear, Ophelia, there will be no absolution."

"YOU MAY WELL be the only one in the hall, besides a perfect stranger, who will speak with me." Rafe winked at his aunt Vertiline.

"Yes, why is that?" Vertiline's fan fluttered about her face. "After all your sins, Raphael, I adore you still."

He leaned in. "Please do own up, Auntie." Rafe spotted the lovely Francine Greyville-Nugent in the corner, in front of several immense potted palms. She was striking in black. Sophisticated. A woman of the world. And that mass of bonny brown hair, all curls and softness twisted up on her head. How he longed to unmake those tresses one pin at a time. And those pouted lips. Good God, had he really forgotten how stunning she was?

"The simple truth is you make me laugh." Vertiline smirked.

His aunt's refreshingly candid answer prodded a further evaluation of his own feelings. The truth was he had pushed Fanny's memory far away. To a place where he did not yearn for her any longer. "Well then, I shall sharpen all my comic traits in order to please you."

Vertiline nodded toward a stately group standing to one side of an ornate turn of stair. "I see your mother has noticed your arrival."

The Dowager Countess St. Aldwyn stood beside the Earl St. Aldwyn, his brother Reginald. His small wife, Bess, who barely reached her husband's shoulder, peeped out at Rafe, sporting a conciliatory expression.

Rafe nodded a cool redress to the chilly stare he received from his mother, then warmed his expression for his brother's wife. "It appears my sister-in-law might speak with me. At the very least I shall have a translator." Bess managed a hint of smile while fluttering a pink fan over pinker cheeks.

A footman balancing a tray of small glasses filled with punch bowed. "I do hope this is spiked," Vertiline said as she raised a glass to sample. Rafe sauntered in the direction of his estranged relations. "Try not to look as if you're off to the gallows, Raphael."

Five years had passed. Even if this sorry handful of family had forgiven his gross misconduct, he would never be pardoned for the embarrassment. He wondered if his mother still refused to speak to him directly.

"Hello, Mother. Difficult to meet under such sorrowful circumstances." He checked her reaction carefully. A slight faltering of the eye, then a quick dart away. A handsome woman, he noted, with a great deal more gray blended through her hair, though she was otherwise gently marked by age. "But then . . . our meetings are always rather cheerless, wouldn't you agree?"

Reginald blustered for a moment before pivoting to their mother. "Rafe says hello. Pity about the circumstances—"

"What am I to make of such an appearance?" Hands trembling, the dowager Lady St. Aldwyn appeared to be on the edge of a swoon. "He'll be the talk of Edinburgh once again. And what of Fanny?" He thought she might choke on the words.

Rafe stepped closer. "Mother."

A single raised brow signaled his brother, who appeared to be counting figures silently in his head. "Oh yes, something about . . . appearances, badly done?"

Bess ceased batting her eyelashes long enough to wink at Rafe. She pressed a hand to her husband's arm. "Allow me, Reggie dear?"

Rafe sucked in a deep breath and exhaled gently. He did not entirely agree with his brother's choice of wife. She had always been an enthusiastic meddler in family affairs. And she was flirtatious with him. At times, most inappropriately so. He nodded a bow. "So kind of you, Bess."

This tedious business of not speaking had gone on for so long no one in the immediate family thought much about these repeated recitations. Rafe so despised the charade, he sought to torture his accommodating relatives by asking questions that required long-winded serpentine answers, which everyone was forced to endure. Twice.

"Please remind my dear mother I ventured home for holidays at least . . ."

His sister-in-law held up a single finger.

He cleared his throat. ". . . *once* in the past five years, enduring several days of—can one really call this *conversation?*"

Mother remained stone-faced, eyes darting about. "What plans has he to stay on after the funeral reception? Shall I have a room prepared?"

"Actually, I'm here in Edinburgh on police business."

Mother's eyes rolled back in her head.

Bess dropped her jaw.

Reginald grunted.

Rafe grinned. "I'm afraid I'm not at liberty to discuss the particulars," he edged his way around his small circle of family. "So please don't inquire." He searched the room for Fanny. Where was she? He scanned the parlor and the conservatory, which today served as a kind of informal supper room. Several buffet tables were piled high with tea sandwiches and sweet delicacies. His stomach growled. Ah, there she was by the punch bowl with a man Rafe recognized. The small hairs on the back of his neck certainly took notice. The attentive gentleman poured Ambrose Greyville-Nugent's surviving daughter a glass of blush-colored refreshment.

"If you'll excuse me." Rafe meandered off for a closer look.

Effacing himself among the guests at the sumptuous buffet, he trailed along in the queue toward the sweets—one in particular. Their eyes met across the table, between tiered platters heaped with delicate desserts. Rafe plucked a candied cherry from atop a petit four, dropped it onto his tongue, and savored the sweetness of her surprise.

Her brows met and mouth bowed before Rafe could brace himself. The expression was so . . . Fanny. She took his breath away, momentarily. Then she slipped into the throng of ravenous mourners and out of sight.

How far he had pulled away these past few years. There was a distance, an almost palpable estrangement from everyone, with the exception of Vertiline. In fact, after his fall from grace, Rafe had set out to prove to the family that he was a most incorrigible degenerate. That he had, in fact, done Fanny Greyville-Nugent a rather unique kindness. One or two of his relations had begun to tolerate him as the family libertine. Every noble bloodline should have one.

Trumping the five-year-old scandal was another equally distasteful aspect of his life—an affront to the legacy of St. Aldwyn and, arguably, the most unpardonable sin of all. He was now Detective Inspector Raphael Lewis. A title that was his alone.

His job was as dangerous as it was rewarding, a vocation that occupied every waking moment of his day. These last years had passed quickly, with very little thought given to the life he had given up in Edinburgh. And too, there were the plentiful and varied distractions of London.

"You've got a lot of nerve, St. Aldwyn—a man in such disfavor. Only a scoundrel would dare show his face on a day such as this."

He pivoted toward a sober-faced fellow of earnest expression. "Indeed," Rafe said, without demur. "I might even go so far as to call myself a cad." He recognized his accuser as the attentive gentleman hovering around Fanny in the supper room. Nigel Andrew Irvine. An old university chum—a rather capricious fellow, who at one time had sought out Rafe's friendship. "Nigel, I might say good to see you, but that would be entirely dishonest of me." Rafe adopted a bored, vaguely amused expression. "In keeping with our history, I shall leave that to you."

His challenger toggled one brow up, and the other down in a bewildering mixture of curiosity and disdain. "Smartest thing Fanny ever did was cry off her engagement to you."

"Ever the patient suitor, Nigel? What is it? Five years and still no answer?"

"Patience requires control over oneself," Nigel smirked. "Something you know nothing about."

Rafe pictured a brutal scenario involving Nigel's broken, bloodied nose, among other wounds. He shook off the thought, and refused to get worked up about an unhappy incident that happened long ago. *Unhappy incident* was putting it mildly. He had suffered through a trial of lies, deceit, and betrayal. A ruse he should have seen through, but hadn't, until it was too late.

"Ready to throw down the gauntlet, Nigel? Just say the word. I'm game anytime you are." He raked a steely gaze over the supercilious man. Irvine had always been considered attractive by the ladies, but he'd thickened some. He could imagine Nigel in a few years, with a potbelly and a harrumph.

"Since you appear to be on friendlier terms with Fanny . . ." Rafe used his most affable grin. "Might I ask you to intercede for me? I desperately need to speak with her on a private matter."

"Fanny is a woman of delicate sensibilities and fragile temperament—"

"So, you don't know her at all." Rafe studied the stiff, arrogant fellow. A wave of longing threatened his composure. He recalled the spirited little harridan of his youth, and the stunning young woman she had grown up to be.

Nigel's neck and shoulders stiffened. "Fanny is indisposed at the moment. Strain of the funeral and your undesirable presence, I'm afraid, has forced a brief respite." Nigel puffed himself up. "What you ask is not only impossible, I find it objectionable. I'm going to have to ask you to—"

"Message for the Honorable Raphael Lewis St. Aldwyn." A footman held out a salver. Rafe picked up the note card centered on the silver tray.

> *Meet me in my father's study. I believe you know the way.*

He smiled. Not quite so impossible, it would seem.

∾ Chapter Three

"How is it you are always around for the worst possible moments of my life?" She spoke with her back to Rafe. The door to the study swept shut with a soft click. Wavy panes of glass blurred her vision as she gazed to the veranda. The veranda. How often she had sat alone in her father's study and watched strangely beautiful ghosts make love on the balcony beyond these French doors.

"If you've changed your mind—" He cleared his throat. "Would you rather I leave?"

Fanny turned in time to catch a gesture. His large, elegant hand crumpled her note and swept backward. She raised her eyes, met his open gaze and raised brow. This was going to be awkward and uncivil. *Very* uncivil. The thought almost quirked a smile. Fanny set her chin high. "Oh no, you don't. I have waited years for this moment. You will stand here and take your punishment."

Those flashing green eyes perused the room as he

pressed his lips to together. She knew this innocent, trying-for-candid expression well. Rafe was hiding something. Likely one of those impudent grins of his.

"Might there be an old torture chamber in the cellar? I'm not as familiar with the town house as I was with your country manse."

She thought perhaps she growled.

"If there were such a dungeon, we might take up my drubbing there. No sense disturbing the guests with bellowing protests and cries of agony." He stepped into the center of room. "Or, I could dash downstairs for a cat-o'-nine-tails." The elusive grin surfaced. "Which would you prefer—Lieutenant Cutthroat?"

"Don't call me that." Her pulse throbbed from temple to toes. He was using their childhood nicknames, characters from the serial *Peter Simple*, to cajole her. Maybe also to pull rank—his moniker had been Captain Savage. But then, he had always relied rather heavily on his charismatic presence. His older brother, the current earl, didn't possess a single ounce of the legendary St. Aldwyn charm. By some peculiar trick of fate, Raphael had gotten it all.

He moved one step closer and she took one step back. "Don't you dare come near. I'll scream at the top of my lungs."

"You have every right to be furious with me. Perhaps you should never speak to me again. In fact, I advise it."

Flippant, deferential, and absurdly charming. And he so often got away with it. She imagined all the fashionable young ladies of London swooned over every self-deprecating word and adorable grin. But did they know the pain he could cause?

"Furious? Furious? I believe I am furious. Brought on by your"—she folded her arms under her chest and he took occasion to stare at her bosom—"infuriating behavior."

"I have fond memories of this room, that is until your father and his mistress caught us on the terrace." He jerked his gaze from her bosom to capture a flutter of eyelash, a twitch of her mouth—most likely every nuance of expression. This close study of his had always been unsettling.

She turned away and paced through the room, winding her way around overstuffed, comfortable chairs and hard-backed settees. "You cut me to the core on the night of our engagement ball. You didn't even have the decency to create some sort of pretense. Five years pass without a word from you, and now today, of all days, you turn up at Greyfriars for the burial?"

"Like a bolt out of the blue, wot? Quite a shock, I admit. Even for me. Gave Vertiline, Reggie, and Bess a stagger. And Mother, of course." He followed her about the room at a leisurely pace, keeping his distance. "You do look a bit jarred, as do Edward and Ophelia. Didn't see Cousin Claire anywhere about."

"We haven't been able to reach Claire. She's always off traveling—on the continent somewhere between countries, we assume."

"On a husband quest, is she? Has she . . ." He tortured a smile into something more sedate. "Slimmed down any?"

Fanny shot him a look. "Claire can't really help her size."

"Sorry. I'm told the Greeks worship the Rubenesque figure. You've filled out nicely, yourself." A slow gaze swept up and down. "In all the right places." He moved up behind her. "I see Nigel is still sniffing about—he's always been the bumptious sort."

"I'd rather you left Nigel out of any discussion between us." She brushed a wisp of curl off her face. "And he is not pompous. He's perfectly—"

"You aren't seeing him, are you?"

"And what if I am?"

He read her expression flawlessly. "None of my business." He snorted a chuckle. "But really, Fan—Nigel? You can't be serious."

She whirled around. "No, Rafe, it is you who can never be serious." She bit down on a raw lower lip. "Why are you here?"

"You will soon find I can be downright humorless when it comes to your safety." Dark green eyes glittered in the dim corner of the room as his gaze narrowed ever so slightly. "Unfortunately, the reason I am here may increase your trepidation, not ease it."

Her throat constricted. She didn't like the sound of that at all. Still, she was curious. "Go on."

"No matter what you or my family choose to believe of me, I did not arrive in Edinburgh—today of all days— to torture Francine Greyville-Nugent. I'm here to protect you."

"Protect me?" Her brow furrowed. "I believe I need protection *from* you, not *by* you."

He didn't crack a smile at her jibe. "I work for Special Branch, Scotland Yard."

"Yes. I've heard as much."

"At this point, I am here as a precaution—until we complete our investigation." Hesitantly, he searched for the right words. "Two men have died recently, both prominent industrialists. Yesterday, the severed head and feet of an MP were found in London. The gentleman apparently made his fortune in railroads. We have sent investigators up to Kent in search of a torso. Sorry to put it so grotesquely, but there it is."

She made a wide-eyed search of his face. "And you therefore believe my father to be the other casualty. Even if that were so, I'm in no jeopardy."

"You intend to carry on your father's various manufacturing enterprises, do you not? You have recently made public statements to that effect." She paled a bit and he moved closer.

"B-but it was an accident." She knotted her brows. "I read the reports, interviews with citizenry who witnessed the whole—"

"My assignment is to guard you with my life."

She was in agony. Her cheeks burned as her heart bled once again for her father. "This isn't fair. I've earned a bloody rant, a good scream at you." She wanted to rage—at him—Raphael Lewis, debaucher and forsaker of Fanny Greyville-Nugent, now returned as her protector? She turned away, then whirled around to face him.

"No, I shall have a good shout and finally get some answers. Why did you abandon me the night of the ball?"

"What did your father say? Did he explain anything?"

"I asked often enough—for a while." Fanny swallowed. "I can no longer badger a dead man—the answers are up to you now."

"Christ, Fan, there was only one course to pursue—allow you to cry off the engagement."

"Indeed. You did your gentleman's duty. But why, Rafe? I thought we had an understanding. I thought you cared for me—a great deal, actually."

His eyes never left her, even when she gritted her teeth and fisted her hands. "I do care, Fanny. I always have and I always will—beyond measure."

Once again, the room filled with ghosts from the past. The faint scent of Father's humidor, an argument barely recalled, the slam of the door as Rafe exited the study. She had always suspected the two men colluded together—to protect her from some hard-to-imagine, horrible truth.

Father had paced the floor of his study, and delivered the news. There would be no betrothal. The marriage was off. She remembered little else of the particulars, just Father blustering about while tears welled in her eyes. He had the appearance of trying not to bark orders, but couldn't help the timbre of his voice. *"It would best if you retired to your room. I shall make the announcement,"* he had said.

Dormant rage broke loose and caused her body to shake off the memory. "What a sniveling coward you are. You are the worst kind of deceiver, Rafe—one who claims affection even as he withdraws his promise."

Rafe swallowed. Apparently it was difficult hearing the truth. "Hard to believe anything could be worse than *sniveling coward*." He edged closer. "Fanny, the fact is I couldn't marry you."

"More pretense and evasion, Rafe? Does it never stop? Everyone wanted the marriage. My father loved you like a son. And certainly your family—"

"Marriage is impossible when one is already married."

A chill went through her. The room around her skewed. For a moment, she thought the earth might have tilted on its axis. "You"—she was aware of a faint ringing in her ears—"are married?"

"I *was* married." His gaze never wavered. "For a time."

The second her knees wobbled, Rafe rushed to her side and lowered her to a nearby settee. "Can I get you a glass of water?"

She shook her head. "Was?" The word rushed out in a whisper. "How can there be a was?" Her eyes darted here and there, blindly searching for answers. "Unless you abandoned her as well."

"Fanny, you're rather pale. I think you should take something."

"Whiskey." Her voice sounded shallow, disembodied. Slumped in a stupor, she watched him pour the Talisker's.

"She died six months after I weaseled out of our betrothal." Amber liquid sloshed about as he held out a tumbler.

"Poor girl." Numbly, she accepted the glass. "I don't

suppose you could have told me you loved another?" Rallying a bit, Fanny tried for something brave and cutting. "Tell me, Rafe, did she die of heartbreak?"

He stared at her for a long time. "Many times I wished to confide in you, Fanny, about my loss as well as my shame." Rafe tossed back his whiskey. "Should I have told you everything from the start—involve you in my disgrace? To what purpose, Fan? Truth is highly overrated when it comes to scandal. You have to let the murmurs and whispers run their course."

Tipping her glass, she inhaled the scent of burnt oak and took a sip. The smoky spirit laid a soft blanket of fire down her throat. "Years ago, you stole my heart, and now I shall never get it back."

There it was—the real tragedy in this whole affair. That she might never be able to trust again, wholly. She hiccupped. Drat. Now there would be a series of them. Fanny gazed at a wall of family portraits, their customary stares colder than usual. She refused to cry in front of him. "I'd like to be left alone."

"The past is done, Fanny. And for that matter, what could I possibly offer now to set things right between us? It seems quite impossible, and I honestly don't deserve your forgiveness."

Once more, Raphael Lewis attempted to muddle the issue. Perhaps the shock was too great, but she couldn't bear to hear anything more from the man. She lifted her gaze to his. "I want you gone from my house this instant. Get out, Rafe."

"I'm afraid you will have to put up with me, like it or

no." A kind of husky burr had crept back into his speech. "I will not bargain when it comes to your life, Fanny. If you do not cooperate with Scotland Yard, you'll be jailed for your own safety."

Her mouth dropped open. "You can't." She couldn't decide whether a grin or a grimace rode above that determined chin of his.

"I most certainly can. And I will."

How was this happening? Her small world had suddenly become too much to bear. Even as she grieved for her father, she was supposed to live in close proximity to this . . . reprobate, who claimed to be her protector.

Fanny sucked in a breath and exhaled. "Everything you've just told me is—" She hardly knew where to begin or what to say. "This worry for my safety is pure conjecture. For all you Scotland Yard men know, these deaths could be coincidental."

"William Melville, director of Special Branch, doesn't believe in coincidence, and neither do I. Hopefully, this should all be sorted out over the next week or two, then—"

She sat upright. "Week or two?"

"I will have to impose upon your hospitality. I'm afraid there is no other way to get round the inconvenience of having me about. You will be questioned extensively. I want a closer look at the scene of the accident. There won't be much preserved to investigate, but one never knows."

"This is ridiculous. I'm to be questioned? For what reason?"

"There are personages in your life, recent acquaintances, possibly, who may be connected to these events. My assignment is to safeguard the heiress to the Greyville-Nugent industrial empire and oversee a homicide investigation. No stone will be left unturned."

Thick with unshed tears and conflicting sentiments, the air in the study stifled. Her fan was missing. She tried another deep inhale and exhale, and still her heart pounded through every part of her body. "The guests will be leaving soon. I must return to the hall."

RAFE FOLLOWED HER down a sweeping turn of staircase to the foyer filled with attendees. The wake did appear to be breaking up. Fanny quietly took charge, directing staff to go after hats and wraps, respectfully thanking each guest. A bit of sniffling went on along with cheek kisses and whispered condolences. Dutifully, Rafe trailed alongside or behind. Fanny made an abrupt turn and nearly ran into him.

"Are you going to be shadowing me about and pestering me?"

Hands behind his back, Rafe straightened. "Yes."

"I suppose that is what detectives do. Trail after people like . . . dogs."

He held a grin in check. Fanny approached a man sporting a great deal of red facial hair and handed the gentleman his bowler. The man tapped the brim of his hat in his palm. "Pardon my intrusion, but might I have a word with you both? In private?"

Fanny darted a glance at Rafe as they retired to a shallow alcove nearby.

The odd, intrusive fellow pulled nervously at an auburn moustache. "Did I overhear Miss Greyville-Nugent call you a detective?"

Rafe edged closer to nudge Fanny.

"Arthur Douglas Poole, please meet Detective Inspector Rafe Lewis." She leaned in and lowered her voice. "It seems Scotland Yard has sent a man up to investigate Father's accident. According to Detective Lewis, I could be in some jeopardy."

"I'd like to keep that information quiet." Rafe eyeballed Fanny, who in turn, rolled her eyes. "No sense worrying anyone unduly."

The wary chap backed away, then hesitated. "Yes, well, I'd cooperate if I were you, miss—strange goings on lately."

Rafe lifted a brow. "Is that so?"

Rather abruptly, Nigel Irvine elbowed into their circle. "See me out, Fanny?"

She accepted the offered arm. "If you'll excuse me a moment?"

Mr. Poole nodded to Rafe and leaned in. "I did not wish to alarm the young lady, but . . ."

Rafe angled himself to better keep an eye on Fanny. She stood outside the door under the portico with Irvine. "But . . . ?"

"There have been several men lurking about the laboratory. James Lazar, my research partner, shooed them off again yesterday. One never knows—a good deal of industrial thievery about—crackpots every-where."

"Are your facilities hereabouts, Mr. Poole?"

"Why, I'm in research, Detective Lewis—at University, here in town."

"Would you mind if Miss Greyville-Nugent and I pay a call tomorrow? Say, late afternoon?"

The man positively beamed—or was that a sign of relief? "Stay to your right, third building west of McEwan Hall."

"Look forward to it." Rafe accompanied Poole out the entry and took up a spot beside Fanny—and a visibly disgruntled Nigel. "Why is he still here? What am I to make of this, Fanny?" Nigel whined.

"Make nothing of it," Fanny cajoled. "Now please, Nigel, say good night."

Rafe nodded affably. "Yes, please do say good night."

Nigel donned his hat, directing a warning glare at Rafe. "Contact me at once, should there be any trouble."

"Pishposh, Nigel, I expect no difficulties." Her scoff was gentle, though she firmly turned him toward his waiting carriage.

Rafe sidled closer. "Do you find that sneery, petulant look of his attractive?"

Fanny nodded to the last of her guests and exhaled a breath. "If you must know, I do not."

He followed her back inside to a set of mullioned doors that opened onto a formal garden. The silver cast to the sky had deepened into evening. Fanny stood with her nose to the squares of glass. A new flush of rose blooms was on dazzling display in the twilight. Rafe reached around her and pressed the latch of the door. Almost at once a myriad of spicy lemony scents drifted inside the house.

Rafe inhaled deeply. "Intoxicating, is it not?" He glimpsed a pretty upturn of lips before she caught herself and turned to him. "Am I to have a room made up for you?"

"I won't require a room—perhaps just a place to wash up. I would like to have a look at your bedchamber." He cleared his throat. "We are fairly certain the London victim was abducted in the middle of the night."

A bit dazed, Fanny turned up the stairs and stopped. "And where, might I ask, will you be sleeping?"

∞ Chapter Four

"Wake up, sir." A tentative prod to his shoulder nudged an eye open. His gaze traced the intricate designs of a Persian carpet and a curved leg of a gleaming side table, then settled on a lone Chinese vase.

Rafe sat up straight and blinked. He was in the Greyville-Nugent town house. Balancing a breakfast tray on her hip, the young maid viewed him curiously. "Miss Francine will be needing her chocolate, sir."

Stiff from sleep, Rafe ordered his body out of the chair blocking the entrance to Fanny's bedchamber. "Let me carry that."

"Oh no, sir—" Rafe whisked the tray out of the maid's hands as she protested, "Please, sir." The girl trailed behind him into the bedchamber. He set the tray beside a pale yellow striped chaise and pulled back the drapes. From the amount of light streaming into the room, he wagered it was late morning.

Straightaway, he inspected every corner and headed for the carved four-poster in the center of the room.

Rafe had fought to stay awake last night and obviously lost. It appeared Fanny, as well, had slept in. Had she tossed and turned until sleep gave her welcome rest from her troubled memories? Rafe supplanted a guilty twinge with something chipper. "Good morning, Fanny."

A shapely lump shifted under the bedcovers. "Get out of my room." Muffled words grumbled from under the sheets. "I mean it, Rafe."

Disinclined to back off, he stayed to see more. "Just making sure—it is Miss Greyville-Nugent I'm speaking with?"

"Rafe." A flutter of bed linens erupted into the air and fell to one side. Fanny propped herself up on her elbows. "Get out!" A head of tousled brown curls framed rosy cheeks, fresh from sleep. Rafe grinned. Every bit as lovely as he remembered, and angry to boot. He'd quite forgotten how stimulating she could be. These past five years, he had neatly tucked her into a corner of his mind and marked the pretty box *out of reach*.

Those drowsy brown eyes of hers narrowed as he backed away. "We have quite a day ahead of us, Fan. A full debriefing, a field investigation or two—"

He dodged a pillow as he checked his pocket watch. "Good God, nearly noon. It appears we've slept the morning away. We'll reconnoiter downstairs within the half hour."

The little maid ushered him out the door. "I'll do what I can, sir."

The carriage was waiting by the time Fanny arrived in the dining room. Pocketing a hard-boiled egg, a slice of ham, and a buttered bun, he took Miss Greyville-Nugent by the arm. "Sorry about the rush. We're a good bit behind schedule today." Once they were settled in the carriage, he unwrapped the napkin he'd placed on her lap.

Her gaze stabbed at Rafe, then the breakfast below. With brows furrowed and her mouth in a pout, she lifted off the top of the lopsided sandwich. "What is it?"

"Egg and ham on a bun." Rafe took out a penknife and arranged slices of egg on the ham, then replaced the top half of the bun. "I have one most every morning on my way into Whitehall."

Gingerly, Fanny picked up the lot and bit into the warm bread. After several bites, she made eye contact again. "Would you mind telling me what the schedule is, and why it is so important I come along?"

"If you can think of another way to guard a person while simultaneously conducting a homicide investigation, please do share. In fact, Scotland Yard would be most interested in any advice you might wish to—"

"I take your point, Rafe." She chewed and glared.

"Cheer up, Fan. The sooner we get to the bottom of all this, one way or the other, the sooner I'll be gone—out of your life."

The remark appeared to perk up her appetite. "This is actually quite good." And he was content to watch her devour the food in silence.

As for their itinerary, he wasn't about to discuss their first stop. They made excellent time to East Lothian while she broke her fast. He mentioned neither the mill nor the granary until they reached Preston.

Fanny quickly realized where they were headed. "Scene of the crime, isn't that what you blokes call it?" Folding up the cloth square, she looked a bit pale. Rafe suddenly felt awful for her.

"I take it you are familiar with your father's demonstration methods?"

Her gaze roamed out the window and back. "Father so loved to show off his new thresher."

The carriage slowed as they approached the mill operation. A jumble of stone towers and wooden sheds surrounded a brick-paved yard. Rafe reached for her hand to help her down from the carriage. He caught a glimpse of white fingers through the crochet-work of her gloves.

"You don't have to go inside, Fanny."

"You said it yourself: the sooner we set aside the notion that Father was murdered, the sooner you'll be gone. Isn't that right?"

They intercepted a mill foreman crossing the yard who did not seem much inclined to show them anything until Rafe handed over his card. "Scotland Yard now, is it?"

The wiry gent walked off toward a barn-sized building. "Name's Jack Gordon. Ye coming or no?" Gordon rolled back one of the large doors. "Local police took several looks about—after the machine ground him up. What makes—"

"Watch your tongue, Mr. Gordon. This is Miss Greyville-Nugent."

The foreman removed his cap. Rafe counted ten or twelve hairs on the top of the bowed head. "Beggin' your forgiveness, miss."

Fanny stepped around both men, a determined set to her jaw. "Apology accepted, Mr. Gordon."

Rafe caught her by the arm. "Let me have a look."

"Don't mollycoddle me, Rafe." She pulled away.

He held on tighter. "Let me go first. Please, Fan?"

She stared for a long moment. "Have it your way, Detective."

Gordon led Rafe into the shadows of the oversized shed. The ceiling was high pitched with a loft that ran the length of building. "Just as well the little lady stays behind. Bloodstains are stubborn. You'll see them about—like that one there on the floor."

Rafe stared at the large rust-colored blotch. "This is where"—he lowered onto his haunches—"the apparatus was?"

"Threshing machine sat right about there, sir."

"Mr. Greyville-Nugent was up above, with a good-sized haystack behind him, pitching the sheaves into the machine. He turns back for another fork, swings himself about, and straight into the thresher below."

"He lost his balance."

Jack Gordon shrugged bony shoulders. "No one else up there with him. Hardly a breeze blowin' through the shed. Can't think of another reason, can you, sir?"

"Mr. Gordon, would you mind telling me why these crates are up here?" The familiar voice came from the second floor.

He craned his neck. "Fanny, I thought we agreed—"

"We agreed you could go first." Her grin sobered. "Join me in the hayloft, gentlemen?"

He and Gordon scrambled up a steep set of stairs and found her sitting upon a medium-sized wooden box beside a very large crate. "Is it possible the wheat was piled here, Mr. Gordon? Exactly where I'm sitting?"

The man leaned sideways to have a look below. "Seems about right, miss."

Fanny stood up and moved to the end of the very large crate and tugged. The end of the crate swung open.

Rafe stepped closer. "Blimey, Fan." He crouched down to fit inside the empty crate. A whiff of urine and cigarette butts and something else. He spied a long oar-like pole, the length of the enclosure. He ran his finger along a thin horizontal window at the end of the crate. Smooth. Cut to look as though a slat was missing.

Fanny poked her head inside. "What do think, Detective Lewis?"

Rafe crawled out from the crate, clapping bits of chaff off his hands and clothes. "I'd much rather hear you speculate on the matter."

"It looks to me as if someone hid inside this shipping box." Fanny paced a small circle, her eyes alive and glistening. "Whoever it was could have paid a crew of workers to cover the crate with sheaves."

Rafe turned to Gordon. "Do you recall how and when the wheat was brought in?"

"Why, that very morning, sir—let the workers in myself. Said they was from the factory—had no reason to doubt them."

Rafe returned his gaze to Fanny. "Proceed, Miss Investigator."

She frowned. "Are you making fun of me?"

"Most certainly not."

Fanny slanted her eyes but continued. "Someone sitting inside this box could have maneuvered that long stick—sweeping the pole back and forth, clearing a small patch, enough to see . . . Father." When the words caught in her throat, Rafe jumped in.

"To prove the young lady's point, all that remains to be seen is whether the bloody poker might reach someone standing near the edge of the loft." He dove back inside the box and slid the oarlike instrument through the slim opening. He pictured Ambrose forking the grain over the side. Each sheaf lifted from the stack would have made it easier to slide the pole through the heavy bundles of stalks.

He poked his head out the crate. "Mr. Gordon, might you take up Mr. Greyville-Nugent's position?"

Somewhat warily the foreman moved to the edge of the platform. Rafe peered out the slit in the crate and extended the pole until it brushed against Gordon's pant leg. He rested the end of the stick on the edge of the opening and joined Gordon and Fanny at the loft edge.

Rafe lifted the pole to the back of the foreman's knee, while he narrated the reenactment. "Ambrose forks up a load, swings around, someone pokes him on his weight-bearing leg—right there at the back of the knee— Hold on to him, Fanny." He pressed the pole sharply to the back of Gordon's knee, which immediately gave way. "Over he goes." Rafe choked on his own words, harsh from chaff dust.

He made eye contact with Fanny. "You all right?"

She nodded weakly. "No one below would ever suspect, would they?"

Rafe spirited Fanny downstairs and back inside the carriage. He turned back to the millworker. "Mr. Gordon. Might I ask you to poke around a bit—without drawing too much attention to yourself?"

"Ye'll be wanting to know something about those blokes who readied the loft that day."

Rafe scratched a wire address on the back of his card. "Seemingly insignificant bits of information have been known to help solve a case." He pulled out a few bills.

"Save your government money." Gordon peered into the carriage and tipped his hat to Fanny. "Ambrose Greyville-Nugent was a fair man who put many a bloke to work, including Jack Gordon." The wiry foreman gave a wink and stepped away. "I'll find out what I can, Inspector."

FANNY SAT QUIETLY on her side of the coach and let the clip-clop of the team and the gentle rock of the carriage calm her nerves. Gradually, the scene at the mill faded some—everything but that last remark in the loft. *Over he goes.*

She thought she might cry, but the tears didn't come. The very thought of a murder plot against her father bothered her more than she could have possibly imagined. Who on earth would conceive of such a scheme? And for what cause?

A week ago, she had picked up the paper and read an account of his demise. The gruesome description had cruelly affected her. But today—when that horrible freakish accident turned out to be no accident at all? Something else had welled up inside her—something much closer to nerves of steel. No matter how discomforting Rafe's presence was, she wanted the brutish monsters who had plotted her father's murder caught and punished.

She returned Rafe's curious stare with a very determined one of her own. "We must find these men who butchered my father, Rafe. They must be put to trial and hanged until their tongues turn purple."

"Pity the poor blokes if you find them first." Rafe wrinkled his brow and sucked in a bit of air—grinning all the while. "I must say that was crack police work, Fan."

His grin had always been contagious. Still, she flattened the upturned corners of her mouth. "You think so, Detective Lewis?"

"I know so." He checked his timepiece. "We have time for a break. A spot of tea and biscuits, then we'll push on to University."

"I'd rather just push on, if you don't mind."

"You always were a stout little soldier." Rafe reached into his pocket and pulled out a pistol. "This is a Webley Mk1. Standard issue service revolver." He emptied the bullets from the chamber and pressed it gently into her hand. "Do you have any experience with handguns?"

"I'm afraid not." She raised both brows. "Are we on our way to see Arthur Poole?"

Beneath thick, lowered lashes his eyes gleamed—and

wheels turned. Very likely Rafe was evaluating what to tell her. No doubt he wished to shield her in some way.

"Mr. Poole complained of unwanted visitors—strangers lurking about. I thought we might have a look around."

The pistol felt heavy, solid, and quite unexpectedly soothing in her hands. And like it or not, there was something comforting about this Yard man, sent from London to protect her. In so many ways, Rafe was intimately familiar to her—a handsome, dashing ghost from her past. She studied his chiseled jaw and the firm, wide-set mouth.

Abruptly, he lifted his gaze to meet hers.

She lowered her eyes and examined the gun. He was also a rogue and a reprobate.

The rascal covered her hand with his and showed her how to squeeze the trigger. An index finger slipped over hers and a tingle coursed through her body. Embarrassed slightly, she looked up to see if he knew—if he had felt her quiver at his touch.

Those dazzling green eyes of his sparkled with mischief. He knew.

How humiliating. Heat rushed to her cheeks. He opened her hand and kissed the pulse point of her wrist. "You have the same effect on me."

She tried to withdraw, but he held on and dropped six bullets into her palm. "Insert them nose first—that's right."

After she loaded the gun, there were lessons in safety as well as how to sight and aim. She raised the gun and held it with two hands, as instructed. "How is it you came to be married, Rafe?"

His gaze swiftly turned black. "Never. Ever. Point a gun at someone, unless you intend on using it."

"And what if I do mean to use it?" Fanny bit her lip. After a good long stare down the barrel, she lowered the pistol.

Rafe exhaled, ducking his head to look out the window. "Excellent, we've arrived at the Hall." Gently, he pried her fingers off the handle and trigger, pocketing the weapon. "I promise you: before we part company, you will have ample opportunity to exact revenge upon me."

"Please make sure of it." Accepting his hand, she stepped down from the carriage onto the University grounds. Skirting McEwan Hall, they wound their way through a nearly deserted campus. It was already late afternoon and few students were about. The laboratory was housed between a hodgepodge of buildings on the third floor.

Fanny stepped inside. "Professor?" Floorboards creaked underfoot and there was the faint hiss of Bunsen burners and bubbling liquids in glass beakers. Late afternoon light filtered through windows veiled by dust. A row of workbenches ran the length of the cramped narrow space.

Rafe moved ahead, shielding her with his body. "Mr. Poole?"

Fanny surveyed the contents of the tables, each piled with odd-looking instruments. They came across an open ledger and a cup of tea beside it.

Rafe laid his hand on a chipped teapot close by. "Still warm."

Fanny craned her neck to peer into a dark corner of the lab. "Professor, please answer!"

Rafe reached inside his jacket and got out his torch. "Glad I brought this." He toggled the switch back and forth. "Bollocks."

"What is that?"

Rafe grabbed hold of her hand. "An electrical torch powered by dry cell batteries."

How was it that Rafe held a device she knew nothing about? Having been raised by an avid inventor and industrialist, Fanny was privy to all the latest inventions—sometimes many years before they were known to the general public. "That's impossible. I would have heard about such an appliance!"

"Experimental. On loan to Scotland Yard for field-testing." Rafe grinned. "No need to be snarlish." He banged the brass object in the palm of his hand. "As you can see, it's not the most reliable of gadgets."

Something crawled along the floor. "Rafe?" Fanny nodded toward the dark end of the lab. A cloud of gaseous material billowed down a few steps and swirled toward them.

The light from the torch sprang to life, causing them both to jump.

Stepping gingerly through the low blanket of mist, they approached the end of the room. Rafe swept the beam of light across a giant metal cylinder topped by a hatch wheel. Clouds of white vapor billowed out from under a dome-shaped lid and down the sides of the chamber. A number of tubes coiled about the unit were covered with frost.

"Have you any idea what this could be?"

Fanny shook her head. "It appears to be a refrigeration unit of some kind." She squinted at the apparatus. "I suppose the professor could be making liquid nitrogen."

Rafe blinked. "Liquid what?"

"If you compress the gases in the air enough, you end up with nitrogen, which at extremely cold temperatures turns to liquid."

Rafe stared. "For what purpose?"

"A myriad of industrial uses, including shrink welding, Detective Lewis."

She and Rafe spun around at the same time. "Mr. Lazar!" Fanny coughed as she introduced Rafe to Professor Poole's research partner.

"We have an appointment with Professor Poole. Might you—" A fit of coughing interrupted Rafe's speech.

"Step back, both of you." Lazar ducked around them. "As liquid nitrogen evaporates, it reduces the amount of oxygen in the air—in confined spaces it can act as an asphyxiant."

Fanny's gaze darted along a counter filled with lab equipment. One after another, Bunsen burner flames flickered and died. Rafe continued to cough as he pulled her away.

Lazar climbed a low ladder beside the tank and turned the hatch wheel. "Either the seals have failed, or someone has tampered—"

The hatch burst open in an explosion of frozen vapor. The sudden blast and displaced air knocked Rafe and Fanny to the ground. Glass beakers and measuring devices slid off tables and crashed on the floor. Lazar lay crumpled in a heap not far away.

Fanny screamed. Her legs and feet scrambled against floorboards, pushing her away from the horrible sight in the tank.

The head and shoulders of a frozen body bobbed up and down at the top of the massive cylinder. Diaphanous clouds of vapor billowed out of the apparatus, which continued to hiss and wheeze. The dead man's eyes bulged from their sockets, with irises that glowed silver-white. The head sprouted red hair frosted pink from ice, and a sardonic grin was frozen in place. There could be no doubt about the identity of the ghoulish corpse.

"Professor Poole." Fanny struggled for breath. The deeper she inhaled, the less oxygen there was. She felt her cheeks. Cold as ice on a warm day. "We must get— outside—"

Strong arms wrapped around her waist, pulling her to her feet. Rafe guided her out of the lab and down the corridor. "Hold on to the banister—you're light-headed. Make your way outside into the fresh air. I'm going back for Lazar."

Fanny caught his arm. "Be careful, Rafe."

Rafe squeezed her hand. "I'll be down in a flash."

On the way outside, she ran into several students who had heard the explosion. She pointed to the lab above.

Still gasping, she stepped onto the terrace and sucked in fresh air.

As she regained her strength, images of death deluged her thoughts. Some kind of monster, or group of fiends, had conspired against her father and now Professor Poole. A man couldn't fall into a vat of gas right-side up—he must have been forced down into the subfreezing liquid gas.

Death and more death. A shiver ran down her spine as she circled the yard adjacent to the science hall. There were one or two business competitors, she supposed, who might have wished Ambrose Greyville-Nugent gone. Fanny chewed a bit of lower lip. Father had also enjoyed a string of women over the years. Many a paramour had set her sights on landing Ambrose Greyville-Nugent. Indeed, her father reigned supreme as the most sought-after widower in all of Edinburgh and had remained so for years. When he jilted those aspiring women, which he invariably did, one or two had become rather difficult. But murder?

Passing the hall entrance, she caught a glimpse of Rafe. He stood beside a recovering Professor Lazar in the foyer. They exchanged a wave and Fanny continued her turn about the grounds. Neatly trimmed hedges formed a Celtic knot in the center of the square. The intricate pathway took her past flower beds and a patch of lawn.

"Miss Francine?"

Fanny turned in the direction of the voice and squinted. She had not noticed that it was dusk, verging on twilight. A young man stood beside the gated entry to the quad. She recognized their new driver—hired last week. At the same time, she heard a door swing open and the murmur of students inside the building. Rafe was out on the terrace and starting down the steps. "Not to worry, Rafe. You recognize Martin—our driver?"

Rafe hesitated, evaluating the young man beside her before turning back. "Very well, Fanny. At all times, you must stay where I can clearly see you. Disappear behind a tree, for even a moment, and I will not hesitate to intrude upon your constitutional." With his eyes locked on her, he walked backward for a bit, then returned to the hall.

She turned to the driver. "What is it, Martin?"

"Lame horse, ma'am. With your permission, I'd like to take the team home and come back with the brougham." The driver opened the gate and she passed into a narrow yard—more of an alleyway.

"Fetch us as soon as you can—" A terrible clunk and a groan came from behind, and she turned in time to see Martin collapse to the ground. Inching forward, she bent over the young man. What on earth? Something—a presence—loomed up from behind. A rough hand went around her face and clamped over her mouth. Another arm pulled her against a hulking frame and dragged her toward the shadows.

She fought back with all her might, kicking and dragging her feet. The toe of her shoe caught on the edge of the gate and slammed it shut. With a grunt, the large oaf who seized her muttered under his breath and squeezed harder. Wrenching her neck, Fanny glimpsed a transport van at the end of the alley. The kind of paneled vehicle used for moving furniture and belongings. The back door was open. Dear God, they meant to put her inside.

She was being abducted.

She squirmed and wriggled and bit to no avail. The brute held on tight, crushing the air from her lungs. How foolish she had been not to take Rafe's instructions seriously. Tossed onto the hard floorboards of the rig, she hit headfirst. Stars swept across her field of vision.

The painful creak of the campus gate crashed open and banged against a brick wall covered in ivy. "Fanny?" The call came from far away.

Thank God for a shout. "Rafe!" The large man in the scratchy jacket flung himself into the wagon and smothered her cry to a feeble gasp.

∞ Chapter Five

Rafe flew out the alley, feet keeping pace with his racing thoughts. Christ, where was she? He took a corner so fast he nearly tumbled onto the bloody pavers. Regaining his balance he lengthened his stride. There, straight ahead, a furniture van wobbled down the street at a blistering fast pace. "Fanny!" Common sense and a nose for crime said he'd find her inside. She had to be.

The clumsy conveyance would have to slow considerably to make the tight turn at George Square. Rafe vaulted over the iron fence and cut across a small patchwork of park surrounded by a quiet row of shops and townhomes. He pulled out his Webley and fired above the driver's head. The man snapped the reins and the horses bolted around the turn.

Rafe sucked in a gulp of air and cursed the day he'd smoked his first cigarette. "Dear God, I'll give up the fags, just let me catch this damned—" Rafe leaped onto the driver's step and pulled himself up beside the man with the reins.

He pressed his revolver to the inside curve of the driver's ear. "Stop the van." The bloke jabbed him hard in the ribs, but his hands were full of reins. The frenzied nags took the next corner at a blistering pace, tilting the conveyance on two wheels. "Bloody hell." He grabbed the man by the collar and used the steep angle to shove the driver off.

As if in a nightmare, the carriage teetered momentarily, then groaned—protesting the pull of gravitational forces before it toppled over. The jarring crash all but hurled Rafe onto the street. But not quite. Thrown to the very edge of the wagon, Rafe pulled himself onto the side panel and crawled back to the front of the vehicle. The overturned van continued down the cobbled lane with great deal of grating and scraping. Sparks flew off the wheel hubs as the terrified horses continued to run, out of control. An eternity of seconds passed before he managed to get hold of the reins. With a firm hand, he pulled back, gentling the horses with the sound of his voice. The drag of the overturned caravan helped slow their forward momentum.

The crash and the horses' high-pitched whinnies brought several men running from a nearby mews. One groom helped steady the animals while the other man worked to unhitch the team from the wagon.

Rafe jumped to the ground and made his way to the rear doors of the van. He squinted back down the lane, but could find no sign of the fallen driver. No injured body lying in the road. Likely ran off, lucky dolt. He reached out and turned the lever on the rear doors. Nothing. He gave it a hard tug.

Jammed.

Bracing his foot against the frame, he wrenched one side free. The open door swung out and hit the ground. Poking his gun into velvet blackness, he held the revolver at arm's length and entered the van.

A streetlamp cast a dim flickering light over the body of a large bloke lying unconscious or dead on top of— Rafe climbed farther inside. "Hello there?"

A muffled cry answered as he wrenched the hefty torso away from a rumpled Miss Greyville-Nugent. Fanny was alive.

"Are you all right?" He rolled the rest of the inert body off her. The deadweight uttered a moan.

She rose up on her elbows. "Captain Savage to the rescue." She coughed, gasped for a bit of air, but otherwise appeared unharmed. Wild strands of curl haloed her head. Rafe swallowed—so relieved he hardly noticed how tousled and, well, beddable she looked.

"Here, let me help you." He reached out a hand.

Gingerly, she picked her way out of the van and onto the pavers. While she fluffed up her bustle and patted down skirts, he checked her ankles and limbs for a sprain. She swatted his hand away.

"Apologies. Don't know what came over me." A lock of hair had fallen in his eyes. He raked it back.

"Are all Scotland Yard men the cheeky sort?" Excellent. She was more than unharmed; she was the spirited young lady of memory.

He returned her grimace with more of a grin. "Regretfully, worse than cheeky."

Though she seemed herself again, he knew from experience the shakes would start soon enough, when the excitement wore off and shock set in. He must get her home and into a hot tub. Good God. He imagined the goddess stepping into her bath—a lovely curve of spine, a plump derriere. She turns to reveal those lovely peach mounds . . .

Mentally, he slapped himself.

She looked up from buttoning her boot and grinned. That devilish pixie grin from childhood—the fairy of Lochree—smiling at him. He checked the urge to yank her into his arms and—well, enough of that sort of thing. What a cruel trick of fate this assignment was turning out to be.

Several new men approached the wreckage to lend a hand. "Right. Could one of you shave off a bit of rein and tie up the large character inside? The sorry bloke just attempted to abduct this young lady." Rafe poked his head inside the compartment to supervise. "Hands and feet both."

The elder man of the group nodded. "Yes, indeed, sir. This here culprit won't get away."

Rafe drew a tuppence from his pocket and called a young groom over. He placed the coin in the boy's palm. "Make your way to the nearest police station. Report what has happened here. Tell them there has been a kidnapping attempt. Have them send a man round to 28 Randolph Place." Rafe took out a card and passed it over.

The young groom squinted, mouthed a few words silently, and gasped, "Blimey, Scotland Yard."

Fanny shivered, crossing her arms under her chest. Rafe's gaze lingered a moment on her lovely figure covered in black silk before he unbuttoned his coat and draped it around her shoulders. He took a deep breath, turned her around, and steered her into George Square.

"Blimey, Scotland Yard." She mimicked the voice and wide eyes of the stable boy. "I suppose all of London's young ladies swoon over a chance meeting with a Scotland Yard detective."

"Depends on the type of encounter." Rafe sauntered happily alongside her. "Ladies do tend to swoon during a rescue or very soon after. I prefer the sturdier lass, like yourself, especially if the lady is on the curvy side."

Fanny laughed. How utterly nostalgic. Her laughter often started as a soft giggle and ended in something wonderfully musical. For the moment, she had forgotten how angry she was with him. He wondered how long it would last.

Rafe opened the gate at the corner and motioned her through.

She waited for him to turn around, sporting her signature pout and accusatory squint. "I suppose this incident means you are thrust upon me for the duration?"

"I am honored to be thrust upon you for the duration."

Lovely doe brown eyes went wide and somewhat dewy. She marched away, shoulders back and chin forward. He paused to admire the sway and bounce of her bustle. "Fanny." He caught up to her. "Please forgive my indelicate humor."

She squinted at him. "Are you capable of being serious for a single moment?"

He tried to look thoughtful. "Aggravated by the job, I suspect. When confronted by danger one simply"—something shifted in the corner of his eye—"makes light of the matter."

A shadow emerged from a nearby alley. The dark figure of a man stepped into the street and took up the walkway some distance away. Rafe put a spurt on their pace. "You have my permission to impart severe discipline in the future. Whip a bit of serious into me—find that switch in the dungeon."

"There is no dungeon at Randolph Place. I don't know why you keep insisting—"

Rafe took ahold of her arm. "Fanny, do pay attention. A man has fallen in behind us and there is yet another across the lane." He squeezed her elbow. "Don't look now, darling."

"Ouch." She wrenched her arm away. "No endearments, Detective Lewis." Still, she leaned in. "What shall we do?" Her sense of adventure never failed—even when she was imperiled.

"Ready your petticoats for a good dash." He ventured so close he had to fight off a sudden urge to buss her cheek. Fanny gathered up the front of her dress as they turned the corner.

He grabbed her by the arm. "Run, Fanny."

They sprinted down a crescent-shaped street of terrace houses, and he pulled her into a basement niche hidden by stairs. Crouched against the stone residence, he held her tight in his arms. "Where might we find a police station?" His words buffeted softly over her ear and she turned her head. In the shadows he could just make out plump lips that bowed so beautifully when she was either deep in thought or in a pout.

"I'm not sure, exactly. High Street, perhaps. Or Waverley station."

Of course, the train station.

"Stay down." He rose high enough to have a look about. The men were gone, but it wouldn't take long before they worked their way back through the neighborhood. "We're going to get ourselves over to Nicolson Street, plenty of carriage traffic and cabs for hire." Wide-eyed, the dear girl bobbed her head and followed him out into the lane.

He caught sight of their pursuers just as he helped Fanny into a hansom. The dark-suited men stepped up the chase, dodging a jumble of road traffic. Rafe jumped in and opened the trap door in the roof. "Double the fare if you get us to the station as fast as possible." The driver snapped his whip and left the men running up on the cab in the dust.

Rafe lost sight of them as they passed several carriages on the road. The driver moved them along at a nice clip, but not fast enough to suit Rafe. Waverley station was blocks away. More than likely, their pursuers would see the hansom turn into the train station.

Fanny's concerned expression echoed his own sentiments. "Get ready to exit up ahead, past the park." She bit her lip and nodded. When street traffic piled up close to the station, he and Fanny left the hansom behind and ran the rest of the way to the station on foot.

"Bollocks." He banged on the door. "Whoever heard of a police station that closes down for the evening?" An echo of footsteps and shouts could be heard across a myriad of train platforms. Placing one foot behind the other, Rafe swept Fanny into the shaded alcove of the precinct's entryway.

"What are we to do?" The plea in her voice made him wish he had a ready answer.

He removed his Webley and spun the chamber. Five bullets. He leaned forward to peer around the corner and quickly retreated. "Not sure."

"Not sure?" She frowned. "I should think a Scotland Yard detective would know exactly what to do at a time like this." Her whispered chide was so . . . adorable.

She peered around his shoulder at the pistol. "Why don't you use that on those men following us?"

"Would you like that, Fan? Set them back, bullets blazing? Even if I didn't give a wit for my own neck, I have you to think about."

She sighed. Loudly.

"Those blokes out there would likely shoot me dead, and then where would you be? Back in the hands of your abductors."

"I can't see that abductors are much worse than faith-less jilting abandoners."

He blinked. A painful silence permeated the humid

air between them. Far off, bursts of steam and the creak of luggage carts echoed under the vast architectural canopy covering the platforms.

She averted his gaze and bit her lip. "That was unkind and uncalled for under the circumstances—"

"No. You're quite right on every count—an inexcusable act of deceit and cowardice, hurtful and very wrong of me. But we are in no position to sort this all out." He ran a hand through his hair. "Fanny, I must ask you for a truce."

Those plump lips pursed into a bow. "For how long?"

"Several days."

She brushed the floor pavers with the toe of her shoe. Her gaze eventually returned his. "You've got several hours, Detective Lewis."

He held out his hand. "Settled."

She hesitated before shaking. "Do not take this to mean you are forgiven."

Rafe nodded in agreement. "Out of the question." He returned his revolver to an inside pocket. "When is the next train out of Waverley?"

"I believe the last train to Glasgow leaves at eight o'clock."

Rafe stared at her. "This evening? Excellent. This is good news."

She rolled her eyes. "Summer schedule."

Rafe flipped open his pocket watch. "Bollocks, eight o'clock." He stole another glance around edge of the storefront. The two natty blokes stood in front of platform five. He recognized at least one of the men as a pursuer. Rather a well-dressed gang of thugs. Minions, he supposed, but whose? He scanned over to the next platform. A porter lifted a heavy-looking chest and handed it off to another man standing in the baggage car.

"Blimey, they've got the wrong train." He motioned her up beside him. "Come." Rafe pointed to the correct platform. "See the luggage cart just to the right?" She nodded. "We're going to make a run for that train."

"We're leaving Edinburgh?" Without having to look, he knew two small frown lines formed between her brows.

"Only for a day or two." He grabbed her hand and trotted silently toward the platform. They hugged darkened storefronts and a telegraph office as they made their way toward the train to Glasgow. The porter signaled the engineer and the locomotive began a slow chug out of the station. Rafe sprinted toward the moving cars. "Stay with me, Fanny." He glanced back as he released her hand. Game little Fanny was only a step behind him, skirts flying.

Rafe reached a passenger carriage door. The evening was warm enough to have the train windows down. Sweat trickled down the side of his brow as he signaled a man having a smoke. "Scotland Yard, open the door."

Rafe leaped onto the step and turned back. The well-dressed thugs monitoring the wrong train had spotted them and were giving chase. Rafe glanced ahead. They were about to run out of platform. The faster man closed in behind Fanny and took a swipe at her.

Rafe leaned well off the step of the compartment and stretched out a hand. "Jump, Fanny."

✂ Chapter Six

The moment she leaped into the air, time reversed itself for a fleeting moment. She and Rafe were at play in the wilderness park of Lochree. He extended a hand to help her up from a tumble she'd taken on the grass. Now, he reached out again—strong arms, pulsing with life, lifted her onto the train and pulled her against his chest. She listened to the pounding of his heart as she gasped for breath. Safe in his embrace, her nose brushed against the smoky tweed of his jacket. Hints of sandalwood soap and man scent. His scent.

Rafe hung his head out the open door. "Ha! Lost the buggers." He turned to her and winked. "You always were a damn fine winger."

"Until your mother found us out."

"And the rugby team was never the same." Rafe pulled her inside and nodded to the gentleman who assisted them. "First-rate service on behalf of queen and country."

He steered her down the corridor until they found an empty compartment. He took a seat and settled in unbearably close beside her. He grinned. "How did Mother discover us?"

She inched away. "I wrenched an ankle. You had to carry me all the way back to Dunrobin Hall."

"That's right." His eyes, once filled with adventure, glittered with desire. "It was you who let the cat out of the bag." Sweeping his gaze over every facial feature, he stopped quite obviously on her mouth. It was the kind of look she imagined a husband might dare in the privacy of the bedchamber. A blazing heat reached her cheeks and she sidled farther away.

"Only after she wheedled it out of me." She patted down her skirts and angled her bustle to one side. "Where are you taking me?"

"Haven't a clue. Where would you care to go, Fanny?" Those teasing eyes had always had a certain way of mocking the world, one that invited others to share the sarcasm, the joke.

She glared. "Why don't you push on to Timbuktu, while I return home?" Nervously, she chewed on her lip.

"Don't do that."

"Do what?"

"That nibbling business." He pointed to her mouth. "Involving your teeth and bottom lip. Most distracting. I can barely keep my wits about me when you—"

"What a hound you are." Her eyes rolled upward. "But then, I suppose you've always been a scoundrel, haven't you, Rafe?"

He stared as if struck dumb by her words, but made a notably quick recovery. He returned a rueful smile and swept a hand through his hair. A nervous gesture that hadn't changed a whit since childhood. Her stomach twitched a bit.

"How is it, Fanny, you never married? No doubt the first year or so after—" He scratched his head.

"I'm afraid the whispers went on well after you'd taken the knock." She tilted her chin. "You did the gentlemanly thing, Rafe. I cried off the engagement, but the announcement shocked all of Edinburgh society. We were so expected, you see. Childhood sweethearts and all." As her voice trailed off, she caught herself. "Do not trivialize the public shame and dishonor you bestowed on me."

"Surely after Edmond Stewart's wife caught him with the telegraph boy, the scandal must have shifted off us—" He corrected himself. "Off you. There must have been a swarm of suitors."

She sighed. "There were none."

"With your father's fortune and your beauty?" Rafe narrowed those golden green eyes. "I don't believe it."

Fanny straightened up. "I do not require a husband. I have found my avocation as an industrialist and suffragist."

"Good God." His words were drowned out by a teeth-rattling crash and thud from above. Rafe poked his head out the compartment window. "Christ, those crazy blokes are jumping aboard from a footbridge."

"How impossible—how on earth could they?"

He placed a finger over his lips and exited the compartment. "A fast carriage could easily overcome us in town." He motioned her to follow. A short creep down the aisle landed them just shy of the rear door. He glanced back at her. "You aren't one of those Franchise League, placard-carrying, grim old maids—" Rafe squinted ahead before glancing back again. "Are you?"

Fanny leaned forward, close enough for a harsh whisper. "If a young lady chooses not to marry, people go to gossiping behind her back—'four and twenty, poor girl'—it's revolting. Cruel."

The door ahead jerked open to reveal one of the dark-suited men who had chased them through Edinburgh. She stared open-mouthed as Rafe's fist smashed into the gaunt man's jaw. A right smarting sock that nearly caused her eyes to water. He shoved the man back out the door of the carriage.

She poked her head through the connecting door. A gusty mist of rain whistled through a gaping slice in the canvas bonnet between rail cars. The man lunged with a knife and Rafe leaped away, narrowly avoiding the swipe of the blade. "Stay back, Fanny."

A forgotten umbrella leaned against the corner compartment. She took it up and followed after the two struggling men, who lost their balance and nearly fell off the coupler bridge. She lifted the umbrella. Rafe recovered his balance and shoved his attacker against the torn curtain, which ripped under the pressure. Fanny swung as Rafe released his assailant. The umbrella caught in the oiled canvas and finished the job. The fabric flapped violently in the face of the attacker gasping for breath. Rafe took a step back and kicked him off the moving train.

A faint shadow passed overhead, distracting her from the spine-chilling shriek of the falling man. "Up above!" she cried and retreated back inside the coach aisle as a second man dropped down on top of Rafe. In the narrow space between cars, punches flying, the brawling combatants rolled from the end of one railcar to the other, each one having a turn at getting his head smashed.

She winced. Holding the umbrella like a cricket bat, she swung it handle first. She smacked the platform inches from Rafe's head. "Sorry." She struck again and got in a good whack to the back of his assailant's head.

"Fanny, get back."

She struck again and hit the mark. *Crack!*

"Bollocks." Rafe wrenched the umbrella from her hands and swiped the wooden handle across the man's face. Blood poured from a broken nose and his attacker collapsed with a grunt. Rafe clambered to his feet, grabbed the bloke by the collar, and propped the dazed man up on the bridge.

"One more for the road, mate?" Rafe lifted the umbrella for a last bash, but before he could strike, the bloody-nosed thug turned and jumped off the train. Fanny sidled up beside Rafe and leaned out the torn canopy between carriages. After a bone-cracking tumble, the man rolled his way down the embankment.

A strong hand gripped her arm. Rafe foisted her back inside the empty passenger compartment and sat her down roughly. "What did I tell you?"

"Stay inside. But—"

"But nothing, Fanny." He placed both hands above

her shoulders and leaned close. "You must do as I say at all times, or I cannot protect you."

Arms crossed snugly under her chest, she thrust out her lower lip. "It seems to me you were the one sorely in need of defending." His tie was askew and the front of his jacket had fallen open. A splatter of blood covered his shirt and waistcoat. She worked her way up to meet his stare.

"Are suffragists always so intrepid?"

"I prefer to think of myself as capable." She raised a brow in defiance.

He slumped onto the opposite seat. "Must have missed that section of the liberated women's manifesto."

Her eyes rolled up and she sighed, loudly. "I'm feeling quite drained, and confused. Where are we going, Rafe? Are we just . . . running away? Do you have any sort of scheme? A plan, if you please?"

"Of course I have a plan. And you do not appear to be greatly fatigued." There was a spark in his eye and a hint of grin. "You always were a daredevil as well as beautiful."

She'd forgotten how he could try a girl's composure. "Your meaningless flattery will only make me more disagreeable. Once again, do you have a stratagem, Detective Lewis?"

Rafe shook his head in dismay. "Christ, you're going to pursue this like a bloody bulldog." A shock of hair had fallen into his eyes. He raked it back with his fingers.

"Only because I suspect you have no plan."

Rafe edged closer and lowered his voice. "There are times

when it is safer that you not know my plans. At the moment, I have no idea who these cockups are, what they're about, why they're after inventors and industrialists—why you in particular. Who their leader might be, their numbers, resources, finances or weaponry . . . I could go on and on. Would you like me to continue?"

The farther he leaned in, the farther she leaned away. "I must admit, that is a great deal *not* to know."

His gaze wrinkled with a smile. "Cease-fire, Fanny." He hooked a finger into his waistcoat for his timepiece. "Half past eight. We have hours of truce left."

"Rather ungentlemanly of you to raise your voice to me." She pressed back into the seat. "And to use vulgar language. *And* to take the Lord's name in vain."

"You might as well know it all, then. I smoke, curse, and drink in copious amounts. And, as you so often enjoy pointing out, I am no gentleman." He reached for his cigarette case and flipped it open. "Dash it." The slim silver container was returned to his inside pocket. "Empty."

"Tobacco is not healthy for the lungs." Fanny blinked at him. "You should give it up."

LESS THAN AN hour ago Rafe had promised to quit cigarettes. Still, he wanted a smoke so badly, he would sell Aunt Vertiline to the Gypsies for a single fag. "Vowed to give them up if I might catch a certain runaway caravan in Edinburgh."

Those exceptional large brown eyes of hers narrowed. She had always met his gaze boldly, bravely. "Why do you pretend to like me so much, when you so obviously do not, Raphael?"

"Now it's Raphael is it? This is grim. First Rafe, then Detective Lewis. Now you sound like Mother."

"If your mother spoke to you."

"As much as I've enjoyed your disagreeable, unappreciative company, I want you to know, Fanny, I got down on my hands and knees and begged them not to send me to Edinburgh." He received a huff and a change of the subject.

"I count four culprits thus far," she mused aloud.

"Possibly more," he warned.

"The two blokes who abducted me, another two chased us into the station and then leaped onto the train. I shudder to think how many more will be sent after us." Fanny concentrated on a delicate piece of torn lace at the edge of her sleeve. "Rather likely those men were involved in the murder of Arthur Poole, as well as my father."

A deep inhale caused a twinge of pain. "It does look as though the Yard's suspicions were correct about you and God knows how many other nabobs of industry." He reached inside his jacket and rubbed a smarting soreness in his side.

A visible shiver traveled up her body to her shoulders. Shock, Rafe supposed. "Even if you haven't any plans, might there be a next step?"

"Send a few wires to Scotland Yard." He rummaged in his pocket. "I'll need to get ahold of a blank telegram pad."

"We make a stop shortly. The ticket collector should have one."

Once again a sudden sharp twinge of pain shot across his torso. He removed wet sticky fingers from his waistcoat. A thick crimson liquid pooled on his fingers.

Fanny squinted. "You're bleeding."

"Must have caught the tip of a knife."

Fanny switched seats and began removing his waistcoat. "You didn't feel anything?" Blood oozed out of a slash in his shirt.

He pulled out a pocket square and wiped his fingers. "A dull ache, perhaps." She leaned close and unbuttoned his collar. "Odd thing about wounds. The pain often grows with a person's awareness of the injury." Gentle fingers inched up his undershirt, exposing his torso. Her fingernails traveled lightly over exposed flesh.

With her lips pursed and brows drawn deep in concentration, her expression triggered memories of a rainy day long ago. Fleeting impressions of a cutthroat game of backgammon in the library. He remembered a fire in the hearth as they lounged on a comfortable window seat. The pale shadow of raindrops, cast from leaded glass, danced across her face. It wasn't the first time he had gotten an erection watching her pink tongue moisten the way for her pearly white teeth.

As if on cue, she bit down on a plump bottom lip.

And here he sat, ten years later, hard as a stone. Rafe resisted the urge to adjust his trousers. When she met his gaze for a quick glance, he sucked in a breath and swallowed. "Bad bit of gash?"

"Hand me your pocket square." She placed the folded handkerchief against the wound on his side and pressed.

"Fanny—" He sucked a great deal of air through his teeth. "Careful."

She bit back a grin and angled his hand over the folded handkerchief. "Keep a bit of pressure on." She covered his knuckles with hers and pressed. "That's it."

He grimaced. "Just keep me wheezing in agony—as long as you find it amusing." The combination of pain and pleasure from this woman was almost inspired. She picked up her skirt and rummaged though several petticoats. "Love watching a woman disrobe on account of me."

Taking up a handful of ruffle, she picked at a bit of loose stitching. "Don't set your hopes too high, Detective Lewis." She gave the edge a good rip and unraveled a strip of ruffle. "There. A nice length, wouldn't you say?" She removed a few errant strings and shook out the cloth. "And a good bit of width as well."

How he longed for her to experience a good bit of length and width.

"You need stitches." She met his gaze.

"It's just a scrape, not to worry, Fan."

She hesitated before slipping her hand around his waist. The light touch of her fingers caused his stomach muscles to ripple. He straightened enough for her hand to slip around his back and wrap the makeshift bandage over the wound. She was so close to him, he could feel the heat of her breath on his neck. If she leaned in just a few more inches . . . His gaze moved to her lips. She tied a knot and tucked the tails into the swath of fabric.

"Quite serviceable and neatly done." Rafe rolled down his undershirt. A large red stain marred the otherwise pristine white garment.

She looked up from her handiwork. "We'll need to find a doctor." Rafe eased back in his seat and she buttoned his shirt. "Any moment now, we should reach Broxburn. Small town. Oil shale mostly."

"I need to get to a telegraph office."

She nodded. "After Broxburn, next stop is Bathgate. Coal mines. Lime and ironstone quarries. Some years ago, Father discovered cannel coal in the Boghead area and opened the Bathgate Chemical Works—paraffin oil and wax." She smoothed the placard of his shirt. "Then of course there's the Glenmavis Distillery."

Rafe rubbed a bruised cheek. "I could use a glass of Glenmavis Dew."

Fanny sat upright and pulled his waistcoat closed. "They'll have an infirmary there. Or—there's Coatbridge farther down the line. Father's hot-blast process greatly increased the efficiency of their smelting ironworks."

As always, smart as a whip, with a memory for detail. He smiled at her. "I see you've boned up on the Greyville-Nugent industrial empire."

"I made a few trips with Father this past year. Believe me, a visit to the Gartsherrie Ironworks is one of the sights of a lifetime." She patted his waistcoat and rose to take the seat opposite. The train braked unexpectedly and she tumbled back onto his lap.

Before she could utter a gasp, he wrapped an arm

around her waist and kissed her. "Remind me to thank our engineer."

She squirmed a bit and pushed away, but without conviction. Those wide, dewy eyes appeared slightly tempted. Her gaze lowered and her lips parted. A gentle exhale of air wafted over his mouth as he brushed soft kisses over that plump pout. He pressed for more, tasting and teasing as he took possession of her mouth.

He tugged up her skirt and ran a hand up silky French stockings. She broke off the kiss and pushed his hand away. "Are you completely mad?"

"I would guess I am. Well, not mad as a hatter." He dragged in a deep breath and exhaled. "Do you see what lust does to a man?"

"It makes him wicked and foolish. Don't do it again."

He held fast to her. "Ah, but I think you'd like me to be wicked and foolish again, wouldn't ye, Fanny?" Her glare fell to his mouth. "Yes, I believe you would."

Chapter Seven

He kissed her again. And though her hands pushed against his chest, her tongue dipped into his mouth and swirled a sensuous little dance with his. The honeyed taste of her conjured up sweet memories.

Shuffled footsteps and a bit of mumbled conversation alerted Rafe to a new rash of activity outside their compartment door. With his mouth still on hers he opened an eye. The ticket collector stood in the corridor chatting with a passenger. Torn between the man in uniform and her luscious mouth, he let her break off their kiss.

"Let me go." She shoved him back into the seat and slipped off his lap, quickly settling on the bench opposite.

His breath matched the heave of her chest as they both labored for air. "Sorry, Fan. It's just that you're so—"

A short rap and the door opened. A uniformed man stepped into the compartment with a perfunctory nod. "Evening." He took a long look at Fanny before he turned to Rafe. "Tickets, sir."

"The lady and I will be traveling on to Bathgate." Rafe reached into his pocket. "Change for a quid?"

"Two for Bathgate." The ticket taker appeared to be having a bit of trouble with his coin changer.

"You wouldn't happen to have a pad of telegram forms on you?" Rafe looked the man over again. After a few years with the Yard, one developed a nose for murky situations. He slipped a hand inside his coat pocket as a precaution. "Turning wet out there?"

"Yes, sir—we've got a spot of weather ahead—"

"Is that right?" Rafe fashioned a rueful smile. "Clear as a bell in Edinburgh."

The ticket man let go of the change machine and pulled out a pistol. "The lady and I will be traveling on without you," he growled.

Fanny slid down the bench, wedging herself in a corner. Her perfectly natural act of self-defense created a moment of distraction.

Rafe fired his Webley and the bullet struck the man's temple. A faint trickle of blood flowed down the side of the imposter's face. Glassy-eyed, the man pitched forward into his grasp. Rafe eased the body onto the floor of the compartment.

With barely a blink, Fanny stared at the frozen expression. "Is he—?"

Rafe dropped the man's wrist. "Dead." She inched around the corpse and reached out to him. Rafe helped her step over an outstretched arm. "You look a bit pale."

"Where on earth did he come from?" Her open-mouthed fascination moved from the corpse to Rafe. "And—how could you know?"

"He must have jumped on board with the other two—worked his way up from the baggage car." He nodded at the imposter's shoes. "The wet trousers and fresh mud didn't seem exactly right. And the man couldn't work a simple change device."

Her gaze swept over the body again. "Shall we search him? Perhaps we might find—I don't know, some sort of clue, I suppose."

"You've been reading the story papers." Rafe grinned.

Her flush colored wan cheeks. "You know very well I prefer a good adventure tale to poetry."

Rafe checked the corridor. "Hard to believe no one heard the shot."

"Frightened, wouldn't you say?" Fanny pressed her nose to the outside window. "Broxburn station is straight ahead. Several constables are standing on the platform." Fanny turned to him eyes bright. "A bit of good news, yes?"

Rafe grimaced. "I'd like to avoid local authorities for the moment." He took up an arm of the body. "Help me get him on the bench."

She did a yeoman's job with her end of the corpse. "You don't believe they are real policeman?"

"At the moment, I trust no one." Rafe lifted the deadweight onto the train seat with a grunt.

They propped the sham ticket taker against the wing of a headrest and set his cap. Rafe glanced out the window. The train would soon slow enough for the officers to jump aboard.

He searched the man's trouser pockets. "Check his waistcoat and jacket. She opened his coat with two fingers. "Quickly, Fan." A grimace readily changed to a triumphant grin when she pulled out a small notebook and billfold.

"You're a damn fine partner, Fan." Rafe took the items from her with a wink. "Come." He grabbed her hand and they moved silently down the corridor. At the end of the carriage, they reached the public water closet.

"Might I?" Fanny looked as though she almost hated to ask.

Rafe peered out the window. The uniformed men had begun to board the train one car ahead. "Make this the fastest piss ever."

He opened the door and she screamed. "Bollocks." A man lay curled up on the floor of the loo, dressed in nothing but his unmentionables. A deep crimson stain covered the back of his undershirt. Rafe slammed the door shut.

Fanny swallowed. "The real ticket collector?"

He nodded. "Poor bloke—"

She backed away from the water closet and reached out. Without a word, Rafe took hold of her hand. He inched the passenger car door open and poked his head out. A few people lingered on the platform, none in uniform.

The silver-gray sky marked a fine, lingering twilight, which would last for the better part of the next hour. He'd not chance a run for the station house. Dark glazing signaled the office had closed for the evening. Rafe and Fanny tiptoed down the steps and struck out along the edge of the platform, holding to the shadows alongside the train. A cool mist hung in the air, and the paved stone beneath their feet was slick from a recent shower. At the end of the platform, he jumped onto gravel-covered ground and helped Fanny down. Behind them, the silhouette of a man exited the train. He looked east and west along the rails. Rafe crouched and pulled her against him.

The dark character, dressed in a natty suit, peered down their way. The man shouted something back inside the train.

"We've been spotted." Rafe yanked her up and they quickly rounded the end of the train. They made a good run along the back side of the track, but there was no exit in sight. They were caught between a retaining wall to one side and the train on the other.

"There, up ahead." A narrow set of crude stairs led up the side of the embankment. Fanny picked up her skirts and they clambered up the steep, uneven steps, arriving in a backstreet behind a terrace of buildings. A horse nickered in a public stable at the far end of the alley.

"You know this town?"

Panting, Fanny nodded toward a break between buildings. "I believe there are several shops and a few pubs up the lane." Racing down the dark passage, they jumped over pools of fetid water and stumbled over a drunk. Out on the street, she pointed farther up the hill.

A group of shabbily dressed men, likely shale miners, bargained with two bawdy street whores. They passed by several quiet establishments before coming upon a smoky, crowded pub. This might prove to be excellent indeed, exactly what they needed for cover. Rafe gripped her hand tight and steered a path through the lively room.

He slid a large coin across the bar to a rough-looking character. The man in charge, it would seem. "Might there be a cabinet particular available?" Rafe didn't have to look; he was quite sure Miss Greyville-Nugent blushed cheek to toe.

"Got no fancy dining room with a hidden bed, mate." After a rude and lusty perusal of Rafe's pretty companion, the man gave him a wink and a nod. "Got rooms by the hour."

"Should anyone inquire, you haven't seen me or the young lady." He dropped a few more coins on the bar in exchange for a key. "Have a good whiskey and sandwiches sent up."

"Up the back stairs. Last door on yer left," the bartender grunted. Rafe led the way upstairs and unlocked a sparely furnished room. A plain cast-iron bed filled all but a small corner of space where a simple wooden chair stood. "Not exactly Claridge's."

She plunked herself onto the mattress. "This is heaven." Fanny looked up at him and smiled.

She forgot his past sins. For the moment. And he forgot about bedding her. For tonight. He tempered a devilish smile into something more benign. "You take the bed. I'll curl up on the floor."

Supper turned out to be mutton roast on a hard bun

and a bowl of strong hot broth. Rafe demonstrated a bit of pub sandwich savvy and dunked the crusty bread into the bouillon. "Mm-mm," she murmured, dipping her own sandwich into the bowl and swishing it around.

"Done like a seasoned pub crawler."

She held out her empty glass.

"One last sip, Fan. Your eyelids are ready to close."

Her hair was a riot of loose pins and massive curls come undone. And her flushed cheeks and somnolent expression? Entirely beddable. Like a child fighting sleep, she jerked upright. "You killed a man today."

"I did." He uncorked the bottle and poured them each another taste.

She chewed on a last bite of bread. "Does it bother you?"

"I learned a hard lesson my first year with the Yard. Took a bullet in the chest. An inch or two over would have killed me." He held up his glass and she clinked a toast. "Here's to cheating, stealing, fighting, and drinking.

"If ye cheat, cheat death." His brogue came out in full force.

"If ye steal, steal a woman's heart," she answered in kind.

He grinned. "If ye fight, fight for a brother."

"If ye drink, drink with me." She tossed back her head along with the whiskey. A beauty who could swill down a dram. Rafe took her glass and set both empties on the wooden tray at the foot of the bed.

"I no longer wait around to be shot at." He stretched

out his legs and adjusted his shoulders against the hard ladder back of the wooden chair.

She sat on the edge of the bed and shivered. He leaned forward and lifted her foot to his knee. "You need sturdy boots and—" He unbuttoned a black *peau de soie* shoe and motioned for the other. "Try not to take offense, but I recommend a change of gown. The natty blokes behind us, along with the local police, will be asking after a young lady in mourning costume."

She thought a moment before nodding. "Good." She perked up and moistened her bottom lip with her upper. "I greatly dislike mourning attire. And I don't believe Papa would mind, under the circumstances."

"Actually, you look rather sophisticated togged up in black silk." He rubbed her toes. "Your feet are cold." She pulled her legs away.

"Can you undo your bustle without assistance?"

Though her eyes widened, she boldly lifted her skirt. She untied a string around her waist, stood up, and wiggled. A leather and metal frame the size and shape of a rugby ball slipped to the floor. As she stepped to the side, he picked up the apparatus and hung it from a single hook on the back of the door. By the time he turned around, Fanny had slipped under the bedclothes.

He sat down on the edge of the mattress. "You've had a long day."

"A long two days." Fluffing the pillow, she turned from him and sighed. "Buried Papa at four o'clock yesterday afternoon, and who of all people makes his unwelcome appearance but Raphael Lewis."

He pulled up the covers. "Bothersome chap, but he means well."

Without looking back she reached out. Icy fingers gripped his hand. A bit of shock had set in. He lay down above the covers and wrapped Fanny in his arms, spooning against her.

She stiffened in his embrace. "You've suffered a shock," Rafe murmured. "As soon as I warm you up, you'll be off to sleep."

After a long silence, she uttered a soft, indignant harrumph.

"May I take your hair down?"

"You may not." She swatted his hand away.

"Might I ease your stays a bit?"

"Will you stop?" Fanny sighed. "I don't believe in corsets—can't catch a breath. Dreadful contraptions whose sole purpose is to repress women."

He scoffed. "Can a corset be any more tragic than that thing I just hung on the door?"

She yawned. "Women's fashion is always a bit ridiculous."

"In defense of Detective Lewis, his only care is for your comfort. And I would like to point out he traveled all the way up from London to guard Miss Greyville-Nugent with his life. And very *appropriately* warn her of the danger she might be facing." He snuggled up closer.

She squirmed in his arms, grinding against him. "What is that?"

He muffled a snort against the fine hairs of her temple. "A good guess would be my cock." He made an adjustment to his trousers. "Actually I'm quite certain of it."

A quick twist of her torso brought her face within inches of his. "Does this sort of vulgar discourse dazzle the ladies in London?" Her glare lingered even after she turned her back.

Rafe grinned. "You seem to believe I do nothing but mingle with the nobs. Attend teas, musicales, and soirees. Let me assure you, Fanny, I have no social life to speak of."

"Curious how you neglect to mention gentlemen's clubs, casinos, and houses of ill repute." She punched up her pillow.

Astonishing, really, that he could find himself lying in bed with Fanny Greyville-Nugent and not make love to her. As if in answer to a second wave of bewildering arousal and frustration, a round little bottom brushed up against him. Her whisper taunted from the land of Nod. "Our truce is over the moment I awake tomorrow."

Chapter Eight

An eye fluttered open, the one not buried in a pillow. Pale light spilled across the tall figure of a man standing near the window. Fanny lifted her head and rubbed both eyes.

"Good morning, Lieutenant Cutthroat."

She knew that voice. Fanny sat up with a start.

Raphael Lewis of all people, held back a shabby curtain. The splash of carriage wheels and clip-clop of horses echoed from the street below. With each waking blink the disturbing events of the last two days flooded her mind. "I asked you not to call me that." Propped on elbows, she yawned. "It's all true then, isn't it?

"What, darling?"

"The funeral. Yesterday. Last night. I was hoping it was all a nightmare. And I much prefer Lieutenant Cutthroat to darling." Rumpled and stiff, she found herself in a strange bed and characterless room, with the exception of Rafe Lewis.

He took his eyes off the street and met her frown with a grin. "Are you always prickly in the morning?"

Cool air drifted into the unfamiliar surroundings. "Rafe, what is going on? I feel as though I've tumbled down a rabbit hole."

"Perhaps we have." He fixed his gaze out the window. "It's imperative I get to a telegraph office and contact the Yard. Zeno and Flynn may have a few pieces of the puzzle put together by now. Who's after you—what we're up against." Rafe left his post and crossed the room. He removed the chair wedged under the doorknob and checked the passageway. "Last night on the train you asked about a plan." He ducked back inside the room and returned to the window. "My plan, at the moment, is to make our way to the shipyards in Glasgow. We have agents stationed there and a safe house."

"But—couldn't we simply go to the authorities here and explain our situation?"

"Rain's letting up." He released the curtain. "Last night, I observed our natty friends in black searching alongside the local constables. What did you see, Fanny?"

"You're saying the Broxburn police can't be trusted." She chewed her lip.

Rafe shrugged. "More likely they've been misled." He removed a pink and white striped paper sack from his pocket and picked out a peppermint. "Breakfast."

She swirled the candy lozenge around in her mouth. "I need to use the chamber pot."

"Ready yourself quickly. I'll be just outside the door."

Her bustle was barely tied before he was back inside their small chamber. "Several men are checking rooms at the end of the hall." He led her to the window. "See that ledge?" She craned her neck and tilted her head. "If you crawl along there, about ten or twelve feet, you'll come to a partially open window. Shove the sash up a bit and worm your way through. You'll find yourself on the back stairs."

She took a quick note of the three-story drop. And a ledge barely wide enough to accommodate an alley cat. "Rafe. How do you know all this?"

He shoved the window up as far as it would go. "Did a bit of poking about last night while you slept. Always like to have an escape plan." He lifted her by the waist. "Knee on the sill. That's it."

Tentatively she crawled out onto the narrow over-hang and stopped. "If I get killed, I am never speaking to you again," she called over her shoulder.

"I say, Mother would approve."

If she so much as snorted a laugh, she'd tumble over the edge. Her heart pattered a country dance inside her chest.

"Push on a bit so I can get behind you." He scrambled onto the roof. "Remember when you climbed the giant oak by the prayer chapel and were afraid to come down?" Rafe was right behind her.

Fanny nodded. "You talked me down, an inch at a time." The window ledge was directly ahead. Gritting her teeth, she yanked her skirt out of the way and scurried along the roof edge to the window. Grasping the open sash, she pushed up the glazing and dipped her head inside.

"Pull yourself through, until you can hitch a leg around." Except for the sound of his voice, she eliminated all terrifying thoughts and followed his instructions to the letter. Seconds later she was safely inside.

Rafe swung through the window feetfirst and landed beside her. "You did wonderfully well." He grabbed her hand and they were down the stairs and out the back entrance before she could catch her breath.

They stayed close together, hugging the back sides of the terraced buildings perched above the train station. In daylight everything appeared completely ordinary and unthreatening.

"One almost feels a bit silly, skulking along like this." She nodded down the embankment. "Might we chance the train station?"

He pulled her into a door niche. "I did a quick calculation. Our chances of escape, should they corner us in the telegraph office, is the grim part of the equation."

Fanny swiveled around in the doorway and read a brass placard. "Mr. Howard, Surgeon-Dentist." She wasted no time ringing the bell.

"Fanny what are you—?"

"Simple, Detective Lewis. The dentist who lives here is also a surgeon. If I am not mistaken, you still require stitching up." Rafe pulled her away from the door just as it opened.

"I'm afraid you've come to the back entrance." A balding, near to middle-aged gent with a good bit of side whisker stood in the doorway. "How can I help you?"

"My friend, the gentleman standing behind me, is in need of medical attention."

Rafe pulled her away. "Honestly, just a scratch—"

Fanny dragged him back. "Mr. Howard, allow me to introduce Detective Lewis of Scotland Yard."

Rafe suddenly stopped their tug of war. "Hold on. I do have a favor to ask." A reach inside his jacket produced a large banknote and his calling card.

The dentist stuck his hand out for a shake. "Rupert Howard, at your service, Detective Lewis." The man's excessively expressive brows traveled up and down as he pumped Rafe's hand.

"I need you to deliver a few handwritten messages to the telegraph office." Rafe handed over a note covered with scribblings. "Wait there. Make sure all the messages are sent, then destroy the originals."

Howard stood up straight, nearly bursting with enthusiasm. "I would be honored to be of service to Scotland Yard."

"Take care, play your part well, Mr. Howard, and you'll have a tale to tell your grandchildren." That said, Rafe moved off, and Fanny yanked him back.

"As I said, Detective Lewis could use a bit of patching up."

Rafe hissed from the sting of antiseptic and yowled with every stitch. Fanny could not be sure whether she was happiest over the much-needed medical attention to his wound or Rafe's obvious discomfort. "Why, Detective Lewis, you're going to draw alley cats." She received a glare followed by a spark of light in his eye. Pure Raphael.

In a twinkling, they were back out in the street and on their way out of town. Following the back alley to the base of the hill, they turned south and wound their way through a run-down district of miner's cottages. Fanny gritted her teeth and recoiled at the sight of fresh laundry lines hanging above open sewer trenches. She studied every detail of the deplorable living conditions, taking mental notes as she and Rafe walked the meandering path between a hodgepodge of crude shacks and stone hovels.

Children dressed in tattered clothing, many without shoes, ran alongside, pulling her skirt and begging for ha'pennies. Rafe managed to distribute a few small coins before a woman chased after the urchins with a switch. Fanny could not take her eyes off the stray children as they ran off, each holding up a copper coin as if it were a gold sovereign.

Rafe pointed at a cluster of oddly pointed hills, gob piles of waste coal heaped along the back side of the shale pits. "Those spoil tips make a lovely picture. Fanny, are you quite sure you want to preside over an industrial empire?" He shook his head. "Honestly, I can't picture it."

His words stirred a cauldron of fear as well as joy inside her. "You haven't been around to know anything about my life, my dreams and ambitions. My interest in women's suffrage, for instance, goes well beyond anything the feeble masculine brain might imagine."

She did not miss the subtle flicker of eyelash and accompanying eye roll.

"If I am to run one of the largest steam machinery enterprises in the empire, I believe I should be able to vote, run for government office, and attend as well as graduate college. Many of the rights gentlemen take for granted."

"But if you wish to be of service, say, to those little guttersnipes, you might do the same good works through a local ladies auxiliary."

"Charity events?" She scoffed. "If I am to help those families in Broxburn, I can do a better job by attending college and studying business economics or passing laws that protect workers as well as encourage commerce. You remember Mr. Lewis; it was the government who treated the workhouse children as pauper apprentices. Besides, I have a very keen interest in what I believe to be a noble experiment. I should like to see if it is possible to create a manufacturing enterprise that can satisfactorily address the interests of the worker and business owner."

He stopped and blinked at her. "My God, Fanny, you'll only succeed in running the factories into the ground—and where will all those street urchins be then? Even worse off."

"I am determined to try, Rafe."

"What did your father have to say about these progressive ideas of yours?"

Fanny marched ahead of him. "My father's opinions are—*were* his. Mine are my own."

Rafe snorted. "He said you'd run the business right into bankruptcy. He did, didn't he?"

Fanny covered her ears and lengthened her stride. She would not listen to another word from him. Still, she wondered if her own ambitions for Greyville-Nugent Enterprises were, well, too ambitious. And there was something else—something her father only suspected before his death. Fanny was secretly enthralled with invention and design. The next generation of machines would be driven by electric and petrol engines. Machines that would replace the horse and carriage, and take the drudgery out of housework.

Father had chided her over the concept, but had walked away pulling on his moustache, a sign he was taken with her ideas. Now, more than anything else in the world, she wanted those machines to be engineered and manufactured by Greyville-Nugent Enterprises.

She walked a mile or two in solitary thought before Rafe intruded, hastening her past a cluster of village shops and a few local residents, who paid them little mind. They kept to the shady side of the street until they reached a crossroads. A church and vicarage were not far down the lane.

She stopped to examine the road signs. "Which way are we going?"

"Southeast." A jumble of arrows pointed in a myriad of directions. Three of them aimed their direction. "Bathgate. Coatbridge. And Glasgow, thirty-seven miles."

The cooling mists of morning had long since given way to another sultry day. Fanny blew a few loose hairs from her face and rued the black dress with its heavy skirt and shelf bustle.

Rafe turned off the main road and started down a cart path. "Just past those bluffs in the distance, I reckon we'll find Bathgate and the next telegraph office."

They soon arrived at a copse of elm trees surrounding a quaint church and a modest vicar's residence. Fanny raised her skirts and stepped through a patch of tall grass. "How is it you came to be married?"

She had nurtured suspicions and a perverse need to know since his startling confession at the wake. And her question did seem to send him farther up the road. He scooped a rock off the path and tossed the stone over a stand of prickly thistle. "Our truce is up, Rafe. And the query is fair enough, given your betrayal of affection."

He settled in beside her and shrugged. "I hardly know how to explain or where to begin, Fanny."

She stopped and stared. "Begin anywhere you'd like. We have quite a long hike over hill and dale to Bathgate." She shaded her eyes against the sun. "I'm going to get freckles without a sun bonnet."

Behind the vicar's barn, Rafe stopped and pulled a white cotton gown dotted with small yellow flowers off the clothesline. Any distraction, she supposed, rather than answer the question. She inhaled a deep breath.

"And I do hope to see a sprinkle of spots across your nose." He shot a wink over his shoulder.

"What a horrid thing to wish for."

Rafe grinned. "I always adored them on you."

"We are not going to steal from the vicar's wife." Fanny crossed her arms and adopted a fierce stance.

"I wager this pretty little frock fits his daughter, not

his wife." Rafe took a pound note from his pocket and pinned it up where the dress once hung. He also pulled down a thin gauze petticoat.

He wrapped the simple muslin dress over the petticoat and slipped the bundle under his arm. A baying of hounds in the distance drifted over the clothesline. They both swiveled toward Broxburn.

She could hardly believe it. "They've set the dogs on us."

"An heiress to an industrial fortune is abducted—possibly by a man posing as an agent of Scotland Yard. Of course they're scouring the countryside." Rafe grabbed her hand and they ran along the dwindling cart path into rugged bluffs dotted with sheep. After a good steep climb, they caught their breaths on a jagged outcrop of rock. A trickle of a creek ran along the base of the hill headed for a loch off in the distance.

He turned to her; a hint of gears and wheels circled behind those distracting green eyes. At one point she thought he was about to speak, but he looked away—far off across the fields ahead.

She sighed.

"All right, Fan. Five years ago I suffered a terrible lapse in judgment—worst of all, I allowed someone to influence my disreputable behavior. And it all ended badly with the death of one young woman and the betrayal of another—sadly, the only person in the world I have ever cared for." He met her gaze directly, his expression so sincere, so anguished, she was forced to look away.

"Not sure if that matters any to you."

She swallowed. "No one had any idea you were seeing someone—least of all me."

His exhale was loud, edged with frustration. "I had a rotten last term at university, including an accusation of cheating." Rafe swept and an errant lock of hair back. "I didn't cheat, Fanny."

"No, of course you didn't. I can't imagine you cheating." She furrowed her brow. "At schoolwork, anyway."

A quick dart of eyes assured her he hadn't missed the jibe. "The class instructor piled a mountain of extra work on me. Enough that I was forced to quit football.

"Then word came down from Queensferry. There was no money for a grand tour—so I cancelled the trip to the Continent with you." A weary smile faded quickly. "And your dear chaperone, Cousin Claire."

He picked up the ball of stolen clothing. "Come on, Fanny, we're on the downside of the mountain." They could barely hear the baying of the hounds. Occasionally, faint barks echoed through the hollows in the rolling landscape. At times, her heart would race and she would gulp in air, not so much from the dog's cries, but from the story that unfolded as they made their way down the last slope of rugged terrain.

Rafe waited for her to catch up. "Who would you say Claire is closest to—as a friend?"

"She has several female companions she chums about with." Fanny paused at the edge of a steep drop. "She thinks of me as her charge, wouldn't you say?"

Rafe lifted her down from the jagged rock. "And her closest male friend?"

"That would be Nigel, of course. What are you getting at, Rafe?"

"During the spring and summer you were gone, I finished up the term, as did Nigel. Coincidentally—or not so coincidentally—he received a number of letters from Claire, two or three for every one I received from you."

"You know how much I loathe correspondence."

"That's because you're a terrible speller." A trace of crooked smile surfaced briefly. "I was at a low point when Claire sent word: 'Exciting news afoot.' Nigel delighted in sharing her letter. 'Fanny is seeing the Duke of Grafton. A whirlwind romance appears to be in the offing, and a formal promise is expected shortly.'

"I suppose I spiraled further downward." Rafe jumped from one flat stepping-stone to another across the stream that fed the loch. "Watch your step."

She picked up her skirts and followed close behind. "But Claire's letter was meant as a tease. You deserved as much . . ." Her speech drifted off. ". . . for not coming with us." Fanny chewed on her lower lip. "Honestly, Rafe, I had no idea . . ."

For a moment, he looked for all the world as if he was about to lose his only friend. "Nigel suggested a village pub crawl. Drink away the misery." His gaze was dark, troubled. "Started off like any other night—letting off a bit of steam—perhaps I was more on edge than usual. Nigel introduced me to a young lady. There's no delicate way of putting it, Fan—I took advantage of her, and a month later, paid the consequences."

Even though Fanny was safely on the bank, she

wobbled and swayed a bit. "I see." Rafe reached out and guided her toward a patch of grassland. She let go of his hand and walked ahead.

"Fan, I didn't know what to do—had no one to turn to. No chance of buying off the girl's family. Not that I would have considered such a thing. Rather ironic, though—if there had been more than two bloody coins in the St. Aldwyn coffers, the family might have insisted on an arrangement."

"But you kept it all a secret, Rafe. And then you . . ." Fanny stopped in the middle of the field and turned. "And then you married."

"Yes." He exhaled a long sigh. "Ceilia was sick for months after. In fact, she was never well. Neither mother nor child, as it turns out." Absently, Rafe whipped a long twig through a tall stand of grass. "No good came from my indecent, immoral behavior, just suffering and death. I caused a great deal of hurt and anger and ended up losing friends and family." He stopped flogging the grass and met her gaze. "And my fiancée."

Once before she had seen him this upset. The night the earl died. Fanny swallowed. "B-but, you never came home to explain—to tell me what happened." Fanny trudged on ahead, her mind awhirl with Rafe's revelations.

Rafe trailed after her. "Honestly, Fan, how well would you have received the news?"

She whirled around. "How could you believe I would do something like that—go off with Grafton? How ridiculous! Claire and I were having a bit of sport—the letter was written in jest." Fanny chewed her lip. "Perhaps it was a stupid joke. But it wasn't meant to be cruel." She blinked back a few guilty tears. "Do you have any idea how old the duke was?" Rafe circled her in the tall grass. Fanny stepped in front of him and pressed a finger into his chest. "Do you?"

He looked at her for a very long time and shrugged. "Haven't a clue, Fan—ninety-one and balding?"

"Fourteen and a carrottop. A freckle-faced. Red-headed. Boy."

Rafe wiped an errant teardrop from her cheek. "I'm so sorry, Fan. Whatever you and Claire did—however it was meant—it doesn't excuse my foolish behavior."

A new deluge of tears threatened to drop. "And how is it you did the cheating and I'm the one who feels guilty?"

Rafe reached an arm around her waist and swept her into an embrace. "Fanny—don't. Exactly the reason I never returned home. I did not wish to force my mistakes on you or my family—more needless hurt and humiliation."

He tried to hold on but she wrenched away and pushed on ahead. Besides the old wounds, new feelings welled up inside, much more disturbing. There were ties that bound them together long before any mentioned engagements or marriage. "I thought we were friends, Rafe."

He caught up and spun her around. "I have always been and always will be your best friend. Years ago I made the biggest mistake of my life—"

"Elephantine."

"I lost you, Fanny."

She swallowed a very big lump in her throat. "Perhaps when you withdrew from our tour, I harbored doubts." Fanny dug down deep and searched her feelings. "You never told me you loved me."

"Neither one of us ever got a chance to say the words." Rafe pulled her into his arms again. "I love you, Fanny. I always have and always will." The sweetest, most wistful smile she had ever seen graced his handsome face. He looked at her as if she were something fine and precious. "And if I told you I was as sorry as a man could ever be, would you believe me?"

A singularly wonderful and curious notion spread through her. She believed him.

He brushed back a few wisps of hair in her eyes. "I would do anything to deserve you again."

Goodness. Something giddy and silly tugged at the ends of her mouth. "Anything?"

His eyes crinkled. "Anything."

She slanted a wary gaze at him. "I must warn you there will be brutal trials ahead."

His nod was honest, serious. "I wouldn't have it any other way."

"And, I might add, acceptance of your apology does not mean you are entirely forgiven. You should expect . . . outbursts."

"Which you have every right to express." He hugged her tight and she surrendered to his embrace. "Ah, Fan. Put me through hell if you wish—just give me a chance to win your heart again." He twirled her above the waving ocean of grassland, as a cloudless blue sky whirled above them.

She couldn't help but add her own breathless laughter to his. "You'll have your chance."

Rafe set her down and neither one of them spoke or touched. A careless word or side-glance might break the spell. He backed away slowly, then turned and jumped onto an ancient stone wall. Fanny raised a hand to shade her eyes.

Rafe stood on the wall, legs set in a wide stance. With his hands on his hips, he surveyed a wide swath of meadow ahead. The statuesque, princely St. Aldwyn was about to be put through the trials of his life. She grinned.

As if in answer to her thoughts, he hopped a jig along the top of the wall and dropped down into the next pasture. Beyond the stone barrier, long-haired cattle and a plow horse grazed the field. "I reckon this sturdy steed can take us well past the loch ahead." Rafe stroked the neck of the brawny workhorse. "We might even shake off the dogs."

Fanny squinted at the brilliant yellow orb high in the sky. "I haven't heard a howl in some time—have you?" Perched on the wall, she eyed the large equine. "And how might you guide this old boy about?"

"Ah, you will be pleased to know, I have a plan." Rafe approached slowly. "I can rig a bridle using your bustle and petticoat."

Fanny narrowed a stare. "Don't you dare smirk." She wriggled out of her undergarments just as fast as you please and Rafe set about reworking the metal truss.

"Tear up your petticoat and braid several long pieces together for reins."

"Aren't you the clever one when it comes to my unmentionables?" She held a piece of slip in her teeth and ripped. A makeshift halter was soon rigged on the animal's head. Fanny tilted her chin. "Not exactly smart-looking, but is it serviceable?"

Rafe lifted himself onto the back of the sturdy equine and took the plow horse for a turn about the field. "Up on the stone wall, Fanny." He maneuvered close. "Side-saddle or astride?"

"Surrender your petticoat, expose a limb." Fanny growled. "I don't believe I have a shred of modesty left." She scrambled on behind Rafe and wrapped her arms around his waist.

"Excellent. I'm hoping for a splash in the loch with a naked pond nymph."

∞ Chapter Nine

$\mathcal{F}$anny leaned back on locked elbows and studied the canopy of rustling leaves above. Dappled sunlight and blue sky wavered in the breeze. "Please do have your bathe, Detective Lewis."

Rafe shrugged off his shirt and stepped out of his trousers. "Come and join, Fan. Water babies—like when we were kids." He made a ripple of small waves and a quiet splash as he stepped into the loch. "Fanny, are you listening?"

The plain cotton dress and petticoat spread out on the grass beneath her made a comfortable makeshift blanket. Fanny picked absently at a patch of clover. Anything but look in the direction of the loch. "Of course I'm listening."

"Come have a splash. I promise not to lay a hand on you."

"How unflattering to be thought such a simpleton." Fanny slipped off a shoe and went to work unbuttoning the other. "I will not be hoodwinked by you again, Rafe."

"It would do your temperament a world of good." He slipped further into the water at the very moment she twisted round to chide, but she yelped—or made a ridiculous squealing wail—instead. He looked back and caught her staring wide-eyed at his backside. With her mouth open.

"Have a handsome bum, don't I?

She swiveled away. "If you say so."

"The ladies in London say so." He dove under the glassy surface of the water and sent a spray of mist into the air. Several droplets cooled the blush on her cheeks. Perhaps she might wash up a bit, just a quick splash, while Rafe had his swim.

From the corner of her eye she watched him take several long, clean strokes toward the center of the loch, then she made her way to a flat outcropping of stone at the water's edge. She removed her stockings and inched closer, dipping a toe in the shallows. She swished her foot about.

A dark head of hair surfaced as Rafe came up for air.

She jerked back. The rock was slippery, and she nearly lost her balance. "You startled me."

He shook back wet hair. "I confess I was hoping you might fall in."

A low growl accompanied her flying stockings. Fanny hurled her rolled-up hose across the water. He caught the unraveling pair in midair. "Shall I give them a rinse? Here we go."

Fanny instantly regretted the loss and reached out. "Rafe, please don't—"

He dipped the pale stockings underwater and rubbed them together. "One really shouldn't toss one's underthings into the drink if one wishes to keep them dry."

She kept her hand out. "Give them back."

Rafe rose out of the water and waded ashore. This time she balked but did not turn away. Rivulets of water ran through the hair on his chest, down a sinewy torso to . . .

She took a faltering step back and forced her gaze upward to meet his.

Rafe Lewis was not going to intimidate her. Fanny once again lowered and raised her eyes. "Brazenly proud of yourself, aren't you?"

Emerald eyes shifted momentarily into something dark and feral. He waded closer, with a member that waved about like a slashing sword. He wrung out her socks and handed them over. "Fanny, your cheeks are red and your brow is beaded with perspiration." Rafe tilted his head, studying her. "Actually, you look like a woman ready to climax. And even though I would like to believe your state of blushing arousal is for me, I advise you to take a cool plunge. Immediately." He launched himself up onto the rock, all naked muscle and manliness as he stepped past her. "I'll keep my back turned."

Fanny bit her lip. "Swear on the lives of St. Aldwyn's Queensferry Dragoon Fusiliers."

Rafe turned his back to her. "I so swear."

PERHAPS IT WAS a good sign that Fanny evoked the name of their imaginary childhood army. And she had mentioned friendship, earlier. If that was all he would ever have of her, it would have to be enough—though he was bound and determined to try for more. His heart leaped for joy inside his chest. He'd been given a second chance. A gift that sprang from the courageous heart of a most extraordinary young woman.

She sighed. "I suppose after that sweltering trudge I could use a bathe." With the first rustle of clothes, he imagined her stepping out of petticoats and unbuttoning her gown. "Do you suppose those hounds will crest the hills beyond and come after us? I would find it most uncomfortable running stark naked over the moors."

He took pleasure in the thought. Fanny. Naked. Fields of heather. He cleared his throat. "Haven't heard them in hours. I wager they've called in the dogs."

He resisted the urge to peek. Well, at least for the first splash or two. No doubt she was down to her unmentionables.

He dropped a shoulder to inspect a pile of clothes on the rock. Good God. Her chemise and pantalets were on top of the heap. How like Fanny—when she decided to do something, she did it full course and with enthusiasm. A furtive glance caught the descent of a round derriere as it drifted underwater. Two exquisite dimples remained visible at the small of her back. His gaze roamed past a small waist and kissable shoulder blades. She adjusted a few hairpins before plunging that lovely spine beneath the glassy surface.

A wonderful long exhale and sigh emerged as the cool water seemed to soothe her skin and refresh her spirit. She used her arms to circle in place. "You swore on the lives of our regiment to keep your back turned."

Rafe scooped up her dress and propped it in front of his ever raucous cock. "Ah, the enchanting naked pond nymph speaks." He neatly folded her drawers and camisole, leaving them on a dry patch on the rock. "Upon risk of death the troops begged their captain for a peek."

Pale shoulders emerged from the water along with the prettiest smile he'd seen from her in hours—years. She paddled effortlessly around in ever widening circles before swimming farther out. Rafe used her old dress to dry off and pulled on drawers.

"I must say you are nicely made, Francine Greyville-Nugent." He tied his drawstrings in a bow.

"And how do I compare to your ladies in London— the ones who so admire your muscular buttocks?"

Rafe twisted a grin into a grimace. "Sorry to tease you like that. Horrid of me."

"I do not accept your apology."

"Why not?"

She splashed her face with water. "Because you don't mean it."

Her faint shadowy figure could be seen underwater, enough to make his fantasy of her complete. She was gorgeous, candidly blunt, and completely bewitching. "Ready to come out?"

She wiped droplets of water off her cheeks and nodded. He held up her mourning gown to block his view and imagined her climb out of the pond. A tug on the dress and he let go. "Would you be so kind as to bring me my new stolen dress and petticoat?" She deftly wrapped the skirt around her.

Rafe pulled on shirt and trousers and hiked back up into the grass. When he returned she was dressed in camisole and pantalets. A few damp spots made the silk fabric transparent and the tempting flesh beneath quite visible. He swallowed.

Fanny tied on petticoats and drew on the gown. She turned her back so he could button it. "You never answered my question."

"I would never compare you, Fan." Rafe hesitated. "For one thing, they aren't exactly ladies."

She twisted round and raised a brow. "Whores?"

"Shall we call them women of experience?" Rafe knew he skirted the slippery slope of her curiosity. "I do not frequent brothels as a customer, but there are . . . courtesans available."

"You can still catch the pox."

"Not when you correctly use protection."

Merry eyes flashing, she bit back a devilish grin. "A French letter?"

"Ah, so you know of such things?"

"Talk, mostly. Gossip and such." She sniffed, chin up. "Many suffragists take the question of contraception quite seriously."

Rafe fumbled with the cloth-covered buttons. "Take a deep breath." Fanny pressed her hands to each side of her waist and thrust her shoulders back. "Might fit a smidge better with a corset."

She snorted. "Serves us right for stealing."

"That pound note I pinned to the clothesline should keep the vicar's wife and daughter in silk for a year."

She fidgeted impatiently. "What do men get out of bedding whores?"

Rafe nearly choked. "Fanny, don't make me laugh."

"Apart from the obvious."

Rafe found the tiny buttons positively nerve-racking. And now discourse with a virginal young lady about . . . sexual gratification. "The obvious, as you put it, is quite enough. Why do women's gowns have so many small buttons?"

Fanny's laugh wafted over her shoulder. "To frustrate lotharios whose only thought is to unbutton them."

She never failed to make him smile. He kissed a spot between her shoulder blades. "Since you brought the unwholesome subject up, ladies of the evening are often rather adept at teaching pleasure."

"Whose pleasure, exactly?

Rafe nearly had to step away. "Are you bent on driving me mad?"

She snorted one of those musical giggles of hers. "An example, please."

"There are hidden places, all over the human anatomy, that are sensitive to a caress, or a kiss. Places that are easily stimulated and lead to greater arousal."

"For example?"

"I can make you tingle in places you never knew you had."

"Show me." Her taunt was husky and caused him to grin. "One."

He lowered his voice and edged closer. "Three or none."

She shot him a stormy look over her shoulder. "I said one."

"Three." His whispered tease caused a tremor. "Remember, I outrank you, Lieutenant."

Silence.

He imagined a plump lower lip being scraped under pearly white upper teeth. A blush rose up her neck— did it color her cheek? Were her pupils dark and wide, aroused with anticipation, her breaths rapid and shallow? "Tut-tut. Losing your courage under fire?"

"I see you haven't lost your swagger, Captain Savage." She sighed. "Three, then."

"Turn around."

"I will not. You said the human body has hidden places all over. Please be quick about it."

"The idea is not to be quick about it." As fortune would have it, he was still ten buttons away from the nape of her neck. He slipped the dress off peach-colored shoulders.

Brushing his lips along the velvet flesh of her upper arm, he moved to her nape. A quick intake of breath followed her sigh. He murmured, "One . . ." along the slim willowy side of her neck. He smiled as small hairs stood up and tickled his nose. "Two," he whispered in her ear.

He kissed a small spot just behind her lobe and licked. A shudder traveled through her body.

"Three." He saw no reason to stop, so he lifted her

skirt and bent down to run a finger ever so slightly behind her knee.

Fanny shoved him away. "You've made your point." She placed the back of her hand on her cheek. It would seem the young lady was hot again, but not from sun or physical exertion. Rafe backed away and found a shaded knoll to pull on his boots and wait for her to finish dressing.

She wrung out her stockings, and glanced up at him. "Rather pleased with yourself, aren't you?" He lifted his hands in a questioning gesture.

"Don't play innocent, Detective Lewis. And please don't get any ideas from that misguided episode a moment ago."

"I take complete responsibility for my actions." He tried to quell a grin, but somehow could not. "Did I sense a tender spot, or was that just a weak spot? A chink in the armor?"

Fanny rolled her eyes. "Did we not agree to a series of trials to restore your honor, Captain Savage?" Fanny slipped on her shoes.

"And what ordeals might you set forth, Lieutenant Cutthroat?"

"Not sure yet, Rafe. But you may start here." Fanny lifted her skirt and stuck out a dainty foot.

He kneeled to button her shoes. "I shall strive for excellence at the doing up of tedious little buttons."

"Even though I suspect your interest is more in the offing . . ." He looked up and met smiling eyes that rolled upward. "Might you?" She raised an elbow and gestured behind her.

"Ah, still more trials remain undone." He stepped around her to finish the job, and caught the reflection of a residence and outbuildings on the mirrored surface of the water. "I mean to try to get us a bed for the night and a meal of some sort. When we tap on this farmer's door, we'll need a story—some sort of plausible legend."

"Lies and more lies." Her stomach growled.

"If you want to stay alive." He spun her around to face him. "You will need to agree to become my wife— or sister"—he nearly choked on the words—"for this evening."

"Oh, very well." Fanny blew a few errant strands of hair off her face and bit her lip. "Shall we say you were driving your sister—that would be me—to the train station, when the phaeton—"

"Broke down?"

She shook her head. "You were showing off your new team."

"Driving so fast I blew off your stockings."

A giggle escaped. "Must have caught them on the fly." She unfurled a fist full of damp hose and shook them out. "One of the wheels hit a large pothole and we veered out of control and overturned."

Rafe's eyes lit up. "Thankfully no one was hurt." He paused to regard her. "You're a rather good liar, Fan."

"Not half as clever as Detective Inspector Rafe Lewis."

Rafe swept his jacket off the grass and flung it over his shoulder. "The story will work as long as we wait another hour or two. If we arrive late enough, there will be nothing to do about the problem until morning."

She nodded. "By then, we'll be in Bathgate."

A breeze stirred a froth of fragrant color as they walked in silence, surrounded by wave after wave of heather. Rafe looked back and stopped once just to look at her. She was a maiden in a painting, framed by an ocean of purple. Sheep grazed in pale verdant inlets of grass and patches of prickly thistle. "You are lovely, Fanny. The frock becomes you." Rafe smiled. "Am I permitted to pay you a compliment now and then?"

She stepped through the tall grass and came up beside him. "Yes, of course. Compliments might well be the rubber match in the event your trials fare poorly."

Rafe barked a laugh. "Come here, my little taskmistress." He pulled her into a small wood and cleared a spot with a view of the water. "Let's have those stockings." He draped her hose over a nearby shrub to dry, then spread his jacket on the ground. Settling himself against a tree trunk, he reached out for her hand. He tugged gently and she sat down beside him. "Be a good crime solver and reach inside my coat pocket for that red leather journal."

Fanny removed the notebook she'd taken from the dead man on the train and leafed quietly through the pages.

"As I recall, you have a talent for riddles and ciphers. Anything revealing, Detective Greyville-Nugent?" He peered over the binding.

"What do you make of this?" She pointed to the embossed symbol pressed into the red leather cover. Her fingertip traced the indentation of a wheel within a wheel. "I've seen these markings before."

"Where?"

"I'm trying to remember." Fanny yawned and Rafe took a turn with the journal. Most of the entries were cryptic, the kind of jottings one made on the dash. "And this?" He returned the open book to her. "Three letters. BVM. Most likely a person's initials, or an organization. They appear on several pages."

She frowned, her lips pursed in concentration. Such a fierce merging of eyebrows. And there were no words adequate enough to describe those plump, voluptuous lips. Of all her airs, this was his favorite. As a boy he had often gone out of his way to provoke the expression.

"Karl Marx once referred to the English factory worker as a mere cog in the wheel of industry. There is a symbol. A small wheel drawn within a much larger one." Fanny lounged on her elbows and squinted up through the branches of the tree. "One often sees the icon at marches painted on placards, either by the anti-progressive party, or one of the trade unions, but the initials . . ." She shook her head. "I'm afraid I haven't foggiest."

"Mull it over. A name might still pop up." Rafe tipped his hat over his eyes. Fanny tucked herself into his side. "Are you going to sleep?"

"A brief catnap—just until dark."

∞ Chapter Ten

Fanny stared at a slice of crescent moon perched above the farmhouse roof. An inky blue twilight was about to give way to evening. She stopped in the middle of a neatly swept dirt yard and greeted a few clucking chickens and a sheepdog. She gave the collie a good scratch behind the ears. "Hello, boy."

Rafe glanced back. "You always did have a way with animals."

"Not all beasts." She shot him a telling look and gave the dog's thick ruff one last tousle.

He pivoted. "Truce, Fanny."

"Our truce was up this morning, Rafe."

"I must ask for another suspension of hostilities."

She brushed down her skirts. "I'm not hostile, exactly, more like curious. It's been nearly five years—you might have written a letter."

He swept back his jacket and placed his hands on his hips. "You're bringing this up now? Honestly, Fan, this is rotten timing." Rafe glanced over his shoulder toward the cottage.

"I can't think which of us is more rotten at timing— you or me?" She folded her arms under her chest. "I wouldn't wish you to fail your first great trial."

He stared at her. "I wrote—many times. I just never posted a single letter."

"And . . . how many letters did you *not* mail?" She tilted her head, waiting.

His gaze moved to the sliver of moon and back again. "Hundreds." He kicked a bit of dirt around the yard. "Might we discuss correspondence later? I mean to try for a meal and a bed."

Skeptical, Fanny swept past him on her way to the cottage door. "And no dodging out on me like you did five years ago," she hissed at him in a whisper.

At the entryway, she hung back and let Rafe do the knocking. He patted the side of his leg. "Come stand by me, kitten."

"Why do you use silly words you obviously don't mean? I can't imagine courtesans of quality answer to such ridiculous sweet talk."

"On the contrary, they speak in oohs and ahs and contented purrs." The sudden throaty gravel in his voice made her pulse jump.

"You always were prone to exaggerate."

"As a sheltered innocent and suffragist, I would not expect you to be familiar with the sounds of pleasure."

"How ridiculous. I am perfectly capable of oohing and ahing."

He put an index finger and thumb to his lips and twisted. "Afraid you'll have to button it—for now."

Rude of him to remind her of his sexual experience and expertise—as well as her lack thereof. And he did it to provoke, quite deliberately.

Rafe turned to knock again, but before his knuckles could manage a rap, the door opened, seemingly on its own. Inside, a hearth burned low at one end of a comfortable room. "Hello. Anyone home?"

"Of course I'm home. Where else would I be?"

They lowered their gazes. A woman of very small stature stood in the doorway wiping her hands with an apron.

Fanny sidled up beside Rafe. "We've had a bit of a spill. My brother was driving me to the station when his new team got away from him."

"Capsized the carriage." Rafe feigned a humble grin. "No one was injured." He rocked his head back and forth affably. "Thank God."

Fanny clamped her mouth shut to prevent a burst of laughter. Rafe was purposely playing the role of a witless toff. "We're looking for a place to stay for the evening. Perhaps a bite of supper?"

Rafe nodded. "We'll gladly pay for any hospitality you might be able to offer."

The middle-aged woman sized them both up and down. "I'll give ye I'm small, but no' short of brains." The diminutive woman slammed the door shut.

Rafe stared momentarily at the heavy wooden barrier. "What do you suppose she meant by that?"

Somewhat amused, Fanny raised and lowered her shoulders. "I thought you were doing quite well, playing the dandy nob—"

The door opened and slammed shut again. A folded newspaper landed on the stone pavers. Rafe reached down and unfolded *The Scotsman*. "You're on the front page, Fanny."

She leaned in close and tilted her head. "I never liked that photograph."

The bare semblance of a grin surfaced as he studied her and the likeness printed in the paper. "It doesn't quite capture that wicked glower of yours."

Rafe dodged her swat with a chuckle. He took a seat on a wooden bench and stretched out his legs. A row of rubber boots covered in barnyard muck stood upright against the cottage wall. All of them appeared to belong to children or people with very small feet.

Fanny straightened a floppy boot at the end of the queue. "It appears we have washed ashore in the land of Lilliput."

He glanced at the muddy column. "I look forward to an attack by wee folk wielding pitchforks. I shall set them on you—have them tie you down with string."

Fanny rolled her eyes. "How easily amused you are."

"Not amused—aroused." As twilight edged into darkness, Rafe squinted at the article. "'Francine Greyville-Nugent and Detective Lewis remain at large.' There's some speculation as to what may have happened to us—captured by unknown assailants appears to top the list." He turned the page. "Ah, here's an article that makes mention of a fatal laboratory accident."

"Poor Mr. Poole." Fanny chewed on her lip. "Might this mean we can go to the authorities in Bathgate?"

Rafe tilted the paper to find some light. "Perhaps."

"You'll be wanting to speak with the constable, then," the husky voice came from above as the small woman poked her head out the window.

Rafe jumped up and turned around. "His name wouldn't be Wee Willie Winkie by any chance?" he asked.

The petite woman slammed the shutters closed.

Rafe pivoted toward Fanny. "Tom Thumb?"

"Stop it, Rafe!" She rapped on the window shutter. "Hello, again. We wish to apologize—that is, Mr. Lewis would like to apologize for his last remarks." Impatient, she waved him forward.

"Come on—Constable Winkie? It was a little droll—" He threw his hands in the air and shouted at the shuttered window. "Sorry."

Rafe plied his regrets to no avail. "Madam of the house, please forgive my thoughtless speech—"

"Brutish." Fanny kept one eye on the window.

A shutter whined and opened a crack. Inch by inch the hinged panels parted enough to shove two wooden bowls onto the windowsill. Rafe took down one and sniffed. "Lamb stew." He handed a bowl to Fanny and took the other for himself. The shutters slammed closed again.

"I thank you. Miss Greyville-Nugent thanks you."

Rafe nodded a bow and settled down on the bench. She surveyed the dish in her lap. "A lovely warm pottage and a large chunk of bread to sop it up with." She looked up at Rafe. "Heaven."

Fanny broke off a piece of bread, sloshed it around, and popped the crusty tidbit in her mouth. "Mm-mm." They ate in relative silence, lapping up the savory hot liquid with bread and using their spoons to scrape ravenously after bits of lamb and carrot.

She finished her last spoonful and closed her eyes.

The now-familiar craggy voice echoed from inside the residence. The front door burst open and lamplight arced over the grounds. The small woman shuffled closer, lantern held high. She was of middling age, sturdily built, and rather unkempt. She eyed Fanny with a certain amount of suspicion and curiosity. "This here is the kidnapped heiress." She shifted her wary gaze to Rafe. "And you're the Yard man, wanted for questioning in Edinburgh, aren't ye?"

She jumped forward and screeched. "Aren't ye?"

Rafe leaned away. "You've found us out, madam." He reached into his pocket and held out a few coins. "May I pay you for your hospitality and your silence?"

Their curmudgeonly hostess considered his offer, then gave a nod.

He placed the coppers in her hand. "Might you have a name?"

"Iona Tuttle." She set the lantern on the ground and dropped the coins in her apron. "Strange folk have been lurking about, asking after the both of yez."

Fanny's pulse quickened as she met Rafe's sober glance. "Men, presumably, and rather nattily dressed?"

Iona Tuttle grunted. "Them and another. Strange character driving a steam-powered machine—almost like a locomotive it was. Saw the smoke cloud it made for miles. Rumbled into my yard, growling and puffing— see there." The small woman pointed to a wide sweep of heavy wagon tracks.

"Can you describe this machine in detail?"

The Tuttle woman ignored Rafe's question and took a seat between them. "*The Scotsman* only printed half the story, aye?" She waited, presumably, for their recounting of events.

Rafe nodded to Fanny, encouraging her to elaborate.

"All right, then." She hesitated, not knowing where to begin. "Yesterday evening I was abducted from one of the University's courtyards. Detective Lewis quite bravely came to my rescue. Soon after, we found ourselves fleeing once again from the horrid kidnappers." Fanny paused in her tale for a yawn. "Sorry. Your wonderful pottage and a long day on the run have quite suddenly overtaken me."

"You can stay the night in the loft." The small woman slid off the bench and picked up the lantern. "Come along."

Twilight had faded into darkness. She led them across the yard and into a large barn. A newly painted hay wagon sat in the center of the stone floor. Paint fumes lingered in the air, along with the sweet scent of new-mown hay. The Tuttle woman looped the lantern handle onto the end of a hooked stick and held it high, along-side a steep ladder. "Up you go. Plenty of clean straw up there. The barn has several good mousers, few rodents about."

When Fanny hesitated, Rafe lifted her onto the first step and encouraged her to climb. "Careful."

After a number of rungs she looked down. "Are you coming?"

He reached for the lamp but the small woman pulled away. "Ye'll not get a lantern." Flickering light fell across a few deep wrinkles and wary eyes. "I'll not chance the likes of you or those sly characters burning the barn down."

"Have it your way, Mrs. Tuttle."

"Not saying whether I'm missus or not," the woman clearly harrumphed.

Rafe stared at the diminutive harpy. "There were several small pairs of boots outside the cottage. We thought there might be—"

Tuttle cut him off. "I'll thank you to leave the bairns out of this."

Rafe scaled the rungs and leaned over to pull up the slatted steps. Before he reached the top rung, the Tuttle woman kicked the ladder over. Rafe made a grab for it and nearly lost his balance.

"Rafe!" Fanny caught hold of flying coattails and pulled him upright. Their only means of escape hit the barn floor with a high-pitched crack and clatter that hurt her ears.

He straightened his jacket and winked at her. "Fast work, Fan."

*   *   *

RAFE PEERED OVER the edge of a crude railing. The small female he now likened to an evil troll glared up at them. "I plan on sleeping tonight. I'll be back for you both in the morning. Good night, Detective Lewis." She nodded to Fanny. "Miss." The circle of lamplight disappeared behind the barn door. Rusty hinges creaked as the door groaned shut.

Enveloped in complete darkness, Rafe reached out and wrapped an arm around Fanny's waist. For once, she cleaved to him, resting her cheek on his shoulder. Their small hostess secured the barn with a clunk. "Salty old witch," Rafe muttered. "Do you suppose she'll try to toss us in her oven?"

Fanny's chuckle was soft, musical, and evocative of their youth. He almost expected to look down and find the freckle-nosed harridan beside him.

"I rather liked her at first." Her voice was gentle, contemplative. "But now, I don't know . . . I don't trust her, Rafe."

Dark shapes emerged from darker shadows, as his eyes adjusted to their surroundings. "Hold on to the railing and don't move." He inched along the edge of the upper story.

"Where are you going?" She rasped a whisper.

"We could use a bit more light up here." Rafe reached out and found the end of the barn. Gingerly, he stepped away from the loft edge and felt his way along the wall until he arrived at what he hoped was the hayloft door. Blindly, he grasped for a latch. "Ouch!"

"What happened?"

"A splinter happened."

"Oh." A soft giggle rippled though the air.

He lifted the crude wooden crossbar and the door swung open. An arc of pale illumination swept across the floor. He smiled at her. "There you are, Fanny."

She joined him to admire the view. The rippling image of the moon reflected off the loch's surface and cast a shimmer of pale light through the loft. Rafe turned toward a nearby stack of horse fodder. "I know a little dove who needs a nest." He sifted through the hay and fluffed up a pile of bedding. Fanny shook out a few empty oat sacks and laid them on top. She lay down and snuggled into the hay. "This will do nicely." She rolled onto her back and sat up. "Where are you sleeping?"

Rafe covered her with his jacket. "I'll catch a few winks nearby."

Fanny nodded absently. "Odd, isn't it? This place."

"The resident is odd. The farm appears normal enough." Rafe picked at the splinter in the palm of his hand.

"That's just it." Fanny scraped pearly teeth over her bottom lip. "Do you remember old Wordsworth? For a time, he lived in the grotto drawbridge housing at Craigiehall?"

Rafe settled down beside her on one elbow. "Of course I remember the small fellow. The name was self-styled, always had a word or quote for the day."

Fanny sifted through a bit of loose straw beside her. "Then you will also remember he had refitted the bridge house to suit his size. The doors were altered, the knobs lowered, the seating child-sized—"

"You noticed." A lock of hair fell forward, blocking his view and he swept it back. Better to watch those large eyes, the color of Belgian chocolate, grow wider.

She lowered her voice. "What do you make of it?"

"Iona Tuttle is the only person of short stature who lives in the cottage, or this farm is not her residence."

She squinted at his hand. "Let me see the sticker."

"It will work its way out. Eventually."

She shot him a perturbed look. "After it reddens and festers and gives you blood poisoning."

He held out his hand, palm side up. "You just want to torture me."

Fanny turned his hand to the pale light and examined the splinter. "If the Tuttle woman is not a resident, then where are the owners?" She reached into the swirl of hair on the back of her head and pulled out a hairpin.

Rafe shrugged. "They might be away. She could be a relative or friend of the family, for all we know."

"Hold your palm very flat." She pressed on his fingers and slid the hairpin behind the embedded splinter. Her brows knitted, and her mouth tensed into a wonderful lopsided bow. She slid the pin along the skin and nudged the wooden shard out. "Hold still. Don't you dare breathe." She grasped the tiny stub with her fingernails and pulled.

"Aha!" She released his hand and held up the fragment of wood.

He examined his palm. "Dandy work. Thank you."

"Rafe, what if she's in with them—the natty horrible men? And what if the family who lives here is being held hostage or worse?" She sucked in a shallow breath. "And what if there are children involved, who could be injured or—?"

"Don't, Fanny." Rafe shook his head. "You must not think the worst."

He reclined onto his makeshift bed of straw and, quite surprisingly, she leaned back in his arms. "We need to find out what is going on inside the farmhouse."

Chapter Eleven

She lifted her head off his shoulder. "Have you thought about how we are going to get down from here?"

"Yes, darling."

"'Yes' doesn't adequately answer the question." Fanny sighed. "And please refrain from using words like *darling* and *kitten*."

Rafe raised a brow and opened one eye. "I promise never to use another term of affection, if you sidle up close and use me as a pillow."

"I'm not tired." She ended a gaping yawn with a growl. "Of course this means you have no plan whatsoever." She closed her eyes and imagined his grin. Horrid man!

Their shocking behavior at the loch stirred feelings she did not wish to think about. Nonetheless, she snuggled into the crook of his arm knowing full well this closeness was completely ill-advised. Out of the dark void of near sleep an image materialized into her consciousness—Rafe Lewis rising from the loch like a Scottish demigod.

The vision taunted her, setting her belly aquiver and her heart to skipping erratically. How extraordinarily beautiful he was physically. She thought of the *Reclining Apollo*, a life-sized statue she often admired in Dunrobin Hall. One muscular leg raised at the knee, the other stretched out from a rippled torso. The pose was angled so one could admire the Greek god's bottom. Frontally, one was afforded the most startling view of the warrior's sword, to put it in polite terms.

With her cheek on Rafe's shoulder, she rode the rise and fall of his chest with each breath. He felt comfortable, familiar, and completely trustworthy. Frankly, it was hard to believe they had ever been estranged. After their failed engagement, she had quite deliberately shoved their friendship into a dusty, cobwebbed corner of memory.

A Hogmanay celebration came to mind. An icy cold evening, the last of the year. Rafe was home from university. The Queen's own Pipes and Drums Regiment hammered a tattoo heralding the pyrotechnics display soon to begin. She and Rafe were out with a number of school chums making merry, reveling in the streets of Edinburgh. The festivities would last well into the early hours of New Year's Day. Rafe had materialized beside her and removed one of her mittens. Clasping her naked hand in his, he plunged both into his coat pocket.

Her cheeks burned remembering the play of his fingers along the inside of her palm. Her heightened senses thrilled to the lightness of his caress, and she had dared to answer in kind, hoping her touch had a similar effect upon him. He turned to her, eyes dark and primal. And there was something else in those lovely green eyes flecked with copper, something more vulnerable. At the time, she read the look as adoring, perhaps even loving. It hadn't taken much, in those days, for her naive little heart to take flight and frolic among the dazzling rockets bursting above Castle Hill.

Rafe tempted her away from the crowd and pulled her into the niche of a building. He lifted her face in his hands and studied every feature, as if to memorize small details. A stray mole? Or perhaps the tip of her nose, reddened from the crisp cold air?

A shower of falling sparks haloed his face. She smiled. "You look like an angel."

"Hard to live up to—being named after an angel. And I certainly don't feel angelic—not around you." He exhaled white puffs of breath and dipped his head. He hesitated, his mouth hovering just above her lips.

"A fire-breathing dragon, then?" She smiled.

He pulled her close and covered her mouth with his. The pounding of her heart drummed a frenetic beat among the bangs and whistles of the pyrotechnics surrounding them.

They huddled in the alcove, wrapped in each other's arms, experimenting with kisses. The image of a fogged shop window flashed through her head. Rafe drew a symbol in the steamed glazing. Two hearts entwined, surrounded by wiggled lines and dots. "Fireworks." He whispered. His eyes shimmered with mischief and desire. He yanked her close and kissed her hard. His mouth, hot to the touch, nipped at her throat and lips. "Open your mouth—just a little." When she complied, he used his tongue.

Shocked, she pulled back and frowned.

He chuckled softly and tried again. This time he licked at the underside of her upper lip, coaxing her to meet him halfway. Their tongues swirled a spellbinding dance, then plunged deep into some sort of wonderful, arousing madness.

"Rafe! Fanny!" The call from the past snatched her from the edge of sleep. Fanny jerked awake and shook off the strange feelings that ran through every part of her body. A sultry warmth radiated through the hay loft. Although rivulets of perspiration ran down her temple, she shivered. Not because she was cold, but because Rafe was gone. She stood up and peered into the deep shadows of the barn.

Odd bits of discarded and broken furniture had been stacked in a corner of the loft. She could see Rafe appraising his reflection in a tall looking glass. He was bare chested. Hints of moonlight haloed glistening skin.

He turned to her. "What's wrong, Fanny?"

"I can't sleep." She swept a few damp wisps of hair of her temple. "Woke up terribly out of sorts and over-heated—this dress is worse than a corset."

His stare made her tingle all over, as if he wanted something very badly.

"You're sweltering. Come here," he turned her around and began to unbutton the dress. "You'll rest more comfortably in camisole and pantalets."

The dress slipped off her torso and rested on her hips. "Hold on to me." She gripped his shoulders and stepped out of the skirt. Strong back muscles moved under her fingers. His skin was warm, like hers—moist. He straightened slowly and both her hands slid down the hard muscles of his chest. Her fingertips slipped through a light mat of chest hair. She had never touched a man so intimately—softness, yet solid underneath. His flesh quivered beneath her touch and there was a sharp intake of air. "Fanny." Gently, he removed her hands and stepped away.

She followed him with her gaze. "Why let London girls have all the fun?" She raised her chin. "Frankly, I don't much care for my virginity anymore. And . . . I was rather hoping you might be the one to . . ."

She caught her breath. Rafe stretched his lean, naked torso against a broken-down highboy and stared. A tingle of wicked arousal surged through her. Had he any idea how thoroughly—Fanny swallowed—masculine he was?

"I am deeply honored, Miss Greyville-Nugent, but alas, I must decline."

She felt a pout coming on. "Why ever not? You seem to have no trouble rallying the little soldier for complete strangers." A sudden, horribly awkward, and terrifying thought caused her to stutter, "Y-y-you don't like me, in that way."

His laugh was more of a scoff.

She flapped her hands. "Oh, you think I'm adorable enough, but you don't see me as naughty—in that way. Someone you would, you know—"

"Fanny, I've been panting after you since you kissed me that day in the boathouse."

She tossed her head and blew back a few errant wisps of hair. "*I* kissed *you*?"

RAFE GRINNED. SHE *was* adorable in those pale silk underthings. And there was something else about Fanny. The promise of a wild, brazen, and perfectly intoxicating creature. A bit of lace rode above a bouncing bosom and that sweet little derriere filled out her pantalets in the most alluring manner. If she only knew the kind of raw need that filled his gut as he watched her. Much too primitive for the word *adorable*, even though she was. "It was your eleventh birthday . . . or was it your twelfth?" He shrugged. "You planted one right here." He pressed a finger to his lips.

"I did no such thing."

"'Rafe Lewis, I shan't be the last girl in my circle to be kissed.'" He arched a brow. "You were quite insistent."

Fanny stared, then blinked. "You kissed me back."

Rafe smiled. "Of course."

Fists landed on hips. Brows crashed together. Lips pouted. "I could make this a trial."

"Trials are supposed to be difficult, punishing tests of a gentleman's character." He pushed off the dresser. "I'd like nothing more than to roger you royally." He scooped her up in his arms and carried her back to the soft bed of straw. "In more polite terms, I'd love to show you a bit o' pleasure, lass." He flopped down pleasantly beside her.

"Then why don't you?"

He smiled apologetically. "No condom."

Fanny propped herself up on elbows. "Don't you randy blokes carry them around on you?"

Quite a cross look, and the pout was back. He laughed out loud and pulled her close. "What put you in such a mood, Fanny?"

She looked as though she might shove him away, but didn't. "I was remembering a winter night in Edinburgh."

He angled his head over hers. "Which night in Edinburgh?"

"Hogmanay." She swallowed and opened her eyes. Moonlight edged a mass of unkempt curls.

"Ah, Fanny. I remember it well." His lips brushed hers, softly. She opened to him and danced a tantalizing, sensual waltz with his tongue. Primed by sensuous memories, his body hummed with desire. No woman had ever made him feel this way. Perhaps no one else ever would.

"I might be persuaded to give you a lesson, of sorts, but it requires a great deal more intimacy between us." He nuzzled her cheek, then moved to her neck and earlobe, which he nibbled gently.

She took his hand in hers and brought it to her breast. "Then, I would have a lesson."

"I will need to touch you in very private places." He cupped a firm breast and brushed his thumb lightly over a nipple. "Here." His fingers trailed down her midriff and belly. "And here." His fingers landed lightly between her legs. "Preferably without these undergarments."

Fanny answered him with numerous soft kisses. "What will it feel like?"

His eyelids lowered, shading none of his desire. "Ecstasy." A husky, whispered promise. With a sudden fierceness, he pulled her onto his lap and sat her astride his torso. The open slit in her drawers widened and there was a glimpse of mysterious curls. Rafe steeled himself and forced his gaze upward. A pretty maiden sat upright, shoulders back, arms crossed over the thin fabric of her camisole. "Must I remove everything?"

Gently, he pried her arms away and pulled on the ribbon. She let go of the delicate silk and the camisole fell around her waist. Her nipples instantly hardened, but not from the warm, humid air. He suspected those pretty peaked tips were not used to being admired.

Fanny tilted her head. "Rafe?"

Rafe leaned back, his gaze locked on the breasts laid bare before him. A slow grin widened. "I am savoring the moment."

Dear God, she was lovely.

Fanny's skin blushed pale rose in the moonlight and she made no move to cover herself. It was as if her entire body steamed with newfound sensuality. He loosed the silky pantalets that fell down past her hips.

He slipped a hand under and cupped a round buttock. She uttered a small moan. "When a man is allowed to place his hand on a lady's derriere . . ." Her scold was soft, throaty. "I believe it is compulsory to give her a kiss."

He pulled her on top of him and kissed her sweetly.

And then again, not so sweetly. "Have you any idea how tempting you are?"

He propped her back up upright and she arched her back. "Touch me," she moaned.

"Yes, my darling little wanton." Until now, he had only dreamed of such delicious behavior with her. His fingers cupped the curve of each breast and traced the faintest outline of ribs. Her midriff quivered from an unseen surge of arousal. He would give her many more.

Using his thumb and index finger, he rolled each rosy tip to a hard point. He wanted to fondle her until she gasped for air and moaned. His voice was husky, urgent. "Show me what you want, Fanny."

She placed her hands on his shoulders and leaned forward. He swirled his tongue over each rosy tip and tugged gently with his teeth. He soothed the bites with a lick of his tongue, then gently drew each nipple into his mouth. With each lick or suckle, she uttered a cry that was part Fanny, part feral creature.

Shamelessly, she guided his hand between her legs. They'd left her pantalets puddled around her hips. The barest hint of feminine triangle edged above the folds of her drawers. His fingers inched along the silky fabric on the inside of her thighs. Brushing softly, teasing a bit, he paused at the entrance to her most private place. "May I?"

He watched a new ripple of pleasure course through her. "You may." She opened wider, inviting his fingers to slide into uncharted territory.

Her warm, slick folds parted as his fingers delved deeper and found the spot that made her moan. He circled his thumb. Soon, this small, magical place would become the center of her universe.

His fingers coaxed a new rhythm from her. And a deeper moan. He guided her hips and showed her how to thrust forward. "Ride me, Fanny." She rocked back and forth across the flat of his stomach, bringing his cock roaring to attention. He groaned. "I take back what I said earlier. This is one hell of a trial."

He alternated fast circles with long gentle strokes. He used his fingers to explore the entrance to her channel but held back, and did not penetrate. He was keeping this as chaste as he could stand it. And with every caress, arousal bloomed in her, each new pleasure building upon the last.

He delighted in her discoveries. "More, please!"

And her less polite commands. "Don't stop."

Rafe sensed from her groans that she had climbed to a new level. He kept the rhythm steady and placed her hand over his, so she might guide him without words, while he kissed her deeply. When he tweaked a nipple, she began to grind against his hand. "Yes." She wanted faster, harder, more.

His own arousal was so great that just the right thrust across his groin might cause him to explode. He exhaled a ragged a sigh. "Let go, love."

There was a soft gasp as she hovered at the peak of arousal. Her body quivered and bucked, then tumbled over the edge of pleasure. He held her close, felt her pulse throb through every fiber of her being, heard the sweet sigh of her climax.

He stroked her back quietly as she drifted in a new land of bliss. A string of kisses led to a lovely encounter with the dreamy, half-lidded eyes of a woman well-pleasured. A second shudder of release nearly triggered his own climax. Hardened to the point of discomfort, he moved his gaze lower. Her breasts swayed ever so slightly.

Good God, there was no place safe to look. He kissed each rosy tip and raised her camisole. Dutifully, he pulled up pretty drawers and tied silk ribbon. As if she could sense the ache in his groin, her fingers played along the buttons of his trousers. He followed her movements closely, knowing that he was ready to burst from his trousers. All it would take was a few buttons.

A low, pleading groan escaped his mouth. "Fanny—"

She kissed him, teasing her tongue over his lips, and laid claim to his mouth—a kind of take-charge kiss that he found extremely arousing. He tried another gasp of protest. "Darli—"

She pressed her finger to his mouth. "It is my turn now."

Sitting up, she pulled the cord on his drawers. "Besides, I'm rather curious. I have never touched—" Uncaged, the beast sprang to life. "My word, and rather eager, I'd say."

Warily, Rafe lay back in the hay. Fanny reached out and trailed her fingers over his chest and along ridges of abdomen muscle. He grinned. "How impossible you are to resist." Delicate fingers moved past his groin and up the base of his shaft. So tentative, and yet so utterly arousing. He sucked in a breath.

Reaching the crown of his erection, she traced a finger over the smooth curvature of the tip. "It feels like the velvet muzzle of a horse," she whispered, her eyes dark and liquid, "only—stretched very tight."

He encircled her hand with his and showed her how to move up and down. There was a wanton vixen inside Fanny. "You always were a quick learner."

He let go of her hand and left her to fondle and stroke and explore. A surge of arousal shot through his body until he thought he might die from the pleasure of her caress. "Be patient, my love, for I wish to prolong the pleasure."

Cocking her head to one side, Fanny smiled at him. "Why?"

He muffled a chuckle, but not his next gasp. "Men are rather easy to please." He showed her how to vary the pressure of each stroke and to gently cup his testicles.

Covering his full length, she put one hand above the other and encircled his cock with her fingers. He came so close to bursting, he was momentarily forced to take her hands away.

"Might I hold you tighter? Stroke faster?"

Rafe quickly returned her hands to his cock, where he encouraged a good deal of tighter and faster.

Chapter Twelve

"Wake up, Fanny!" Rafe shook her gently.

Sleeping beauty stirred. "It's still dark out."

"All the better to sneak up on the cottage." He grinned. She would call herself a fright. He would argue otherwise. Half-lidded eyes and untamable curls with a few bits of straw poking out. Last night, her unskilled touch had been astonishingly powerful and stimulating. Her every innocent moan had affected him strongly, and her pleasure had enlarged his own.

Rafe shook off libidinous thoughts. "Here. Have a sip of this." He held out a tin ladle.

A pert nose wrinkled. "What is it?"

"Rainwater from a barrel below."

She sat up straight. "You found a way down?"

Rafe nodded toward the center of the barn. "See that rope and tackle hanging from the rafter? Hooked it with a pitchfork and lowered myself down."

A yawn turned into smile. "Aren't you the sly one?" Fanny sipped, then gulped thirstily.

"Had a skulk around the cottage as well." Her gown and petticoat were draped over his arm. "They train us well at Special Branch."

She stopped drinking to catch a breath. "I had no idea Scotland Yard ran a detective school."

"Not a school, more of an apprenticeship."

"I'm sure the dowager Lady St. Aldwyn is thrilled you've taken up a trade."

Rafe snorted. "You know very well she isn't."

"As a commoner I feel quite differently about your vocation." Fanny handed back the ladle. "The fact that you are a Yard man, and quite a competent one at that, might be the single most attractive thing about you." Seemingly surprised and amused by her own remark, Fanny raised both brows.

Rafe was equally amused, in a different way. "That's not what you said last night, lass."

A flood of color blushed her throat and cheeks and there was a squint, much like a hunter's eyes before he fired upon a buck in the forest. She enhanced the look by chewing on her lower lip. "What happened last night—"

"Was rare and wonderful, Fan."

She rolled her eyes. "Indeed, so rare we shall never speak of it again. Promise me, Rafe."

"I meant rare as beyond compare—without equal." He pulled her onto her feet. "And what happened is strictly between us." Fanny brushed off bits of straw and stepped into the simple country frock. The little vixen had whipped up a tempest of desire last night, and now, just looking at her . . . Rafe shook off the thought as he buttoned her up. They had work to do, a mission to accomplish.

At the edge of the loft, he turned to her. "I'll go first and steady the ladder." Fanny gamely followed on behind, until they were both safely on the ground. "This way." Skirting several empty stalls, he led her into a dusty room, some sort of tool shop.

Rafe opened the door a crack and surveyed the farmyard. A pale glow rimmed the bluffs east of the loch. Dawn was breaking. He angled Fanny in front of him. "See the wood pile?" All eyes, she nodded. "There's a window at the rear of the house I can crawl through. Give me to the count of one hundred, then make your way quietly around to the front door and knock just as plain as you please.

"Where will you be?" she whispered.

"Somewhere inside. Not sure exactly. Your knock will bring Wee Willie's wife to the door, hopefully with her back to me and the Webley here." Rafe pulled out the revolver and counted his bullets.

"Why don't you just barge in and overpower her?"

"Fortunately for you, you are divertingly comic and lovely. Which means I shall answer your impertinent question." He picked two pieces of straw from her hair. "We have no idea who is in there with the little missus. I'd rather not injure an innocent with a stray bullet. And what if the natty blokes are about?"

She frowned. "It will be my neck they're after."

His grin widened. "And my bullets they'll get. Poor chaps, they have no idea what they're in for." He returned the pistol to his jacket pocket. "To one hundred. Slowly."

Rafe lowered his profile and dashed quietly across the paddock. Behind the house, he used the blade of his pocketknife to lift the window latch. A sturdy fat log angled against the cottage wall lay right where he left it. He used the makeshift stepladder to get a look inside. A small room, likely the larder. He hoisted himself onto the ledge and into a sitting position, more inside than out.

He waited for his vision to adjust to the darkened room. Jars of preserves and sacks full of staples filled the deep shelves in front of him. A narrow door to one end would likely lead to the living quarters. Inching off the sill, he made the three-foot drop to the floor as quietly as possible.

The cat's tail went unseen until he landed on it.

Much like a torture victim with his cock in a vise, the feline's scream resounded through the larder and presumably the rest of the county. Large yellow eyes blinked at him from the shadows. He grabbed the growling minx by the ruff and tossed a flurry of gnashing fangs and swiping claws out the window. Another angry yowl came from outside.

Rafe sat on a large sack of grain and sucked the bloody scratch on his hand. Christ. One had to assume the current tenants, whoever they might be, were now fully awake. He heard a stirring in the next room—and something else. The floorboards beneath the grain sacks shimmied. Rafe swung around and squinted into the darkness. Another mouser perhaps?

A rapid hammer of muffled taps resounded through the cottage. Fanny's knocks. Rafe moved to the larder door and turned the knob. Nothing. He reversed directions. Bollocks. The door was locked from the outside. He searched wall hooks and shelves for a key.

FANNY STARED DOWN the cold steel barrels of a shotgun. At the other end of the gun Mrs. Tuttle was looking rather cross and bleary-eyed. Both she and the weapon swayed. Was she bladdered? Could a person wake up and still be drunk?

Squinting hard, the Tuttle woman craned her neck to see the barnyard. "Where's that detective friend of yours?"

Fanny crossed her arms under her chest. "That was a rather unkind thing to do, Mrs. Tuttle, leaving us up in the loft without a ladder."

After a wobbly peering about, the small woman grunted. "Inside."

Fanny pressed forward, forcing the dwarf in skirts to shuffle backward. But the disagreeable woman didn't fall or trip. Blast it.

"Not so fast, deary."

Fanny stuck her chin out. "What have you done with the people who live here?

The small woman narrowed beady eyes on her. "Like to know, wouldn't ye? Where's the Yard man?"

The gloves were off, but the ruse might yet be on. Fanny's gaze darted about the room. "Left in the middle of the night for town. Promised he would bring back the constable." Fanny inched away from the barrel of the gun, searching for signs of life. The layout was simple enough. The cottage consisted of a main room with a pantry and kitchen to one end. A plain stairway with unadorned railing led to sleeping quarters above. Where was Rafe?

Fanny lifted her shoulders and shrugged. "He appears to be a reliable sort. Although we girls can never be sure about a bloke, can we?" She raised her voice and loosed a smile; perhaps she could win over Tuttle, if that was her name.

The dwarf woman pointed her gun toward the rear of the kitchen and shoved Fanny backward. Fanny placed one foot behind the other. "Yes, well, why bother with Detective Lewis when it is me you're after?"

The little woman sidled up to a narrow door. She dropped a skeleton key on the floor. "Pick it up and open the latch." The shotgun remained poised while Fanny inserted the key. With a click, the door swung open.

The Tuttle woman lifted her chin and gestured with the tip of her weapon. Fanny stepped inside and pivoted. "Tell me, Mrs. Tuttle, why does BVM want me so badly?"

The small woman's mouth dropped open as her fingers tightened on the trigger.

A hand came out of nowhere and shoved the barrel

of the gun to one side. The blast was deafening. Gun pellets tore into a large sack of flour, filling the air with a cloud of white dust. Through the pale mist of flour particles a masculine form leaped between Fanny and her captor.

Rafe. She heard a dull sort of punch, a grunt, then a thud. The large grayish frame whirled around. "Are you all right?" His voice sounded as though it came from a distance.

She pointed to her ears. "Ringing."

He nodded and spoke louder. "You were spiffing. Just brilliant." He dropped onto his haunches. Fanny could just make out the fallen lump on the ground, the unconscious body of Iona Tuttle. "There's a coil of heavy twine on the shelf in the back. Bring it here, Fan."

Rafe dragged the old girl inside the larder. Fanny passed the cord and watched him tie several neat loops around her neck. "I believe she's alone."

"Most likely left here to keep watch. I wager this is the only north-south route into Bathgate. Travelers have to pass by here on their way into town." Rafe rolled the woman over and looped the ties around her ankles. He tested the knots. "There. If she tries to wiggle her way out, she chokes herself."

Fanny turned her head to admire his handiwork. "Cook does up a roasting goose in similar fashion."

"We need to get to a telegraph office in Bathgate." Rafe grinned. "I would say the initials BVM mean something, wouldn't you?"

Fanny's eyes brightened. "You saw it, too?"

"An instant before she was prostrate." Rafe placed both hands on his hips. "Quite a brave little charade, Fanny. Please don't do it again. I had no idea the woman had a shotgun pointed at you."

"And where were you and your Webley, Detective Lewis?" She tried a frown of annoyance, which quickly reversed itself. "I have a knack for sleuthing?"

"A bit too fearless but . . . quite extraordinary, actually." Ever the ready charmer, the gleam in his eye was a mixture of pride and something else. Lust, she suspected. The thought made her uneasy. He had made love to her last night without actually—doing the deed, as it were. And it had been pure pleasure. Warm thoughts and the memory of his touch actually caused her knees to wobble a bit. Her gaze darted away and back again. "I believe this adventure has aged the two of us." She began to laugh.

Rafe jerked upright and tousled his hair. "A bit of gray might add a dash of sophistication." A halo of white flour floated about his head.

"To my mind, you are quite dashing enough." She brushed flour dust off her cheeks and felt the heat of her blush.

A hopeful smile tugged the ends of his mouth. "Give me a moment." He took a step or two backward and began to drag heavy sacks of grain from one side of the small room to the other.

"What are you doing?"

"If I am not mistaken, beneath the larder we will find

a root cellar. And in the cellar . . ." Rafe shoved a large flour sack over and pulled on an iron ring. The trap door opened.

"Please, sir! Do not take my wife and children. Ye can have me and do as ye wish, but I beg ye do no harm to my family."

Rafe leaned over the opening. "Now, why would Fanny and I wish to harm anyone, Mr. Tuttle? You are the real Mr. Tuttle, I take it?"

A long moment of silence passed while the man looked them over. "Gavin Tuttle," he offered. "And who are you, sir?"

Fanny peered down into the cellar. A young man and woman huddled together holding two small children in their arms. Frightened smudged faces looked up at her. "It's perfectly safe now. This is Detective Inspector Lewis from Scotland Yard and I am Francine Greyville-Nugent." She smiled. "We are friends."

Rafe held a hand out and the couple passed the boy up to Rafe and the girl to Fanny. "Mrs. Tuttle." Rafe lifted her up out of the trapdoor. Last man out, Mr. Tuttle climbed up after his wife.

A good-looking lot. The family appeared shaken, but no worse for the wear. Mr. and Mrs. Tuttle reached out for both towheaded children "Come, Duncan. Effie."

Rafe handed over the boy. "I'm afraid we have no time for acquaintances. Your family cannot stay here alone without protection. We must all travel to Bathgate and report this incident to the township's constable."

"That would be Clarence Ferguson." Mr. Tuttle laid

a protective hand on his young son. "Good man, retired Royal Scots Lothian Regiment."

"I take it the men who forced you into the cellar also borrowed your equipage?" Rafe nodded past the window to the road and fields beyond. "Is there an inn close by where we can hire a carriage?"

Tuttle shook his head. "The MacClarys live down the road. They've a fine team of mares and a good-sized dog-cart."

"How far away?"

"A mile and a foot south."

Rafe frowned.

Faintly, the snap of reins and hooves could be heard pounding on the road. On tiptoe, Fanny could just make out a serviceable old barouche stirring up dust as it turned down the drive. "Who do you suppose this could be?"

Rafe glanced out the open window and waved Mr. Tuttle over. The young father stepped over to the window and squinted. "That's my rig and them are the blokes who took my house over."

"Natty dressers, were they?" Fanny blurted out.

Taken aback, Tuttle blinked and turned to his wife, who nodded. "Right smart, I'd say." Outside, pounding hooves slowed to a trot.

"Well now, it seems we have visitors." Rafe turned to Mr. Tuttle. "Help me get these bags of grain up against the door."

Tuttle stared at him. "We're barricading ourselves in, then?"

"We're going to make it look that way."

Fanny caught the furrowed brows on the farmer's wife, who rocked the whimpering little girl in her arms. "I'll not go down in that hole again."

Rafe shoved the bag of grain against the door and tossed a look over his shoulder. "Fanny, tell them I've got a plan."

She folded her arms across her chest. "You tell them." Hoisting a sack over his shoulder, Rafe stopped to raise a brow.

"Oh, very well, then." She helped push a large bag over. "Detective Lewis, generally speaking, devises reasonably good plans—at least he's managed to keep us alive thus far."

"Not the kind of glowing account I'd hoped for." He turned to the young farmer, his mouth firmly set. "We'll not be leaving you and your family behind." Rafe grabbed another grain sack.

Gavin Tuttle set the boy down and joined in. They quickly had a stack of staples pressed against the larder door.

Rafe clapped flour dust off his hands. "How many men last time?

"Three plus the wee woman." Tuttle pointed to the lump on the floor.

"Did all of them carry weapons?"

The farmer nodded. "I believe so."

Rafe broke open the shotgun and checked both barrels. "You've got one shot." He handed the gun off. "I've always found the butt-end makes a handy bludgeon." He dragged a milking stool over to the window. The moment the carriage rolled past the rear of the house and entered the farmyard, he climbed onto the sill and leaped to the ground. He reached up for Mrs. Tuttle. One by one, everyone made it through the small window and safely to the ground.

Rafe hunkered down to speak to the children. "Your father and I are going to disappear for a few moments, but you mustn't be afraid. Your da is going to help me take back your carriage so we can get away from the bad men." Both children stared wide-eyed. "You must promise to be very quiet." Rafe dipped his head. "Effie? No more tears." The child nodded from behind her mother's skirts.

Rafe approached Fanny with brows drawn and a glint in his eye. "Keep the troops calm and quiet. No bugles or screaming from young cadets." He pressed an index finger to his lips and winked at the children. "The next time you see us we will be driving up close to the side of the house. Be prepared to let fly and cast yourself and the wee 'uns into the gig. We don't mean to slow down much as we pass by."

He nodded to Mrs. Tuttle. "Ladies."

◌ Chapter Thirteen

Fanny took the boy, Duncan, by the hand and Mrs. Tuttle carried her daughter on her hip. The young mother shushed the sniffling girl. "Chin up, Effie. Remember what Detective Lewis told you." The young woman managed a thin smile. "My name is Lara."

"Lara, lovely name—much better than Iona. I'm Fanny." She queued the Tuttle family up against the cottage and waited. After several tedious moments, loud thuds and a strangling noise could be heard from the yard. Fanny peeked around the corner.

A man lay on the ground, but she couldn't see who lay in the dirt—pray God it wasn't Mr. Tuttle or Rafe. Several shots fired and Fanny caught a glimpse of Rafe struggling with one of the natty blokes.

Mr. Tuttle climbed onto the driver's seat and unhooked the reins. "Hurry, Rafe!" Her harsh whisper carried. She chewed her lip, knowing full well she had broken silence.

"Bloody hell, Fanny, give a me a moment, I'm trying

to finish this last one off." Rafe got in a few crushing blows to the man's face and rolled out of the clinch. The natty bloke righted himself and pulled a gun. Rafe raised his Webley. She had no idea how many bullets were left. Rafe fired and the man fell to the ground. Her pounding heart welcomed a sigh of relief.

Mr. Tuttle slapped the reins and Rafe jumped aboard. Fanny signaled to the young mother beside her. "Come." As the vehicle slowed, she scurried farther into the yard. Running beside the carriage, she lifted Duncan up into Rafe's capable hands and helped to secure Lara Tuttle and her daughter into the rear seat. Rafe reached out and pulled her up onto a carriage step. "My skirt—" Fanny gathered her dress and yanked it away from rear wheel spokes.

"Slow us down!" Rafe shouted to Tuttle as he lifted Fanny into the vehicle.

The Tuttle's collie ran alongside the carriage and yipped. "Orkney!" Duncan leaped off his mother's lap and nearly tumbled over the edge of the carriage. "Here, boy." Tongue lolling, the old herder picked up speed and made a leap for the carriage. Fanny set the child back on the bench and leaned out to grab the child's pet.

"Fanny!" She heard Rafe over her shoulder. She reached for the dog but her hands barely brushed his head and front paws. "I've almost got him." The children began whimpering.

She leaned farther out. "Hold on to me!"

Rafe's arms went around her waist. "Quickly, Fan, there's a bridge ahead."

Alarmed by Rafe's warning, she glanced up the lane. In mere seconds her head would be lopped off and the dog cleaved in two by a stone bridge pillar. She grabbed the dog by the ruff. Front paws splayed, and rear legs scrambled. Fanny held on and tugged harder. At the last moment, strong arms yanked both woman and canine to safety.

Out of breath, Fanny looked up at Rafe. "Thank you." She might have predicted a cross retort accompanied by a few curse words. But the look in his eyes was something akin to relief.

She directed his attention to the child on the floor of the carriage. Duncan hugged the panting collie, who licked the boy's cheek and wagged a ragged tail. "Lovely sight, is it not? A boy reunited with his dog?"

Rafe rocked with the sway of the carriage as Gavin Tuttle snapped the reins and steered the team onto the main road. The ends of his mouth made a sudden plunge downward. "Never do such a thing again."

She could not fathom why, but she found his snappish words rather endearing.

Shots whistled overhead.

Fanny peeked around the canopied top of the buggy. Two figures ran down the long drive firing wild shots after them. "I thought you got them both."

"Apparently not." Rafe grabbed Tuttle's shotgun. "Stay down." He popped off a shot that presumably sent the men scurrying for cover. At a runaway gallop they entered the cover of a small wood. Mr. Tuttle skillfully slowed the team and brought the horses under control.

Fanny settled herself on the narrow bench of the rear seat. Mrs. Tuttle and the children appeared rattled but otherwise hardy. Rafe glanced back at Fanny. She thought he meant to say something, but then changed his mind. His gaze left her breathless and shivering. And her reaction was not entirely due to the morning's excitement. Rafe had always been athletic and awfully clever, but this Yard man was both wily and courageous. And he had heeded her concerns about the Tuttles, when they were only a possibility. A figment of her worried imagination.

She returned his wink with a smile.

"DETECTIVE INSPECTOR RAPHAEL Lewis, Scotland Yard." Rafe handed a card to the officer at the front desk of the constabulary. A middle-aged man sporting a neat gray beard and moustache poked his head around the corner of a back office and gave them all a long look. The man nodded at Tuttle and boldly approached Fanny. "Yer the missing heiress, Miss Greyville-Nugent?"

Fanny nodded, "I am, sir."

"Clarence Ferguson, constable here in Bathgate." The man examined her disheveled appearance. "No worse for the wear, I presume? The detective here has acted the proper gentleman?"

Rafe eyed Ferguson as the constable questioned Fanny. Rafe thought about their afternoon at the loch, and last night in the loft. Perhaps he hadn't acted the perfect gentleman, but then she hadn't acted the demure young lady, either. Fanny had turned into a wanton goddess.

She squared her shoulders. "I have been well protected, Constable."

The headman surveyed the motley assemblage and settled his gaze on Rafe. "Been expecting you."

Rafe buttoned his coat. No doubt they appeared a ragtag lot. "On the run for two days from Miss Greyville-Nugent's would-be abductors and, I'm sorry to say, West Lothian law enforcement."

The man turned to Rafe. "Ye dinna need to tell me my business, Detective Lewis. I am in receipt of several messages from authorities in London and Edinburgh."

Rafe exhaled. "Excellent. Then the confusion has been cleared up?"

Constable Ferguson gestured toward his office door. "Will be soon enough." He ushered them all into a plainly furnished office, which included a government-issue desk and a few chairs. A small cast-iron stove took the morning chill off the room. The man in charge settled into a desk chair on wheels and looked as though he expected to interview the lot of them at his leisure.

Rafe cleared his throat. "The culprits after Miss Greyville-Nugent are, at this moment, in the area of the Tuttles' farm, doing their best to acquire transport into Bathgate. They are armed and dangerous, and there may well be more of them here in town."

Ferguson stared at him. "Ye canna mean these malefactors would dare attack the constabulary?"

Rafe didn't blink. "How many men are on duty this morning?"

"That would be myself and Sergeant Wallace here. I can marshal deputies given an hour or—"

"Not fast enough. I'm afraid we are all in danger." Rafe turned to Tuttle. "Do you have friends or relatives in town?"

Tuttle nodded. "Lara's brother is a collier, has a flat between here and the mines."

Rafe turned back to the constable, who grunted a sigh. "Have it your way, Detective Lewis. I am in possession of several telegrams addressed to you in care of this station." The man sorted through a stack of wire envelopes before handing them over.

Rafe tore into the missives, sharing something of the messages with Fanny and the others. "Detective Kennedy of Scotland Yard has alerted law enforcement from Edinburgh to Glasgow as to my identity and the threat to Miss Greyville-Nugent."

Ferguson looked as though his troubles might soon be over. "Ye should be safe in the city once again, miss."

Rafe glanced up from the wire. "Except that I am ordered to bring her to London."

"What?" Fanny's eyebrows collided in a straight line.

"And I am to make contact with another inventor, a Professor Minnow. You wouldn't by any chance—know him?" The constable shook his head. Rafe took a swipe across the desk and grasped a pencil. "May I?"

Ferguson kept an eye on his scribbling. "Deciphering one of those coded wires?"

Rafe tapped the side of his head with the writing instrument. "I do those in my head." He scrawled a brief sentence or two, transposing letters as he went along. "I'm writing a reply."

"You use a military code?"

"A centuries-old encryption, actually." Rafe continued to work his squiggles. "I think it might be best if Fanny and I leave Bathgate as quickly as possible."

The constable checked his pocket watch. "Glasgow train should be here within the hour. Ye've got just enough time to get to the station."

Fanny pivoted in her chair. "Constable Ferguson, I wish to return to Edinburgh posthaste, with or without Detective Lewis." Her eyes darted over and he tried a wounded look, but it was no use. She saw right through it. "Rafe, I do not wish to further endanger anyone else on my account." She returned to Ferguson, all beseeching eyes and mournful pout.

Before she could utter another word of entreaty, he was forced to dash her hopes. "I'm afraid you have no choice, Fanny. You are now in the custody of the Crown." Rafe passed the wire over the desk.

Ferguson dug out a pair of spectacles and read the directive. Sorrowful eyes peered over the rim of the reading glasses. Shaking his head, the constable offered her the wire.

"Come here, lad." Mr. Tuttle reached out a hand and Duncan slipped off her lap.

Fanny accepted the missive and slumped back into her chair. There was a gasp, a hiccup, then a bit of sob.

"The writ is for your own protection."

She turned her head. "How is that possible, Rafe? Why would London be any safer than Edinburgh?"

"I don't know." He sucked air quietly through his teeth. "Fanny, no matter where you go, you'll expose someone to danger." He wondered, frankly, if there were other motives behind this request of hers. To elude him—quite likely. All that intimacy last night no doubt made her skittish. The thought, however, turned the edges of his mouth upward.

"Fan . . . I must ask a favor. While I encrypt this message—which takes more than a bit of concentration— might you give the constable a description of the horrid natty blokes?"

Ferguson leaned back in his chair. "What's this about horrid natty men?"

Fanny rolled her eyes and colored slightly. "A description of mine—a silly one. The men after me all dress rather smartly."

"Have ye noticed they wear black waistcoats?" Ferguson seemed pleased with himself. "Quite formal in appearance when it comes to attire."

Lara Tuttle perked up and nodded. "Almost like they were militia or clergy."

Rafe looked up from his ciphering. "Might be a uniform of some kind."

"Caused a bit o' trouble the other evening at the Nag's Head." Ferguson lowered his voice. "Declared themselves member of some order—the Utopian Society." The constable scoffed a chuckle. "Raving lot. Several of them talking nonsense. 'The machines will destroy us.' I tossed the worst troublemaker in the lockup 'til he sobered up. Daft man tried to lecture me. 'Britain's reign is over. Greatness wasted on a system of domination and exploitation.'"

Rafe exchanged looks with Fanny. Hurriedly, he finished his secret missive and stuffed the paper into his coat pocket. "We'd best be on our way, Constable." He lifted the warming plate from the cast-iron stove and tossed in the telegrams from Special Branch.

"Best see you out this way." The constable escorted them all to the back of the station. "See to yer family, and be back here within the hour, Mr. Tuttle. We'll take a ride out to the farm." The farmer nodded as the collie scuttled through the door with the young family right behind. The Tuttles dashed across the narrow alley, made a turn at the first lane, and disappeared. Ferguson turned to Fanny and Rafe. "Follow this alley straight up the hill to the train station."

Rafe nodded to the constable and grabbed Fanny by the hand. They kept to the shadowed side of the lane and periodically took cover in doorways. Fanny peeked around the corner. "Station straight ahead."

Rafe handed her a small pouch of coins. "Purchase our tickets and board the train the moment it arrives. Try for a compartment."

"Where will you be?"

"Takes a bit of time to send an encoded message. I must see it through and destroy the original." He indicated for her to proceed on ahead of him. "Don't worry, Fan. I'll find you."

*   *   *

FANNY FOLDED HER hands in her lap and sought to disappear into her corner by the window. Several passengers occupied seats in the compartment, including an elderly vicar and two ladies. With no hat, gloves, or coat of any kind, she attracted stares from the other passengers. She clutched the train tickets in one hand and used the other to smooth her hair.

In no mood to face off their cool stares, she gazed out the window. Why oh why was this happening to her? Always on alert now, she peered up and down the tracks looking for dark-suited pursuers. She wanted to go home. Back to her life before all of this . . . turmoil. Before Father died.

Fanny had not yet come to terms with her father's death, not wholly. A heavy blanket of horror shrouded her mind, smothering both her grief and her loss. Days ago, she'd confronted the truth of the gruesome murder, even vowed to see her father's assassins brought to justice. So what had happened to her? Last night with Rafe had happened. She hadn't expected the intimacy to be so—intimate. Her body trembled at the very reminder of his pleasuring.

And the Tuttles. Those dear children put at such risk, and such a lovely young family. All because someone with a private army was after Ambrose Greyville-Nugent's daughter.

Incredible. Impossible. Nightmarish.

Fanny inhaled a deep breath and exhaled quietly. She

scraped her upper teeth across her lower lip and contemplated the question of her further cooperation with Scotland Yard. In point of fact, the local police appeared woefully undermanned, no matter how well intentioned. A hiss of steam and the gentle bump of train cars rolling forward caused her empty stomach to lurch. Where was Rafe?

The fates had been perversely mischievous of late—case in point, Raphael Lewis. She felt a smile coming on. Of all the devilish, philandering scoundrels in the world to come to her aid, why did it have to be—

"Here you are, darling." His lips bussed her cheek. "In your dash to board the train, you forgot these." He plopped a blue peplum jacket, a pair of crocheted gloves, and a small but jaunty enough chapeau in her lap. Rafe smiled his signature winsome grin at the middle-aged spinsters across the aisle. "A bit late rising this morning. Almost missed the train." He might as well have winked. "Newlyweds." The ladies tittered and the vicar turned the page of his newspaper with a snap.

Fanny pulled on an open-weave glove. "You had time to shop, Detective Lewis?"

Rafe used his new ruse to touch her cheek and sweep a few errant hairs back into the coil of hair on her head. "Hand me your hat, love."

She examined the high-crowned fedora on her knee. One side of the brim included a spray of poppy and cornflowers tucked into a grosgrain band. He set the hat on her head and adjusted the tilt. "There. Every bit as cheeky as my lovely new wife." He removed a long hatpin from the ribbon and fastened the crown to her topknot. "After you were safely away, I took a separate route to the station." His words whispered over her ear. "I happened to find a shopkeeper opening her doors. The jacket and hat came straight out of the window and the gloves off the counter. I tossed two crowns at the confounded woman and was out the door in under sixty seconds."

"You always were foxly fast." She flashed her eyes with a smirk.

Rafe sat back. "Do you think so?"

"I know so."

He grinned. "Handy trait in my line of work, but hardly clever."

The morning sun had quickly warmed the compartment. She tried fanning herself with a loose glove. "Clever enough, Rafe, and I think—rather thoughtful of you."

Rafe settled back beside her. "Crikey blimey, Miss Greyville-Nugent, does this mean I have reason to hope?"

"Don't pop the corks yet, Detective Lewis." She glanced out the compartment window as brickyards and smokestacks were replaced by the hills and dales west of Bathgate. "Many trials are yet to come."

Fanny sighed. Perhaps, for the moment, she would go along with Scotland Yard's directive. But she wanted answers. "What news from London? Might Special Branch have anything to say about my—*our* dilemma?"

"Nothing half as brilliant as your insight on the matter, which I wired them. I will say the mounting casualties have confirmed suspicions."

"My father, that chap in London, and Mr. Poole."

Rafe nodded. "They're off collecting inventors and industrialists in London, housing them in a secret enclave somewhere in town. They've instigated a roundup here in Scotland as well. Peter Guthrie Tait, Lord Kelvin, and someone named Waterstone are in protective custody."

She was going to need a salve for her lower lip if she kept on chewing. "Good God. Tait and Lord Kelvin in the same cell together. They don't get on. William can be quite insufferable."

Rafe's eyes wrinkled. "They'll likely put them under house arrest."

"And how is it I am ordered to London, while they reside comfortably in Edinburgh?"

"Can't say for sure." When she slanted a glare, he shrugged. "They must fear you've been singled out in some way." His gaze wavered slightly over her face. "There is a lovely blush of sun across your cheeks and nose, no doubt from all that frolicking in the loch and the heather."

"But no spots?"

He squinted and made quite a show of examining her cheeks. "Alas, there are none."

Exasperated, Fanny crossed her arms over her chest. She caught a glimpse of her new hat's reflection as they passed through a small tunnel. She adjusted the brim slightly.

For several miles, she gazed out the window. It would not be difficult to loll about in a reverie over yesterday's swim in the loch and the astounding pleasures of last evening. In fact, she wished to curl up against Rafe's broad shoulder and forget the morning's excitement.

The train lurched and she squinted down the tracks. Something was wrong. "We're slowing down."

Rafe pressed close to the window. "Bollocks."

∽ Chapter Fourteen

Fanny groaned. "Now what?"

Rafe reached for her hand and pulled her onto her feet. He nodded to the passengers in their compartment. "Excuse us, ladies."

She trailed Rafe out the compartment and down the aisle. At the rear door of the railcar, he stopped abruptly and turned to her. "The train is being flagged down."

Her pulse raced. She should be used to this kind of disruptive scenario by now. Back at the station she had sensed something afoot but had dismissed her apprehension. "By them—the natty blokes?"

"We're not waiting to find out." Rafe struck the heavy door latch and it swung open.

Fanny pulled back. "We're still moving."

Rafe nodded. "Don't worry, I'll catch you." With those discomforting words he was down the steps and off the train. She squinted through fluttering lashes. A blur of coattails flew through the air. He managed to land on his feet, which was hopeful, until his body folded under him. He rolled onto his side and disappeared down the embankment.

"Rafe!" Panic set in and she froze, momentarily. She was to be the next one off the train, but there was no Rafe to catch her. Biting her lip, she stepped down the metal stairs and hoped for a grassy patch of hillside. Something with a bit of cushion.

His voice barely carried over the shrill squeak and hiss of the train. Something about a hill and a bit of encouragement. "Jump, Fanny."

Gathering her dress around her knees, she let go of the handrail. She couldn't think. She just had to close her eyes and . . .

The knoll wasn't nearly as soft as it appeared. Her landing, if one could call it that, was bone jarring and teeth rattling. She tumbled head over heels before smoothing out into a sideways roll down the grass.

Every rock bruised.

Every burr pricked.

Finally she slid to a stop. Shaken senseless from the fall, she lay prostrate on the ground, arms clutched fast to her sides. Her head throbbed, and she sucked in short, labored breaths. She waited for the shooting pain to come, signaling a broken limb or two. The slightest whimper escaped her throat. She licked her lips and tasted blood.

With a bit of effort, she raised her head. Her dress had flown up around her thighs, her stockings were torn in several places, and both knees were skinned.

"Fanny!" Rafe clawed his way up from the base of

the hill to her side. "Are you all right?" The strength and comfort of his embrace surrounded her, and she burst into tears.

He rocked her in his arms and rubbed her back. Gently, he kneaded some of the aches away. This time, with permission, he checked her arms and limbs for injury. The concern in his expression blurred through damp eyelashes. He wiped tears off her cheeks. "I should have been there to catch you."

She hiccupped. "No broken bones?" She wiped her eyes with a gloved hand and blinked.

"No permanent damage to either one of us." He grinned, she was almost sure of it. "I'm afraid your new bonnet has not fared quite as well." She unpinned her hat. "See—a dent in the crown, and you've lost a few posies."

She stabbed the hatpin into the brim. "Help me up."

Rafe's arm wrapped around her waist and he stood insufferably close as he lifted her to her feet. He also held on too long. "I'm perfectly fine." She pushed him away, teetering on weak legs. He tried to steady her. "Let me walk about, Rafe." After a few wincing steps, she turned around and hobbled back.

"You're hurt."

"Nonsense, a bit of a sprain is all."

Rafe lowered to his haunches. "May I?" She lifted her eyes along with her petticoat. He craned his neck for a look. "Ah yes, there is a swelling." His fingers gently probed her ankle. "You mustn't try to walk on this."

She dropped her skirt. "I shall not prattle on about a

simple sprain." She took a few tentative steps and started down the hill. "We'd best be on our way."

He rose from his crouch. "Fanny. Let me carry you."

"Ha!"

Rafe trailed along after. "I rather liked your tears. I was able to witness this lovely softening—a sign of maturity, I think."

She spun around and struck him in the face with her ruined fedora.

"Ouch!" He hunched away from her.

Instantly regretful, she bit her lip. "Sorry. Are you all right?" She noted a red welt under his eye. She dropped the ruined hat.

He gazed at her between furious blinks. "Quite all right, only half-blind."

"But really, Rafe, that business about softening and maturity? I greatly dislike those kinds of remarks. Gentlemen often think to compliment a lady on her gentle ways and girlish sentiments." She took a moment to huff. "But it is often an insult, is it not? 'Little lamb, how wonderfully biddable you are.'"

Rafe stared at her. "I take it all back. I meant to remark upon how contrary and troublesome you can be." He turned away and surveyed the field in front of them. "This grass is not tall enough to provide cover. We need to cross the field and get to that small copse of silver birch."

After a bit of slow going, he fell in alongside her. Fanny winced with every step. "Truth be told, I dislike your suffragist rhetoric as much as you hate my flattery.

Besides the vote, what do you possibly hope to get out of it, Fanny?"

"I'll take the vote for a start. And it is my intention to study engineering at university. That is, if I survive this gruesome adventure."

Her revelation appeared to knock the wind from his sails. They walked along in silence for a number of strides before a chug and hiss signaled the train pulling away. Rafe looked back across the field. "Entirely too much exposure."

"What?" Her breath was strained and harsh from pain.

"Are you up to something faster?"

Fanny nearly choked. The very thought of faster caused her eyes to moisten and burn again. She stepped up the pace for several strides, limping so terribly she had to bite her lip to keep from crying out.

"Unbelievably muleheaded of you." He swept her off her feet. "Arms around my neck—that's it." Lifting her higher, he adjusted his grip, and quickened the pace. "I fully understand your anger, Fan. It must seem as if every time I enter your life I bring with me some form of difficulty."

The marvelous brawn of his arms and shoulders thrilled and her throbbing ankle seemed greatly relieved. She tilted her head and studied his handsome profile. "Perhaps it hasn't been all misery."

Rafe's grimace shifted to a grin. He stepped up the pace again, something less than a jog, but they covered a good deal of ground before he spoke again. "Even though we're in a bit of a mess, might I just say . . ." Rafe slowed down to look at her, adjusted his grip, and walked on. "I'm not unhappy about it. Not in the least. In fact, I am grateful to be the one assigned to your safety."

Over Rafe's shoulder she spotted a man at the edge of the meadow. Her heart moved from a girlish skip to a rapid patter. "We must make the woods, quickly." She scanned the field again and gulped. "There is a dark-suited man on horseback, by the train track." Rafe returned to a jog.

Fanny glanced ahead. The copse was still some distance away. She arched back for a scan about the grassland and spotted two more riders entering the western slope of the meadow. Her voice croaked out a whisper. "Second enemy position, due west."

RAFE PUSHED HARDER, increasing his speed. Less than a hundred feet to the stand of trees. Up ahead, he could just make out a road edging the field. If he could get her to cover . . . A bullet whizzed overhead. That would be a warning shot.

At a second crack of gunfire, Fanny ducked her head into his shoulder. Rafe sucked a harsh breath into burning lungs and forced himself to run faster. The pounding thud of hooves crossing the field drew closer.

Less than fifty feet from the copse, another man on horseback emerged from the wood, riding straight for them. Rafe slowed his pace and halted. "Reach into my pocket and remove the gun." He eased her slowly onto the ground and folded himself into a crouch in the tall grass. She slipped him the pistol. "Stay down, Fanny."

He stood up, took aim, and fired. The rider barring their entrance into the wood collapsed and fell to the side of his mount. Rafe ran forward to try and capture the skittish animal, but the horse shied away and bolted into the trees. Another whistle of bullets sailed past his shoulder and he took aim at the approaching riders. He pressed the trigger and the revolver clicked. No more bullets. He dropped the gun on the ground and raised his hands in the air. The sign of surrender.

Placing one foot behind the other, he backed over to the dead man in the field. He reached for the man's pistol as a shot rang out. Rafe tossed the gun to Fanny in a lateral rugby pass. Quickly righting himself, he raised his arms again.

The riders were nearly upon them.

Fanny picked up the revolver.

"Hide it between your legs." She raised her gown and inserted the weapon between her hose and garter.

"Listen to me, Fan. No matter what happens, we are going to survive this."

Three men in dark uniforms reined in their steeds. Each one pointed a pistol at Rafe. A tall, wiry-framed man with high cheekbones and hollow cheeks lifted a thin, sneering upper lip. "What's wrong with her?"

Rafe lowered his arms. The man's pocked skin further marred a skeletal appearance. Not long ago he had bumped into a rat catcher in the Docklands of similar veneer. Some of these blokes weren't quite so natty up close.

"Keep your mitts up there, mate." Rafe turned his head. Another rider on a large gray approached from behind. The heavier set man removed a silver object from his inside pocket and held it to his mouth. A shrill sound, much like a police whistle, pierced the air.

The burly man dismounted. "Answer the question." A staggering blow to his back nearly tumbled Rafe on top of Fanny.

He recognized the fear in her eyes and forced a wink. "Remember what I said earlier." Wide-eyed, she gulped and nodded.

Rafe straightened, keeping his hands upward in surrender. "Miss Greyville-Nugent has injured her ankle. It's rather difficult for her to—"

Another blow to his shoulder spun him around. He faced the barrel of a pistol inches from his nose. "And whose fault is that, mate?"

He eyed the bulky chap, whose jowls were covered by copious amounts of whisker. "Since you dregs are the malefactors, I would have to say yours, actually." The punch grazed his chin and caught some of his cheek.

Rafe braced for more blows and they came in a flurry to his midsection and head. Feigning a stagger, he reached out for balance and grabbed his assailant's gun hand. He swung the culprit around to use as a shield.

A shot rang out and a fine spray of red splattered his face. The large bloke in his hold spewed blood from his mouth. Glazed eyes stared back at him. Rafe tore the gun from the dead man's grip as he collapsed. With revolver in hand, he aimed at the remaining grim-faced man on horseback.

The elegant rat-catcher clicked his tongue and tutted. "Now see what you've made me do?" He leveled his pistol at Rafe's chest and cocked the trigger. "The question remains . . . will it be me?" The glint from yet another gun barrel caught his eye. "Or you?" Rafe's gaze fell to a second pistol aimed at the ground. "Or her?"

He searched the pitted, gaunt face. Highly unlikely he would kill her. Not after going to such arduous and tenacious lengths to capture her. Still, what would stop them from causing her pain? Rafe lowered his arm and something cold and hard struck the back of his head. He fell to his knees and heard her cry out.

"Rafe, don't you dare leave me!" Fanny's muffled, distant decree faded into darkness.

∞ Chapter Fifteen

A bombardment of artillery shells went off inside his skull. His head lolled backward onto his shoulders as he jerked awake. He began a muddled inventory of the pain. Throbbing temples. Sore ribs. Incessant, prodding elbow. "Rafe!"

The shrill whisper came again. "Rafe, wake up."

His eyelids remained half-closed as he tried to make sense of dark shapes and blurry surroundings. A groan, not unlike the last utterance of a dying elephant, bellowed out of his dry, cracked lips.

Ache by ache, his body came alive. Rafe inhaled musty air and triggered a spate of painful coughs. Dark figures on horseback came to mind, as well as shots from revolvers. He gritted his teeth. "Where exactly am I?"

"*We* are at the bottom of a mine shaft." He recognized Fanny's voice. There was a tremor in her whisper. A frightened echo to be sure, but resilient nonetheless.

A familiar poke jabbed his side and something shifted

across his back. "They have us tied together. All the better to flatten us both."

Half a smile caused his bottom lip to crack. The sting of warm blood rushed into his mouth. Rafe squinted into nothing but blackness. Gradually, as his vision improved, he was able to make out walls of chiseled rock, equipment strewn about. He craned his head back and followed a shaft of dust motes up to the surface. "Christ. How did they get us down here?"

"Steam-powered lift. Carries miners and equipment up and down."

"Something of your father's design?"

Silence. "I believe so."

"Ah, let me guess." Rafe detailed their immediate surroundings. "Thick cables and an odd variety of wheels and pulleys. I wager we are positioned somewhere under the contraption."

"Directly under the lift."

He licked a split lip and sucked in a deep breath. His chest strained against the bristle of hemp rope. "Hence the remark, 'all the better to flatten us.'"

"I have come to understand they are quite excellent at threats."

Along with a hammering headache, his senses returned. A tug came from behind his back. "What are we to do, Rafe?"

He made a brief assessment of their bindings. His hands were tied behind his back and his feet bound separately. Another heavier rope strapped the two of them together. They appeared to be cocooned in hemp. "I'm relieved you didn't ask if I had a plan."

Fanny huffed. "Well, do you?"

He pictured the knotted brow and the pout on her lips and quickly shuttered all trepidation aside. For her safety. For their lives.

"First off, we need to get out of these ropes." Rafe hunkered down and extended his legs. He found he could swing them side to side. Now, if they were both tied in similar fashion . . .

"What are we sitting on?"

"An old skip loader, turned upside down."

"Stroke of luck. Possibly." Rafe was thinking out loud. "Well then, we're going to move together—like good soldiers. Be prepared to take a tumble onto the ground if this works." He sat up straight and pressed his feet to the floor. "Brace yourself against me, place your feet on the ground, and raise your bum off the loader."

Quite miraculously, they both rose off the metal container until Fanny's feet slipped out from under her. She plopped back down, taking him with her. They both landed with a hollow thud. Rafe exhaled. "You all right?"

"Don't be ridiculous, of course I am." There was an exasperated breath before she leaned against him. "Let's try again, only this time don't push quite so hard."

With backs pressed together and feet planted squarely on the ground, they pushed upward in sync. "On the count I am going to do a kind of toe-to-heel step to my right. Simultaneously, you will wriggle your feet to the left, and we are going to shuffle along, until we reach the edge of this metal bin, and then . . ."

The rope binding them together snagged on one the cart's wheels. A struggle to break free ensued, tipping the loader and themselves onto the ground with a crash.

"Here now, what goes on below?" The gruff query echoed down the long shaft.

Rafe froze. "Who's that?

Fanny wriggled herself upright. "Rats."

The voice from on high queried again. "A rat in a copper mine? Never heard of such a thing."

"Sorry. I forgot they're all aboveground here."

Rafe snorted. Fanny always had been a stouthearted lass.

Her voice returned to a whisper. "Can you feel my fingers, Rafe?"

Good God. A lovely tickle along his wrists. "Yes. Yes I can." Their fall to the ground had twisted them so that their bound hands were in close proximity to one another. "Fan, if you could manage to find the tail of the knot, that would be a start."

Rafe inched his hands closer. Pressing hard, he strained against the bindings even as they cut into his wrists. "Can you reach it now?"

Tentative fingers made several blind attempts to get a grip on the rope. "Wait, yes, I believe I've got it."

Dear God. Rafe closed his eyes. Prayer was something he admittedly invoked only on rare and deserving occasions. However, twice now in so many days, he had asked for the Almighty's assistance in saving Fanny Greyville-

Nugent. Her fingers tugged at his knot and her elbow pressed against him in a jerky fashion.

To ease the tension in the rope, he pressed his wrists together to allow the smallest bit of slack in the prickly hemp. He felt a long pull, and the rope eased. "I think—" Rafe pulled hard, twisting his hands. "That's got it." He wrested a hand loose and was able to push off the bindings. Easing his arms to his sides, he wriggled his hands up through the coils of rope binding them together.

"Patience, Fan, I'm almost free." Rafe loosed the bindings around his ankles, untied her wrists, and pulled her upright. "We need to find a way to get him down here." He chafed a bit of circulation back into her wrists, then untied her feet. "I'm going to need you to cry out, like you did before. Louder this time, and quite desperate."

Fanny nodded and stood up to yell. "Wait a moment." He pulled her off to one side of the mine shaft—away from the path of the lift. "Just in case their desire to kill us is greater than their curiosity."

"Ready?" Fanny didn't wait for an answer. She inhaled a deep breath and let loose an ear-piercing shriek.

"I say, what be the trouble down there?"

Fanny turned to Rafe and raised a brow. He held an index finger to his lips. As seconds of eternity passed, they waited in silence.

"Hello down there? Miss?"

Rafe pulled her close. "How many guards, do you think?"

She stood on her tiptoes to whisper in his ear. "I believe some of them went off, not sure how many were left behind."

Another voice, different this time, came from above. "Don't make us come down there, lass. Ye will no' like it much if we do."

His hand remained at the small of her back. "Do you still have the gun?"

She raised a brow. "You mean the one digging a hole into my leg?" She turned away and drew up her skirt. Fanny's momentary lapse into modesty caused a grin. Pivoting back, she passed the weapon to Rafe.

He released the cylindrical chamber and counted bullets. Overhead, the gasp of steam signaled the lift engine was engaged. The pulley system began to lower the metal cage. Her large round eyes shifted up from the revolver. "How many?"

"Two." Rafe winked. "No pressure." He motioned her back into the shadows and bade her stay, while he crouched behind a queue of empty skip loaders and cocked the pistol.

As the iron cage descended, he made out a pair of legs, and then another pair. And another. Drat. Three men were in the metal cage and they were almost upon them. Belching a hiss of steam, the heavy platform groaned to a stop four feet above the shaft floor. Good. They assumed he and Fanny were still tied up below. The gate retracted, and one of the guards dropped to the ground. The man drew a weapon and ducked under the lift.

Rafe stepped out of hiding and slipped under the platform. He used the butt of his revolver to strike the back of the man's head and caught hold of deadweight.

The body slumped soundlessly over the upturned skip loader. Rafe pocketed the man's pistol and took cover behind the unconscious guard.

A second man landed on the ground with a heavy thud. This one, a burly stout bloke, turned and fired a shot into his own man. Rafe returned fire and brought the guard down. With a hiss and a clunk, the lift began to rise overhead. Rafe leaped onto the skip loader and into the air. He caught hold of the edge of the platform and pulled himself up. The guard at the controls stepped away and kicked Rafe's shoulder, sending him back off the lift. Rafe barely held on to the ledge as a booted foot stomped. Bruised fingers slipped off the platform and left him dangling by one hand. He looked down. Pain knifed through his upper arm even as crushed fingers numbed. Soon the lift would be high enough that the fall alone would either kill him or break both his legs.

Rafe swung a leg up, meeting his attacker face-to-face. The guard moved to crush the bones of his other hand. The crack of a pistol shot zinged overhead, but he was almost certain it came from below. Rafe stared as a dark hole appeared under the man's eye above him and blood dripped from an open mouth. He fell forward, then plunged head over heels off the platform. The body landed facedown on the floor below. A frightened, wild-eyed Fanny stepped into a shaft of light, holding a pistol with two hands. The gun still pointed at the lift.

"Brilliant work, Fan, but lower the gun, darling, if you would?"

"Don't you dare fall, Detective Lewis."

He clenched his teeth, ignored throbbing fingers, and raised himself onto the lift. A lantern sputtered from the cage ceiling. With no one at the controls, the lift continued to rise. Willing himself to stand up, he stared at the tubes and levers that made up the control.

He shouted into the darkness, "Which way do I push the lever?"

Fanny's strained voice carried up to him. "The engine must be in neutral before you can change directions. Find a midpoint."

Aching fingers gripped the brass handle and pulled the lever back to an upright position. Neutral, he hoped. The cage jolted to a stop. He poked his head out of the steel chamber and found her ashen face below.

"Groaning men are starting to flail about." She stood in a shaft of light, shading her eyes. "Rafe, please come down."

He rubbed his bruised hand and returned life to several swollen fingers. "Should I push the lever past neutral in the opposite direction?"

Her head bobbed a yes. "Try it."

Rafe pressed the lever down and a burst of steam came from above. The iron cage rattled, groaned, and gasped, then started down again. Near the bottom, Rafe brought the lever back to neutral and the lift stopped. Rafe leaned out the open metalwork gate. "Hop aboard, Miss Greyville-Nugent."

Rafe lifted her into the cage and shoved the gate closed. He wound his arms tightly around her and pushed the lever. "Look." He nodded upward. From a tiny square of light, high above, a rose-colored sky poured soft rays down on them. "Nearly dusk outside." They had been down in this hellish pit for most of the day. Fanny clung to him as the groaning, creaking platform slowly climbed up the shaft. "Now what, Rafe?"

He stroked the small of her back and spoke softly. "We charge ahead, Lieutenant Cutthroat. Onward to Glasgow."

∞ Chapter Sixteen

The grind and squeal of metal pulleys and the shudder of the lift bore a strange semblance to her own fatigue. She was weary of being chased around Scotland's industrial corridor by this bizarre band of malefactors. And this cat-and-mouse game—this seemingly endless struggle—had grown well beyond tiresome. The foppish malefactors had murdered her father and two others. Now they skulked after her. But why? Even though her body ached, her mind retraced what little they knew of these devious, malicious men.

It wasn't as if she was going to become an inventor. She was more of an engineer, if truth be told, with a keen interest in mechanical devices. She had even helped her father out on a design or two. Child's play, really— hardly genius. Besides, how would these criminals know anything of her hopes and dreams?

She nuzzled close to Rafe. She couldn't help it, the man brought out the wanton hussy in her. Worst of all, she suspected that he knew it. His jacket smelled of copper dust and gunpowder, reminding her she'd just held a pistol in her hand. Good God. She pushed away. "I believe I killed a man."

"It was either him or me." His grin was oddly reassuring. "Glad you chose to save me." The cage rose aboveground and a rush of air swept through the open ironwork. They clung to each other and gulped deep breaths. Fanny exhaled a sigh.

"The fresh air should help revive us." Rafe spoke in low tones as he opened the retractable gate and peered around the gravel yard.

Some distance away, a man sat in a wagon, his back to them. His snores suggested their lookout might have had a wee too much drink. Rafe reached for Fanny's hand and stepped out of the lift. They circumvented massive wheels and pulleys and exited the shaft house.

A steep incline covered in loose shale girded the mine entrance. They kept to the deeper shadows and made their way around a curve of foothill. Once they were shielded by a slope of knoll, they headed toward the setting sun. West, Glasgow way.

"Look here." Rafe pointed to a boarded-up shed. A couple of two-wheeled contraptions were parked against the building.

Fanny's eyes sparked with recognition. "Velocipedes!" Bicycles were often used to move about large mining operations.

"A couple of old Rovers." Rafe rolled out one of the wobbly-wheeled bicycles and dusted off the seat.

"A bit drossy, don't you think?" Fanny squinted at the rusty Rover.

"Maybe a bit worse for wear." He held the metal frame upright and motioned her on. "Shall we have a go?"

Fanny gathered up her skirts and settled onto the seat. She tucked a bit of skirt under her bottom and away from the wheel spokes. "Ready?" She nodded and Rafe shoved her off.

On her first turn, the handlebars of the teetering two-wheeler proved loose and unworthy. Rafe frowned. "How's the steerage?"

Fanny leaned forward and pedaled faster. "Improves some with speed." At least the pedals worked fair enough. Fanny steered the bicycle in ever-widening, wobbly circles until she got a good bit of steam up. Passing Rafe, she made a turn down the country road and waved. "See you in Glasgow."

Rafe jumped on the other bicycle and chased after. He rode close behind, keeping a lookout, as they quickly put a good bit of distance between themselves and the mining operation. Fanny silently gave thanks for long summer days. The luminous silver twilight would linger for some time to come. At least she would be able to see the road ahead.

Once they were well away and onto a good length of flat road, Rafe pulled abreast. "You've become quite the pedaler."

"A machine can just as easily do the pedaling. A German inventor, Gottlieb Daimler, has attached a petroleum engine to a bicycle. He calls it a *reitwagen*." She offered a smug little smile, and raised her chin in the air. "He based it on the four-stroke internal-combustion engine invented by an engineer, Nikolaus Otto, except Otto's uses town gas. Petroleum is lighter."

"Ah yes, more of your inventor chaps."

Fanny inhaled a deep breath. The exercise had improved her mood even as a bit of heat flushed her cheeks. "I should like to manufacture motorized bicycles."

Rafe checked the road behind them. "I will say that last batch of natty blokes were a sorry lot."

"With heavy brogues as well." She stopped her pedaling to coast around a gentle curve.

"Nefarious locals, recruited out of a pub."

"Who are these vulgar anti-progressives, Rafe? They fancy themselves a Utopian Society or Empire or whatever, but machines won't destroy us. This age of industry assures our advancement as a civilization. What used to take a man weeks to accomplish can be done by a machine in a few hours. Did those wires from London tell you anything more?"

"If they know anything, they're not sharing it by wire. I forwarded on your insight regarding their cryptic symbol—as well as the initials BVM."

For a time, Fanny chewed on her bottom lip and rode on in silence. Their escape from capture was just starting to sink in. "Why didn't they kill us?"

"Waiting for orders, perhaps? I suspect they wanted me alive to find out what Scotland Yard knows. Torture me until I spill the beans."

"You were rather grandly heroic back in the mine."

She managed a shy smile. "I fancy you'd stand up to torture rather well, Rafe."

"After they yanked out the first fingernail, I'd tell them everything." He answered her shiver with a grin. "Don't worry, Fan. They won't torture you. I wager you'll be put through some sort of—" He hesitated.

"Flesh chopper of my father's invention?" She giggled madly. "One way to press the wrinkles out of a girl's skirt."

Rafe barked a laugh before he could stop himself.

Then she snorted. Good God! One laugh led to another and as fast as her legs could pedal, she pulled ahead of Rafe. A sudden memory catapulted her back to a moment in their youth. She was riding Jewel, her gray hunter. She had galloped over a bluff ahead of Rafe. They were both laughing, but she could not recall why.

Fanny glanced over her shoulder and there he was, right behind her—pedaling his rickety Rover. She smiled at him. How brave as well as resourceful he'd been these last days . . . and nights. She shook off indecent thoughts.

"What shall it be, Rafe, death by meat grinder?" They both let loose another belly laugh, but thoughts of her father torn apart by that bloody thresher sobered her quickly. "What wretched creatures we are."

"A bit of gallows humor, Fan."

"No doubt common in your profession, Detective Lewis." She broke off conversation to cycle up an incline. After cresting the hill, she yelled out a challenge. "Race you to the bottom!"

Pumping furiously, Fanny set the pace and held her

lead until they neared the bottom of the slope. Just as Rafe was about to pass her by, something happened to his bicycle. A high-pitched clinking and an awful grinding noise, metal upon metal. Rafe swerved into her, pushing her front wheel toward the ditch. She tried to brake.

No brakes.

Fanny skidded off the road and stopped with such a lurch that she went flying over the handlebars. "Ouch!" She felt the scratch and sting of brambly thistle. "Ooof!" She landed with a thud in patch of weeds by the roadside.

She suffered a faint buzzing in her ears. "Fanny! Are you all right?" Her eyes opened in a flutter of lashes. A fuzzy-looking Rafe danced overhead. Had he any idea how many times he had asked her that question over the last two days? She narrowed her gaze into slits. "No, Rafe. I am not all right."

"What happened?"

She gritted her teeth. "You knocked me over into the ditch and now you steal my question?" Her speech was calm, if more than a bit clipped, given her inner turmoil.

Rafe enveloped her in his arms. "The sprocket must have seized—then the drive chain broke—I'm so sorry." He cradled her head against his shoulder. Absently, she picked a few burrs from her hose and examined a tear in her dress.

Rafe dipped his head to look into her eyes. "Fanny? Talk to me."

She finally met his gaze and sighed. "I give up. I am

going home to Edinburgh. You can follow me if you want, but I am done with this nightmarish little sojourn." She pushed away and stood up on her own. "I have enough money to hire my own private army, if need be, and I am quite sure they will be more effective than one rather inept inspector from Scotland Yard."

She wobbled and Rafe leaped to his feet to steady her. "You blokes are always five steps behind the culprits, aren't you?" She shrugged off his grip and climbed back onto the shoulder. Disoriented in the darkness, she looked up and down the roadway.

"To your right, Fanny."

"Shut up, Rafe." She purposely turned in the opposite direction and began heading up the grade. He trailed behind.

"We just raced down this hill. You're headed back toward the mine."

She whirled around and released an ear-piercing scream that went on interminably.

He jogged up the road. "Stop, Fanny!"

RAFE GRIPPED HER shoulders and shook until the screams stopped. He could just make out the burn of fury on her cheeks. She was breathless, angry, and unbelievably tempting. More than anything he had ever wanted in his life, at this moment, he wanted to kiss her. Savagely. And then he would toss up those skirts and take her right here on the road.

She met his gaze and seemed to sense his frustration—his raw lust, which likely subdued her hysteria. She continued to gasp for air. "I don't believe . . . you have enough imagination . . . to conceive of how much I'd like to . . . to . . ." She shoved him off.

He swept back a lock of her hair and brushed his thumb across her lower lip. "To what?"

In the twilight, her eyes narrowed to slits. "Box your ears."

"Well, I for one would like to kiss yours." He dipped his head, but at the last second she pushed him away.

"I bet you would, you, you—" she sputtered.

"No objections last night, if my recall is correct."

With a sharp intake of breath, she said, "How quickly sentiments can change, Detective Lewis."

Rafe studied a few bright stars in the evening sky. He placed his hands on his hips and nodded. "All right, Fan. If it will do you good, have at me."

She punched him in the jaw and his head snapped back.

He rubbed his cheek. "A lefty. I'd quite forgotten what a wallop you pack in that dainty little—" Fists flying, she let loose a flurry of punishment, which he tolerated until a jab to his nose drew blood.

"You little devil." He picked her up and tossed her over his shoulder. She continued her drubbing, with blows to his back and kicks to his shin. Then her toe slammed into his balls.

His testicles smashed into his intestines. His stomach pressed on his lungs, making it hard to breathe. Rafe staggered a bit and fell to his knees. Fanny rolled out of his hold.

On the ground with his knees drawn to his chest, he released a groan that sounded more like a howl or a bellow. Vaguely, he was aware she watched him writhe in agony. Time passed. He couldn't be sure how many seconds or minutes. He covered his groin with his hands, unsure where his balls had gone or if they might one day venture outside his body again. He glanced at Fanny. "Just checking on the manly parts."

Sprawled out beside him, Fanny brushed hair from her face. "Rafe, I'm tired of being chased like a wanted criminal by a gang of . . . criminals! Why are they picking on me?" She exhaled. "What's going on?"

Rafe stared at a black sky sprinkled with pinpoints of light and traced a pattern of stars. He raised his head and turned his body toward her. "I wish I knew, Fanny." He threw a leg over her body and watched storm clouds form in her eyes.

Brows knit. Lips pouted. She was ready for battle. "Is this how you Yard inspectors subdue your prisoners?"

"Only the most dangerous ones." His voice a gruff whisper.

"Let me up."

Rafe groaned. "You may have finally succeeded in emasculating me."

She brushed hair from her face. "The Women's Franchise League would be proud."

"Why, you incorrigible— You're not the least bit sorry."

He grabbed both of her hands and pressed her arms to her sides. How he wanted to kiss her again. He must be hallucinating. She smiled. Even in the dark, her face smudged by road dust, Fanny was irrepressibly Fanny, doing her best to drive him mad.

"After two days on the run, you've left me bruised from head to toe, Rafe."

"Shall we have a contest? We'll remove our clothing and count up the black-and-blue marks." He grinned. "Bruises are good. They remind us we are alive." His groin still throbbed and his throat was dry. "However, I would sell you to a white slaver for a drink of water."

She added a nod. "And I'm ravenous beyond words."

Rafe's gaze traveled up and down her body. "As am I."

"Such a brute." She pushed him off, angling her body away. Her stomach growled loudly.

He leaned back on his elbows. "My word, you are hungry." Over Fanny's shoulder, he caught a glimpse of a dark, odd-shaped . . . mechanical . . . something shambling down the road. He instantly forgot about his aching balls and scrambled to his feet.

"What do you make of that?" He clapped road dust off his hands. "Fight or flight, Fan?"

Eyes glazed from fatigue, she twisted to look down the road. "Good God." She sat up straight. "Rafe, I'm too tired to run."

"Then we hide." He pulled her to her feet. "Behind those shrubs."

Off the road, they hunkered down behind a clump of brush. The night air remained balmy and comfortable, yet her body trembled. Instinctively, his arm went around her waist and he tucked her in close. "We're going to be all right, Fan."

"At least one of us believes that." She peered through a crisscross of branches and studied the ominous contraption rolling toward them. "I've seen plans in my father's study for machinery on wheels. All of it rather hush-hush. Most of the devices were designed for farm use or mining. But there were others. Great machines designed for battles—'engines of war,' Father called them."

The rumbling behemoth moved steadily closer. The chug and hiss of the engine suggested the vehicle was steam-driven. Fanny turned to him. "Have you ever heard of a pedrail wheel?"

Rafe shook his head.

She frowned. "I don't suppose anyone has. It hasn't been invented yet." She sighed.

"Fanny, you're speaking in riddles." The ironclad machine rolled along on large wheels with a number of podded feet attached to their circumference. As each wheel turned, a rubberized foot swung into place with a hiss and hit the ground with a *ker-clunk*. Hiss, *ker-clunk*, hiss, *ker-clunk*.

"It's an armored landship, designed to transport artillery and troops over rough terrain—break through enemy trenches." A gleam returned to her eyes. "I've only seen sketches on paper. I had no idea anyone had built one."

As the metal-on-metal noises grated ever louder, a porthole cover slid back in the vehicle's front end. A powerful ray of light poured onto the road. The beam swept over potholes and ruts searching for . . . Rafe swallowed. "Fanny? Back at the farmhouse last night—"

"Was it last night?" A bit dazed, she stifled a laugh. "Seems like a year ago."

"The batty dwarf woman prattled on about a strange vehicle. A steam-powered machine that had rumbled into her yard, growling and puffing."

Wide-eyed, Fanny turned to him. "She called it a locomotive on large metal wheels."

"And whoever was driving the blasted contraption was looking for us." While they studied each other, the hiss and *ker-clunk* rumbled closer. "What do you think, Fan? Shall we raise the white flag?"

Chapter Seventeen

Fanny stood beside Rafe in the middle of the road and waved her arms. Her flailing about became a good deal more frantic the closer the armored monstrosity loomed. Rafe, as well, swept his arms up and down. "Ahoy there, landship!" His only answer, the steady hiss and *ker-clunk* of the behemoth.

She shaded her eyes. "Can't you see us here in the road?" A bright beam of light passed over them, hesitated, and swung back.

"Best step away." Rafe grabbed her by the arm and tugged. They shuffled outside the circle of light. The glaring beam followed them.

"And get that blasted light out of our eyes!" Rafe blinked and pulled her farther to the side of the road. He cupped his mouth. "Stop this contraption before you run us down!" The giant wheel's podded feet took a step and then one more before grinding to a halt.

S-s-s-s-s-s. The machine exhaled a huge belch of steam.

High atop the odd parallelogram-shaped vehicle, a wheel rotated and the hatch opened. This time, Fanny reached out for Rafe's hand. In the darkness it was hard to make out much more than the head and shoulders of a man. Fanny squinted. Bearded with a wild crop of un- kempt hair, partially pulled off his face. Broad—almost burly—by the look of his shoulders.

The shadowed figure pulled a whiskey bottle out and took a long slurp. He wiped his mouth on his shoul- der sleeve. "Well now, lass, ye wouldn't be Francine Greyville-Nugent by any chance?"

Fanny squinted at the unkempt man. "And what kind of straggly, disheveled, reprobate wants to know?"

"Hoo-hoo!" The man drained the bottle and tossed it into the field. "Feisty one, ain't she, Detective Lewis?" The drunken sot rested his chin in the palm of his hand.

"She asked a simple enough question." Rafe placed his hands on his hips. "Who are you?"

The stranger stared at Rafe for a moment and then focused his woozy gaze on Fanny. "Ye probably don't remember me, lass, but yer father and I, bless his dear departed soul, were fast friends for a time." The man dis- appeared down inside the belly of the beast and popped up a moment later with a new bottle. He popped the cork. "Where was I? Ah yes, fast friends—before we were rivals."

"Bloody tippler." Rafe cursed under his breath. "Mister—?"

"Professor Hamish Mulvaney Minnow." The man

tipped an imaginary hat. "At your service. Or should I say—to your rescue?"

Rafe nearly choked. "Minnow?" He pulled the wire from a jacket pocket and checked the name. "Bollocks." He rolled his eyes and raised his voice. "Professor Minnow, Scotland Yard has ordered me to place you under protection."

"You . . . are going to protect me?" A perpetual grin broadened. "Well now, that remains to seen, Detective." The burly man tossed down a crumpled paper.

Rafe unfolded the note. "It appears we both received a cablegram from Scotland Yard."

"Been searching for the two of you since yesterday." Minnow took a hefty swig. "Meantime that throat o' yers sounds a mite scratchy." He learned out of the hatch and offered the bottle. "Better yet, why don't you and the lass join me inside? We're headed for Glasgow, are we not?"

With a bit of guidance from the professor and Rafe behind to catch her, Fanny climbed the machine and dropped down into the hold. She stood in a narrow corridor surrounded by endless tubes and levers and switches. The steerage cabin was lit by a single arc lamp in the ceiling. A long tubular steam engine compartment appeared to take up the rest of the craft, with some kind of lookout post in the rear.

"Right behind you." Rafe's voice, comforting under the circumstances.

Fanny edged forward. "Professor Minnow, what sort

of— I distinctly hear the hiss of a boiler on board, but the toggle switches?"

"Steam conversion, lass. There's a dynamo electric generator in the rear of the ship, under the gunner's seat. Powers the searchlight and the onboard lamps." Minnow threw a lever and, with a shudder and hiss, the vehicle started up again. "Have a seat. You can be my navigator." The large man gave her a wink and patted the space beside him.

Fanny hesitated.

"Come now, I could use another pair of eyes." She marveled at how he could see anything out the narrow slits for windows, bladdered or not. She crawled into the cabin and lowered herself onto a thinly padded bench. "Not that I have to worry greatly about us running off the road." He winked. "Built for a rough ride, she is."

"Might there be a view out the rear?" Rafe yelled over the rumble of the engine. "I'd like to keep a lookout for the dark-suited blokes." He leaned farther in. "You wouldn't by any chance know who they are?"

"You're the detective, Mr. Lewis, not I. You'll find a chair underneath the Gatling gun in the stern," Minnow called over his shoulder. "As ye pass by the furnace, shovel in a bit of coal, would ye?"

Fanny squinted through the mechanism in front of her. She could swivel the apparatus from side to side and imagined that in daylight one could scan a wide range of terrain. The dark gray road before them wound its way across a flat plain. Far ahead, she could see dots of light. "Professor Minnow, those lights ahead—"

Minnow squinted through the crack. "We'll be upon the Clyde and the Port of Dundas shortly." He turned to her with brow raised. "And soon after?"

"Glasgow." Fanny smiled. She wasn't sure why she felt such elation. Maybe it was because she had formulated a plan. Orders or not, if Rafe continued on with this ridiculous plan to try for London, she would just have to take matters into her own hands. Once they were in the city, she would slip away and catch the first train back to Edinburgh. She neither wanted nor needed the protection of Scotland Yard, and she had certainly put Rafe through enough. She tried adding up the number of times he might have been killed or injured these past two days and quickly lost count.

Fanny sighed. All this dangerous life-risking behavior of his was having its effect. She was being won over, completely and utterly. And she wasn't forgetting how his body nestled with hers, or how heavenly his mouth felt when he lightly brushed his lips over hers. A warm heat prickled up her neck to her cheeks. She fanned herself. "Boiler keeps it nice and cozy in here."

Minnow steered the behemoth with handled sticks that rose up from the floor. "A bit too cozy on a summer's day, if you take my meaning."

She had detected his meaning the moment she sat down beside him. The man needed a bath, sooner rather than later.

"What ho!" Rafe's shout traveled through the inner workings of the landship. "Three riders brandishing weapons approach from the north."

Minnow unhooked a speaking tube from the ceiling. "Release the lever at the side of the chair—you and the gun will pivot. Let me know when you're in position."

Fanny peered out of her window slit. She made out three men—likely the ones who'd chased them down and left them at bottom of the mine-shaft. If anything could scare these blokes off, it would be a Gatling gun pointed at them.

"Aimed and ready, Professor." Rafe's voice sounded far away and tinny.

"Now then, listen carefully. You've got no real accuracy, lad, so fire well above their heads. I'll not have ye bring down one of God's finest four-legged creatures." He winked at Fanny. "I'm a gambling man by nature." Minnow returned to the speaking cone. "A long-odds filly as fast as the wind and as pretty as you please financed this here rig, so watch yourself." Minnow crossed himself. "Fire at will, Detective."

Minnow turned to Fanny. "You'll want to cover yer ears, miss."

IT TOOK ALL the strength Rafe possessed to keep the gun firing and not let it spin wildly out of control. Empty shells spewed out of the repeater and dropped to the floor. He was so preoccupied with the unwieldy mechanical gun, he forgot to let up on the cranking mechanism. Only when the barrel began to smoke did he become alarmed. "I've got a very hot gun back here!"

"Let up on the crank, Detective." Instantly, Rafe let go of the handle. His entire body throbbed from the release of tension in his arms and back. He squinted through a haze of smoke. The natty blokes had turned tail and were retreating at a gallop.

Rafe loosed a battle cry of triumph. "This is a fine war machine you've made here, Professor Minnow." He sat back in the rotating chair, released the lever, and spun around, scanning the terrain. Flickering lights from several cottages a ways off meant they were approaching civilization.

Glasgow. He removed a stack of folded wires and found the decoded address of the safe house. 19-B Oswald Street. Undercover Special Branch men would offer shelter and help get them safely out of town. He hoped for a cozy room in a nice, out of the way hotel. He hadn't slept much in these last two days, and all he could think about was a bath, a bed, and a dram. He swallowed, remembering how thirsty he was. "Professor Minnow, you wouldn't by any chance have anything to drink up there?"

"Pressure's down, laddie. Stoke the fire and I'll send the lass back with yer reward."

Rafe removed his jacket and shoveled coals into the furnace. His gaze followed the funnels and pipes from furnace to boiler. Inside the horizontal cylinder the steam would drive the pistons—which in turn cranked the wheels of this great beast. Rafe wiped a bit of sweat off his brow with his sleeve. "What a marvel."

"Thank you very much for the compliment, Rafe." Fanny dipped her head through the hatch. She held a bottle of whiskey in one hand and a covered container in the other.

He reached out for the metal pail. "Water?"

She handed it over. "Somewhat tepid I'm afraid, but it's liquid." He poured the water down his throat and splashed another handful over his face. Fanny leaned against the hatch opening. "Once again, Detective Lewis, you saved the day."

Rafe grinned. "Not me. This machine—this beast is the absolute future of war. And I, for one, am very glad Professor Hamish Mulvaney Minnow is on our side."

"He's quite the character." She ducked her head into the rear compartment. Rafe took her by the hand. "Have a go at the gunner's post." Ignoring her protests, he climbed up into the chair and pulled her onto his lap. He placed her hand on the crank and released the lever. "Sight through the notch here."

While Fanny took aim over a sea of dark grass, Rafe rotated the turret. "My word, this is excellent. Will the gun do a full rotation?"

He spoke softly in her ear. "Three hundred sixty degrees, Lieutenant." She jumped and accidentally cranked a spray of bullets into a field alongside the road.

"Sorry, Professor, Fanny got carried away." Rafe removed her hand from the gun's trigger mechanism.

She poked him in the ribs. "Not exactly carried away. You whispered in my ear." Fanny moved to slip off his lap. "It tickled."

"Don't go." He held on to her arm. "Rest here a moment." He encouraged her to lie back against his body.

She shot him a look over her shoulder. "For a little while, then I must return and assist Professor Minnow."

"Call me Hamish, and take yer time, lass." Minnow's voice barked through the speaking cone dangling overhead. "The river now lights our way. Fix your turret north-northwest, Detective Lewis, and have a look." Rafe released the lever at the side of the chair and rotated the hand crank.

"Look, Fan, as lovely as can be," Rafe said softly. The river Clyde snaked a silvery path through the darkened landscape. The road they traveled would soon take a turn and run alongside the broad waterway.

"In London, I often walk home along the Thames. It reminds me of home—the path along the firth that connects Lochree with our deer park."

She rested her head back against his shoulder. "Rafe?"

"Hmm?" His breath blew softly across the delicate hairs of her temple.

"I want to apologize for my very rude behavior, back on the road." She hesitated. "All that screaming and fisticuffs and such."

"I'm quite recovered, Fan."

"In fact, you've been so wonderfully kind and devoted these last few days, I believe you deserve a bit of tribute."

Rafe turned her in his arms. "A few trial credits, perhaps?"

"Oh yes, a fistful." A slash of brow came together. "But you are not yet entirely forgiven."

"I will strive for entirely before we reach London." He stole a quick kiss and then another.

"Rafe, when we reach Glasgow, I shall return to Edinburgh. You may carry on—catch and arrest the natty blokes and the dastardly man with the initials BVM, if the monogram is indeed the man behind this"—Fanny jerked upright on his lap—"ghastly business." Her brows crashed together.

"Rafe, there was a man last year—rather an eccentric fellow. I've only seen him once. He was speaking to an unlawful assembly of millworkers. I believe his name was Bellecorte Mallory. I have no idea what his middle initial might be. Father called him a crackpot."

His slight uptick in pulse rate signaled an important clue. "Good God, you may have just given us our first big break in the case."

She leaned back against his shoulder. "Rather a woolly bear sort, with a bit of drool around the mouth. Mr. Mallory hardly seemed the type to be plotting the grisly demise of the most prominent citizens of the industry."

"Mild-mannered but half-mad anti-progressive gathers around him a close-knit group of misguided souls—"

"The size of an army." She sniffed.

"And these minions join in his scheme to rid the world of steam engines and motorized machines by eliminating their fiendish creators." Rafe rubbed the top of her head with his bristled chin. "Seems irrationally . . . reasonable."

"What is not reasonable, or rational, is how my dilemma continues to endanger innocent citizens, to say nothing of the burden I place on you."

"Fanny—"

"In protecting me, you put yourself in great danger. I shall return home, hire my own private horse guard, batten down the hatches, and wait for this whole bloody business to be over."

Rafe exhaled. "No, you will not."

"*Yes*, I will."

Rafe sighed. "No-o-o-o, you will not."

"Ye-e-e-s-s, I will." Fanny chewed her bottom lip. "How impossible you are." She slipped off his lap.

Rafe snorted. "*I'm* impossible?"

"Detective Lewis," Minnow's voice squawked from overhead. "Port of Dundas, straight ahead, and I'll be needing to head upriver apace. You'll be wanting to get Miss Greyville-Nugent to safety while I park this here Iron Lady in a storehouse."

Rafe and Fanny moved forward into steerage. "Meet us at 19-B Oswald Street."

"Know the area well." Minnow rose from his seat. "Down the lane from Ivory Black's—a fine gaming establishment." The professor gestured upward and Fanny started up the ladder. "I'll see the lass safely down while you stoke me a few more, Detective."

Dutifully, Rafe shoveled coal before he climbed out of the leviathan landship. Skipping the last few footholds, he jumped to the ground. Good God. He craned his neck. Hamish Minnow was a mighty-sized Scot, the kind built for wielding a claymore or tossing a caber. Reasonably tall in stature, Rafe found he had to step back a bit to make eye contact with the giant. "My orders are to escort you and Fanny to London."

Minnow grunted his acknowledgment, grabbed a side rail, and lifted himself up the craft with surprising agility. Rafe shouted after the man, "Don't make me come after you, Professor Minnow!"

Chapter Eighteen

"This safe house, as you call it, on Oswald Street. What is it exactly?" Fanny trotted up beside Rafe, who set a blistering pace along Clyde Street. The cobbled thoroughfare bustled with carts and pedestrians even at this wee hour of the morning.

"It's a kind of hotel for detectives working undercover. A secure location for witnesses or undercover operatives in danger—usually on the run," He glanced over at her.

Her brows knit together. "Like us."

The tall masts and rigging of the merchant ships moored along the river wharf painted a macabre criss-cross of webbing across the night sky. Rafe reached for her arm at the street corner. "When agents are found out, they need a place to hide until they can be brought safely into headquarters. The Yard men who work the Glasgow docks are after arms dealers and explosives traffickers, mostly. Deadly dangerous work. Two operatives were killed last year. A rat-catcher found the bodies in the hold of a ship, partially—" The last detail trailed off as he checked the sign post. "Hold on. Here we are, Oswald Street." They made their way down a row of shop fronts and boardinghouses.

At No. 19, they entered the foyer of the residence and used the door knocker on the apartment lettered B.

"Will I have my own room?" She moistened her lips. "Will there be food and a bath?" Fanny allowed herself to hope for a few creature comforts.

"Perhaps *hotel* was the wrong choice of words." Rafe's mouth twitched. "More likely pub food brought in and a quick washup—we'll see what can be done." They waited in silence. And waited.

Rafe lifted the knocker and rapped again.

Fanny leaned in. "Do you suppose the house is not in use at the moment? Might there be a key we could ask for—from a neighbor?" She detected a whiff of fresh paint in the air and noted the clean runners on the polished wood floor. Perfectly respectable. She tilted her head back to check the brass letter again. "You did say 'B'?"

"B as in bollocks." Rafe tried the knob. Locked. He rapped on the door, this time with bare knuckles.

"Rude of Scotland Yard to direct us here and have no one to—what would you call it?"

"Bring us in. And rather typical, actually, the rudeness." Rafe stepped away from the door, only to jerk back with a start. Fanny pivoted in the direction of his gaze. A rather swarthy-looking man dressed as a gentleman leaned against the rail post at the foot of the stairs. He pointed a pistol at them.

When Fanny opened her mouth to speak, Rafe grabbed her hand and shook his head. The man pushed off the banister. "If you would walk on ahead—this way." He gestured with the gun—Fanny to go first and Rafe to follow after. They made their way down the corridor behind the stairs to a service entrance. The strange man crossed ahead and held the door open. He motioned them both inside.

They were in a kitchen, with a large kettle of water steaming on top of the stove. Fanny brightened at the thought of a cup of tea, no matter how unsettling their taciturn host might be.

He bid them follow and wound a path through the kitchen and down a corridor, where he opened a door revealing a narrow stair closet. She raised a brow as he pointed upward. Up close, he was strikingly handsome in a dangerous, brooding sort of fashion. As she squeezed by him he regarded her with an amused half smile.

She felt his eyes on her as she climbed the angled wooden treads. Feeling her way in the dark, hardly able to see the next step, she ran headlong into—"Ouch." She rubbed her nose.

"You will find a latch to your right. Slide it back." The man's accent, though well-educated and thoroughly British, held traces of another dialect—something close to home, perhaps?

She found the pull and stepped into the upstairs apartment. There were a number of angles to the ceiling and one heavily draped gabled window. Straight ahead, she could just make out a table beside an overstuffed chair.

Familiar with the placement of furnishings, their armed escort slipped into the room. The strike and hiss of a safety match revealed an oil lamp on the table. He tipped the flame to the wick and replaced the funnel. The imposing gentleman nodded to Rafe and spoke in a low voice. "Please, come in."

After adjusting the wick the stranger took a moment to study them. Rafe appeared calm enough, as though he waited for something. She found the room a bit musty and cleared her throat.

"Detective Lewis." The man's dark eyes gentled when they reached her. "And you are Miss Francine Greyville-Nugent. The engraving in the paper does not do you justice."

She swallowed. "I never much cared for that photograph."

"I must ask both of you to remove whatever is in your coat pockets."

Rafe pulled a revolver from each pocket and set the weapons on the side table. He also produced a number of folded papers and the red leather journal taken off the dead man on the train. There were also several satchels of coin.

Their enigmatic host gestured them over to the settee while he swept up the papers and journal and took a seat opposite.

Rafe sat down beside her and gave her a comforting wink. She leaned close. "Rather a great deal of intrigue, wouldn't you say?"

"Standard procedure, Fan."

The mysterious gentleman glanced up from his reading. "Sorry for the subterfuge, Miss Greyville-Nugent, but as the detective says, we must follow procedure whenever possible. You'd be surprised how often it keeps us alive." He closed the journal, and refolded the papers.

"I am Hugh Curzon, on assignment for the Office of the Admiralty. Here in Glasgow, bored out of my brains, awaiting the arrival of a large shipment of explosives." He nodded to Rafe. "Scotland Yard, perennially understaffed and always at a loss for agents, asked me to step in." Setting back in the overstuffed chair, he stretched his legs out and folded his hands in his lap. "How may I be of service to you?"

"Have you a wire or some form of communication that might confirm you are who you say you are?" Rafe's polite smile appeared rather clenched.

Curzon removed a missive from his jacket and passed it over. "From Detective Kennedy, addressed to you in care of me."

While Rafe ciphered through the message, Curzon turned to her. "And you, miss—how might I make your stay here at 19-B Oswald a pleasant one? I take it you've been on the run for the better part of two days?"

"I would very much like a bath, a change of traveling clothes, and something to eat, in that order, Mr.—Agent Curzon."

Rafe looked up. "Fanny, I would be happy to—" he began.

Curzon's dark gaze never left her. "It would be my pleasure to see to a bath for Miss Greyville-Nugent." He turned to Rafe. "You both look like you could use a hot soak and a good rest. As long as Miss Greyville-Nugent's abductors and are still in pursuit, neither of you should be seen on the streets."

Rafe nodded. "I've another man under my protection, a Professor Hamish Minnow, an inventor the Yard wants brought in. I expect him here shortly. If he does not turn up soon, I shall have to go after him."

"You have an address?" Curzon asked.

Rafe shook his head. "Said something about a warehouse upriver."

The intelligencer wrinkled a brow. "One of hundreds, I'm afraid."

Rafe leaned forward. "He can't very well sneak a landship the size of a locomotive and twice as loud into storage without someone noticing."

Curzon turned to Fanny. "I'm afraid this refuge is very much each bachelor for himself. I had just put a kettle on when you arrived. Perhaps you'd enjoy a cup of tea while Detective Lewis and I scare up a tub?"

They all descended into the kitchen, where the intelligence agent filled a teapot and brought out a tin of biscuits.

Fanny set about heating more water, and Rafe located a nice-sized copper tub in a pantry closet. "I believe I shall bathe here." She hesitated. "With the door and all . . ."

Curzon bowed. "You will at least have privacy, miss." A bell rang among a line of servant's bells. "Ah, we have another visitor." He cracked open the service door, and motioned to Rafe. "Shall we have a look?"

Pleasantly perched on a stool by the large worktable, Fanny sipped an entire cup of tea and devoured two biscuits before Agent Curzon returned. She forced a swallow midchew. "Where is Detective Lewis?"

"It seems your inventor chap is in some difficulty." Fanny stood up to leave. Curzon held up his hand. "His trouble is with the local authorities. Detective Lewis left a moment ago with an officer from the constabulary."

"Whatever does Professor Minnow need Rafe for?"

Curzon added a drop of cream to his tea. "Bail."

Disquietude did not quite describe her unease. Very much alone with the spy or agent, or whatever he was, Fanny suddenly found it impossible to meet his gaze—for long. There was something attractive as well as dangerous about this strange virile man. Fanny bit her lip and busied herself checking pots of water on the stove. Steaming hot. She wiped her hands on an apron hanging near the dishpan. She could feel Curzon pass behind her. He wrapped a towel around his hand and picked up the first pot of water. He made several trips from the pantry to the stove until all the warm water was in the tub.

He unwrapped his hand and nodded a bow. "Your bath awaits, miss."

Fanny dipped a finger in the bath water and motioned to Curzon, who adjusted the temperature with a pan of cool water. Fanny tested the water again. "Yes, that's lovely. Thank you."

He turned to leave the small room and closed the door after him. "Agent Curzon." The door slowly swung back open. "I'm afraid this is rather awkward."

The man's smile twitched a bit.

"Could you—?" Fanny lifted her arm and pointed behind her. She even twisted around a bit to show him the length of buttons running down her back.

With his hand still on the knob, Curzon leaned against the doorjamb. "You want me to undress you?"

Cheeks aflame, Fanny turned her back. "Just the buttons, please. I can manage the rest myself." How utterly humiliating and difficult. Rafe had left her here, alone in the house, knowing there was a bath on the way and this . . . man for company.

Occasionally, his fingers or knuckles would brush against the flesh on her back. Warm hands. She laughed softly, nervously. "So sorry to put you through this."

"The pleasure is mine, Miss Greyville-Nugent." His voice was soft, playful. "You may apologize for so many, many buttons, however."

"Yes, Rafe complains of the same—" Fanny bit her lip and cursed to herself. "I suppose you think I let gentlemen disrobe me as a matter of course."

"No, Miss Greyville-Nugent, but I do detect an undercurrent of familiarity between you and Detective Lewis. Am I not correct?" He turned her around and held her with both hands. Her dress slipped off an arm. His gaze fell to her bare shoulder.

"Good God, it's no wonder he loves you."

"Do you think so, Agent Curzon? You are dealing with a man who betrayed my trust—who called off our betrothal the night of our engagement ball. And yet, I still care a great deal for him." Fanny bit her lower lip. "Many people would advise me differently. They would argue that if a man truly loved a woman, he could never do such a thing."

Curzon studied her. "That's not entirely true, miss. I have loved many women in my life and never married one of them."

They stood in close proximity—too close. Fanny dipped her fingers in the water. "I suppose I must press on or my bath will grow cold."

Dutifully, Curzon backed away.

"Might you leave the door open a crack and sit inside the kitchen—a ways off?" She blushed again, just asking the question. "This is a strange house." And the look in his eyes—they were too piercing, too dark and full of . . . well, she didn't wish to think on it.

He left a sliver of space between door and jamb. "If I am to sip tea and listen to you splash about in your bath—I will require a distraction. A story, I think." A kitchen stool dragged across polished floorboards. "It seems you and Raphael Lewis have a history together. Shall we call it 'The Princess of Industry and the Scotland Yard Detective?'"

"I'm afraid it's a very long tale, and nothing very dramatic happens until the last few chapters." She stepped out of her dress.

"*'Begin at the beginning,'* Miss Greyville-Nugent, *'and go on till you come to the end: then stop.'*" His husky voice carried through the crack in the door.

A furtive, puzzling sort of man who quoted Lewis Carroll. She unpinned her hair. "Then I suppose you really ought to call me Fanny."

∽ Chapter Nineteen

The moment she slipped into the bath a moan escaped her throat and skimmed the surface of the water.

"Honestly, Fanny, moans and sighs?" The agent exhaled a tut-tut. "Don't get me wrong, all perfectly delightful, but I was expecting 'once upon a time.'"

As the steaming bath calmed scrapes and soothed bruises, she lathered up a cake of soap. "Your story, Agent Curzon, begins with a rather idyllic childhood."

"Now that we have become intimates, please call me Hugh."

Scrubbing off layers of dust and grime, Fanny recalled summers spent riding far up into the hills, games of cricket that lasted until well after dark. Lawn pins and croquet—all played ferociously and with abandon.

"Then Reggie went off to college and it was just Rafe and me."

Hugh Curzon slurped his tea rather loudly. "I never once played cricket with my sister. Bookish sort."

Fanny caught a length of pant leg through the crack

in the door. Long-legged, this one. Rafe, too, had wonderfully long muscular legs. No doubt de rigueur for
lady-killers. She squeezed out a washcloth. "In winter
there was chess and backgammon." Fanny smiled. "And
Dunrobin Hall golf—an eighteen-hole course, up and
down stairs." The centuries-old wainscoting in the great
hall had suffered a number of unfortunate scrapes and
dents. "Golf was outlawed after a wild ball of mine broke
a Ming vase."

"Don't tell me, young Lewis took the blame." Hugh
taunted.

"Yes." Fanny paused. "Rafe went off to college a year
later."

"You were lonely."

"Very." She submerged her head into the water. A moment of oblivion. She resurfaced and pushed wet hair off
her face. Raising her knees, she pressed her fingers to her
eyes. "Mother died when I was very young. Barely three."
The only face she knew was an image of her mother
from an old tintype. "I was left with Father, who was
kind, but awfully busy. My uncle and his wife were always about, and my cousin Claire, who was . . . bookish."
Fanny soaped her hair. "When Father announced our betrothal, I was the happiest girl in Victoria's Empire."

"I can imagine the St. Aldwyns were equally thrilled.
Your dowry must have been sizable."

"Whopping." Fanny reached for a pitcher of fresh
water on the floor. "I didn't give a fig about the title."
The ceramic handle slipped out of soapy fingers and fell
over. "Drat."

"Everything all right?" Hugh's query came from just outside the door.

"I could use another pitcher of clean water—to rinse my hair."

She tilted her head and caught a glimpse of him through the narrow slit.

"There should be warm water left in the kettle."

The door opened a crack wider. "If the bath water is soapy enough to provide cover, I might come in and pour if you'd like. I promise not to—"

"Such a lie. You all peek."

Hugh snorted a chuckle. "All right. Then I won't touch."

Fanny pulled her knees against her chest. "You may come in."

He opened the door and didn't stare, exactly. He admired. "You sure?"

She nodded, even though her cheeks were hot. "Shall we get this over with?"

"Lean forward, Fanny." Warm water splashed over her hair and back.

"Rafe came up from university just for the engagement ball. He spoke privately with Father." She supposed she would never know exactly what transpired between the two men. "The next thing I knew, Rafe was gone and Father stood on the stairs in the great hall and . . ." She swallowed. "He announced to the entire assemblage that I was calling off our engagement—that I had quite made up my mind. Father claimed it was for the best . . ." Her voice drifted off.

"Just days ago, Rafe finally confessed his reasons for calling off our betrothal. 'One can't marry someone, Fanny, when one is already married.'"

Hugh stopped pouring. "Jesus."

"I stood in my father's study and thought, 'This cannot be my life.' I was in shock, paralyzed."

"Lean back." His husky voice was oddly soothing.

She raised her chin, resting her head on her shoulders. Warm water poured over her scalp. Hugh's handsome angular face appeared overhead. "A man can love a woman with all his heart and still make mistakes—do things he might deeply regret."

She frowned. "But how could that be?"

"Life often has a way of spiraling out of one's control. A man finally meets the love of his life, and then makes a grave mistake—something irrevocable. He might have . . . killed the lady's brother, for instance."

Her eyes flew open and searched his face. Hugh's piercing gaze met hers and softened. She swallowed. "Does she know?"

His smile was hesitant, gentle. "I believe so."

He lifted the pitcher. "Close your eyes." Once more, water flooded over her head and into the tangled curls plastered to her back. He piled up wet hair and wrapped her head in a towel. "Such a darling little thing. I more than half envy Rafe."

"Why do you continue to believe Rafe cares for me?"

"For one, he threatened to rip my balls from my scrotum should I dare scrub your back." He laid a bath sheet by the tub and turned to leave. Fanny gurgled a laugh and looked up.

Rafe stood in the doorway to the pantry.

There was something dark and menacing in his eyes, like nothing Fanny had ever seen before. His deadly gaze traveled to Agent Curzon.

"My word, this is unfortunate timing." Hugh approached Rafe cautiously, hands up in casual surrender.

"You should have told me you had no further use for your testicles, Curzon, I would have picked a different organ—close by."

If Rafe's eyes could slash and cut, Hugh Curzon's most prized masculine body part might soon be served up as dinner. On a roll.

Fanny gripped her knees tight to her chest. "Rafe!" She lifted her brows and forced a pleasant expression. "Would you be kind enough to leave us alone, Hugh?"

Reluctant to leave, the agent's protective stance caused Rafe's eyes to bulge.

"I'll be perfectly fine. Rafe would never—"

Rafe grabbed Hugh by the lapels and leaned into his chest. "I do not take advantage of women, nor cause them any—"

"Not exactly true, is that, Rafe?" Fanny cut in sharply, then gentled her words. "Please let him go."

RAFE LOOKED HUGH up and down. The man was every inch as tall as himself, with a bit more brawn. But he could take him in a fair fight.

Reluctantly, he eased back and Fanny nodded to Hugh, who closed the door with a wink. Rafe spun around. "What the hell are you doing, letting a strange man into your bath?"

Fanny rolled her eyes. "Hold up the towel."

A demigoddess arose from her primordial sea. Rivulets of foaming water ran down her breasts. The glistening droplets traced a path between luscious mounds, a narrow torso, and a sweet belly, only to be caught in a nest of soft brown curls.

She unwound the towel from her head and turned slowly while she fluffed a tangle of hair.

A lump formed in his throat. Not the only thing that was rock hard.

He noted those wonderful dimples just above the round plumpness of that enticing derriere. She turned full circle before she stepped into the towel. He covered her in the warm sheet and held her, wrapped in his arms.

"There now," she whispered. "You are the only man I would ever let see me."

"Fanny, I love you."

Searching his face, she bit her lip. "Funny, that is what Hugh said."

Rafe blinked at her and gritted his teeth. "Blasted, deceiving operative—cuckolder. Love at first sight, was it?"

Fanny blushed from temple to toe. "How you jump to conclusions!" She giggled softly. "Hugh said, 'It's no wonder he loves you'—he meant you, Rafe, not himself."

She nodded toward the floor. "Take note of the puddle

of water you are standing in. My pitcher of rinse water tipped over. Hugh offered—"

"I bet he did."

She raised both brows. "Nothing happened. And even if—" Fanny broke off midsentence and stepped out of the tub. He grabbed hold of her arm to steady her.

"You were about to say?" He stuck his chin out.

"You are the only man who has ever seen me naked—entirely. You have touched me in places no lady should ever allow a man to know without a ceremony. Quite an advantage, wouldn't you say, for a dodgy ex-fiancé?" Fanny carried on drying her hair. A mountain of curls cascaded around her shoulders and down her back.

"Good God, you are lovely."

"'Good God, you're lovely—Fanny, I love you.' What does it mean? Words, Rafe, empty words—"

Rafe yanked her into his arms and kissed her. And she returned his ardor with a surprising passion, slipping her tongue into his mouth, tangling, retreating, chasing. He caught the plump bottom ledge of her mouth between his teeth and tugged. And she rallied to his game of kiss and release with her tongue and teeth.

He slipped his hand under the sheet and brushed his thumb over the tip of her breast. The towel loosened and fell below firm mounds as he teased up one nipple with his fingers, the other with his tongue. She spoke in incoherent, musical utterances and trembled in his arms.

He returned to her mouth and whispered over her lips, "There are times when words just won't do."

Her eyes searched his. "If I thought for a moment, you might truly love me . . ."

"It doesn't matter to me that you have doubts, or that it might take me a lifetime to convince you of my affection. All that matters, Fanny, is that you let me try. I love you with all my heart, and with no idea how I might ever fully make amends."

"As we've discussed, Mr. Lewis, there are ways for you to redress your sins." Fanny backed away and slowly pulled up her bath sheet. "Would you hand me my undergarments, please?"

Hugh rapped at the door. "While you two are reconciling—and I do hope you are faring well, Detective Lewis—I shall attempt to find something edible for supper."

"Yes, you do that." Rafe tossed the remark over his shoulder.

Fanny butted past him and opened the door a crack. "Might there be a confectionary nearby where you could purchase some chocolate?"

"At this hour I should find the cooks at work. They might take pity, for a sixpence."

Fanny's eyes brightened. "I believe we have sugar. We'll need a jar of milk and perhaps some soft meringues?"

Hugh smiled through the crack. "I will endeavor to bring back all the items you need to make your hot chocolate, miss."

She returned his smile. "Thank you."

Hugh looked her up and down, sizing up her figure.

"I'm afraid I'll not be able to find you any suitable attire until morning."

Rafe tossed a few shillings through the crack and slammed the door. He leaned back and folded his arms over his chest. "Do you enjoy that man's company?"

Fanny tied on her drawers and slipped on her camisole. "You do him a disservice, Rafe. He has been very kind."

"How kind?"

"At the moment, very much kinder than you." Fanny picked up the pretty summer frock, now sadly splattered with mud and torn along the hem.

Rafe stared at the floor, his jaw clenching. "When the shops reopen in the morning, I will purchase all new traveling clothes."

She stepped into petticoats and pulled on the ruined dress. "Hugh knows all about you and me."

Rafe raised a brow. "How is that possible?"

"I told him."

Rafe rolled his eyes. "No wonder he's crawling all over you."

"I asked him how it was possible for a man to declare his love for one woman and be unfaithful to her with another."

"A man in a very dark place, one who was betrayed himself, by a rival who called himself friend." The words had slipped out, and there was no way to grab them out of the air and take them back.

"Hugh said, 'A man can love a woman with all his heart and still . . . '" The words died away as Fanny slowly turned around.

He waited for her gaze to meet his. "You heard right, Fan." The knot in Rafe's throat threatened to choke off his intake of air. Her eyes, already large and round, glistened. Fanny was confused, shaken. But then, why wouldn't she be?

Her mouth moved to frame a word then hesitated. "Who betrayed you?"

Rafe chose his words carefully. "It was Nigel." There. He had finally spoken the name out loud. "In collusion with Claire. I didn't allow myself to believe it at first." His lungs contracted with the accusation.

Fanny blindly reached back for the edge of the tub to brace herself on the rim. "Nigel?" The name rushed out in a whisper. "How can that be?" Her eyes darted here and there, searching for answers.

He sucked in a bit of air. "To this day, I don't know if it was a game between them or if it was deliberate."

"Nigel has always been a bit resentful—even envious of you, at times." She shook her head. "You used to shrug it off, Rafe." Rallying a bit, Fanny tried for something brave and cutting. "Was a knock to your manhood all it took to drive you into another's arms?"

He bit back a remark he was quite sure he would regret. So many times he had wished to confide in her about his loss of faith as well as his shame. He opened his mouth to answer and quickly shut it again. He had never been able to forgive himself, so why should Fanny? Even though he believed the ruse to be deeper and more insidious than she realized, the argument still rang shallow. She was right, all it took was a blow to his confidence and he was off with the first village chit that had batted an eyelash.

She stared at a wall of empty pantry shelves. "I'd like to be left alone."

Rafe pushed off the door. "Do you need me to button your dress?"

Her gaze traveled over to him, eyes welled with tears. "Please leave."

He backed out. And quietly shut the door.

Rafe pumped a bit of water into the kettle and placed it back on the stove. He pulled out a stool, took a seat at the table, and pressed his forehead into the palms of his hands.

Her muffled sobs tore into his gut. He forced himself to listen until he couldn't stand it any longer. He yanked open the pantry door and picked her up in his arms.

Chapter Twenty

"Put me down." She hiccupped.

"Cry as long and as hard as you need to." Her arms crept around his neck, and he hugged her close. "Just let me hold you."

Five years' worth of pent-up tears had finally let loose. She thought the waterworks might never stop. And when the sobbing gradually lessened, a great deal of sniffling took over. Rafe rocked her gently in his arms. For once in her life, she had nothing to say, was utterly speechless.

The floodgates had opened up inside her. These past few days, what with all the sudden danger and adventure, Rafe's presence had filled the vast dark cavern inside her. At last she cried the tears she hadn't allowed herself to cry. For her father. For herself.

For Rafe.

Now, more than ever, she was determined to go home. But not to Edinburgh. She would return to Lochree, the estate in Queensferry. She would raise the drawbridge, blockade herself inside the castle, and let the horrid natty blokes lay siege.

A key turned in the kitchen door. Rafe reached inside his jacket for a revolver.

"Don't shoot. I've a hamper stuffed with chops and stout, and chocolate for our lovely guest."

Hugh unpacked the basket and set out supper. Fanny retrieved hairpins from the pantry shelf and arranged her hair while Rafe buttoned what was left of a dingy frock.

She held a cold compress to her eyes and Hugh angled for a closer look. "Much better, swelling's down. No more puffy eyes." He pulled out a stool. "Mademoiselle."

They were all hungry—famished actually. The men set about devouring a half dozen meaty chops each and several tankards of beer. Fanny ate even though she thought she might retch up the lot of it. Happily, supper had the opposite effect and calmed her roiling stomach.

Hugh sat back and studied the both of them. "It appears you were unable to reconcile."

Rafe glared at Hugh.

Fanny glared at Rafe.

Hugh didn't glare, he grinned. "Come now, tell the love doctor."

Hands fisted, Rafe shot up so fast his stool fell over.

Fanny shook her head in disbelief. "I don't know which of you is worse. The man who refuses marriage because he is already married." Her scowl moved from Rafe to Hugh. "Or the man who admits to killing his fiancée's brother."

Rafe eased back. "You cut down her brother?"

"We weren't promised. Never made it that far. Her brother was an unapologetic, murdering anarchist. What I did, I did for queen and country." Hugh's narrowed gaze met Rafe's. "I take it you're married, Detective Lewis?"

"*Was* married." His frown flattened into a thin grim line. "She died four years ago."

Fanny sighed. "What a sad and ghoulish pair you are."

"And you're stuck with us, I'm afraid." Rafe righted his stool.

She fluttered an eye roll toward the ceiling. "What luck."

" 'Tis a mystery how fortune smiles on us." Hugh settled back on his stool. "I was stationed in the Punjab for several years—no doubt you've heard of the very ancient concept of kismet? It is used among Persians to express the idea of fate, specifically the inevitability of events occurring. Both what we do and what ultimately happens to us are preordained. We play out a story invented for us."

Hugh munched on a few leftover tidbits. "Sikhs, on the other hand, believe in Karma. The concept of action or deed, which affects causation and effect. One simply earns one's luck, or lack thereof, by the actions and deeds of one's life."

Rafe stared. "And what does this bit of unsolicited wisdom have to do with us?"

Unfazed, Hugh tipped his kitchen stool back on two legs. "I fall somewhere in the middle. More of a hedonist philosopher, as it were. We are all sinners, perfectly capable of effecting our own redemption. A man's destiny is what he makes of either his good fortune or his worst folly." A self-satisfied grin widened as Hugh's scrutiny moved from Rafe to Fanny. "Don't end up like those flimsy characters in Anthony Trollope novels—quibbling over mistakes, misunderstandings—losing track of what is truly important."

Fanny looked up to find Rafe gazing rather intently at her.

Hugh locked fingers together and stretched out his arms. "There's a pack of cards upstairs. I don't play unless we play for money." It was a short reach across the table to squeeze Fanny's hand. "Make yourself a hot chocolate and come try to lighten my pockets at *vingt-et-un.*"

Even as her body ached for sleep, her heart raced at the very thought of escape and home. If she was to evade these two, she must do so quickly. And she would need a sizable bank. Enough to hire a carriage and driver. At this juncture, possibly the safest way to return home and evade the natty blokes. Especially if she was on her own.

Feeling brighter, she clasped her hands together and rubbed. "If either of you two gentlemen would be kind enough to advance me a small sum, I would be happy to beat the pants off the both of you."

With all the intensity of high rollers at a London gaming club, they played for several hours, Fanny often coming out ahead. "I believe my jack and nine beats your paltry ten and seven, Detective Lewis."

Rafe tossed his cards over. "Pisser."

Fanny scooped up the coins in the kitty and placed

them neatly on the stack in front of her. She covered a yawn.

Hugh tilted his chair back onto two legs. "I will make a few discreet inquiries about Mallory. Lieutenant Colonel Bellecort Mallory, if it's the same character I'm thinking of. Cashiered out over a disturbing bit of misery. An explosion in the armory—killed several men. Blew half his skull off . . ." Hugh hesitated as Rafe's eyes darted her direction.

She returned a flat sardonic grin. "Wouldn't want to upset the lady's delicate sensibilities. Not after her father was ground to mincemeat by a threshing machine."

Rafe stared at her. "Why don't you get some rest, Fan?"

Hugh's chair touched ground. "Just there—the door in the corner. Quite a soft bed and clean sheets. I don't mind sharing."

"Another remark like that one, Curzon, and you'll have nothing left to share." Rafe tore his glare away as she rose from her chair.

"I'd like to say it's been lovely." Fanny brushed her winnings into an empty coin pouch. "Because it certainly has been profitable." With her heart racing and knees knocking, she walked toward the bedroom steady as you please. At the door she turned back and smiled. "Good night, gentlemen."

The room was small and gray. Not the least bit attractive. In fact, it was perfectly uninviting. Fanny headed straight for the gabled window. Dawn was breaking over the eastern rooftops of Glasgow. There was no time to concoct a plan. She must go now, before the whole city was up and about. The leaving part was going to be easy. She was angry with Rafe, now more than ever. Why had he not written to her in Italy? She bit her lip. Nigel could be spiteful and Claire was capable of malicious gossip. But Rafe knew all this. She unlocked the window latch. And now there was Hugh Curzon. A lost, world-weary man in search of his soul, which he had long ago sacrificed for queen and country. Rafe would no doubt end up just like him.

The window sash lifted enough to get her fingers under and give the frame a shove. She looped the coin purse over her wrist and lifted herself onto the sill, swinging her legs over the ledge. The roof shingles were dry as bread and gave good footing. She crept to the edge of the roofline and looked down. Nearly three stories. She experienced a tinge of vertigo and willed herself to concentrate on finding a way down.

She spied a downspout with plenty of brick outcroppings. Footholds, she hoped. The trouble with this aspect of her escape was the pipe ran down the corner of the building, very much in plain view of anyone in the street.

She sidled over to the corner of the roof and had a look down the side of the house. Nothing. Not even a rose trellis. Drat.

She swung her legs over the roof and rolled onto her belly. The hardest part would be hanging off the edge until she managed to find a ledge or crevice. And try as she might, she couldn't seem to find a brick out of place. Then suddenly, a toehold! Her foot slipped into a crack in the mortar. Fanny held on to the drainpipe and inched downward. She craned her head over her shoulder, searching for the next protruding brick or gap in cement.

"What the devil do you think you're doing up there, lass?"

Fanny mouthed a silent prayer before risking a glance below. Professor Minnow stood on the sidewalk with his hands on his hips.

She lifted a finger to silence the big Scot and slipped down the pipe. She couldn't help it. She let loose a loud yelp. Grasping desperately at pipe and bricks, she reached a thick bit of ivy and held on.

"Don't let go, lass! Wait for me to get under you." Hamish Minnow trotted along the walkway yelling at the top of his lungs. The man's booming voice would carry down the River Clyde, sail the Irish Sea, and awaken every living soul between Glasgow and Belfast. Fanny cringed. She might have burst into tears, but she was rather occupied at the moment hoping to live.

"Fanny! Are you mad?" Rafe's voice. She bit her lip and realized it was possible to be humiliated to the point of wishing one could die and fearful about dying in the same moment.

She gritted her teeth, "Shut up, Rafe. Just—get me down. Or up." A quick look above found Hugh at the edge of the roofline.

"I can't reach her, Rafe. You'll have to climb up from below."

The ivy broke away from the wall. She dropped through the air until the thicket of sinewy branches held again. Eyes squeezed shut, Fanny hung on with all her might.

The stand of ivy creaked, and then arched over. "He-l-l-l-p!"

∞ Chapter Twenty-one

Rafe positioned himself under a thick tangle of ivy. The mass of foliage snapped, groaned, and bowed over slowly, dropping her into his arms.

"Rafe. Please get me down from here." Her eyes were tightly shut and she clung to a few broken offshoots.

"You are down, my darling."

She opened her eyes. "What happened?" His grin must have vexed her thoroughly, because she growled, "Set me on the ground, please."

Rafe held on tighter. "Not until you promise never to do such a thing again."

She looked away and sighed. "Promise."

He pressed his chin against her forehead. "Promise, what?"

"Don't treat me like a child." Her fists dug into his chest.

He removed a sprig of leaves caught in her sleeve. "Then don't act like one." He let her wriggle out of his grasp.

"I'll not be going to London with you, Rafe. I'm set on returning home—to Lochree."

He placed his hands on her shoulders. "Once we're in town we'll sort this all out and you'll be free to return home again. I promise." Rafe took a quick look around. The sun glinted above rooftops and the street was near to bustling. "Might we continue this argument inside?"

He nodded at the bleary-eyed professor. "I was beginning to wonder if the Dundas police had decided to keep you." Rafe motioned for him follow. The big man lumbered behind as they reentered the building and traversed the kitchen.

"Stopped off for a pint or two." Minnow squeezed his hulking frame up the winding closet stairs. "A man gets a mite thirsty sitting in jail."

They joined Hugh Curzon at the window overlooking the street. "We can't stay long. Not after that little spectacle."

Rafe exhaled. "You believe our location is compromised, then."

Hugh stepped back from the curtain. "Dundas has its share of spies and informants. Word will travel fast."

"Aye, yer right about that, sir." The large man reached out a hand. "Professor Hamish Mulvaney Minnow."

"Ah, you must be Detective Lewis's other charge." He stepped forward. "Hugh Curzon."

Minnow bent an ear. "Of—?"

Hugh grinned. "Not really necessary for you to know, Professor. Suffice to say I am friendly."

Minnow winked at Fanny. "Secretive lot, aren't they?"

"I don't give a fig where you all are headed—to hell for all I care." She approached Hugh. "I would like you to place me on the first train back to Edinburgh, Agent Curzon."

For once, Hugh didn't flirt or smile. "It is my understanding you are being transported to London, for your safety, in the custody of Detective Lewis. I would have to have received a countermanding order to interfere. Do not ask me again." He hesitated. "You could have been gravely injured just now, Fanny."

She uttered a rather disturbing wail, stomped her foot, and threw herself down on the settee. A flurry of dust rose up and caused a sneeze. Rafe bit his lip. Her dilemma might be comical if the poor miserable thing weren't so . . . miserable.

How brave and resourceful Fanny had been these past few days. For the life of him, Rafe could not think of another woman who could have borne up under such a hellish ordeal. And last night he'd blurted out that nasty bit about Nigel and Claire. He wanted to kick himself. All of it could have—no, *should have*—waited until this case was over and the danger past. He would have gone to Fanny afterward, laid out the foolish tale in its entirety, including his suspicions.

"There, there." Minnow sat down beside Fanny, discharging a larger cloud of dust. "Have a tipple o' this, lass. He pulled a bottle from his coat pocket. "Now, it willna hurt ye to take a short little junket to London with Professor Minnow. I'd like nothing more than to have the daughter of Ambrose Greyville-Nugent help me demonstrate the submariner at the Exposition." The man's eyes lit up. "I've an underwater ship, lass. Wait 'til ye see her."

"Oh dear." She took a swallow of whiskey.

Rafe moved closer and took a seat near the sofa. "What is it, Fanny?"

"The London Industrial Exposition." She crinkled her brow. "What with the funeral and being on the run and all, I'd quite forgotten about it. Father had a machine sent ahead to London." She turned to the professor. "There is to be a competition, with a good deal of prize money."

Eyebrows raised, Minnow nodded. "Five hundred and a hefty defense contract to the winner."

"Very kind of you to invite me, but I've had quite enough excitement these past days, thank you very much." Fanny squared her shoulders.

Minnow took a long swig, wiped the bottle on his sleeve, and passed it over. "Take your adventures now, while you can, lass. Someday soon there will be bairns, and after they're grown, a pack of grandchildren—and what tales ye'll have to tell."

"Professor Minnow, do you always talk in such heroic terms? Some of us would rather go along in life a little less greatly."

Minnow's eyes crinkled. He reached out and tipped her chin. "Ah, but not you, Fanny."

Her liquid brown gaze traveled from Minnow to Hugh and landed on Rafe. An interminable silence ensued, one that brought a very long sigh. "I made a promise myself, in Edinburgh, to seek justice for my father's murder."

Rafe reached out and squeezed her hand. "We'll get them, Fanny, I promise you."

"Very well. I will travel to London." She chewed on that plump bottom lip again. "The moment we arrive, Detective Lewis, you will take me directly to Scotland Yard, where I will demand my rights as a citizen. I am quite certain my detention is unlawful and unwarranted." Fanny tilted her chin. "There are plenty of excellent solicitors in London. I will file suit against Her Majesty's Royal Empire if I am not released. And promptly."

Rafe's mouth twitched. "Spoken like a true mogul of industry."

She crossed her arms under her chest. "And I want a new change of wardrobe—proper traveling clothes and a straw boater." She leaned forward with a glare. "Straightaway, if you please, Detective Lewis!"

Hugh grinned. "It occurs to me you could wire staff in Edinburgh, have a trunk of Fanny's things shipped here before she wakes this afternoon."

Rafe shook his head. "I say we catch the first train south. We'll purchase a sleeper or a compartment. Fanny can rest on the train."

Hugh checked his pocket watch. "If you leave now, I can accompany you as far as the border to help with protection." The naval operative shrugged on a topcoat.

Rafe turned to Fanny. "There is no reason why a trunk could not be delivered to London. Small recompense, after what you've been through, but still, your own things will bring some comfort." He tried an encouraging smile.

Her eyes narrowed to slits. "I suppose that means I wear this sad little frock all the way to London."

Rafe sighed. "Smile, Fanny, and no one will notice."

"We'd best get going, then." Hugh unlocked a traveling chest and removed two double-barreled rifles along with a number of shells, which he stuffed in his pocket. He passed one of the long guns to the professor. "Two triggers. Here and here." He pointed to both finger pulls. "Take care, Professor—these guns are custom-made by John Rigby—paid a bloody fortune for them." Curzon kept the other rifle, grabbed a pistol for himself and a box of ammunition, which he tossed to Rafe.

Agent Curzon led them down every rat-infested alleyway in Glasgow until they reached George Street Square. Hugh nodded across the thoroughfare. "Queen Street station." Huddled together behind the Willow Tea Room, they watched the entry into an annex of the station.

Minnow hiked the rifle under his long coat. "Trains headed south leave from platforms at the far end."

Rafe nodded to Hugh. "You and the professor go in first. Locate the train with the most immediate departure." Rafe reached back for Fanny's hand, which he received. "Fanny and I will slip in quietly and find you."

Hugh and the professor dodged a few cabs and carriages and walked straight in the entrance as casual as you please. "We'll give them a few minutes to check the departure board and locate the platform." Rafe leaned back against rough brick. "Is something the matter? You are entirely too quiet and cooperative." He felt her forehead. "Are you well?"

She slapped his hand away. "You know how I feel about pushing on to London. I put all of you at risk—don't argue with me, Rafe. Plainly, you do not care about my feelings on the matter. I find this most disloyal of you and rather wormlike—scuttling there and about at Scotland Yard's bidding." Fanny sniffed.

Rafe exhaled a sigh of relief. "The worm part hurts, Fan."

Her gaze rolled skyward. "A devilish, lowly worm at that."

"Worms are, by definition, lowly." He grinned. She could hurl all the names she wanted at him. The adorable, spirited Fanny was back. "Come." He took up her hand. "Save your vitriol for when we're safely aboard and on our way."

Weaving through a tangle of travelers milling about the station, they worked their way to the far end of the train shed. Fanny leaned in. "The large man ahead, isn't that the professor?"

"I see him." They were almost upon the platform when he caught sight of Hugh behind a baggage cart. The secret service agent's rifle rested on a traveling trunk and pointed directly at them . . . until the barrels swiveled. The hairs on the back of Rafe's neck stood on end. Curzon was quietly signaling that they were being shadowed. He released his grip on her hand and drew his pistol. "Quickly, Fan, run on ahead."

In an attempt to draw their pursuers off, Rafe dodged his way through a bustle of passengers scurrying in the opposite direction. He caught a glimpse of the professor. Minnow whisked Fanny inside a passenger car and stationed himself on the steps. Rafe scanned over to Hugh, who lifted his firearm and retreated back toward the railcar. The sight of a man brandishing a long gun sent the crowd into a panic and the travelers began to stampede. *Good man, Curzon.*

Rafe glanced behind him. There—several passengers back, he spotted the familiar pockmarked face of their pursuer in the field outside Bathgate—the man who had pointed a gun at Fanny. And there was another dark-suited, surly chap right beside him.

Swept along in the rush of the crowd, Rafe fought his way through the teeming masses. A shot fired from the rear. The poor man next to him grunted and dropped to the ground. More screams as the horde swelled and began to scatter in all directions. The train was leaving. In fact, the last railcars were approaching the end of the platform.

He had to make that train. Rafe ducked between travelers and headed for a great ironwork stairway that led to the street above. He launched himself upward, taking two steps at a time. The two blokes behind him jostled past commuters as they chased after him.

As soon as the pedestrian traffic cleared, Rafe turned and fired his revolver. One of the gunmen slumped and rolled down the steps. The other culprit leaped over the tumbling body, menace in his eyes. Rafe made the landing and vaulted over the railing. There was a breathless moment of free fall and then a terrible thud as he landed on the roof of the departing train. He rolled onto his side, and peered behind him.

A hand shot up from the back of the last railcar, then everything went black. Rafe sat up and shook the buzzing from his ears. The chug of the engine and shrill whistle echoed through the tunnel, along with the smell and taste of cinders and smoke. He could just make out a head and shoulders rising from the rear of the train. Where was his gun?

As quickly as they were plunged into darkness, it was light again. The ruddy-faced man pulled himself onto the roof, pistol in hand.

A desperate, quick scan located his Webley. The revolver had skittered along the edge of the railcar's roofline. His beady-eyed pursuer flashed a maniacal grin. "Well now, I finally get rid of you, Detective Lewis."

Chapter Twenty-two

Rafe lunged for his revolver. Sliding along the edge of the railcar's roofline, he grabbed the gun just as a shot fired overhead. "On behalf of Scotland Yard, I'm afraid I'll have to ask you to surrender your weapon." Rafe hardly knew which way to look. Arching backward he caught sight of Hugh Curzon with a smoking rifle. He rolled onto his back and sat up. His stunned attacker sank to his knees, a red crimson spot widening on his chest.

Hugh climbed onto the roof and walked toward them, rifle aimed at the natty bloke whose eyes glazed over and rolled up into his head. Hugh lifted his boot, and tipped the dead man onto his back. A pool of blood oozed from around the upper torso. Crimson rivulets ran down shallow grooves etched in the roof. Hugh offered a hand up and stayed with Rafe to make sure he was steady on his feet. "All right?"

"Grand timing, Curzon." Rafe nudged the corpse with his foot. "Shall we?" Trailing a thick smear of red, they dragged the body to the edge of the car and rolled him off. The body hit the adjacent rail tracks just as a northbound train whistled past. Hard to know what happened next as both trains swept past each other. Rafe enjoyed a fleeting fantasy—something bludgeoning, gruesome, and disturbing. He was becoming as bad as the natty blokes.

Hugh nodded ahead. "Another tunnel coming." They both dropped down between cars, and climbed from baggage to passenger carriages. "In here." Hugh opened the door to a private sleeper compartment.

Fanny sat comfortably on a plush leather seat opposite the professor with a platter of biscuits and a teapot beside her. "You never told me Scotland Yard travels first-class, Rafe." She chewed her biscuit. "Is everything all right?"

Rafe sat on the other side of the tray and sampled a small cake. "Two less natty blokes to worry ourselves about. I plugged one in the station and Hugh got the other, saving my life in the process."

Fanny's eyes widened above a tipped cup. "I suppose I should thank you for that, Hugh, only I'd rather not." She returned cup to saucer with a clink.

"Still angry with us, Fan?"

Fanny tilted her chin. "My displeasure with you, at the moment, is boundless. One might even say it reaches infinitude."

Rafe raised a brow. "My, that is a great deal of vexation."

Hugh placed his double-barreled rifle in an overhead

rack and settled in beside the professor. "Infinitude . . . would that be longer or larger than an eternity?"

She cast a glare across the aisle. "For the moment, I am locked in a terrible dilemma. Either be abducted by horrid Utopian Society minions or be imprisoned by Scotland Yard."

"You are in custody, darling." Rafe reached for another cake. "And our accommodations are so much more . . . accommodating than theirs, unless you'd like for me to tie you to a skip loader at the bottom of mine-shaft."

"Not amusing, Rafe." She stared out the window, hands clenched in her lap.

He was laughing. "Really? I find it rather droll." The look on her face stopped him cold. "Come now, Fanny, I'm only teasing . . ."

She continued to gaze out the glass, and refused to speak.

"Is there a pack of cards about?" Hugh poured himself a cup of tea from the tray. "Adorable as it is, I'd rather not listen to the two of you bicker for the next few hours."

Rafe settled back. "I'd like to conduct a debriefing first—starting with Fanny."

She looked alarmed. "Must we?"

Rafe tempered a grin that might put her off. Minnow had hunched himself up in the corner and was nodding off. "Professor, feel free to join in anytime."

Minnow cracked an eye open. "If I have something to say, I'll say it."

Rafe turned to Fanny. "Could Mallory's interest in you, if indeed Mallory is our man, have something to do with your father's secret invention? Do you have any idea what kind of machine it is? And where it might be housed in London?"

Fanny licked a few biscuit crumbs from her bottom lip. The sight distracted Rafe no end. "I can't think of anything offhand. I believe the exposition's theme this year is *A Better Britain, A Better Life.*"

"I have it on good authority yer father's entry was no war machine." Minnow resettled his large frame on the compartment bench. "Do a bit of industrial espionage on my own, Detective."

"And might I ask about your entry, Professor? You mentioned a submersible?"

Minnow's eyes twinkled. "A three-man submersible, twelve tons on her. Powered by a seventeen-horsepower Brayton engine and armed with pneumatic tubes for the launching of torpedoes at enemy ships."

Rafe blinked. "My word, Minnow, that is impressive."

"She's tied up in the Oxford canal at Lucy's Ironworks, being fitted with arc lighting and stainless steel plates. I'll be needing ye to drop me off in North Oxfordshire so I can motor the *Horatio* down the Thames in time for my demonstration." Minnow grinned. "Plenty enough room for the three of us, Detective Lewis."

Rafe frowned.

Hugh leaned forward. "Might be safer than the trains."

Fanny arched a wary brow at the elder Scotsman. "You've tested this submariner well? I'd hate to be sitting twenty feet underwater and have the main ballast tanks fail."

Professor Minnow grinned. "So, it's true, then. Ambrose had a nautilus of his own in the works. Ha! I knew it! Did a bit o' testing in the inlet there along Queensferry, I expect."

She grinned. "Father had a large boathouse built on the firth. Houses a number of mysterious seaworthy conveyances." This time it was Fanny's turn to wink.

Rafe considered Hugh's words. The trains coming into London from the north would likely be monitored. "Yes, why not?" He perked up. "We'll take the submariner."

Fanny fidgeted. "Is the debriefing over, because I wish to prepare a wire home. I was promised a trunk of clothes shipped to London, was I not?"

"Bollocks. I'd quite forgotten." Rafe reached in his coat for a pencil stub and notepaper. "Fire away."

Fanny moistened her lips. "I suppose I should prepare for the worst. At least a week or two of wardrobe."

"Depends on how long it takes us to run down these culprits. Might be months."

Fanny glared. "Do you have to be so bleak about it?"

Rafe flattened a grin. "Your list, Fan?"

"I'll have the blue and white striped traveling dress with the matching pelisse and the straw skimmer with the cornflower blue ribbons. That will require white petticoats and chemise. White or slate gray stockings and blue garters . . ."

"Matching garters?" Rafe quirked a brow. "Who the devil even knows what color garters you're wearing?"

She stared at him. "I do."

Rafe tempered his retort. "Do you always plan your wardrobe down to the color of your unmentionables?" He watched her face flush. "Never mind, of course you do."

"I'll need at least at least five day frocks. The plain blue muslin and the pale yellow pinstripe with the pink and white paisley waistcoat." She detailed a shirt and jacket and skirt combination before stopping with a sigh. "And I suppose something respectably black."

Minnow snored comfortably from his corner and Hugh settled back into the plush bench seating and tipped his hat over his eyes. Rafe noted a half smile from the agent whenever Fanny detailed matching underthings.

As her day and evening selections proliferated, Rafe developed a kind of shorthand: five day frocks, one black. The train slowed as it pulled into the station. He needed to wire Scotland Yard, as well as send off Fanny's trunk list. He folded the note.

She frowned. "We're not done. I haven't selected shoes and jewelry."

"Oh yes, you have." Rafe unfolded the paper. "Coordinate shoes, gloves, and jewelry with wardrobe." He neglected to mention he had already added undergarments to his list of color-coordinated accessories.

He rousted Hugh and the professor, who took up weapons and followed him out the door. Rafe dipped his head back in the compartment. "Lock us out, Fan."

"Address the telegram to Mrs. Lockley and tell her to have Fiona do the packing." She rose to secure the door.

"You might also send a cable to 7 Abercromby Place, to a Mr. J. Silas Connery, my father's solicitor. He will know where the exposition machine was shipped."

Rafe smiled. "Very helpful of you."

"Anything to facilitate the demise of the Utopian Society." She slid the latch.

Fanny plopped back into her set and yawned. The sun had broken out over the lowlands and warmed the compartment. For the next few hours, she might try to get some sleep. She folded her jacket to use as a pillow and tucked herself into a sunny corner by the window. A myriad of suppressed questions, mostly regarding Rafe's ill-fated marriage, came bubbling up and she was left with no distraction but to consider yesterday's revelation.

Of course, things made better sense now, especially if Rafe had somehow been duped into thinking he'd been jilted. If she recalled correctly, it had been Claire's idea to write Nigel and mention Fanny's acquaintance with the Duke of Grafton. Rafe was sure to hear about it secondhand. She bit her lip. The letter had implied a flirtation—enough to nettle Rafe for not making the trip, but nothing that might plunge him into deep despair.

She felt upended by Rafe's obvious distress, but also nettled. The longer she thought about the now infamous missive, the more puzzling Rafe's response to their prank became. And it was quite impossible to confront either Nigel or Claire at the moment.

Fanny adjusted her makeshift pillow. Her eyelids grew heavy. Three raps. She jerked awake. Three more raps. Grumbling, she got up and let her bodyguards in.

During various stops, either Rafe or Hugh busied themselves sending or collecting telegrams. The farther the train traveled without trouble, the more everyone was able to catch a wink or two of rest.

"Fanny." She felt a tug on her sleeve and opened her eyes. "A quick good-bye, before I return to Glasgow." She blinked and peered out the window. The sign on the station read *Lockerbie*. They were near the border.

Hugh leaned over and kissed one cheek, then the other. She reached out and stroked the stubble of beard along his jaw. "It was very nice making your acquaintance, Agent Hugh Curzon."

A slow smile curved the edges of a strong mouth. "Likewise, my dear." He covered her hand in his and brushed the inside of her wrist with his lips. "Love is not love unless it is tested in some way." He winked at her and backed out the door.

Hugh hoisted both long guns over his shoulder and wove a path through the travelers on the platform. She thought he turned back once, to look their way, before he disappeared into the crowd.

She sat back and met the darkest green eyes she had ever seen. Her gaze shifted to the professor. Still snoring. Reluctantly, she returned to Rafe. "Don't look at me that way."

He crossed his arms over his chest. "You can't suppose I enjoyed watching that intimate little tête-à-tête."

His jealous words could not have touched her more. She inhaled a deep breath and kept her voice down. "I find it rather sweet, this sudden possessiveness of yours."

"You are spectacularly lovely, Fanny—even when you try your shrewish best to bedevil me." Rafe shook his head in wonder. "It's no wonder men are drawn to you like hounds to the scent. Frankly, I am still a bit bewildered you remain—"

She interrupted. "Unwed, on the shelf? A spinster?"

He snorted. "For God's sake, Fanny, you're four and twenty. And quite the beauty, as well as the richest heiress in all of Scotland. You could have your pick of the most eligible men in the empire."

Rafe settled into his seat like he expected a good story. "So, what exactly kept you on the market all these years?"

Fanny averted her eyes briefly. "Well, it wasn't because I never got over you—that's what you'd like to hear, isn't it, Rafe?"

They both sat facing each other, arms crossed.

"I'm not sure, actually. I was surprised to see Nigel still sniffing about." Rafe tilted his head. "I thought some handsome fortune hunter would come along for sure.

"There were plenty of those. And I consider Nigel a friend, nothing more." She huffed. "I just never thought I would marry anyone else, I suppose."

"Anyone else but me?" The most irritating smile edged the corners of his mouth.

"Could you possibly do me a favor and wipe that dull-witted grin off your face?"

He lifted a finger to his lips, rose from his seat, and sat beside her. "Come here, you." He snaked an arm around her waist and pulled her against his chest. "You're a bit overwrought." She straightened her shoulders and tried to resist, but he stroked her back with a gentle hand. "Rest your head on my shoulder and sleep."

She closed her eyes and didn't remember much after that. A dream, perhaps, in which she was carried from one moving train to another. She awoke to find herself lying across an upholstered train seat, covered by a coat. Fanny inhaled his potent male scent. *His* coat.

She propped herself on an elbow and wrinkled her nose. The compartment air felt a bit swampy. The professor had a rosy glow about him. There must be a whiskey bottle somewhere close by. She wrinkled her nose. "Where are we?"

∞ Chapter Twenty-three

Rafe couldn't help it: there was something wonderfully sensual about Fanny when she woke up. Her mop of curls, always a bit askew, and those heavy-lidded sleepy eyes inevitably caused his manly parts to stand up and take notice.

He glanced out the window. A gray sky and a few dark clouds loomed overhead. "I was just about to wake you. We're in Oxfordshire, almost upon our stop, Port Meadow Halt—just up the lane from Lucy's Ironworks."

"A pleasant ten-minute stroll, lass." The professor returned to his racing reports in *The Sporting Life*.

Fanny rubbed her eyes. "I dreamed I changed trains."

"You did. In Birmingham." Rafe folded his paper. "The professor bought our tickets and I carried you from platform to platform without so much as a peep from you."

Fanny blinked at him. "Your eyes are bloodshot—you've had no sleep in days."

Rafe smiled. "It is nice to know that even though you

withhold absolution, you still care about my health. I've even given up tobacco, in case you haven't noticed."

The train braked and she leaned sideways to look ahead. "I believe we have arrived, gentlemen."

Rafe and Professor Minnow combed the country station for natty blokes and left Fanny to repair her hair and button her jacket. Upon their signal she debarked, and they proceeded down the lane toward the canal. The skies had clouded some since Ayrshire, but there was no rain as yet.

The ironworks factory was not huge by Greyville-Nugent standards, more of an artisan foundry, Rafe guessed. A maze of iron beams and massive walls surrounded huge smelting ovens and other production equipment. It was at least ten degrees warmer inside, and the smell of molten ore mingled with that of machinery grease as they crossed the shop floor. Fanny took it all in stride, commenting on the steel-plating equipment and a plethora of copper fittings, each of which she seemed to find fascinating.

"We transport raw materials as well as finished goods by canal." The ironworks manager, a Mr. Huxley, steered them onto a pier, with a number of moorings that ran the length of the building. "Hull's been reinforced, plus your arc lights and batteries are installed, engine has plenty of petrol. She's all ready for you."

Rafe halted midstride, as did Fanny. A low whistle escaped his mouth. "Blimey, Professor! What is she? Twenty, twenty-five feet?" Nearly half the submarine rested above water. The crew deck on the cigar-shaped craft swept up to a four-foot hatchway at the center. Several pipes and a periscope protruded even higher. The sight was so strangely futuristic, one could only stand in awe.

Fanny stood on the gangplank that led to the submarine's deck. "Can we go inside?"

Rafe turned to the foreman. "Any strangers about, asking after the submarine or Professor Minnow?"

The man stroked his chin. "Seems to me there was a couple of blokes nosing around last week. Had to ask them to leave."

"Both of you, on board." The professor leaned closer to Rafe. "We'd best be leavin' right away. Give me a moment to settle the bill and I'll join you."

Trailing Mr. Huxley into the business office, Minnow called over his shoulder, "Don't touch a toggle switch on her."

Rafe followed Fanny down the ladder and entered the craft. A shaft of light from the overhead hatch revealed intricate pathways of brass tubes and copper wires, which traveled along the walls and roof of the ship connecting power sources to valves to gauges in the steerage compartment. Two large bulbous portholes looked out over the placid canal water. Rafe hardly knew which fantastic piece of apparatus to look upon next. He took in the size and volume of the sub and exhaled a low whistle.

"Due to its relative compactness and efficiency, the gasoline engine will far surpass the steam engine in the future." Fanny pointed to an oval-shaped bulb mounted to the ceiling. She reached overhead to flip a switch and hesitated.

"Go ahead, lass." Minnow climbed down the ladder. Fanny turned on the lamp. A pinprick of light sparked from each end of two metal filaments, then an arc of electricity connected inside the glass. The tube glowed with ever increasing light intensity until the single lamp illuminated the entire steerage compartment.

Minnow wedged himself down a narrow corridor and opened up the engine compartment. With two swift cranks of a brass handle, the engine sputtered, then purred to life. "Cast off, Detective Lewis."

Rafe had barely reeled in the line before the underwater craft quietly motored into the canal as smooth as silk. They were in the middle of the waterway, a good twenty yards past the ironworks, when Huxley ran out the huge open doors of the factory waving his arms.

As the sub took on more speed and pulled farther away, Rafe couldn't make out a word. He shouted into the main hatch. "I believe Mr. Huxley is trying to tell us something. Shall we come about?"

"Get yerself down here, Detective." Minnow's words echoed through the interior and out into the air. Fanny appeared in the aisle and waved him in. Rafe climbed down and dipped his head into steerage. "You have any idea what Huxley wants?"

"About fifty quid." Minnow looked happily relaxed at the helm. "He'll have the rest of his money just as soon as I win the competition." He winked at Fanny. "And what do you think of my chances, lass?"

"There are inventions—and then there are very great inventions." She smiled. "Your submarine is a marvel, Professor."

Minnow was so pleased that he passed the bottle around. Rafe took a long nip, and wiped the lip. "Are you going to take her down?"

"Canal isn't reliably deep enough. Wait until we're past the lock and out on the river—perhaps when we reach Henley-on-Thames."

Rafe passed the whiskey to Fanny. "Aunt Vertiline owns a charming place in Nettlebed, just down the lane from Henley. I spend weekends there when I'm off. Do a bit of rowing, even started a vegetable garden."

Fanny managed a swallow before she sprayed whiskey over him. "Good God." She gasped from the whiskey fumes. "I can't picture it, Rafe. You and some little doxy from town toiling in the garden." She snorted. "Really?"

"King's lock ahead," Minnow called out. "I need the two of you above deck to raise the gates."

"Aye, aye, Cap'n." Rafe swiveled around in tight quarters and ran straight into the cold steel of a pistol pointed at him. He did not recognize this minion. The dark suit identified him as one of Mallory's men. One who had obviously tucked himself away in the rear of the sub and awaited the professor's arrival.

Rafe shoved Fanny behind him. "We've got a stowaway." These blokes were patient, as well as resourceful, and there appeared to be an army of them. They had the manpower to track them over distance and the intelligence to anticipate every possible move. For the first time since this cat-and-mouse game began, a current of fear shot through his bones.

Minnow glanced over his shoulder. "Hold on there, I'm going to have to ask ye to leave my ship."

The man with the revolver ignored the request. "Hands up, where I can see them." He rifled through Rafe's jacket and pocketed both weapons. He nodded upward. "You heard the professor. Lock's ahead." Fanny climbed up first. As he passed by the gunman, Rafe noticed several missing fingers. The gunman addressed the professor. "If you want to see your crew alive, mind you keep your eyes ahead and your hands on the controls."

The moment the *Horatio* glided into the Thames, the submarine accelerated with the current. The dark-suited man prodded them down the hatch and into steerage. "Just keep this bucket of bolts above water and head downriver." He stood watch just outside steerage and waved his pistol about.

Rafe squeezed onto the bench seat next to Fanny and the professor and kept his own vigil on the fingerless bastard. When Minnow reached for a lever he got a pistol stuck in the back of his head. "Leave me be! I'm adjusting the ballast, we're forward heavy."

Rafe knew this section of river. They were almost upon Henley-on-Thames. He probed their captor again. "Since you've got the big stick—where are we headed?"

He received little more than a thin-lipped grin.

Fanny elbowed him in the side and he caught a wink from Minnow. Rafe waited for his next cue. Obviously, the professor had a diversion in mind. He just prayed he saw it coming two seconds before the tight-lipped natty bloke.

The craft rocked violently to one side as the sub's nose dove underwater. "Ho there! Something's wrong," Minnow yelped.

Rafe sprang from his seat and made a grab for their captor's gun. The force of his lunge caused a brief, mid-air wrestle before they landed on the floor and skidded down the narrow passageway. He two-handed the man's gun hand as they rolled side to side with the sway and lurch of the watercraft. Minnow shouted something to Fanny as he struggled to regain equilibrium. The back of Rafe's head cracked against the hull and he saw stars. Blindly, he struck out and managed a blow to the assailant's head.

Rafe blinked several times—Fanny was overhead wielding a giant wrench. Good God. Rafe got in another punch before he squeezed his eyes shut and hoped for the best. A loud *thunk* did the job. The natty bloke slumped on top of him, deadweight. Fanny helped roll the gunman off. "Bloody brave of you, Lieutenant Cut-throat."

Normally that would have gotten him a smile, at the very least a grin. But Fanny's worried gaze darted toward steerage. "I'm not so sure the professor has the sub under control." She set down the heavy tool. "In a moment or two we might all drown."

Rafe scrambled to his feet. Holding on to both sides of the passageway, Rafe made his way into steerage. "What's wrong, Professor?"

"I canna get the valves to shut. We're taking on too much water." Rafe squeezed in next to Minnow and they both put their weight against the hand crank. Nothing.

Minnow shook his head. "We'll be sunk soon if we don't lighten the load."

"There's at least twelve stone of deadweight in the back. Let's start with that." Rafe moved to dispose of the gunman as Minnow called after. "Watch the hatch, Detective, we're nearly under."

Lifting the body up through the hatch proved close to impossible. Chilly water poured in as the river lapped against the very edge of the raised opening. Rafe poked his head out. It was nearly dark. Just ahead, the few soft gaslights of Henley reflected off the river's edge. "Fanny, I need you to help me keep the body upright." Fanny pressed her back into the job, enough to keep the body vertical so Rafe could shove the man up through the hatchway. The surge of cold river water revived the unconscious gunman, who began to cough and spurt water. Rafe hauled the moaning man onto the deck and rolled him off the submersible.

Back inside the sub, Rafe closed the hatch. "I wager he'll swim ashore and live to stick a gun in my face another day."

Fanny frowned. "Let's hope not."

"Did that help any?" Rafe shouted down the passage.

"Not near enough." Minnow grumbled. "Might be able to keep her afloat if she were unmanned." As if on cue, the ship nosed down again. "I'll be steering her ashore, Detective."

The professor throttled the engine down and headed the craft toward the riverbank. "Going to try to beach her." Their captain looped a tie on the steerage wheel. "Best abandon ship straightaway. I won't chance running aground in a bad spot—don't want us trapped under a boat slip."

Minnow was up the ladder in a trice. "Either we go now or we never get the hatch open again."

Water gushed into the hold. They were soon, all three, soaked to the bone. Minnow pressed his sturdy back to the hatch cover and Rafe squeezed past the large man and through the opening.

He stood on the deck in a foot of river water and held the door open for Fanny and Minnow. "Christ almighty, she's headin' downriver. If she sinks, I'll never find her. I need to turn her in." Minnow stepped back down into the hold.

"Be quick about it, Professor."

"You two go ahead, I'll be right behind you."

Fanny shook her head. "We musn't leave him, Rafe."

"I'll get you to the bank and go back for him." Rafe had no idea if his impromptu plan was even possible. He only knew one thing. Fanny would be safe on land. Rafe shed his coat. "Come on now. The worst is over." Reluctantly, she stepped to the edge. Rafe grabbed her hand. "We're already cold and wet. On the count of three— jump."

Fanny swam well until her dress tangled in her legs. "Rafe!" She reached out to him and he grabbed hold before the heavy skirt dragged her under. He pulled her close. "Keep stroking, Fan—kick if you can." Slowly, they paddled their way to shore. With their last ounce of strength, they climbed the muddy bank and found a spot of lawn. Fanny was a mass of shivers. She swept wet hair from her eyes and glanced over her shoulder. "Whose park have we intruded upon?"

He shook his head. "I hardly know a soul here. I'm more of a weekender."

Rafe could just make out the sub, barely afloat, some hundred feet downriver. "I must try and help the professor. Stay put and don't move—no matter what. Minnow and I will work our way back here."

Rafe took off at a run, crossing the broad expanse of lawn, until he was even with the sub. He slipped and slid down the bank and into the water. Either he was swimming extraordinarily fast or the sub wasn't moving. A few more strokes and he reached the underwater craft. The hatch was now entirely underwater. Rafe turned the wheel and the round cover opened easily enough. "Bollocks." The hold had completely filled with water. His heart as well as his hopes sank. An inventor drowned by his own invention. The maniacal madmen could not have planned his demise any better.

The sinking submersible groaned and exhaled a last pocket of air from deep under water. In a burst of bubbles, the professor erupted from the open hatch much like a whale breaching in the sea.

Rafe stared, mouth open. "Christ, Professor, you had me worried! I thought you'd neatly done Mallory's job for him."

Minnow turned around in the water and gasped for more air. "I couldna open the hatch from inside. I found a small air pocket to catch a few breaths, but I'm glad ye came along when you did, Detective."

He and the professor swam back to dry land. That is, Rafe swam, and the professor did something that resembled a paddling crawl. From the bank they both turned for a look back. The only evidence of the submersible was the periscope that poked above the Thames's surface.

"She's caught up on something underwater. There may yet be hope to salvage her." A bit of light glowed in the professor's eyes. Rafe helped Minnow scramble up the side of the bank.

Fanny stood up and waved. "There she is." Rafe returned the gesture.

Minnow looked him in the eye. "How did you ever let a lass like that get away?"

Their waterlogged shoes made squishing sounds with every step. Rafe shook his head. "It's a rather long and foolish tale."

"I've no doubt of that, Detective Lewis."

Shivering from head to toe, Fanny hugged herself. "Rafe, where—" She wrinkled her nose and sneezed. "W-w-where do we go from here?"

He sighed. "Aunt Vertiline's little country manor. It's no doubt the safest place we could stay tonight. Our man overboard likely made it to shore and has already wired his cohorts."

A breeze whipped up off the Thames and appeared

to travel straight through Fanny's wet clothes. Her teeth chattered. "How f-f-far?"

Rafe scooped her up in his arms and started up the curved mound of lawn. "Not far. Coming, Professor?"

Minnow cast a longing glance back to the water and followed after them. They trudged inland from the river, along a narrow dirt lane dotted with old brick homes. Walled yards and thick foliage sheltered them from the river's chill. By the time they reached the service entrance to the house, Fanny was nodding off.

Rafe knocked before entering to warn the housekeeper. "Mrs. Coates?" He carried Fanny inside the larder, up a few stairs, and into a warm kitchen. "Have a seat, Professor."

Minnow stretched out along a table bench, kicked off waterlogged boots, and peeled off soggy hose.

"Lord have mercy, Mr. Lewis." His housekeeper shuffled along the brick floor, fastening her robe.

"Ah, Mrs. Coates. We're going to need blankets and a bottle of whiskey—immediately."

Minnow grunted. "Now yer talking, Detective."

Rafe looked down at Fanny, who could barely keep her eyes open. She'd gotten a few hours of sleep on the train, but could use a long night's rest. Rafe yawned. They all could. The personal revelations could wait another day.

⚭ Chapter Twenty-four

Fanny awoke to birds chirping and pried an eye open. From the looks of it, she was in a strange room, in a strange bed. But the mattress was soft and the comforter most comforting. Several chatty wrens perched on a ledge just outside the windowsill. Her gaze traveled from small panes of wavy glass, along a swirl of flowered wallpaper to—

She started at the sight of a small person standing in the room. A child with large round eyes stared without blinking.

She lifted her head. "Hello."

No answer, only a hint of a smile in green eyes flecked with copper. The short pants and the bowl haircut gave him away. "My name is Miss Greyville-Nugent. But you may call me Fanny."

Still no response, but the eyes did appear to grow wider, if that was possible. "Shall I try to guess your name, then?" Ah, now there was a familiar sort of grin.

She rolled her eyes up to the ceiling and pretended to think very hard. "Might your name be . . . Fenwick?"

The boy shook his head violently.

Fanny wrinkled her brow. "No, I suppose not." Propped on an elbow, she realized she had no sleeping gown on. Whoever had put her to bed had taken off her clothes. She remembered soaking wet garments and drew the covers close. "Might you be a lieutenant colonel in the dragoons? A Melvin Stewart?"

The child laughed, a golden sparkle in those emerald eyes. Just like—Fanny's gaze traveled to the man standing in the doorway.

Rafe entered the room in clean shirt and trousers, his waistcoat unbuttoned. "Guessing games are his favorite sport. He's relentless. He'll keep you at it all morning."

Rafe's hair was damp, glossy—just out of the bath. He looked vibrant and so very masculine. He stopped at the foot of the bed and lowered his gaze. "Sneaking into a lady's bedchamber?"

The child looked up, unafraid. "You are in a lady's bedchamber."

"Yes, but I am quite sure Mrs. Coates has taught you better." Rafe lowered his chin for a scowl. "Introduce yourself, then go downstairs." Rafe turned to Fanny. "You take chocolate?"

"Please, with plenty of hot milk and sugar."

"Have Mrs. Coates ready a breakfast tray." The boy dipped a polite bow and ran from the room.

"No running in the house." Rafe leaned against the

foot rail and turned to her. "He knows better, I'm sure of it."

"Father?"

Her heartbeat quickened as her gaze left Rafe and traveled to the little boy, who stood in the open doorway. She felt light-headed. In need of air. As though all the oxygen had been sucked out of the room.

"What is it, Harry?"

"I wished to ask about meringues in her chocolate— but now you've gone and told her."

"Yes, I'm afraid she knows everything." Rafe's gaze briefly met hers. "Why don't you tell our visitor your entire name? The long one."

"The very long name, or the one with two names?"

"Whichever you'd like."

The boy turned to her and smiled. "Harry Lewis."

"I should have guessed Harry. Had you given me a hundred more chances, I would have. Pleased to meet you, Harry." The ends of her mouth tugged upward. "And I would very much enjoy a nice soft meringue in my cocoa." Long after Rafe closed the door she stared at the entryway, unsure if she wished to flee or stay.

She felt the mattress dip as he sat on the edge. "Fanny?"

Her gaze slowly scanned the room until their eyes met. She swallowed. "You have a son."

His eyes were steady, careful. "No one knows, Fanny. Not even Vertiline. Just Mrs. Coates—and now you."

She very much did not want to cry at this moment,

but her eyes insisted on welling. "Might I ask why?" She hardly recognized her own whisper.

Rafe lowered his eyes. "He'll not pay for my mistakes. I won't stand for the raised brows, the chilly treatment, especially the cold stares from Mother. I won't have him treated as the mistake, a burden the St. Aldwyns can ill afford."

She blinked hard. "Many families take in bastards, Rafe. You were married—"

"To a village smithy's daughter. If I hadn't married— just bore the child off to raise—Harry might have had a fighting chance."

His gaze traveled out the window, past singing birds and into the void. "It seems, in trying to do the right thing, I did the one thing my family might never forgive."

"But . . . we were to marry, and I'm a commoner, of sorts."

His grin was wry, cynical. "You come from landed gentry—an ancient, well-respected family. With a dowry the size of a princess."

It was all suddenly clear. "I had no idea your family needed the money so badly."

"Harry was barely four months old when Ceilia died. I traveled to London looking for employment. Vertiline wrote and apprised me of the impending St. Aldwyn ruin, and I asked if I might make use of this cottage." He glanced at her somewhat sheepishly. "During that time I tried to write. I wanted to confess everything to you and my family. But when I learned how empty the coffers were—"

He shrugged. "Eight months later, Reginald married

Bess. I do not know the size of the income, but her dowry has likely kept the estate in credit."

In her mind's eye, Fanny conjured Dunrobin Hall, sitting on a hill above the firth, the picture of elegant disrepair. Her heart continued to beat erratically from the depths of a sinking stomach. There had been rumors of financial difficulties after the earl died.

Rafe grimaced. "They'll never forgive me for not marrying you. Can you imagine what Harry would go through?"

A tapping came from the door. "Your breakfast tray, miss."

"Once you've had your chocolate and a nice hot bath, come and find me." Rafe opened the door for Mrs. Coates.

A spry woman with steel gray hair and a warm smile entered the room. "Your shoes and stockings, dear." Fanny vaguely remembered the housekeeper from last evening. "I washed them out and let them dry by the stove."

Fanny glanced out the window. Sunny and bright. "What time is it?"

"A bit after two in the afternoon." Rafe smiled, exiting the room. "Mrs. Coates washed your clothes. They're likely dry on the line. I'll go check."

"IF YOU PULL up every one of those, there won't be a morsel left for the rabbits." Rafe bent over a row of turnips. "And I'd like to know how it is I get the tiresome weeding job while you have all the fun harvesting."

Harry shook soil off the pale orange root, and placed the carrot in a wooden basket. "But I do weed. Mrs. Coates forces it upon me or—"

Rafe chucked a handful of weeds into the heap beside him. "Or no sweet cream and berries at tea?"

Harry darted up from behind frothy carrot tops and tossed a dirt clod at him. Then another.

"Watch it." Rafe tossed one back. And another. Within moments a colliding salvo of garden soil projectiles arched across orderly rows of vegetables. "All right, enough, Harry." Rafe made his way across the garden, dodging chunks of dirt. "No sweet cream and berries for this lad." He tackled his son and lifted him into the air.

Harry flapped his arms and made like a bird. "Higher!"

"Demanding little devil."

"Here they are, miss." Mrs. Coates escorted a freshly washed and dressed Fanny into the garden. His housekeeper gave him and Harry a look—her grim one. "I'll not have time to make a decent tea if you keep me busy heating water for baths."

Rafe brought his son gently back to earth. "I'll scrub him up, Mrs. Coates."

"Again!"

"One last fly." Rafe whirled the agile little body into the air over his shoulder. Harry squealed in delight. "Shall we have a chat with our guest before you're off to your tub?"

Rafe plunked himself down on the garden bench beside Fanny. "Careful, he can be a monster."

"I must say a very charming monster."

Harry wriggled off his lap to sit between them. "Yes, that's just it. Monsters are often charming. That's how they worm their way into your heart," he said.

Fanny's smile seemed thin—forced, actually. She turned to Harry. "Can you tell me the names of all the vegetables you grow?" She rose from the stone seat. "Better yet, why don't you show me?" Harry slipped off the bench and held out a dirty hand.

"Look at those filthy little digits." Rafe relaxed onto the bench. "Most girls wouldn't hold hands with you."

She took the small hand in her own and winked at him. "Where is the professor? Gone off to dredge up his submersible?"

Rafe nodded. "He was up before me this morning. Found a bloke just south of here with a bilge pump. I thought we'd have a bit of tea and catch up with Professor Minnow at the tavern later."

"What about this row?" she queried Harry, then turned to Rafe. "You've made arrangements to meet?"

Rafe grinned. "There are four pubs in town—five counting the Rose and Crown Inn. We'll find him."

Harry pointed to a feathery clump of green. "Radishes." He looked up at Fanny. "Is Professor Minnow a fish?"

Fanny knelt down to finger the fernlike leaves. "The professor is the inventor of a ship that can sail underwater."

"Oh, *like* a minnow." Harry smiled knowingly.

Fanny laughed. "Very much like a fish."

Rafe stretched his legs out and savored the sight of

Harry and Fanny stepping carefully between the cucumbers and wax beans. He knew well and good he had left questions unanswered. Even now he could see the wheels turn in that wickedly clever brain of hers.

History to ponder.

Timelines to puzzle over.

Half-truths to ruminate on.

Sins to atone for.

She would have a million questions about all of it. Emotions were likely to run deep, far deeper than any simple explanation he could provide. He had wanted to wait until this whole frightening episode in her life was over. Until he had this crazy lot of anti-progressives, Bellecorte Mallory included, tossed into the Newgate jail. Case closed.

Rafe entered the house to check on Harry's bath. Perhaps the pub was a good idea, where a few drams of whiskey couldn't hurt. A public place where she wouldn't cry or wail or carry on. Much.

Chapter Twenty-five

"Are you quite sure?" Rafe raised a brow. "What about the motor?"

"If the seals hold to the engine compartment, the Brayton will be bone dry." Professor Minnow lifted his glass of stout to another man at the bar. "I'm telling ye, she's nearly afloat. Mr. Roger Spottesworth here has called up another pump from Reading. Be here in the morning. She'll be seaworthy by afternoon."

Rafe paid for a bottle and two pints. "Have another on me, gentlemen." He scooped up two small glasses and headed for a table placed near a large hearth. Glowing embers added a rosy hue to Fanny's cheeks.

"The professor says the submariner will be ready to shove off by afternoon tomorrow." Rafe kicked out a chair and set their glasses down.

Fanny frowned. "I'm not in any mood to go below-decks, are you? Not until I'm assured he's solved his ballast problems."

Rafe uncorked the bottle and poured them both a

glass. "You do seem rather concerned with ballast problems. Apart from our sinking yesterday, what makes you so wary?"

She sipped a drop of whiskey. "Father also experienced ballast tank problems. Rather tricky managing fore, aft, and main tanks on a vessel less than fifty tons. It's my theory the trouble would disappear with a larger warship, where small displacements of air—that is, changes in buoyancy—wouldn't cause such unmanageable effects."

Rafe sat back in his chair and grinned. "Tell me, Fanny, how involved with your father's work were you?" He swallowed half a dram. "Truthfully, this time."

Fanny's eyes narrowed slowly. "*Truth*, is it?" She raised her drink and held it to her lips. "All right. If it is truth you want—truth is what you shall receive. But I will require the same of you." She emptied her glass and set it on the table. "Truth for truth, Detective Lewis."

Rafe met her narrow squint with one of his own. "Me first."

She nodded her go-ahead.

"You refer to a submarine as a warship—why?"

"Can you think of any other use, apart from scientific studies, for such a stealth ship?"

Rafe shrugged. "Spying?"

"A line item the size of a submarine on the Home Office ledger?" She rolled her eyes upward. "That would be an allowance in the Ministry of War budget, would it not?"

"Spoken like a defense contractor." Rafe grinned. "Scotland Yard might make use of such a craft."

"Irish Americans financed a submarine project in America. I believe it sank—weighed down by too much dynamite, I expect." Fanny's eyes danced from the firelight. "I'm trying to picture you trolling the Thames for anarchist bombs."

Rafe poured and she picked up her glass. "My turn. How is it . . ." She hesitated. "How is it you waited until the night of our engagement ball to call off the marriage?"

Rafe took in a breath and exhaled. "I suppose I could have sent a wire—'Sorry darling, but I can't marry you. Stop. Got a girl bagged. Stop. Already hitched.'"

Fanny's eyes glistened. The sight made him swallow. He reached across the table and rotated his glass. "I had a mind to come to you in person. But I was late getting to Edinburgh. Ceilia was having a rough time—the pregnancy was difficult. As you well know, I arrived just hours ahead of the ball."

Rafe shook his head. "I remember walking into the hall, joking with family and friends and thinking, 'Dear God, what have I done?'" He picked up his glass and tossed it back, welcoming the whiskey burn. "Then you walked out on the terrace." A faint smile tilted the corners of his mouth. "You were the loveliest little thing—exquisite, actually."

"Ravishing." She swallowed. "I believe that was the word you used." The blush on her cheeks didn't come from the warmth of the hearth.

"All of that and more." Rafe stared at the beauty across the table and pictured the dazzling lavender gown she had worn that evening. Shoulders bared, her alabaster skin glowed in the moonlight. "I nearly had you right there on the balcony."

"Yes, if it hadn't been for Father and Eliza Murray—quite an inopportune moment, as I recall. What exactly did you and Father discuss, afterward, in his study?"

Rafe uncorked the bottle again. "I believe the next question is mine."

Fanny crossed her arms under her chest and raised a brow.

"What kind of machine did your father have shipped to London?"

"Ha!" She leaned forward. "I have no idea. Sorry, Rafe." He frowned. "Truth?"

She raised her pledge hand. "On the lives of Her Majesty's Fusiliers, if any of our foot soldiers are left alive." Her eyes teased momentarily.

"I did sacrifice a few men at the loch. Good cause, though."

"Honestly, Rafe, I'd tell you if I knew. Father called it a surprise—for me. We'll find out soon enough when we reach London. You haven't heard from the solicitor, Mr. Connery?"

"Only one wire today." His eyes shifted away. "They've discovered another body. An industrialist, or so they believe."

Eyes wider. "What happened?"

"Is that your question?"

"Yes."

Rafe filled both their glasses. "All this truth requires liquid courage."

He tilted his chair back. "This time, they found parts of a torso. Head's missing—parts of hands and legs. Grisly, as if the man was drawn and quartered."

Fanny slumped in her chair. "Sounds like Mallory."

"Our villain likes to keep things interesting. A bobby on patrol found a bloodied piece of waistcoat in Savoy Row. There was a card in the pocket with the name of a munitions factory in Newcastle."

"Newcastle." Fanny pressed her lips together and squinted. "I might have a name for you."

Rafe rocked forward. "Who?"

"Is this your question?"

He nodded.

Fanny looked up from her glass. "William George Armstrong. He owns Elswick Works. Hydraulic machinery and heavy artillery. The Armstrong gun is a rifled cannon, which gives the gun gyroscopic stability and improved accuracy. 'Tis a very powerful cannon with range as well." Her voice grew faint and a bit raspy. "Reportedly, projectiles fired from the gun can pierce a ship and explode inside an enemy vessel, which would increase the damage, and casualties." She drained her glass.

Rafe started to pour then tipped the bottle up. "How much more can you handle?"

"One more. And I will count that as a question. Now I have two." Fanny leaned forward. "What exactly did you and Father discuss in his study, after he and Eliza caught us on the balcony?"

"I confessed everything—well, most everything. When I finished, Ambrose was actually rather civil. He told me he'd never forgive me for such a betrayal. For injuring you so—and then he said a funny thing. He said, 'God damn you—you've done the right thing, Rafe.'"

Fanny's mouth dropped open somewhere along the telling. "Father never said a word." Her gaze traveled the room. Glazed eyes that focused nowhere until, at last, they connected with him. "Did you . . ." She caught her breath. "Did you . . . love her? Ceilia?

"Very sadly." His eyes never left hers. "Yes."

"Why is that sad?" Her speech was nearly a whisper.

"Because I didn't love her . . . not at first." Fanny's eyes filled with unshed tears. Rafe handed her his pocket square and she pressed it to her eyes. "Thank you." She continued to dab at the evidence of her sorrow.

"I came to love a young woman who had made a terrible mistake. Quite as terrible as the one I made. There we were, two people quite miserable in a marriage neither one of us wanted, with a child on the way. My affection no doubt began with empathy—we were so . . . pitiable."

She reached for the shot glass and he covered her hand with his. "Fanny . . . I never loved her as I love you—as I will always love you."

She stared at him for a very long time. "How tragic for

us, Rafe." She lifted the glass and tossed back the last of her whiskey. She stood and wobbled a bit.

He caught her wrist. "Let me explain."

Her eyes darted about the pub, as a few people began to take notice. "I believe I've endured quite enough truth for one evening."

Fanny dipped a dismissive curtsy and had to steady herself on a passing gent. "Sorry."

The man grinned. "My pleasure, lass."

"Excuse us." Rafe downed a shot, picked up the bottle and followed her to the door. "Fanny, wait." A shiver ran up his spine. He had risked everything to reveal the truth to her and he must see it through to the end. It was his only hope of ever winning her back.

Rafe signaled their leaving and the professor raised his glass in salute. He set the whiskey on the bar. "Mr. Spottesworth, at the end of this bottle, might you point the professor in the direction of Catslip, last house in the lane?"

"I'll have him home in a wheelbarrow if I have to, sir."

"Good man." Rafe dashed out the door and located Fanny trudging down the road. She tilted to one edge of the lane, overcorrected her balance, and wobbled to the opposite side. Her state of inebriation caused him a brief smile.

FANNY KEPT MOVING. If she stopped, the ground underfoot moved and the earth whirled around her.

Rafe caught up and fell in beside her. "You know why God invented whiskey?"

She glared at him. "So the Irish would never rule the world." She hiccupped. "You still tell that joke, Rafe?" She stopped in the lane and stared at him. When she listed to one side, he reached out to steady her.

Fanny yanked her arm away and marched down the lane. "What's the difference between an Irish wedding and an Irish wake?" She looked over her shoulder at him and nearly fell in the ditch.

"One less drunk." He jogged to catch up. "Really shouldn't pick on the Irish—especially when we Scots match them dram for dram." He put his arm around her waist and dragged her up beside him. She didn't protest, much. "Except for this Scot. You're a cheap date, Fanny. What was that? Half a dram over four?"

"Where's the Talisker's?" She swayed. "I could use another."

"Back at the pub, I'm afraid."

She swayed and squinted at him. "But you paid for it."

"Hamish Minnow has dedicated himself to reaching the bottom of our bottle. Here we are." Rafe guided her through the wooden gate at the end of the lane.

Fanny stood on the brick walkway while he closed the gate. A tilt of her head brought a thousand stars into view. All . . . whirling . . . around . . . in . . . the . . . sky. She steadied herself and sighed. "I dream about you every night."

Rafe pivoted slowly. Even though his face was something of a blur, he looked . . . hopeful.

"Well, nearly every night." Fanny shrugged and loosed

an apologetic giggle. "How embarrassing. I have no idea why I blurted that out."

He swept both arms around her. "You're in my thoughts by day and my dreams at night."

A tingle ran down her spine, numb as it was. She thought she managed a thin smile before stepping away. "Rather foolish of us, wouldn't you say?"

Rafe opened the terrace door and they crept inside the darkened house. An oil lamp sputtered on a side table near the stairs. He adjusted the wick, picked up the lamp, and signaled for her to go up ahead.

At the top of the stairs, a door swung open. "Oh, Mr. Lewis, I'm afraid young Harry has had a terrible night terror. Might you take a turn with him, sir? He's been asking for you."

"Yes, of course." Rafe turned to Fanny. "Your room is on the left, and mine is another two doors past on the right. In case you have a nightmare of your own—you did mention you dream of me." He winked at her and entered the nursery.

Fanny leaned against the wall, and exhaled.

"Have you checked under the bed, Harry?"

"Yes, Father."

"The wardrobe as well?"

The conversation made her smile. She imagined a soft shake of hair as Harry nodded.

"Once or twice?"

"Twice."

"And you still didn't find him?"

"He's here, I know it," the little boy whispered.

The sound of furniture being dragged across the floor prompted her to peek into the room. Rafe pulled the child's bed over to another wall.

"There, now. When the Nettlebed Troll arrives, he will believe he's under your bed. That is when we'll get him." Rafe spun around. "Where's my old cricket bat?"

Harry stood in the middle of the room in his nightshirt and pointed to the corner. The bat leaned against a child's cupboard, its shelves filled with toys and storybooks.

Rafe grabbed the bat with one hand and hoisted the child under his other arm. "There, now." He settled Harry in his bed and pulled up the covers. "You hold on to this." He placed the cricket bat in his son's small hands.

"What if he comes when I'm asleep?"

Rafe sat on the bed. "I'll wake you."

"Will you help me get him?"

"Of course. That's what fathers are for, chasing off trolls."

Fanny closed her eyes and smiled. How could this be happening? It seemed as though there were no sins too great to be forgiven. All the anger she had ever harbored toward Rafe was falling to pieces and evaporating into thin air. She would blame the whiskey in the morning, but for tonight, she was quite sure she had never been more in love with Raphael Byron Lewis. He had been honorable once—a young man with a generous and noble heart. In a very reassuring sense, in this fleeting stolen moment, Rafe became the man she had loved since childhood, utterly steadfast and familiar.

And there was something else. She wanted him. Dear God, she wanted him more than she had ever wanted any man in her life. And that was rather odd. Fanny peeked back into the nursery. He reclined against the headboard, his arm wrapped around his son. It was odd because Rafe Lewis was the only man she had ever wanted. Ever.

His voice filtered into her fuzzy brain. ". . . I'm quite certain the only way little boys can get to the Land of Nod is by moonbeam."

"Tell me how to catch a moonbeam."

"You know how."

"Yes, but I want you to tell me again." Harry yawned.

Fanny slipped away from the nursery and opened the bedroom door on the left. Her gaze, however, ventured down the corridor to the second door on the right.

∞ Chapter Twenty-six

Rafe entered his bedchamber and disrobed. Fanny had always been a wicked tease and a bittersweet torture, but tonight she had blurted out something extraordinary. Something that actually gave him pause.

I dream about you every night.

Rafe tried sleeping on his stomach. When that didn't work, he tried his back. With each toss and turn, a picture came to mind. A lovely water nymph dipped into the loch. He lay on his side. A voluptuous beauty bared her breasts in the loft. He punched up a pillow and changed sides. An earth goddess emerged from her bath.

Steaming hot, he tossed off bedcovers, swung his legs off the mattress, and walked to the dresser. He ran his hands over beard stubble as he leaned over the basin. He lifted a pitcher and splashed his head and neck. Cool water dripped down his shoulders and chest, bringing some relief.

He tried thinking about the case. All the events of the past few days, which included a small army of anti-progressives, whirled in his head on whiskey wings. It seemed obvious the shadow-faced minions wanted Fanny for something special—a grand statement of some kind. As Rafe puzzled over the meaning behind their relentless pursuit, he became more and more convinced they would find their answers in London.

He returned to bed and slowed his breathing. Turning onto his side, he faced the wall of the house and stared past the clouded, wavy window glazing. He counted a few evening stars before rolling onto his back with a grunt.

The dull aching throb of a very visible cockstand pitched an impressive tent under the bed linens. Cursing to himself, Rafe kicked off the covers a second time to yield wholeheartedly to the temptation of his oh-so-turgid flesh.

He heard the click of his door latch, and rolled over to find Fanny standing just inside his chambers. "Might you help me with these?" He was getting used to the enchanting sight of an awkward elbow up in the air as she tried pointing behind her.

He quickly covered himself and spoke softly. "Come here." He patted the edge of the bed.

"Sorry to be such a nuisance." She hiccupped.

He grinned. "I'm beginning to have a greater appreciation for these tiny, unmanageable buttons." When he got to the base of her spine, he kept his touch light and helped her slip out of the gown. He kissed the top of an ivory shoulder. "Sleep with me, Fan." He nuzzled a pretty length of neck.

She raised her arms overhead and he lifted off her camisole. His hands went around her waist and traveled under the curves of her bosom. She turned to him, a sensuous arch to her back, breasts silhouetted by moonlight. "You may let down my hair." He removed a handful of hairpins and a mass of curls tumbled down her back. For a time he lost himself in a tangle of corkscrews and coils. The intoxicating scent of her. His fingers gently wound their way through the soft curls and pulled her close. She leaned against him and hiccupped. Again.

Rafe sighed. Fanny was inebriated. He couldn't possibly take advantage. If and when he took her virginity, he wanted her full, sober—and wanton—consent.

He lay back against pillows and inhaled a deep breath. His pulse felt as though it tripped over itself when she slipped under the sheet. Pulling her close, he cupped her breast as his fingertips played over a silken nipple, which quickly ruched into a hard point. She moaned and the small of her back rubbed up against his cock—velvet soft, skin on skin. The randy boy danced a pretty dance between the two dimples above her derriere. He ran his hands up and down the silky smooth curves of her. Having little experience with the sexually uninitiated, he reminded himself to take it slow. Not just because Fanny was an innocent, but because he knew very well she had only to touch him and he would erupt like Mount Etna.

He exhaled slowly. "Close your eyes, Fanny."

"If I close my eyes, the room spins."

Rafe propped a few pillows behind them and tucked

her into his arms. "Better?" Her head nodded against his chest.

He pulled out a drawer in the bedside table and removed a tin of condoms, purchased this morning on his way home from the wire office. Wishful thinking, he supposed, until now. Not that he'd expected something this wonderful to happen in his room, but Fanny was in his bedchamber.

Rafe smiled to himself and pulled her close. Here's hoping his luck would hold until morning.

JUST SHY OF sunrise, Fanny awoke to pleasant arousal. A pale gray light filtered into the room. Rafe slid his hand along the curve of her belly and pulled her close from behind. His touch was so delicate—so delicious— it sent waves of sleepy, sensuous pleasure through her. *Yes.* She held her breath and waited for his next move. *Please.* His hand reached her breast and cupped. *More.* His thumb lightly stroked the nipple. A sleepy moan escaped. *Mm-mm.* Oh yes, please—she wanted so much more. He kissed her shoulder and moved up the side of her neck. His teeth nibbled an earlobe, sending shivers down her spine.

She purposely turned onto her back. As she turned, his hand slipped down her rib cage, his fingertips brushing a circle around her navel before moving between her legs. She sensed him above her and opened her eyes.

"How lovely to awake and find you in my bed." His

mouth lowered to her breast and she arched. Circling his tongue, he teased, kissed, and nipped.

"Make love to me." Her whispered demand caused a hard nipple to pop from his mouth.

A shock of hair fell over his forehead. He answered with a slow smile. "Sure?"

She nodded.

His hand nudged her inner thigh, and she wantonly opened to him. She would give him access to her body—but could she hold on to her heart? Fanny shivered when he parted moist folds and circled delicate flesh. "Oh, yes, Rafe."

He gently explored her opening. A finger pushed inside, shallow at first and then deeper. All the while his thumb continued to circle the wondrous, swollen part of her. Waves of mysterious desire pulsed through her body, causing her stomach to flutter and her hips to thrust. Inviting him to play—urging for more.

She spoke between breathless moans and sighs. "What is the name of the place you touch to make me moan?"

Rafe swept a trail of kisses across the bridge of her nose. "Mmm, the Latin word is *landīca*." He appeared to be amused as well as aroused by her curiosity.

"You always were handy with Latin."

His lips continued down her throat. "I plan on discovering where all your pleasures lie."

Ignoring the chill of early morning, Fanny pushed the covers off. She wanted to see him look at her again—yes, that look. His eyes narrowed with a kind of hunger that made her tremble. "You are a vision. All peachy flesh and rosy tips." He trailed a finger over her nipples and then moved lower. "And no pantalets." He encouraged her legs to part. His fingers played along the inside curve of her thighs, and a tremble shot through her body. Rafe pressed her back onto the sheets and held her arms while his tongue traveled over breasts and belly. He hesitated before delving deep between her legs. "I must taste you."

He delved inside her most intimate place using slow, laving strokes. Shocked at first, she stiffened. "Think of nothing but pleasure. My fingers, my lips . . ." He dipped and took a gentle lick. "My tongue."

Rafe licked. Much to her surprise, she moaned in response, squirming with pleasure. She wanted him to explore every petal and fold, every forbidden place. Each surge of arousal built upon the next until all she could think about was his touch, his kiss—and those fingers that patiently widened and stretched her entrance. She arched back and raised her hips to him.

Rafe could feel that she was ready—more than ready. He reached over her sweet little torso and lifted a tin of rubbers from the top of the side table.

He straddled her belly and his cock jumped in response to her gaze.

"Such a great angry beast."

His eyes flicked upward, but he also growled. "If you insist, Fanny." He opened a packet and rolled on the condom. Hovering above, he took a moment to brush a few strands of hair off her face. He gazed at every inch of her body and she arched up to meet him. "No rushing, Fan. I wish your first time to be as pleasurable as possible."

Her gaze returned his bravely as he poised over her, cock in hand. "Is this the part of pleasure meant to tease—drive me near to madness?" Fanny sighed, her pretty face haloed by a mass of rich brown curls. And her lovely body, plump in all the most wonderful places, lay open and waiting for him. Good God, it was a dream come true, a fantasy long-imagined come alive.

As much as he might try to hold back, Rafe was quite sure this was going to be a quick pleasuring. He would bring her to climax, linger at the apex, then tumble her over the edge. He pushed just inside the moist, warm sex of her, slippery with excitement. She gasped and then slowly opened, stretching to accommodate the girth of him.

"I can stop if you wish." His voice was husky.

"Don't you dare stop."

Her head fell back. She drew up her knees, and her warm, tight sheath enveloped him. "Good God, you are heaven." He withdrew and pushed in, until her body trembled and her hips rocked with his motion. He dipped down, caught a nipple between his lips, and suckled. She arched her back and offered the other.

He continued his slow, deliberate thrusts, and she wrapped her legs around his body. She wanted more. More lips. More tongue. More—Rafe.

He dropped between her legs and, without missing a stroke, brought her with him as he sat back on his haunches. Fanny rode his thighs as he held her quite impaled upon his cock. He cupped her buttocks and guided the thrust of her hips. Her pleasure rose to a new level as her chest turned rosy pink. "We are so right for each other, Fan." He pulled out enough to rub *landīca* with the tip of his cock—his own fervor building as he stroked her slippery magical spot. They were both a breath away from release.

A cry escaped her lips and she added a groan.

"We're going to wake the whole house." He laughed softly. Pressing his fingers into the flesh of her buttocks, he brought himself deep inside her hot, tight sheath. Fanny arched and quivered and bucked in euphoric throes of pleasure.

Hovering at the brink, Rafe pulled her down for one last thrust, then roared his climax.

He could not speak—not for many seconds. He had tried to be gentle, but the sex had ended in a wild, lusty position. Deep and passionate, but not for beginners.

He admonished himself for being such a brute. He held her, clung to her, for he feared he had hurt her. She was not ready yet for such rough sex. Finally, he managed an apology. "I'm so sorry, love. Things got quite—heated. Are you well enough?"

She leaned back onto the pillows, wearing an expression of divine pleasure. "I am very well, sir." Her breath was still harsh from exertion. The room was as warm as toast, and the small window by the bed was actually fogged from condensation.

"No pain?"

"Very little, and I came to pleasure with you inside me."

Rafe smiled. In the pale light of dawn, her skin glowed

with the sheen of *lumière de l'amour.* Her chest rose and fell, nipples relaxed and rounded, opalescent pink in color. He lifted a finger to one tip and watched it respond to his light manipulation.

Fanny rolled onto her side and tucked herself into the niche of his body. Resting her head on his shoulder, she closed her eyes. "Well done, Raphael."

FANNY LAY IN bed and ran a hand over her belly. A smile tugged at the corners of her mouth. They had made love. Something she had thought about—dreamed about—for years. And she was not disappointed. Far from it.

Her fingers slipped between her legs, where proof of his invasion remained. A slippery translucent substance moistened her fingers. She sat up and tossed the covers back, searching for evidence of her lost innocence. Nothing much to speak of, perhaps a bit of pink on the sheet.

Fanny swung her legs over the side of the bed and her toes brushed the floor carpet. The room tilted back and forth. Her head hurt. Rubbing her eyes, she vaguely remembered Rafe kissing her temple. "Sleep in, darling. I'm off to find Professor Minnow."

She washed up and dressed, leaving the buttons on her frock for Mrs. Coates downstairs.

"There, now." The kind woman's nimble fingers fastened her dress. "By the looks of you, I'd guess a strong cup o' tea and toast might be just the cure."

Fanny tugged up a lopsided smile. "A bit green, am I?"

She sat at the kitchen worktable and eyed a pile of carrots. She took up a knife. "Would you like these sliced or diced, Mrs. Coates?"

"Oh dear, never mind the chopping."

"Even as a child, I enjoyed helping out. At first, cook chased me out, but she gave in when I kept pestering."

Mrs. Coates placed the tea service on the table. "Dice them up, then—but drink your tea first. I'll not have you cutting yourself and bleeding all over my kitchen."

The housekeeper sliced into a loaf of bread. "Young Harry likes to help shuck peas. Such a sweet child, misses his father something terrible when he's in town." The woman laid the bread on top of the stove to toast. "We almost lost him as wee 'un. Child was a sickly infant. Mr. Lewis fretted over him so. But the lad pulled through, and will you look at him now?"

Fanny gulped her tea and poured another cup. "Where is Harry?"

"Down the lane and across the dell at the pond— digging up worms. The two of 'em fish off Angel Bridge. They've been known to bring back a line of perch a time or two, but I don't count on it for supper."

Fanny looked up from her chopping. "Is there a study in the house I might use? I need to write a letter of some urgency."

"Why, yes, I don't believe Mr. Lewis would mind. The first door down the hall past the parlor."

Rafe's study was small and lined with bookshelves. Pale light from a north-facing window poured over a simple secretary desk. Circling the room, Fanny ran her fingers over well-worn spines. Familiar names: Haggard, Stevenson, Cooper. Many of his favorite authors were hers as well.

Something Rafe had said in the midst of their harrowing journey had continued to niggle at the back of her mind, something vaguely unsettling about Claire's letter. Rafe recalled a missive that implied her impending engagement with the Duke of Grafton. Patently absurd, but nonetheless disturbing, for Rafe would not have made up such a thing. In point of fact, he had fully confessed his betrayal of affection and made no excuse for his lack of morals.

She took a seat and opened the top drawer of his desk in search of notepaper. It was true that she and Claire had been writing to Nigel, knowing full well what a gossip he was—every word was bound to reach Rafe. But the letter was meant as a tease, something she and Rafe would laugh over once they returned from the Continent.

Setting aside two letters from Vertiline, she removed a sheet of stationery from the drawer. Dipping pen into inkpot, Fanny scratched out a brief message. She bit her lip. If Claire were back in Edinburgh, a cable would reach her faster. Perhaps she could ask Mrs. Coates to send a wire. Fanny finished her message and reached for a blotter. Finding none, she opened the deep desk drawer.

She spotted the blotter behind several tall stacks of letters. As she lifted one of the bundles she recognized the hand as Rafe's. The top envelope was addressed to Francine Greyville-Nugent. Fanny's heart fluttered in her chest. Gingerly, she fingered the soft twine that held the missives together and pulled the cord.

Sifting through the pile, her fingers trembled. Every one was addressed to her. Fanny swallowed, remembering their argument at the farm. *It's been nearly five years—you might have written.* She shivered as though he stood beside her this very moment. *I wrote—many times. I just never posted a single letter.* She opened the top envelope on the stack.

> June 10, 1885
> My dearest Fanny,
>   How I miss you. I hope this letter finds you well. The gunshot wound to my chest continues to heal without infection. Doctor says I shall soon be fit enough to return to duty. As much as I have enjoyed the company of my toddling son and housekeeper these few weeks, I am also anxious to return to work and the distractions of London.

There were several charming paragraphs about Harry. Apparently Rafe had been keeping a one-sided correspondence with her. Fanny skimmed down.

> There is a void in my heart and an empty place in my soul where you will always reside—I shall never find another in all the world like you, nor do I deserve to—

The words blurred, and she had to squint to read his last lines.

> Last night I held you in my arms. Heaven.
> Then I awoke from the dream.
> All my love,
> Rafe

She allowed herself a brief, quiet weep. It was as much a cry of joy as it was of sorrow. When this nightmare was over, she and Rafe would have a good long talk, make amends, and refer to these days together as their adventure. Fanny wiped away a lagging tear and sighed. They might take up the life they had set aside five years ago, the one that, God willing, still awaited them.

She retied the bundle of letters and put them back into the drawer. If, one day, Rafe wished to show them to her, she would sit down and read each one carefully. Fanny inhaled a deep breath and exhaled a gentle sigh. For now, it was enough to know he had cared enough to write. *Hundreds*, he had said.

She folded her note and returned to the kitchen. "When you get the chance, Mrs. Coates, would you send this off for me—at the wire office?" Fanny smiled and patted the skirt of her dress. "I'm afraid I haven't a farthing on me."

The housekeeper pocketed the note. "Don't worry, miss. I'll take it out of the household kitty."

"Thank you." Fanny took in a deep breath. "I thought I might join Harry for a bit of worm pulling."

"Just down the road on yer left."

The sky above Nettlebed was clear, and the sun was warm as Fanny walked down the narrow gravel road and into a field of clover. The pond, more of a large puddle, was nestled into a slope by a giant spreading oak.

A chestnut head of hair bobbed up and down behind the tall grass at the pond's edge. "How many so far, Harry?" she called out to him.

The lad sprang up out of the tall grass. "Come and look." The boy held up a tin. Fanny peered inside the can. "Ooh, I see a few lovely fat ones," she said.

He picked up a spade and moved to a muddy spot along a stand of cattails. "There's always more down here."

The long low limbs of the oak spread out overhead. "Quite a good climbing tree, wouldn't you say, Harry?"

He looked up. "I'm allowed up to there." He pointed to a thick low branch that hung out over the pond. "Father says if I fall, I can't hurt myself too badly."

The boy smiled and it took her breath away. A miniature version of Rafe. "As a matter of fact, your father once had to talk me down from an old oak tree. I climbed so high, I became frightened." The boy stared at her in the curious way a child does. Fanny smiled. "Would you like me to dig, and you can pull?"

In short order they amassed a tin full of worms, enough for a nice long afternoon of fishing. Goodness, an entire afternoon of leisure. She realized that Rafe must have made up his mind to wait for the professor's submarine.

They started back along a narrow trail through the meadow. Harry ran ahead, chasing after something. Fanny craned her neck to see. He marched out of the grass triumphantly holding a bright green frog for her to examine.

"Marvelous creature." She stroked the pale green stripe down its back. "Put him back now. He has a wife and tadpoles at home on the lily pad."

Walking along the gentle winding lane, she found the neighborhood delightfully charming. "Are we in the Cotswolds?"

Harry looked up at her. "This is Catslip Lane."

The squeak of carriage springs and the clink of harness rattled down the road. Fanny glanced behind them. A carriage wound its way through the quiet neighborhood. She smiled. "I'll ask your father."

"He's gone to Henley."

The tiny small hairs on her neck stood on end. Fanny turned back to take another look. The carriage swayed around a curve and increased speed. Alarmed, she turned to the boy. "Shall we have a footrace? First one to the garden gate wins." Fanny picked up her skirt and ran after the boy, who sprinted down the lane ahead of her, oblivious to any danger.

Creaky wheels and pounding hooves signaled that the carriage was right behind them. She swept Harry up in her arms and tossed them both into a hedgerow by the side of the road.

The carriage swept past them at a furious pace. For a split second, Fanny breathed a sigh of relief. But the carriage slowed and, worse yet, stopped quite close to the house.

Harry's tin of worms rolled into the drainage gutter. "We must find your father." She pulled him close. "Can you run all the way to Henley?"

Wide-eyed, the boy nodded his head.

Fanny grabbed Harry by the hand and they ran down the road in the opposite direction.

"Halt right there. I'd rather not shoot you or the boy."

Fanny slowed to a walk, then a stop. She and Harry pivoted toward the threat. Not one natty bloke but two. Both of them stood at the rear of the carriage, weapons raised.

She squeezed Harry's hand. "Get ready to run again."

There was a sharp bend in the lane just yards away. If they could reach that turn, the men wouldn't have much of a shot. How she and the lad would ever outrun these men she had no idea, but she meant try.

She backed away as the gunmen stepped forward. "Run, Harry!"

Chapter Twenty-seven

"By any chance . . ." Rafe shouted over the motorized pump. "Have you seen Professor Minnow?"

Mr. Spottesworth throttled down the motor on the bilge pump. "Left him outside the Bird In Hand last evening."

"The professor is nowhere to be found in the village."

"I walked him down the lane, pointed him your way." The man wiped his hand on an oil-soiled rag. "I expect he'll turn up, sir. A man can't go missing for long in these parts."

The underwater craft bobbed peaceably in the river. Rafe tried not to look too wary. "I shall have another look along the road." He turned, then pivoted back. "Might you be able to tow the submersible to London?"

Spottesworth removed his cap for a scratch. "Well, now, I suppose that could be arranged, sir."

"Arrange it." He borrowed a pen and slip of paper. "Deliver the submarine to Harbor Patrol and tell them to alert Special Branch, Scotland Yard." He handed over the message along with near half a quid.

Rafe hurried his pace, ruminating over his missing charge with an increasing sense of dread. He searched a ragged length of hedgerow along the lane just in case the professor had fallen into the shrub and passed out. Peering through a tangle of greenery, he thought of last night—just before dawn. The lovemaking had been nothing short of astonishing. Fanny had always been sexually appealing—even sensual in a natural, unaffected way. But how wonderfully receptive and adventurous she was as a lover.

At a curve in the lane, he heard the distinctive lurch of a carriage and an ear-piercing scream he'd recognize anywhere. Rafe froze at the sound.

"Let go! Get off me."

His heart leaped into a hard, fast pounding in his chest as he rounded the corner. The carriage driver snapped his whip over the heads of the team hurtling down on him. Rafe jumped to one side of the road and caught a glimpse inside the vehicle. Fanny struggled with someone, he was sure of it.

"Rafe!" Her cry was muffled in a cloud of dust.

He dove for a loose baggage strap at the rear of the carriage and pulled himself onto a luggage platform. Poking his head around the side of the coach, he looked for a foothold somewhere. Rafe heard a click, and looked up into a blast from a pistol.

The bullet missed.

The surly fellow angled himself farther outside the carriage and Rafe grabbed for the revolver. He wrenched the gun from the man's hand, but it flew out of his grasp and into the dirt by the side of the lane.

Rafe made a split-second decision and let go. A painful landing on his shoulder signaled something else was wrong. He sat up and checked his arm. His sleeve was red. Bollocks, the man had winged him.

He rolled onto his feet and ran back to recover the gun. He passed a rusty old tin in the road. A scattering of worms squiggled and squirmed in the dirt. Rafe slowed and stared.

Dear God. They'd got Harry as well.

A charge of energy shot through his body. He dashed across the meadow and around the pond. Catslip Lane curved in a near half circle before straightening out toward Henley. He scrambled up the old oak, ducked a few low-hanging branches, and stepped out onto a limb that overhung the road. Rafe waited for the carriage to pass under and vaulted onto the roof,

The driver turned and Rafe fired. Nothing but a click. Christ! Jammed or empty. He pocketed the gun and threw himself at the driver, only to be tackled by another bloke from behind.

The carriage turned onto the faster, straighter road and picked up speed. The driver tossed his friend a weapon. Rafe lunged for the pistol as did his attacker, and they rolled to one side of the carriage. Gripping the barrel end of the revolver, the man pressed down the trigger. Rafe two-handed the barrel and shoved it aside.

A blast of gunpowder covered his cheek and eye. The hearing in his ear cut out.

Rafe swung and connected. The man struck back, but Rafe dodged the blow. Bare knuckles connected with the roof of the carriage. The man yelped and Rafe pushed him off and scrambled away. Where was the gun? The dark-eyed natty bloke with the weird grimace rolled over and pointed the weapon. Rafe struck out with his leg and kicked the man off the vehicle.

As the desperate man fell, he reached out and caught Rafe's ankle, pulling him off the roof. Twisting in midair, Rafe grabbed hold of a ridge at the roofline and dangled alongside the vehicle. He stared through the coach window into the eyes of his terrified son.

This time when Rafe landed, there was a nasty crunch and a thud. He managed to lift his head. The carriage rolled away in a cloud of gravel dust and . . . stars. Drifting at the edge of consciousness, his head fell back.

Rafe willed himself out of darkness. They had Fanny and Harry.

The stars faded and his sight returned. An odd-sounding exhale blew across the nape of his neck. Rafe shot up off the body of his attacker and scrambled to his feet. Swaying, he looked down at a contorted grimace, frozen in death. The twisted body lay on the ground, eyes straight ahead, the skull turned at a disturbing, unnatural angle. The fall had broken the man's neck.

Good riddance.

Rafe struggled for breath. He wheezed every inhale

and there was no exhale whatsoever. He waited until he could draw breath more naturally.

With nothing to be done for the dead bloke, Rafe turned toward the road. Something caught his eye—a sparkle in a rough brown patch of earth beside the body. He blinked and the shiny object blinked back. He picked up the jewelry piece and turned it over in his palm. A circular tiepin. Two golden circles—a wheel within a wheel. A large round sapphire had been set into the precious metal where the two circles came together. A badge signifying rank, or some sort of medal?

Rafe pocketed the pin and checked the revolver. There had been no malfunction—the chambers were empty. Rafe jogged down the road in hopes of finding the gun he had kicked out of the dead assailant's hand.

Now that Mallory's men held captives, he was quite sure they'd keep to the carriage rather than risk the train stations. What he needed was a fast mount to catch them. Rafe gave up his search for the second gun, picked up his pace, and ran straight for the village.

Turning onto High Street, he spied a rider and nice-looking mount readying to leave town. Rafe pulled out the revolver and grabbed hold of the reins.

Startled, the disgruntled rider took a slash at him with his riding crop, and the horse reared.

Rafe yanked the whip away. "Pardon the inconvenience, but I need your horse." He caught the man by his jacket lapels and yanked him off his saddle.

The wild-eyed equine snorted and pranced, but Rafe managed to lift himself onto the steed's strong back.

He toed into the stirrups—about right, not too short. He spun the horse around. "Wire Detective Kennedy, Scotland Yard, tell him Miss Greyville-Nugent has been abducted along with a child."

Rafe dug his heels into the horse's flanks and the animal moved out nicely. Excellent. In no time at all, they would make up lost ground.

FANNY NARROWED HER gaze on the man across the aisle. "Let me have the boy."

The bug-eyed brute holding Harry leered at her. She hardly knew who was worse, this ogler who made her skin crawl or the bearded and grim-faced man beside her, whose long fingers wrapped around her neck and tightened.

Stuffed in the opposite corner of the carriage, a bound and gagged Professor Minnow appeared miserable enough. His eyes were red and swollen, and not all of the damage had come from drink.

Their two captors were different from regular infantry. Both men appeared to be higher-ranked persons of authority. She didn't quite know how or why she surmised this, but it seemed to Fanny there had been more ordering about than carrying out of commands. She wondered, frankly, if there were mostly chiefs left and only a few remaining Indians. It rather pleased her to think that she and Rafe had actually managed to deplete their resources. It might even be comical if these blokes weren't so horrid.

Determined to make their lives as difficult as possible, she did the one thing she knew worked every time. "I'm going to vomit."

She began to choke and her captor's fingers loosened around her neck until—"Stop the carriage and let me out." Fanny coughed. "I'm afraid I'm prone to the traveling sickness." She produced a gagging sound and a convincing spasm of dry heaves.

The grim bearded man checked the roads before stopping the carriage. Shoving her out the door, he followed after, pistol drawn. "Toss it up now, or get back in the carriage."

Fanny traipsed out into the field and uttered the most god-awful retching noises she could muster. If Rafe were conscious he'd stop at nothing to come after them. Dear God, let it be so.

Her captor approached from behind. "Back inside now." She whirled around and wiped her mouth with the back of her hand. Suddenly, she actually did feel a bit queasy. She lurched forward, spewing her breakfast of tea and toast on the ground—some of it on the natty bloke's boots.

Excellent, another delay while he cursed and wiped off his toes. Fanny gripped her knees—and scanned the road that ran alongside the grain fields. Nothing more than a few slow-moving carts and a single rider on horseback.

Long, thin fingers gripped her arm and turned her back. "Inside, miss." Stepping into the carriage, she stole another glance at the lone rider. The man on horseback wasn't flying after them, but she could swear it was

Rafe. Something in the way the rider sat his horse, like a prince among men.

She took her seat quietly even as her pulse raced. So what was keeping him? Fanny tasted bile and wet her lips. She took heart in the fact that he was with them in spirit—biding his time, perhaps. Outnumbered and out-gunned, he waited for the right opportunity for a rescue. She looked at brave little Harry and winked.

Wretched men. No matter what happened, she and Rafe would see every last one of them swing from the gallows at Newgate. Fanny turned to the bearded men-ace beside her. "If you do not let me care for this child, I will scream and struggle and bite without end." She stuck out her chin. "Let the boy sit with me and I prom-ise to be quiet and cooperative all the way to London." She even forced a pleasant look. "Your choice."

The grim bloke studied her. The frown appeared to be permanent. "What makes you think we're on our way to London?"

Fanny shrugged. "Aren't we?"

He nodded to the man across the aisle. Fanny reached out for Harry, who jumped into her arms. She sat him on her lap and smoothed back his hair. "Much better, yes?"

The child snuggled against her but continued to stare wide-eyed. "Don't let the awful man frighten you." Fanny glared at the ogler. "He is going to hang by his neck until his tongue protrudes, his eyes pop, and he def-ecates on himself."

The man's gaze finally shifted off her.

She could have sworn Professor Minnow winked.

*   *   *

RAFE HUNG BACK far enough to keep an eye on the carriage. It had taken every ounce of willpower to keep from riding up on Fanny and one of Mallory's henchmen. She appeared to be taking some sort of necessity break, bless her. Just like her to try to slow the blokes down, make it as difficult as possible for them. A ragged smile tugged at one side of his mouth. Headstrong, defiant, unruly—all traits Fanny had in abundance.

These last days with her had been some of the most harrowing, frustrating, and punishing days in his life. They had also been a wonder. Such wicked punishment doth God mete out when he knows he's got you good. He could never live without her now. And tucking Harry away like he had, hiding from his family's scorn. The rationale for his retreat from life had worked up until a few days ago. Now it seemed absurd—perhaps even cruel and cowardly.

Rafe straightened his shoulders. When this was all over and he had Fanny and Harry safely tucked in his arms, he would never let them go. He pictured both of them together in the carriage. More than likely the professor was with them. He took some comfort in knowing the three captives at least had each other. But he did not dare to dwell long on the subject. His heart jumped inside his chest. Those men held on to Harry for only one possible reason.

To keep Detective Lewis at bay.

They were nearly upon Windsor, little more than an hour to London now. He would wait to make his move until they reached town and a bloody snarl of traffic. He toyed with the idea of following them as far as their lair—directly into the hands of Bellecorte Mallory himself.

∞ Chapter Twenty-eight

Rafe closed the distance as the carriage veered off Bishopsgate and merged into the traffic on Ratcliffe Highway. Their entry into London was perfect; the avenue teemed with traffic. As they traveled deeper into the East End, Rafe's view was obscured by a tall paneled wagon. Without much difficulty, he maneuvered around the hulking vehicle, and caught sight of the carriage as it turned onto Commercial Road. They would soon be dead center in the middle of the Docklands.

Rounding the corner, he lost them momentarily. The carriage must have sped ahead and made a turn. Rafe pressed his borrowed mount for a bit more. The horse, a hearty chap, was tired but willing. Generally, the thicker the traffic, the more erratic—which definitely seemed to be the case this afternoon. Several carts jostled onto the road in front of him. Undaunted, Rafe wove a circuitous route through the snarl of drays and hansoms. He could just make out the battered road sign ahead, and turned onto the row of warehouses.

No carriage to be seen. He didn't worry greatly, not at first. Cautiously, he guided his mount up and down the dead-end row. He squinted down back alleys and questioned warehouse workers. This was impossible.

"They've disappeared," he muttered to himself. Even though his pulse raced, he kept his head.

The carriage had been out of his sight for fifteen, perhaps twenty seconds. Rafe recalculated those seconds over and over. How much time would it take for a carriage drawn by two horses to vanish? The doors of these great warehouses were tall and wide enough. Christ, one could easily drive a vehicle inside and lock up quickly. How much time? He sighed. Apparently, just enough.

An imposing tobacco warehouse took up one side of the street—a good five hundred feet long divided by strong partitions, each with double iron doors. A smaller storehouse, however, seemed the likelier candidate. Rafe checked every door. Locked and likely bolted from inside. The whole of the district was under the care and control of the officers of the customs. Rafe looked around. Nary a customs man be to found this afternoon.

Rafe considered his options. He was three miles from Whitehall and could use reinforcements. If he stayed, he might try shimmying up a drainpipe. He could climb into the storehouse through a skylight, or crack open a back door. But that sort of illegal entry was best left until dark.

Flynn and Zeno Kennedy had been working the case from London. Zeno had not shared much in his coded wires, but it was likely they had information and resources that could help him get to Fanny and Harry faster than lurking around Henry Street on his own. And there was the Yard dog. Rafe could not shake the idea that Alfred's olfactory talent might be useful here. Most of these great warehouses had extensive underground vaults storing thousands of pipes of wine and spirit. Who knew what the talented bloodhound might sniff out?

"WHERE ARE YOU taking us?" Fanny lifted Harry and stepped around the fetid waters of—whatever it was they traveled through. Neither bloke answered. Some time ago, they had passed through acres of wine cellar. But the acrid stink of old port and sherry had been replaced by something far worse. A sewer, or at least it smelled like one. And it looked like what she would imagine a sewer to look like: crude and cavelike.

Fanny hitched the boy up on her hip and he pinched his nose to block out the stench. She dipped her head. "Could you hold my nose as well?"

Harry reached out and placed a thumb and finger to each side of her nose. "Ah, what a relief—so much better," she said. He snickered softly at the nasal sound of her voice.

Minutes passed like hours as the group trudged through pools of fungus and nameless sludge. They halted at last before an iron door. The grim bloke rapped on the metal plate with the butt of his gun. The small hairs on Fanny's arms and neck rose as they entered yet another dark, unwholesome cavity. A single sputtering lantern hung from a chain in the center of the room and shadows loomed in every corner.

The heavy door slammed shut behind them with a clunk.

Fanny hugged Harry close and waited for her eyes to adjust. She made out a group of men: their two abductors and two more—one very short, the other somewhat portly—all of them standing near a wall of sturdy tea chests. Her nose twitched at the strange scent of moldy tea leaves—oolong, she thought.

The very short man leaned forward for a better look. In the gloom, his only discernible features were a horrid sprig of red hair and ruddy cheeks. Fanny squinted before leaping back in shock. "Mrs. Tuttle!" she exclaimed. The man let loose a sinister chuckle.

"How is this possible?" Her speech rasped from a scratchy throat, no doubt caused by the wretched foul air.

"Come closer, Miss Greyville-Nugent."

Her heart jumped erratically as she inched forward again. She pictured the odd, disagreeable creature in a frowzy gray apron and dress from the farmhouse. She stared at the small man—a dwarf, she supposed. He leaned across a stack of tea chests and smiled. Nothing very amusing about that sardonic grin. "Spent many years performing in the most degrading sort of theatricals. I find it simple enough to change my gender in the course of an operation—for the cause."

"How wonderful to be so . . . talented." Fanny hesitated. "Might you explain something about this *cause* of yours, Mister—?"

Less amused, the dwarf shook his head. "The cause is our business and none of yours, miss."

Her gaze narrowed. "Since my own father was a victim of your cruel purge, I believe I have every right to ask the question."

The portly bloke standing nearby cleared his throat. "Perhaps you could answer a few questions first." He moved in beside the dwarf, who opened a red leather pocket journal complete with insignia and took out a fountain pen.

The corpulent man's coat was ill fitting and his waistcoat buttons were ready to pop. Rather disheveled for one of the dapper minions. "The location of your warehouses here in London, for a start," he said. The man's fleshy lower lip protruded—a meaty sort of ledge where drool collected in corners like viscous cobwebs. He was abhorrent, all right, but far from forbidding.

Fanny studied them both before speaking. "I suppose you would have to believe your *cause* was righteous, to go about your killings in such a crude, sensational manner." She fought off shudders and backed away. She wasn't entirely foolhardy. She knew enough to be wary of them. "Perhaps you might be more specific about what you are looking for? Greyville-Nugent Enterprises has several manufacturing facilities about the greater London area."

Fanny raised her chin and stared back at the not-so-very natty blokes. Whatever these two wanted, they wouldn't be getting much from her, not if she could help it.

A wooden stool whined and creaked as the largish

gent settled himself on the smallish seat. "Your company's entry in the London Industrial Exposition, miss. Just tell us where it is and we will leave you and the boy"—his beady eyes shifted to Harry—"unmolested."

Her pulse raced but she answered mildly. "Be delighted to, gentlemen." Fanny hiked the child up her hip and hugged him tighter. "I shall tell Mr. Mallory whatever he wishes to know—in trade." She paused to take in the gobbler's belly and the ink-stained sausage fingers of the dwarf's pen hand.

"Do you act as secretary for the cause? If so, please note my willingness to negotiate." She tried for a demure smile. "Surely one of you is brave enough to deliver my offer to your master?"

"Negotiate?" A weary sigh, like a rush of wind, escaped the shadows of the cavern. "I'm afraid I do not listen to offers, miss." The voice was deep, even gravelly, and yet as low as a whisper.

All eyes shifted to a break in the rock wall. Someone moved—or rather descended down a crude set of steps. Fanny strained to see this new apparition. A man of normal size and build, perhaps taller than average. She wondered how long he had been standing there on the stairs spying on her.

The dark figure prowled closer. Flickering lamplight caught the prominent angles of cheekbone and jawline. The light above sputtered to brighter life and haloed the top of his head. Fanny blinked from the startling sight—he was completely bald, and there was a ghastly zigzag scar that ran down the side of his skull.

Her knees knocked as she edged backward.

Dark eyes smoldered like glowing coals. He gazed at her with suspicion and no small amount of curiosity. "Tell me, Miss Greyville-Nugent, what terms did your father make with the steelworkers in Motherwell?"

Unlike her previous inquisitors, this was a man to be reckoned with. In the weak lamplight he appeared almost handsome in a macabre sort of way. And he moved like a panther after prey—fierce and muscular. The word *devil* popped to mind, an accurate description of those savage eyes that never left her.

Fanny met his fire and ice gaze. "Who am I addressing, sir?"

"Oh, I think you know very well, miss." The firm-set mouth twitched slightly. "I am Mallory."

∞ Chapter Twenty-nine

Rafe stumbled inside the office, ushered to a chair by Melville himself, director of Special Branch. The head-man nodded to Mr. Quincy, his secretary. "Would you collect Mr. Kennedy? I believe he's in the lab with Mr. Bruce."

Rafe coughed up a bit of road dust as Melville settled into his old leather chair with its familiar squeak. "We've been expecting you for days, Mr. Lewis."

"Sorry to take so long." Rafe cleared his throat before continuing. "Ran into a bit of trouble on the road."

Melville leaned back and pulled absently on a bushy sideburn. "Is that your blood or someone else's on your jacket sleeve?"

Rafe glanced down. "I was grazed by a bullet earlier this morning."

Melville grunted. "And where is Miss Greyville-Nugent?"

"Abducted, along with my son."

"Christ Almighty." Rafe hunkered down, ready for an

onslaught of invectives. "The last I heard," Melville went on, "you and the heiress were on your way to London by some sort of underwater craft. When did this all happen?" Melville puffed himself up. "And what about the other chap, the inventor of the submersible?"

"Missing, presumed kidnapped." Rafe rubbed the stubble on his jaw. "You didn't receive a wire from Henley?"

"Some sort of backlog in the telegraph room." Melville slumped in his chair and stared. "In your absence, we've rounded up the lot of them: magnates of industry, inventors—an uncommon bunch—rather extraordinary, really. Got them sequestered in a safe location. I'll be glad when this damned industrial exposition is over." Melville halted suddenly and blinked. "You have a son?"

"Who has a son?" Zeno Kennedy stood in the doorway with Melville's secretary.

"I do." Rafe shot up out of his chair. "I tailed the kidnappers to London. Lost them off Commercial Road." Rafe tried to slow down—he knew he appeared wild-eyed and raving. "They disappeared into a block of warehouses on Henry Street. We must go after them. Is Flynn available, by any chance?"

"I believe so." Zeno eyed Rafe. "Have you eaten anything all day?"

He shook his head.

Zeno pivoted toward Mr. Quincy, who had already anticipated his every request. "I'll have Flynn Rhys called in." The secretary exited with a bow. "And order a plate and pint from The Rising Sun for Mr. Lewis."

"Very good, Mr. Quincy." Melville's signature scowl

eased. "Mr. Lewis, you'll eat a bite of roast beef and get that arm looked at before you leave this office." The cracked leather of the director's chair whined as he settled in. "Sit back down. I'll have the whole bloody story—and make it a good one."

Zeno turned to Rafe with brows raised. "Might be wise to debrief, perhaps do a bit of strategizing—formulate a plan?"

"A plan." Rafe almost smiled. "I daresay Fanny would approve."

Zeno pulled up a chair, opened a file, and shook down his pen. "Take us through the last few days, Rafe. We need to know what you know."

Between bites of roast beef and gulps of ale, Rafe went over the high and low points of the past few days, beginning with his investigation and the chase through the streets of Edinburgh. He recounted his and Fanny's trek from Broxburn to Bathgate, leaving out the bath in the loch. A picture of Fanny tramping through the heather came to mind. Then he detailed their capture and subsequent escape from the mine-shaft outside Coatbridge. How could he ever forget the look on her face as she pedaled the old Rover down the lane—and their crash of bicycles?

Images of Fanny barraged his mind until someone cleared his throat. Rafe snapped back to reality. He realized both Zeno and Melville were waiting. "Sorry," he said, continuing on with the tale of their chance meeting with Professor Minnow and their brief respite at the safe house in Dundas.

Zeno looked up from his scribbling. "The last wires I received were from Glasgow, one from you and one from Agent Curzon."

"Good man. Saved my life in the Glasgow train station." Rafe ended his story in Nettlebed, with the tale of the sunken submarine and his chase after the kidnappers.

Zeno closed one file and opened another. "How old is your boy?"

"Not quite five."

"His name?"

Rafe eyed the file with his name on it. "Harrison Gabriel Lewis."

Zeno looked up from the folder. "Is there a . . . Mrs. Lewis we should know about?"

"Deceased."

A rap at the door brought a lab technician in to look at his wound. Zeno closed his file. Reluctantly, Rafe shrugged out of his shirt. He turned to confront stunned looks on the men's faces. "What?"

"Christ, Rafe." Zeno shook his head. "Is there a place on your body that isn't wounded or bruised?"

He looked down at his torso. "Those last two tumbles off the carriage did a bit more damage than I thought."

Zeno blinked. "You rode all the way to London in this state?"

"I can tape the ribs for now, but—" The technician got out several rolls of muslin cloth from a medical kit. "You should see a doctor."

Melville grimaced. "Sorry we didn't get more help out to you."

"I understand we're short on manpower." Rafe winced as the lab man pulled the bandage tight.

Flynn poked his head in the door. "Blimey—you get hit by a train?"

RAFE PRESSED UP against the warehouse. Under cover of fog, he and Flynn were back in the warehouse district along with Alfred, the Yard's trusty bloodhound. Getting to Henry Street had been tediously slow. During a black fog, emergency workers with large torches slowed every vehicle at main intersections throughout the city.

Flynn emerged from the brownish-yellow haze wielding a pair of bolt cutters. "A real pea souper this evening. Spot of luck, wot?" Rafe stepped back. Flynn snapped off the padlock. "You're sure this is the storehouse?"

"More like a guess, really." Rafe led the Yard dog through the door of the warehouse. "Alfred will let us know quick enough." The floor was sticky, as if it had been newly tarred. Alfred sniffed and licked.

Flynn lowered onto his haunches and rubbed the sticky substance between fingers. "Sugar residue—leaks through the wine casks."

Rafe toggled the switch on his torch. Nothing—as usual. He slapped the metal cylinder in the palm of his hand and a swath of light lit up the floor in front of them. Rafe peered into the vast surroundings of the warehouse. "We could use more light," he said.

"Sorry. Broke mine over a dynamiter's head a month ago." Rafe had to imagine the grin on Flynn's face. A swath of low-lying dark mist crept under the cracks of the warehouse doors. The dense fog invaded everywhere. "I put a requisition in for another."

"That will take a year." Rafe passed a stack of tea chests a full story tall. The larger warehouses were partitioned off in sections. Rafe's nose twitched from the pungent smell of tobacco mixed with tea leaves and rum—an intriguing brew.

Alfred strained on his leash. "Here we go—what's up, old boy?" Rafe asked. The dog sniffed along the stone floor and arrived at a pile of horse droppings. Flynn stepped around the hound.

Rafe noted the wheel tracks and hoof prints. "So they brought the carriage into the midsection." He swung his torch over to a wide set of doors. "Likely exited there as well."

Gingerly, they both walked the approximate perimeter of the horse and carriage, looking for footprints, a trail of some kind—something, anything. Best they could make out were three sets of scuffs that led away from the carriage in different directions. One group of prints was their own. That left two others that went . . . nowhere. Rafe squinted at every mark on the ground while the Yard dog sat and watched.

Rafe turned his torchlight on the hound. "Anything, Alfred?" He swept the floor with a circle of light. Drool pooled in front of the dog. The beam passed over a small white dot.

"Hold on," Flynn said, squatting beside Alfred. He

picked up the small white object and turned it over in his palm.

Rafe swung the light back. "What is that?"

"Looks like a button."

Blood pounded through every part of his body. "Bring it closer." Flynn wiped off the dog spittle and handed it over. Rafe could hardly contain himself. "This button is from Fanny's dress." She'd worn the damn dress for days. He knew every little posy on the thin muslin frock. And he'd rather not think why buttons were missing from her dress. He clenched his teeth and focused on finding his son and Fanny, bringing them safely home and never, ever letting them out of his sight again.

"This has to have her scent all over it." Rafe held the button to Alfred's nose and the hound snuffled around the tiny button.

The animal stood up and Rafe urged the dog onward. "That's a good boy. Show us where Fanny and Harry are." Alfred led them in a circuitous route through bales of tobacco. At the rear of the warehouse the canine stopped to sniff around a stack of tea chests six feet high and nearly as wide.

The hound sat down with a groan.

Rafe scanned the area with his torch. Sure enough, another round white button. This one had a small yellow flower on it. He swallowed.

"Give us a bit of light—this way." Flynn motioned him over. Rafe turned the beam toward his partner. Fresh scratches on the floor suggested these crates of tea had been moved recently. "I'll hold the torch." Rafe pointed to his sore ribs with a grin. "Lucky for you, tea chests are light."

Flynn rearranged tea chests until he uncovered a metal door made of iron bars and steps leading downward. "One would suppose the stairs lead to the wine cellars belowground. Odd that the only access would be blocked."

Rafe grunted. "Then again, maybe not." He gritted his teeth and helped shove a few more chests aside, enough to lift the grate.

They descended into pitch-blackness. Pervasive wine fumes and the moldy smell of dry rot pervaded the deathly still air. Rafe ran his torch beam floor to ceiling over the narrow, cavernlike tunnel.

"Blimey." Flynn whistled. "Let's hope those batteries hold out."

At a fork in the passageway, they searched the ground. The Yard dog growled and ran off after something. The lead slipped through Rafe's grip and trailed after the animal. "Hold on, Alfred." Rafe and Flynn followed as fast as they could with only a bobbing torch to light the way. The hound trotted back with a dead rodent in its mouth and dropped it at Rafe's feet.

Rafe exhaled. "Perhaps we should rent you out to the rat-catchers? Might pay for your horsemeat, save the taxpayers."

Alfred whined and cocked his head.

"Never thought he was fast enough to be a ratter," Rafe mused aloud. Something was odd about this.

Flynn shook his head. "Perks up when he's on the scent, though. Led us straight to the body in Canterbury at a blistering clip. Not that it was difficult. The torso was just as you called it. Lying neat as you please between the rails."

Alfred used his large proboscis to nudge the dead rodent several times. Rafe sucked in a breath. "Rats pretty much eat anything—don't they?"

"Dog's bollocks." Flynn stuck a thumb under his cap and scratched. "You think he could smell a button in a rat's belly?"

Rafe unfolded his pocketknife. "There's only one way to find out."

HARRY INCHED OFF Fanny's lap to explore the dingy cell they were locked in. Rumblings from the next room sounded like the professor had argued with his inquisitors. The minions wanted something from the inventor, perhaps the whereabouts of the submersible. And their curiosity bordered on maniacal with regards to her father's entry in the exposition. She thought it likely that she and the professor were inadvertently thwarting some scheme of Mallory's. No doubt the man wanted to make a big splash—some sort of grand and gruesome execution. Not that she could fathom what he had in mind, but she was intrigued by the idea that they might be able to interfere with his plans.

A jangle of keys and the whine of rusty hinges caused her to jump. "Come, Harry." The boy returned to her side as a string of unfamiliar men paraded into the room. One held a dress—something in deep shades of sapphire. And there was a steaming bowl of water with soaps and towels.

The last man, who carried himself like a butler, set down a bench and looking glass. He arranged the soaps and bowl, a comb and brush. After laying out towels, the man turned to her. He wore an eye patch. She nearly rolled her eyes. What a motley crew of well-dressed pirates these blokes were.

"I am Aubrey." His bow was more of a brief nod. "Your presence is required at dinner. Mallory has provided you with these small comforts, as well as a change of gown." The man's one good eye traveled up and down her tattered frock. "Please refresh yourself. I will return within the hour to escort you to his suite."

The door clunked shut and Fanny sprang into action. She stripped off the dingy white frock and removed every last remaining button. Harry stashed them all in various little boy pockets.

She washed up first and then gave Harry a good scrub and toweled him off. "When you see your father, I want you to remember to tell him something for me. Could you do that?" she asked.

Harry nodded, his eyes brightened. "Is Father coming for us?"

"I believe he is trying very hard to find us this very minute—but we must help him." Fanny hesitated, not knowing exactly how much to reveal to the child. "Just in case your father can't find us right away, I am going to make a bargain this evening. If I am successful, you will be able to help your father—so he can locate the professor and me."

She held him by his wee little shoulders. "Listen very carefully, Harry. What do you hear?" A muffled assortment of sounds filtered down through the low, arched ceiling.

Harry's eyes rolled upward. "Noisy."

Fanny smiled. "Harbor hubbub. Tell your father I can hear the sailors singing boisterous songs from a Yankee ship. And there is a cooperage nearby—lots of hammering and empty casks rolling along cobblestones. Will you remember, Harry?"

The boy pushed his arms into shirtsleeves and repeated back nearly every word to her. Fanny buttoned his shirt up the back, turned him around, and ran a comb through his bangs. "Very handsome—like your father."

Rafe would find them. He must.

Until then, they would, all three, soldier on. Fanny left hook and eyes closed and lifted the new gown overhead. "Pull down hard, Harry."

The child took hold of the skirt and tugged from the back, while she gripped the front and sucked in a breath. She refused to ask those horrid men to fasten the dress. Ugh! One last wriggle and she squeezed herself into the bodice of the gown.

She picked up the vanity mirror for a look. Watered silk—lovely—with a rather daring décolletage.

No femme fatale by nature, she would nonetheless play Bellecorte Mallory with every bit of wit and sangfroid she could muster. A violently nauseous stomach nearly overcame her. She must seduce the very man who had ordered the execution of her father. She could not dwell on the thought for long; it was too disturbing. Fanny pinched her cheeks and moistened her lips. She was in the game of her life and would play it fearlessly.

∞ Chapter Thirty

The man named Aubrey escorted Fanny through a cata-
comb of tunnels and connecting rooms. She lifted her
skirt to climb a rise of stair and arrived at an iron door
rounded at the top and bottom like a ship's hatch. The
butler ushered her through the opening. "Watch your
step, miss." She entered the boudoir of a sultan.

The cavernous room appeared to be a reflection of
the man in charge. Simple elegance with a rugged, dis-
tinctively male sensibility. More like a pirate's den than
the private quarters of a—what might this strange man
be called? An anti-progressive, surely, but his comport-
ment was that of a leader, the self-styled autocrat of his
very own anarchist movement. At least it would seem so,
what with Mallory's private army of minions.

The ceiling was low, vaulted. A sumptuous bed, sized
for Henry VIII, dominated the room. Fanny quickly surveyed the rest of the quarters. A small library was in one
corner; a sitting room and dining area occupied the rest
of the space. Covering the stone floor, plush, red Persian

carpets had a warming effect. Her gaze traveled back to the heavily draped four-poster. She disciplined her mind to stay in the moment—not to roam into abhorrent, fearful territory.

"There is wine and stronger spirit on the breakfront by the table." The one-eyed butler bowed. "Mallory will join you shortly." The door clanked shut behind the manservant.

Fanny waited a moment and checked the door. Locked.

It was a short walk across the room to the whiskey. She opened amber-filled decanters until she found something smoky and poured herself a tumbler. She tossed back half a glass of—what had Rafe called it? Liquid courage.

"You favor good whiskey, Miss Greyville-Nugent. Might I ask you to pour another?"

Fanny spun around. A man she did not recognize set down his hat and crop and strode into the room. He wore riding clothes. She examined long legs in breeches, covered to the knees with top boots. He looked every inch the polished English gentleman. He paused at the dining table, removed a dark-haired wig, and peeled off a rather dashing, close-cropped beard.

She turned back to the buffet to pour his drink and a splash more for herself. "I rather liked the shaved head with the beard."

"Yes, a gold ring in one ear and the picture would be complete. Shall I have Mr. Talbert bring in his glue pot and costume jewelry box?" He stepped closer and his eyes grew darker. Not the cold fire of their first meeting. This time his gaze swept over her figure with a kind of heat that made her weak-kneed with terror. And yet there was also a sense of empowerment in his need. He wanted her badly.

"Unnecessarily sociable of you, Mr. Mallory."

"Just—Mallory."

She forced her eyes to look straight into those searing black orbs and was scalded by his gaze. She offered him his drink. "Mallory, then."

He slipped a hand over hers and accepted the glass.

"Is Mr. Talbert the dwarf or the very corpulent gentleman?" She tilted her chin. "At least some of Mallory's minions appear to hail from a traveling theatrical of some sort. Or am I wrong?"

She could not be sure, but she thought he stifled a laugh. He gestured toward the parlor area with his glass. A grand chaise longue and several side chairs were arranged for conversation in the center of a large area rug.

"I thought I heard you speak once at a worker's rights gathering, but I must have been mistaken," she chattered on a bit nervously.

"I often use a decoy to deliver my speeches, whilst I mill about amongst the disgruntled. I handpick all my recruits." Mallory patted the cushion beside him on the settee. "One or two of the men have a good deal of theater experience and enjoy public speaking. I also find their knowledge of makeup and facial appliances useful in my endeavors."

"Do you fancy yourself a Robin Hood?" Fanny asked.

"Neither knight nor peasant, but most certainly above the law." He studied her as a talented roué might observe a future conquest. "Robin Hood is entirely too romantic for this day and age, wouldn't you agree? The citizenry of Britain long ago made their decision—replace a man's horse with steam, give his job to a child—" Mallory reached across the chaise and turned down the lamp wick. "Abandon the soft glow of gaslight for Mr. Swan's electrical light bulb."

As he leaned away, she studied the brutal zigzag scar that curved down the side of his head and disappeared behind an ear. She wanted to gulp her whiskey, but sipped instead. "I don't believe electricity will ever replace the beauty of a dancing flame." Over the rim of her glass, she connected briefly with a flicker of light in his black gaze. Fanny abandoned sipping for a good gulp. "Tell me, Mallory, do you mean to put an end to progress in general or do you terrorize selectively?"

The slightest uptick at the ends of his mouth suggested a kind of world-weary amusement. "As I mentioned, the citizens have voted. Keep the wheels of industry turning at any price. In 'the age of the machine, Britain has become the workshop of the world,' or so Thomas Carlyle says."

Mallory settled into the curve of the chaise while those piercing eyes evaluated, questioned. "It is one thing for children to labor on farms or help with the spinning. But to put a child in the narrow air shaft of a coal mine to open and close the ventilation doors, or crawl underneath running machinery—perhaps lose a finger or two . . ." He seemed to drift off momentarily.

"Young children are gone from the regulated workplace for some time now." Fanny squirmed a bit. "With each successive decade the industrialists have made progress."

"When forced to it."

"Granted, change hasn't always come willingly." She lowered her eyes before raising them again. "Why do you not choose to make your argument through legislation, Mallory? More equitable pay for women, for instance, and more funding for public schools."

"My brother was killed, crushed by one of your father's huge machines." Mallory resettled himself to look at her more directly. "He was nine years old."

Stunned, Fanny drew herself upright. "So, an eye for an eye, is it?"

He finished his glass and got up for more whiskey. "Ah, but there is more to this tale of woe." He returned to the couch with the decanter and Fanny lifted her glass. "One fine October morning, my entire family was killed in the Jewell Gunpowder Mill explosion. One hundred and nine men, women, and children dead—many more injured. Happened years before you were born."

"In 1863, actually, the year I was born." Her whispered words barely registered.

Mallory rubbed the side of his temple. "At the time of the explosion, I was in the infirmary getting my hand stitched. Saved, ironically, by an earlier mishap."

A heavy heart thumped inside her body. "You lost everyone?"

"God spared no sorrow for me. By the time I returned to the factory, the building was on fire. A few of the injured managed to crawl out alive."

Fanny bit her lip. "I suppose it's no wonder you took it upon yourself to rid the country of this popular new form of modernization." Her world spun slowly out of control. How could one ever recover from such a blow? She supposed one never did. "I do not mean to in any way take away from your very painful loss, nor the terrible misfortune that befell your family, but I must argue for at least some of the good that comes with industrialization. The machines have created a new working class, which Robert Peel referred to as—"

Mallory sighed. "'An additional race of men,' who are pressed into factory work and obliged to become respectable, hardworking laborers." He sipped from his glass. "And since you quote Peel, allow me the poet and critic Matthew Arnold: 'This strange disease of modern life with its sick hurry, its divided aims,'" he quoted.

There was a distance in his eyes—it was nearly always there, she thought, as if Mallory was not quite of this world. Aware of her study, he returned to her. "Another unsightly by-product of greed and mass production—is the whole of Britain's landscape soon to be despoiled?"

Fanny found herself evaluating Mallory, viewing him as she never thought she could—more as a damaged soul than an adversary. His opinions, those of a crusader, were not the ravings of a mentally disordered man. In fact, they were entirely rational. Even his madness seemed to have lessened, cloaked in a delicate shyness and hidden in some secret place, away from scrutiny. At first, she had been intimidated—overawed by the man. And now, disturbingly, in these moments alone with the leader of the Utopian Society, she found him as pitiable as he was dangerous.

Sitting close beside him, she found he exuded a quiet control, a coiled serpentine presence, nearly overpowering at times. Well-built through the chest and arms, with muscular legs covered in tight-fitting deerskin breeches and gleaming leather boots. The sheer physicality of him was . . . unsettling. Something akin to a faint tremble ran through her. "I don't suppose anyone likes the look of smokestacks, except titans of industry. But must you punish so brutally?" Nervous, she moistened her lips, and his gaze moved to her mouth.

Inexplicably, the very next thing Fanny found herself doing turned out to be as shocking to her as it was to the man beside her. Before she could gain any control over her hand, she reached out and stroked the smooth-shaven side of his head, tracing the ragged cream-colored scar.

"Whatever I do, I do to make a point—" He trailed off in surprise. Her guileless, candid gesture had stopped him midsentence. Somewhat awkwardly, Fanny became aware of her unfathomable behavior and withdrew her hand. The humiliation of such outrageous deportment caused a wave of heat to rise from her neck to cheeks.

She managed an uneasy laugh. "I don't know what came over me, please excuse me . . ."

"No, please." Covering her hand in his, he guided her

fingers across his stubbly jaw and large, well-formed mouth. Gently, he turned her hand palm up and brushed his lips down to the faint pulse on the inside of her wrist. "Forgive me, Francine." He swept a hand over her cheek. "Your name is Francine, is it not?"

Most disturbingly, she did not shrink from his touch. She swallowed. "Most everyone calls me Fanny."

She had never seen him smile, really. He appeared vulnerable—human. And she was positive she had felt him tremble, earlier, when her finger had traced the awful scar down behind his ear. She had touched him in a special place, like the ones Rafe had touched at the loch. Good God . . . *Rafe*.

In a faraway place, in the far reaches of her mind, she could hear him. *Jump, Fanny. Run, Fanny—hang on, Fanny!* She blinked back any show of emotion. She would make love to a nine-headed hydra if she had to— to survive. And this man was most assuredly a monster with a wounded heart and tortured soul.

The devil swept a few strands of curl off her brow, and took a very long moment to examine every feature on her face.

There was a rap at the door. Without taking his eyes off her, Mallory answered. "Enter."

The butler, Aubrey, rolled in a cart laden with a number of covered dishes and several bottles of wine.

"Ah, supper. Are you hungry?"

Even though her stomach pitched like a ship in a storm, she would eat at a snail's pace and drink a good deal of wine. "Famished."

Mallory uncrossed black leather boots and stood. "The lady and I will serve ourselves."

From her seat in the parlor, she saw that dinner appeared to be simple, elegant fare. There was a piece of fish, a leg of beef, boiled potatoes, and buttered vegetables. Fanny marveled at the spread, but wondered, frankly, how much cooking could possibly be done in these caverns.

She rose and tugged at Mallory's hand. "I must ask a favor—a simple act of kindness." She quelled a current of fear that caused a racing heart and shallow breath. "About the child, Harry . . ."

"The boy will be returned to his father tomorrow." He escorted her to a chair at the table. A wave of relief flooded through her. "And now it is my turn to ask a favor." He reached around her waist and pulled her against him. "I want you to come to me willingly, consciously—" He turned his chin slightly, his mouth so close his breath buffeted gently against her lips. "And with pleasure." Those eyes of his, burning coals of controlled rage, searched her expression for the slightest sign of guile. "Will you do that for me?"

Fanny masked her hesitation by admiring his well-defined lips. She thought about a kiss but held back—too much. Too readily given. She opened her mouth and curled the tip of her tongue over the edge of her upper lip. Her gaze lifted. "I will."

The ground shook underfoot and a great blast of thunder buffeted the air around them. Fanny lost her balance and reached out. Mallory covered her body with his. The deafening roar of an explosion blew the door to his suite open. The shock wave sent them both flying onto the carpet. He rolled her under the table. "Stay here."

Fanny coughed. "What just happened?"

"Intruders." He let go reluctantly and crawled out from under the table. Fanny lifted the tablecloth. Mallory helped the man called Aubrey up off the floor. Several more of his minions entered the room as the dust settled. "Came from one the cellars below, sir," one said.

Mallory took a cursory look about the room as Fanny crawled out from under the furniture. "No harm done."

While Mallory and his men huddled near the entrance, Fanny eyed the buffet cart full of food, and sidled over. She slipped a silver compote off the table and emptied dried fruit into a napkin.

"It appears Scotland Yard might be onto us." Mallory turned just as Fanny stuffed a roll in a dress pocket.

She straightened up and raised both brows. "I found them to be brighter than one might think." She smiled, thinly.

Unfazed, even amused, he moved to the doorway. "Then again, it could have just as easily been a rat. They've been known to chew on fuse wire." He glanced back at the supper tray. "Take what you like back to your quarters."

Mallory bowed to her. "Until tomorrow night."

*   *   *

RAFE GROANED. SOMETHING moist and warm slithered over his face and cheeks. Hacking dust and dirt from his lungs, he opened both eyes. The Yard dog panted inches away. The dripping tongue lapped upward, slathering him again. "That's enough, Alfred." A ticklish wheeze in his chest forced him up on his elbows for a look around. "Flynn?"

Like some sort of uncanny beacon, the dog's nose swung toward a pile of rubble. Several bricks tumbled onto the floor beside him. Rafe struggled to his feet and sucked in as much particle-filled air as he dared. His lungs burned and his ribs ached. He felt under his shirt and ran his fingers over the tape that wound around his rib cage.

He leaned over the great mound of mortar and stone and began tossing off bricks. Within a few minutes, he uncovered a pair of boots attached to two legs. He took up both feet and pulled. A yell came from deep under the pile. Rafe checked in with Alfred. "Good news. He's alive." The Yard dog sat down beside him. Rafe couldn't be sure, but he thought the hound looked pleased.

Rafe labored near to half an hour uncovering his partner, who emerged from the debris scuffed and bruised, but in relatively good health. After a long fit of coughing, Flynn scanned the cellar.

Several pipes of wine had been blown to smithereens. Most of the casks' contents had drained through grates in the floor, leaving a few dark red pools spotted about. Flynn dabbed his finger in a puddle and tasted.

"Pitiful waste of a lovely vintage." His partner sucked in a wheeze. "We must have set off the dynamite." He coughed out more dust.

Rafe nodded. "Some kind of rigged wire or land mine. Lucky we didn't both get blown to pieces. Along with Yard dog here." The hound whipped a tail against his side.

He helped Flynn up from the ground. His partner took a few steps and winced. "Bollocks. I can't put any weight on this leg." He teetered slightly.

Rafe stepped up beside him. "You've likely cracked a bone." He looped Flynn's arm across his shoulders and the two hobbled away from the pile of bricks. Gingerly, they made their way back out of the underground cavern and shut the warehouse door. Once outside, he and Flynn stepped over a drunken warehouse worker in the alley.

"Hold on." Rafe swung them both around and gave the old bird's shoulder a shake. "Say there, Jasper, know anything about the deeper caverns—below the wine cellars?"

The drunken sot squinted at him. "Under St. Katharine Docks. Seen 'em myself. The river pirate caves, hundreds of years old. Used them to stash contraband and treasure."

Flynn shook his head. "Poor old sea dog."

Rafe squinted through fog as thick as ever. "Nothing to be done here. It'll take days to clear out the rubble. We're going to have to find another way in."

∞ Chapter Thirty-one

Rafe blinked several times and Zeno Kennedy came into focus. The number two Yard man appeared overhead, haloed by the harsh light that poured through a sooty glass skylight.

"Wake up, Prince Charming."

"Bugger off, Kennedy." Every inch of bone and muscle felt the hardwood bench under him. Rafe sat up and recognized absolutely nothing about his surroundings. Sore ribs forced a grimace.

"You managed to get Flynn to Harley Street last night. The surgeon is with him now." Zeno grinned. "Glad to see you were able to catch a few hours' sleep."

Rafe rubbed his eyes. "Eventually, if one does not obey the laws of nature, one just—passes out." He exhaled. "And how is Mr. Rhys?"

"Fractured tibia. They're plastering him up as we speak." Zeno nudged his shoulder. "Come, grab a bite of breakfast with me."

They found a pub nearby and tucked into a hearty

plate of egg and kippers. "Flynn says you're determined to find another way in." Zeno buttered a warm bun.

"There's no other recourse. I've got nothing to go on—all my leads have dried up." As the waitress passed, Rafe ordered another pint. He reached in his waistcoat pocket and pulled out a bit of change. Picking through copper and silver coin, he came across the sapphire stickpin. "What do you make of this?"

Zeno leaned forward to examine the trinket. "More like a medal than a piece of jewelry."

Rafe forked into his remaining kipper. "Picked it up in the dirt beside a dead man. One of Mallory's blokes."

"Quite a large gem—do you think the stone is genuine?"

"Can't think why it wouldn't be. The Utopian Society appears to be extremely well financed." Rafe stopped chewing. "Why?"

Zeno tossed a bit of change on the table. "I might have an idea."

LARGE DROPS OF summer rain pattered quietly on the roof as the carriage rounded Oxford Circus. "Where are we headed?" Rafe settled in beside the number two Yard man.

"Nineteen Chester Square, Belgravia."

Rafe lifted a brow. "Tony address. Who's the chap again?"

"Phineas Gunn. Interesting fellow. I knew him distantly some years ago—we were both in Her Majesty's

Scots Greys together. Bruising rider. He once beat me by several lengths in a race around the parade grounds. Got himself stationed in the Raj, the Punjab region. Suffered a rather bad event, hasn't been the same since."

A bit of rain slanted inside the coach and Zeno lifted the latch and closed the window. "Somewhat of an odd duck," he went on. "An acute recluse at times, and yet he continues to take on assignments now and then. He's a top-notch criminologist and quite a talented writer of crime fiction—penned several novels. Scholarly works, as well, in the field of forensic science."

Rafe frowned. "That might be useful if we had a body." He couldn't think of it, not with Fanny and Harry in the clutches of a madman. He clenched his fists and concentrated on Zeno's briefing. Anything to avoid spiraling into a demoralized state.

"Mr. Gunn is also a gemologist—more of a gentleman's hobby. I'm told the nobs seek his advice on purchases and pay him handsomely for appraisals. Scotland Yard has him under retainer—actually, we share him with military intelligence. Perhaps he can help. At any rate the man's bound to have some unconventional thoughts on Mallory, as well as the murders." Zeno flashed a half smile. "I believe you will get on with him."

"I thought he was an odd duck." Rafe said.

Zeno nodded. "Precisely."

As it turned out, the uncommon Mr. Gunn employed a rather eccentric butler, who accepted their cards, rolled his eyes, and abandoned them to a small reception parlor. While Rafe paced, Zeno made himself comfortable on the settee. "I know it's difficult under these trying circumstances, but you must keep your head about you. A needless waver or wrong move at this juncture—"

"We can't afford another setback," Rafe bit out.

Zeno's reply was measured. "Exactly why we're here—we need the best mind we can get on this."

"Sorry to keep you waiting, gentlemen."

Rafe turned toward the deep, resonant voice with a touch of gravel—a familiar voice. He nearly jumped at the sight. "Hugh Curzon?"

"One of several names used in service to queen and country." The imposing man in the entry smiled. "I assure you, Phineas Gunn is written in the birth register at St. John's Anglican, Helmsdale."

Rafe looked him up and down. "Well, this is . . . a bit of a shock." He turned to Zeno, and found his grin an equal irritant. "*He* is the man you described as the brilliant recluse?"

Unruffled, Phineas Gunn leaned against the door frame. "My nervous spells wax and wane. I've had a good long respite, of late, from my infirmity."

A rather striking woman darted past the open door. "Until next week, *chéri*." Gunn reached out and caught her. A half stride took them down the passage, out of view. An audible kiss and a faint titter of laughter wafted back into the receiving room.

The man returned to the parlor and nodded to them both. "Miss Hébert takes good care of me."

"Indeed, Mr. Gunn." Rafe didn't give a fig whether

this man was Hugh Curzon or Phineas Gunn—not if he could help him find Fanny and Harry.

"Please call me Finn." The man's gaze softened and he cleared his throat. "Very sorry to hear about your son—as well as Miss Greyville-Nugent. You have both my sympathy and support."

Rafe faltered slightly. "You've been briefed on the matter?"

"Only what's in the papers. I just got back in town myself," Finn added.

"Christ, the press has gotten wind of the kidnapping." Zeno's dislike for the newspapers and scandal sheets was well-known. In fact, the detective was nothing short of famous around town, having been written up by the yellow newssheets on many occasions.

"Would you both care to join me for a cup of coffee—or something stronger?" Phineas rang for his servant. "While we refresh ourselves, you can fill me in on all the details the press didn't get."

FANNY FOLDED SEVERAL slices of roast beef and placed them on a linen square. "You take the rest, Harry. I'll have the roll."

She divided what remained of the dried fruit, pocketing a few pieces for later. She had managed to take away a small platter full of food last night and their jailors had even allowed her to pass a bit of nourishment on to the professor. The wink Hamish gave her through the peephole in the door of his cell had helped sustain her through the night.

If Rafe had been the one to set off the dynamite, she prayed he was not gravely injured. She could not allow herself to even think such things for long. She refused to believe he might be gone. Injured, perhaps, but not gone. Harry had asked about the explosion and she had reassured him he would soon be reunited with his father.

Fanny bit into her roll and watched his little legs swing back and forth from the wooden bench that had doubled as their bed last night. Nearly sick with worry, her fears spiraled into a vast nightmare of woe.

Last night, she had returned from Mallory's suite and found Harry huddled in a corner, shivering. Quickly re-purposing her soft cotton frock as a blanket, she sat him on her lap and fed him bits of dried fruit and a lovely sliver of fish. After several repetitions of "Diddle Diddle Dumpling" and "Ding Dong Bell," he had curled up in her arms and slept as soundly as she had fitfully. In the middle of the night she had awoken and felt his little hand in hers.

She smiled at Harry. "You're awfully quiet. Cat got your tongue?" He chewed on a piece of meat, and man-aged a smile with a mouthful.

A bone-chilling moan drifted through the walls of their cell.

Harry swallowed. Fanny swallowed.

The brassy clink of keys at the door was already famil-iar. Two minions: the fat bloke and the dwarf this time. Fanny inhaled a deep breath and stiffened her resolve.

The immense chap seemed larger and the dwarf smaller than she remembered. "We've come for the boy."

Harry jerked upright, his wide eyes darting toward her.

"I will not release the boy to the likes of you."

"Oh, I believe you will, miss." The gluttonous belly shook in amusement, the kind with no laughter.

Fanny reached out and clasped Harry tightly in her arms. "Oh dear, I'm afraid Mallory will be very displeased. You see, we struck a very private bargain last night. If he wishes me to honor our agreement, I will need to speak with him." She dared raise a brow, slightly. "I would make it my business to get him down here at once, if I were you."

The fat man turned shellfish red and the dwarf stopped swinging that huge ring of keys long enough to slam the door.

She looked down at her charge and winked. "Soon, Harry." She kissed the mop of hair on his head and waited. She wasn't a very good judge of time passing—not in this small dungeon. It seemed like eons before there were footsteps in the corridor and another jangle of keys.

The door burst open and Mallory stepped into the room. He set his stance wide and crossed his arms over his chest. "You've taken me away from important business."

"Like killing people?" Fanny bit her lip. The moment the words left her smart mouth she regretted them. But she met his gaze and did not falter.

Mallory angled his chin and narrowed his eyes. "In the interests of preserving our agreement . . ." He sauntered farther inside the small chamber. "How may I be of service?"

Fanny swallowed. "You must deliver the boy to Scotland Yard."

Mallory stopped and stared. "I do not run errands."

"And *I* do not trust your men to see the boy safely to his father. They would just as soon toss him over Westminster Bridge and call the errand done." Fanny sucked in a breath of air. "I trust you, *and only you*, to see the boy returned."

Mallory, of all people, blinked. "Why?"

His dark, angry eyes continued to stare, forcing her to look away, collect her thoughts. "You suffered terribly—needlessly—as a youth. Even though your rage is misdirected and your remedies cruel beyond measure, there is something in your cause that deserves respect. I pray God I will find some sort of honor amongst thieves—or anti-progressives, as it were."

Fanny steeled herself. Her gaze met and held his with as much composure as she could muster. "I trust you will not harm the boy, but see him safely returned to his father."

Mallory stepped closer and lifted the child from her. Harry whimpered quietly.

Fanny stroked his cheek. "Be a good boy."

Mallory examined the child in his arms. "Can you ride a horse—if I put you in the saddle in front of me?"

The wide-eyed boy looked to her. She nodded. "It will be all right, Harry."

* * *

RAFE STOOD BY the desk as Finn examined the sapphire under a jeweler's magnifying glass. "A wheel within a wheel—any reasonably talented artisan could craft the stickpin." He turned it over. "Ah, we have a motto. *Actus Reus* neatly engraved along the edge of the larger wheel."

"Wrongful act," both Zeno and Rafe translated the Latin simultaneously.

"I see we all stayed the classical course and made it to university," Finn teased gently. "The terms *actus reus* and *mens rea* are covenants of English law, derived principally from the axiom *actus non facit reum nisi mens sit rea.*"

Rafe nodded. "An act does not make a person guilty unless his mind is also guilty," he translated.

"The general test of guilt as recognized by the courts is one that requires proof of culpability both in deed and thought." Zeno sat back and removed a cigar case from his inside pocket. "Mind if I smoke?"

"Please do." Finn left his chair at the desk and perused a wall of reference books. Rafe and Zeno had gone over every detail of the case—twice. Rafe's patience this last hour had dwindled to somewhere between little and none.

Zeno offered a smoke to Rafe.

Rafe shook his head. "Quit tobacco. Fanny hates it."

Zeno's thumbnail flicked over the match head. "Over the course of these last days together, did you manage to reconcile with the lovely young heiress?"

"I believe so. Partially."

Zeno puffed on his cheroot. "Partially?"

Finn's mouth twitched. "If constant bickering is a sign of affection, I'd say they are fully restored." He plucked down a leather-bound volume. "Here we are." He thumbed through pages and stopped. "Royal Horse Artillery. Lieutenant Colonel Bellecorte Valour Mallory, 17 Regiment Royal Artillery—there's your BVM initials, Rafe.

"The man was cashiered out after an explosion in his unit caused a volley of accidental returned fire—killed several men. Blew half his own skull off . . ." Finn shook his head. "Odd, wouldn't you say? A man so gravely injured is dismissed in disgrace?"

Rafe shrugged. "Fratricide and negligence are serious charges."

Finn raised a brow. "Well, it appears you've identified the right man." He snapped the book closed. "And very likely the leader of this . . . Utopian Society."

Their consultant sat down and flipped the pin right side up. "The gold work is simple, unexceptional, but the sapphire may be rare, indeed." He invited them both to view the stone under magnification.

Rafe and Zeno each took a turn hunched over the man's desk. Finn leaned back in his chair. "I am acquainted with a jeweler in Hatton Garden—Eastern European chap, goes by the name Nandor Fabian. A skilled cutter who specializes in sizing down stones from much larger, rarer gems." Finn paused, an amused look on his face. "Shall we pay him a visit?"

Rafe straightened. "By all means—that is—" Rafe looked him up and down. "If you feel up to it?"

Finn grimaced or flinched, perhaps both. "You won't have to ask—you will know very well when I am not 'up to it.'"

Zeno snuffed out his cigar. "I'd like to get back to the office. Mind if we pick this jeweler up and take him in for questioning? A trip to Scotland Yard will loosen the man's tongue quick enough."

∞ Chapter Thirty-two

Rafe folded his arms across his chest and leaned against the bleak walls of the interrogation room. He listened rather intently as Finn sifted through Nandor Fabian's story.

"The stone is one of seven matching sapphires. All in the four-carat range."

Finn languished in slat back chair, legs crossed. "And what of the original?"

The jeweler's gaze darted about. "The original?"

Finn lowered his chair so he might loom over the interrogation table. "The mother of all mother sapphires."

"Ah yes, of course." Fabian wiped perspiration off his upper lip. "The original stone was a gift from a maharaja to an actress who shall go unnamed. Less than a year ago, she sold it to me for a very good price."

Finn stared interminably. "Would you say . . . too good a price?"

The jeweler shrugged. "I had no choice but to cut down the stone."

Rafe grinned. Phineas Gunn had a way of using his deep voice and unhurried manner to prod the man in mysterious ways. Rafe not only admired it, he studied it. If he'd been the one doing the questioning, the jeweler's *jewels* would be roasting over a meat pit right about now.

"And once the pins were completed, who returned for them?" Finn asked.

Fabian sat in a cold sweat. "Why, the very same gentleman who placed the order."

"Bear with me once more. Might you describe this man as—?" A strong rap at the door halted Finn midsentence.

"Yes, what is it?" Rafe answered, impatiently.

A guard pressed the door open. Melville stood in the entry, holding the hand of a much smaller figure standing beside him.

Rafe blinked, hardly able to trust his own eyes. "Harry?"

His heart did a somersault inside his chest. He launched himself off the wall. Melville released the boy, who ran toward him.

"Father!"

Rafe caught his son in his arms and held on tight. He kissed the soft hairs of his head. His eyes blurred—hardly able to control his emotion. Vaguely, he was aware Finn and the jeweler had stepped out of the room, into the corridor.

"Thank God you're safe." The part of his life he had tucked away in his heart and hidden from the world for years hugged him with all his little might. The overwrought father in Rafe released all the fear and uncertainty—the abject terror of the last day and night. He could not stop the tears that flowed.

A bit light in the head, he sank to his knees and settled against the wall. Harry's little arms around his neck never felt as precious as they did in this moment, nor his child's soft whimpers of relief. As soon as he could see clearly, Rafe swept his hands through the boy's bangs and examined his arms for bruising. "You're all right? They did not touch or hurt you in any way?"

Harry shook his head in that energetic way of his, dislodging a few tears. "She—Fanny—told them no."

Rafe swallowed. "And how is Fanny?"

Zeno opened and closed the door softly. "Do you mind? I've a bit of news."

Rafe waved him inside.

Zeno lowered onto his haunches and smiled at Rafe's son. "Hello, Harry." He held out his hand. Somewhat hesitant, Harry removed an arm from around Rafe's neck and shook hands. "Quite a brave lad."

Rafe hugged his son. "Brave, indeed."

Zeno removed a pocket square from his waistcoat and offered it to Rafe. "Finn thought you should know that one of ours chased after the man who dropped Harry off—a gentleman riding a fine hunter. A dead ringer for the customer described by the jeweler."

"I take it we didn't catch him." Rafe dabbed his son's cheeks and eyes. Harry's stomach growled. "You're hungry."

Harry nodded. "And I need to use the water closet."

Zeno stood and offered Rafe a hand up. "What about a bit of fish and chip?"

Harry nodded. "Yes, please."

"Right, then." Zeno patted Rafe on the back. "Melville wants a briefing—nothing too taxing. Collect yourself, see to the boy's needs. We'll meet in his office."

The walk upstairs from the lockup and interrogation rooms took them past a number of department offices. Several of Rafe's colleagues popped out to say hello to Harry.

"My word, you are quite the celebrity," Rafe said to his son.

Harry looked up. "What's a celebrity?"

Rafe managed a tense smile as he guided his son into the director's office. "In your case, Harry, a celebrity is a kind of popular hero." Melville stood near the library table with Finn, who swung around and held out his hand. "Hello, Harry. Phineas Gunn."

The boy reached up to for a shake. "Do you like guns?"

Finn nodded. "Nothing grandiose, more of a selective arsenal."

Zeno arrived at the door with a stack of file folders. Rafe sometimes wondered if Special Branch would have any records but for Kennedy's hurried scratches.

"Have a seat, gentlemen." Melville gestured to a smattering of chairs around the table. "As you all know, a rather splendid exhibition of machines is set to open in the Royal Polytechnic Institution tomorrow morning."

Melville paced behind Rafe's son. "As I speak, one

of our lab teams is combing the Hall of Manufactures, top to bottom. We're looking for all the usual types of hidden explosives. We also have most of the competing inventors and engineers assembled. Each man shall inspect his entry—check for evidence of tampering." Melville pulled out his pocket watch. "Mr. Bruce is late. I expected him here to fill you in on the specifics."

Zeno looked up from his file scribbling. "I caught a glimpse of Archie downstairs. He should be here any moment."

Melville's gaze shifted from man to man. "Even though the hall will be guarded this evening, I have added additional police patrols."

At the end of the table, Harry forked a large chip into his mouth. The potato wedge fell back onto his plate. Rafe stood up to help, but the director had already taken up a knife. "Tomorrow we'll have over a dozen plainclothes officers milling about in the crowd. I plan to personally brief these men before the doors open." Rafe could not quite believe his eyes when Melville sliced a fillet of fish and several chips into smaller pieces. "What am I going to tell them?" Melville groused as he returned Harry's fork. "Might I give them a description of our culprits? I'm told we've got one—finally."

Rafe shrugged. "The followers, or Mallory's Minions, as we've come to call them—"

"Better than *natty blokes*." Finn shrugged off Rafe's glare.

"They're dark-suited, and wear plain waistcoats. I'm afraid they'll blend in to a crowd of spectators." Rafe leaned forward. "And they do appear rather dapper, actually."

"What about the latest man?" Melville asked. "The one who delivered the boy."

Zeno read aloud from a file. "Tall, well built, stylishly dressed in riding attire. Midthirties, dark hair—neatly trimmed beard."

Melville grunted. "Doesn't sound much like one of your Utopian Society militiamen, Rafe. Conducts himself more like a peer of the realm than one of the proletariat."

Finn leaned back in his chair. "Pure speculation, but it may have been Mallory himself."

Harry jerked upright. "Mr. Mallory let me ride his horse with him."

Rafe's gaze moved from his son to Finn. "Are you saying that man walked my son into Scotland Yard?"

Finn exchanged a grim look across the table. "Right in the front door."

Rafe analyzed the audacity inherent in the act itself—a thumbing of the nose. "Bollocks."

Harry finished his milk and set the glass down. "Bollocks."

Rafe's glare moved to Harry. "You're not allowed to say *bollocks*."

"Why not?"

"Because I say so."

Rafe leaned closer to his son. "You and Fanny were held somewhere—together?"

Harry's eyes grew big and he nodded. "A very scary

place." He forked a piece of fish into his mouth and chewed slowly. "Fanny made a dress into a blanket to keep me warm. And she brought back food."

Finn angled his chair. "She went away for a while?"

The child nodded. "When she came back, she made roast beef on a bun."

Rafe didn't like the way Finn avoided eye contact. Of course they were all thinking the same thing. Where had they taken Fanny and what had they done to her? Once again Rafe's heart thumped wildly inside his chest. "Did she—did she tell you something, a message possibly—for me?"

Beaming, Harry quickly swallowed a piece of chip. "She can hear the sailors' songs from a Yankee ship. And there is a cooperage—lots of hammering and empty casks rolling . . . . along the cobbles." His rote recitation rang true.

"I imagine she made you practice?" Finn prodded gently.

He nodded and ate another piece of fish.

"Good lad." Finn turned to Rafe. "Obviously somewhere under the docks—St. Katharine possibly?"

Melville opened a large cabinet. "We've got several good charts of the Docklands." Searching through cubbyholes and flat drawers, he pulled out two maps and spread them out on the tabletop. Rafe traced the aboveground route from the warehouse on Henry Street to the nearest mooring. "Has to be St. Katharine Docks. But where, exactly?"

Finn rubbed beard stubble and shook his head. "Won't

be as simple as finding an American merchant ship and a cooperman."

Rafe nodded. "The dock is teeming with both." He recalled the old man outside the warehouse last night. "When Flynn and I were under the warehouse, just before the explosion, we found a passage that took us below the level of wine cellars—much older. Once we got ourselves back aboveground, I nearly stepped on an old sea dog lying in the street. I asked if he knew anything about the lower levels. The old sot rambled on about ancient underwater passages and river pirate caves."

"I heard water." Harry licked a finger. "Like the river at Henley."

Rafe inspected a near empty plate and glass of milk. "An order of fish and chip and Harry is restored." Rafe marveled at the resilience of children. Honest and always in the moment. No guile, and very few judgments. "I take it you enjoyed supper?"

Harry exhaled. "Better than Mrs. Coates'."

"I would not mention that to her, if I were you." Rafe gave him a wink and leaned back in his chair. "All right, even if we could locate the Yankee ship and the cooperage, who's to say we'd find a passageway down into the caverns?"

"Blimey, I have just been inside the most amazing vessel." Archie Bruce, Scotland Yard's crime lab director, poked his head in the door. "Sorry I'm late. Got delayed dockside with Harbor Patrol. A Mr. Roger Spottesworth just towed in a twenty-four-foot submarine. Left your name, Rafe, and a Henley-on-Thames address."

"When Professor Minnow went missing, I asked Spottesworth if he might tow her into town." Rafe bolted upright. "If there are indeed underwater passages leading inland from the docks—we could use the submarine to get to the caverns."

"Bloody hell you will!" Even with the office door closed, Melville's bellow carried down every passageway on the third floor. "I'll not send the best men I've got off half-cocked—into an as yet unknown underwater passage—in an experimental vessel." An angry finger pointed to each man in turn, while a red flush climbed the director's neck.

After that blast, Rafe sucked in a bit of air. "It is imperative we try for a rescue tonight. Tomorrow may be too late. We have no idea what kind of machine or contraption these blokes are planning to use for their ghoulish executions. And they have three more coming, by my calculations," he addressed his superior.

Finn tried another tack. "As we are well aware, the signature Utopian Society murder theme is 'the master's demise by his own machine.' The bittersweet irony of Dr. Frankenstein done in by his own creation."

Melville snorted. "You make it sound like Shakespeare."

The Yard's cocky consultant grinned. "More of a nineteenth-century aesthetic—Mary Shelley with a bite of the Bard's own wit."

Rafe rolled his eyes. "Let's assume, for a moment, that the sapphire stickpins are medals—job well done, lads, that sort of thing.

"Fabian confirmed the pins," Finn added.

"Mallory's men have thus far been awarded four out of seven. There have also been two failed attempts—Fanny and Minnow." Rafe grimaced at the thought.

Finn pushed out of his chair and moved around the table. "In Minnow's case, they more than likely planned to scuttle the sub by tampering with its ballast controls. The professor would have been found, eventually, at the bottom of the Thames if Rafe hadn't fished him out of a sinking ship. Pun intended," Finn added. "There is also the possibility that Fanny is to be number seven in some kind of grand finale. Whatever the scheme, the Utopians under Mallory did not foresee Special Branch getting onto them so quickly. Sending Rafe up to Edinburgh like you did must have vastly undermined their plans. And Rafe is correct, we must keep the pressure on."

Rafe gathered Harry in his arms, anxious to get going. "Can we at least attempt to take the submarine under the docks—a trial run?"

"Does anyone know anything about how to operate this craft? And who's going down in that bucket of . . ." Melville drew a deeper frown. "It's not even seaworthy by last account."

Rafe nodded to Finn. "Grab that old map." He bit his tongue and made a great effort not to raise his voice to his boss. "Might we argue about this on our way to Docklands?"

Archie Bruce stepped into the fray. "I've had a look at the controls. With a bit of practice up and down the river, we'll get the knack of it, sir."

"Hold on." Melville opened a desk drawer and took out several new pistols and a box of shells. "Brand new Webley Mk1s. Arm yourselves, gentlemen." Melville loaded a pistol and handed it over to Rafe. The director looked him over with a kinder eye. "Do try to hold on to your weapon for a change, Detective Lewis."

"I'll do my best, sir." Rafe slipped the Webley inside his jacket. "Any of those battery torches left?"

Archie pocketed his weapon. "We've got two in the lab—just take a moment to collect them."

Outside 4 Whitehall Place, Rafe hailed a hansom and sat Harry on his lap. Finn squeezed in beside them. Zeno, Archie, and Melville followed after in the director's carriage. Finn spread the map out on his lap and toggled a switch on the torch.

Rafe grinned. "First try and you didn't have to bang it around—good sign."

Harry blinked at the magical torchlight. Rafe took in the look on his son's angelic face. "Quite an adventure you're having."

Exiting Blackfriars Underpass, they turned onto Upper Thames Street. Rafe pointed to the massive construction site out on the river. "See there, Harry. They're building the Tower Bridge."

"Actually, we may have only one boat basin to search, and a small one at that—take a look." Finn hunched over the map tracing the route from Henry Street to the docks. "Assuming the underground caverns were made by nature and the passages connecting them by pirates—as the crow flies—" His index finger stopped at a triangular basin.

They soon ditched cabs and carriage for a river taxi, which got them to the Port of London Authority Harbor Patrol Pier in no time. Framed by the dark silhouette of the looming Tower Bridge construction site, Melville paced the length of pier, eyeing the submarine suspiciously. "Blimey, indeed."

Rafe approached Zeno. "You're about to become a father. Perhaps you'd like a bit of practice?"

"We'd be delighted. Cassie has just finished the nursery, you can sleep in nurse's bed." The detective smiled at Harry.

Rafe smoothed silky bangs and tilted his son's chin. "I'm afraid I'm going to have to ask you to be brave a few hours longer. I must find Fanny and bring her home." Harry nodded solemnly, none too pleased about it. "This very nice man and his wife will take good care of you while I'm gone." Transferring the boy to Zeno, he turned away quickly and joined Archie and Finn dockside.

"You believe you can control this thing?" Rafe searched Archie's face. Not a risk taker by nature, their young lab director shrugged. "Only one way to know, I suppose."

Rafe ran a hand through his hair and turned to Finn. Glistening beads of sweat dotted the man's forehead. "Crikey, this is a bit nerve-racking."

Finn stared at him. "You have no idea."

Chapter Thirty-three

$\mathcal{F}$anny picked up the skirt of her new dress and climbed the stairs. Silk again, in a mysterious shade of claret. She dreaded every step, as though she made her way toward the hangman's noose—even the procession surrounding her felt like a gallows walk. The manservant, Aubrey, led the way, with another burly man close behind her. Mallory had sent an order—in the form of a request—that she leave her hair down. She had complied, tying her unruly mass of curls behind her head with a ribbon cleverly garnered from some trim on the gown.

Aubrey rapped tentatively and gestured her through the door. Something was wrong. She sensed it almost instantly. The suite was deathly quiet and darker than she remembered. The grind and clunk of a heavy door latch made her flinch. She trembled with each step as she ventured farther into the room.

Mallory lounged across a high-backed settee. His head lay against the sweeping curve of an arm, his long legs stretched across the other wing. Moving closer, she could not help but notice his waistcoat and shirt were unbuttoned to his trousers. The narrow gap exposed a sliver of masculine flesh with a mat of dark fuzz that trailed from chest to navel.

She hesitated as he turned his head. His gaze swept over every inch of her figure before settling on the gown's décolleté. He lifted a finger in the air and circled. "Turn around."

On display for his personal pleasure, she pivoted slowly. A blaze of heat rushed to her cheeks.

"Come closer."

His eyes appeared strained, and much redder than the usual black orbs that studied her with unblinking intensity. "You look unwell, Mallory." She feigned a note of concern.

"I'm afraid a blistering headache is coming on." He grabbed hold of her wrist and guided her around the side of the chaise. He rested his head back against the upholstered curve of the arm. "Place your hands on each side of my head—the temples." She did her best to keep her hands steady. "Mm-mm, cold hands are soothing." He closed his eyes. "Circle slowly." Gently, she massaged his temples and he exhaled. "I suffer the occasional supraorbital neuralgia, due my head injury. Press harder." He lowered his gaze. "Are you always so brave?"

"I hardly think of myself as brave. Might I try a different spot?" She moved her hands over his shaven head to the base of his skull and circled her fingers. "Here, perhaps?"

"God, yes." He groaned with relief.

"What caused such a terrible wound? Surely you could grow an excellent head of hair to cover the scar."

"A long and painful military tale."

"Yes, but why choose to display such a mark?"

Mallory sighed. "After I lost my family, an uncle took me in—a military man who had sired a bevy of daughters. Raised me as a son—in his footsteps. I suppose I took to the military life with its order, its clear directives. I rose up the ranks rather quickly until the accident."

He brought her hands forward again to his temples. "A mortar cannon exploded. Set off a chain of return fire. I don't remember much after that." Mallory gasped for air, as though bracing for a wave of pain. "There was a long period of unconsciousness. I thought I had died. No one could have been more surprised than I to wake up in hospital.

"As commanding officer I was assigned blame—cashiered out for negligence. They sent me to a mental hospital to be long forgotten. Over the next few years, I recovered most of my faculties."

Fanny bit her lip. So, the men in dark suits and pointed collars were Mallory's own private militia. "Your life does appear to be fraught with injustice."

"Exactly the kind of life that turns an orphaned guttersnipe into an anarchist." He reached up and drew her near, pressing her hands to his chest.

He showed her where he wanted her hands to go. Encouraged her fingers to travel over the soft mat of hair that covered a hard-muscled chest.

"Lower." A whispered demand as he pulled her closer.

Her fingers traced the trail of hair down a flat torso. His belly quivered, and he groaned softly.

She was nearly cheek to cheek with him, her lips a breath away from his ear.

If she was his lover, she might whisper naughty promises of things to come. If she were his enemy, she might tear into the flesh of his ear—add her mark to his mutilation. Instead, she withdrew her hands from his belly and moved to press her lips to the scar on his head. Gently, she traced the zig, then the zag down the side of his skull.

IN THE DIM light of the submersible, Rafe studied his shipmate. Something a bit twitchy about Finn. The cool-headed Mr. Gunn was noticeably agitated.

"Don't look at me that way. I'll get worse if you keep looking at me that way."

Rafe suppressed an urge to mock. "What way?"

"That bug-eyed, racked with concern way."

Their trial run up and down the Thames had gone so well, Melville had waved them along. Tensions had eased, some, until they submerged. They were now well into the triangle basin. As the water grew progressively murky and strangely oppressive, Finn had begun to sweat bullets.

"Are you a hydrophobe, by any chance?"

A rolling of the eyes accompanied Finn's sigh. "Normally, I'm more of an agoraphobe. Crowded spaces, enclosed public places—squares and the like. If I was the self-diagnosing sort, which I suppose I *am*, I'd call this particular bout claustrophobia."

Rafe puzzled over the man's affliction. He recalled a rooftop facedown as the train pulled out of Glasgow. Finn had shot down old Ruddy-face as cool as you please. He sucked in stale air and exhaled. "What can I do to help?"

Hunched over, Finn braced himself in the hatchway. "I cannot just stand here and watch Mr. Bruce fumble about with the controls. Give me work to do."

Rafe straightened as much as he could in the sub. "I believe Archie's got things working fairly well now." Their submarine pilot continued to toggle switches in an effort to find . . . something. Archie flipped a switch overhead and a swath of light beamed through the bilgy green basin water. "There we are. Much better, wouldn't you say?"

Finn ducked for a look out the observation window. "At last—we can see three feet in front of us."

Rafe agreed with Finn's bleak assessment. "Thick as a black fog down here."

Arch turned to Finn. "Near as I can tell, we're not more than a few feet under the surface. The rear observation dome will give us a view higher up. I could use another set of eyes if we're to find this old pirate route."

Archie unhooked a cone-shaped speaking tube attached to a rubber hose. "Should be one of these back there. Give us a shout if you see anything."

Finn nodded his head. "Right."

Rafe took the seat beside their intrepid pilot and

strained to see through the flotsam and jetsam. A hail of squawks blared out of the cone above Archie's head. Rafe took down the speaking tube. "Say again, Finn?"

"I've a herd of river rats swarming about the glass up here—love to take a few nips out of my head. Have a look above."

Rafe craned his neck toward the surface. A myriad of undulating shadows and tiny, clawed feet paddled just underwater. "Blimey. Hundreds of them."

Arch motored alongside the immense black hull of a moored ship. "The rodents are attracted to the light, possibly? Ask Finn if he can get a direction—where they're coming from."

Before Rafe could speak, Finn's voice filtered through the device. "As soon as we pass this ship, throttle down a bit and head us starboard thirty degrees."

A trail of rodent legs and tails led them into the oldest section of the dock. The crude stone basin wall grew more rugged until . . . it just fell away. An entire section of wall appeared to break off into darkness. "You see what I see?" Rafe spoke into the cone and waited for an answer. "Finn?"

"Christ. Tell Archie to take us lower—and another ten degrees or so starboard."

As the submarine slipped into what they hoped was a passageway, Rafe strained to see into the unknowable darkness of the gaping hole. "Can you reverse our direction?"

"If there is a reverse lever I haven't found it."

He wiped away a few beads of perspiration off his forehead. "Excellent."

Archie took a quick glance at Rafe. "There must be a back lever around here somewhere." A stomach-lurching grinding noise came from below ship. Archie grimaced. "We're scraping bottom."

Finn's tinny voice actually had a reassuring effect. "I can see air pockets throughout the tunnel. The dome is partially above water—with more room above—you can take her up a bit."

The next terrible clunk and crunching noise came from the top of the sub. They were now partially above the waterline. The search beam illuminated rugged walls that closed in from both sides. Rafe's gaze traveled up, over, and down. "Narrow bugger."

"Rather tricky, these small adjustments in ballast." Archie tugged on several wheels and levers. At the moment, the most reassuring aspect of their cruise down this ancient passageway was the constant putter of the submersible's engine.

Finn's voice shouted from the cone. "Stay your course, Mr. Bruce. If I'm not hallucinating, there may be a grotto ahead."

Rafe fixed his eyes forward. The passage grew even tighter for a time before it opened, rather quickly, into an expansive cavern.

Archie whistled. "Blimey. And to think this quiet cove is hidden beneath the Docklands."

The moment they surfaced, Rafe cranked the wheel of the overhead hatch and poked his head up. The pungent odor of decayed organic material mixed with stale air—mustier, moldier than topside. The sub chugged softly into the cavern, gliding through dark waters. "Heave ho, mate." Finn urged from below.

Up on deck, Rafe stepped through a thin sheet of water. He pivoted in a slow circle, peering into cracks and crevices. Long ago, by the looks of it, a stair and walkway had been constructed up one side of the cave. And there were hints of passageways lit by torches. Archie nosed them toward a grotty old pier.

Finn joined him. "Awfully quiet. Do you suppose anyone's home?"

Rafe removed his revolver from his jacket. Out of habit he checked the cylinder. Six bullets. And he had more in his pocket. "Let's knock on a few doors."

"SUCH A HEAVENLY angel . . ." Mallory reached up and brought her around to his side. "And what trouble you are."

"Trouble does seem to follow me of late." Fanny perched herself on the edge of the settee and tried to make small talk. Much more difficult, face-to-face. Like now—when he captured her gaze and held it.

She knew that look of desire very well. On her dearest, most darling Rafe. "You delivered the boy safely to Scotland Yard?" This forced flirtation with Mallory had worked her stomach into knots. She drew her lower lip between her teeth. Mistake. His eyes locked on her mouth and she heard a groan.

"To their door." He pulled her to him and did not ask permission. "A kiss."

Every fiber of her being reacted to the soft pressure of his lips. Warm, passionate, they traveled lightly over her mouth and then pressed harder with more intensity.

She grew frightened and pushed away. He leaned closer, never taking his eyes off her mouth. "I am not finished."

Mallory seized her and kissed her angrily. Fanny shut her eyes tight and tried not to resist. He assailed her mouth with his own, plowing the depths with his tongue. He pulled her onto his chest, the press of his erection more than obvious. If only she could just let him do as he wished. His breath was ragged and his words even more so. "Say yes, Fanny."

She declined with a shake of her head. "Please, Mallory." Her voice husky from fear of this strange, unholy attraction. He reached out and pressed her hand to his groin.

"Shall I tie you down and take you here on the settee? Look at me." He was so arrogant. So aggrieved. He grabbed hold of her chin and forced her to look at him. "What happened to willingly?"

"I made a bargain. I will do what I must, but I'm not sure about the pleasure part." Fanny swallowed. "You murdered my father. Not something one can easily overlook."

Mallory slumped back onto the arm of the chaise. "Yes. I did." She found both his shrug and grin disturbing. A kind of madness seemed to overtake him at times. "Not something one can easily apologize for."

A volley of bullets rang out in the passageway. Her heart quickened with the thought of what might be happening outside the door.

Much like a sudden bolt of lightning is followed by a downpour of cold rain, Mallory's reaction to her shifted. His glare deepened as his black eyes once again blazed a deep crimson red, not unlike they had during their first meeting. He made no mention of the disturbance, and yet she knew he listened.

The echoing ricochet of more gunshots. Closer, she thought.

He drew his mouth into a thin cruel line. "So, it appears the lady's protector makes yet another attempt at rescue." Mallory shifted her off the couch and traversed the room.

"It is comforting to know someone looks out for me." Fanny bit her lip and tried to look as though she regretted the remark. Impossible when her heart had grown wings and soared with hope. Until Mallory slid open a desk drawer and removed his pistols.

He tossed a coat and hat her way and shrugged into a frock coat. He grabbed her by the hand, and paused at the door. "Cry out, make any attempt to communicate, and I will shoot him dead."

He opened the door a crack. No guard standing watch. It seemed this outlaw post was rather understaffed this evening. Fanny wondered why. Had Mallory sent them all away? But why would he do such a thing? He took her by the hand and hauled her toward a set of spiral stairs carved into the rock of the cavern.

*   *   *

RAFE SPOTTED MOVING shapes at the end of the passage—two people, a man and a woman. Dear God, one of them must be Fanny. He thought his heart would pound out of his chest. "Scotland Yard! Stop right where you are." He climbed the stairs.

"Rafe!" His name was muffled. But it was she—it was Fanny.

He raised his gun. "Let her go."

The two figures were so close together in the dark, he couldn't chance a shot—not yet. The man yanked Fanny to his chest. One hand covered her mouth while the other placed the barrel of his pistol to her temple. "Oh . . ." The man grinned and shook his head sadly. "I think not, Detective."

Could this ghoulish creature be Mallory? If he took his gun off Fanny and fired, Rafe might have a chance at a very dangerous shot. But would he risk taking it? Rafe hesitated, then lowered his pistol.

Several pistol shots zinged by him from the passage below stairs. Rafe slipped down the steps and flattened himself into a shallow alcove. More bullets ricocheted off the rock wall next to his head. He swung out from cover and returned fire.

He'd left Finn in the middle of an attack of nerves, and now he was caught in the cross fire. Rafe rolled onto the ground and let fly a hail of bullets, taking the gunman down. Now he faced another, with pistol drawn, just feet away.

A gun fired—and then another shot. The bloke standing over him dropped his weapon and fell to his knees. Finn stood behind the fallen man, his pistol smoking. "Sorry I'm late. I do hope I haven't missed out on all the fun?"

Rafe rolled onto his feet and started up the stairs. "Mallory's got Fanny." The curved rock stairway led them directly out of the cavern into an anteroom. A very small iron door opened onto an alley. The clever exit was hidden by the stone footbridge overhead.

"Hold it." Finn picked up the broken end of a crate and jammed the opening. Rafe checked the alley. In one direction, the masts and rigging of ships docked in the basin could be seen a hundred feet away. At the opposite end of the alley, a carriage turned the corner at a fast clip.

"That's got to be them." He and Finn sprinted down the row, leaping over cartloads of tea chests and cotton bales. They made the corner only to lose the carriage in the crush of traffic on Commercial Road.

"Bugger me." Rafe walked in circles, panting. "Bugger me. Bugger me."

Finn hunched over, hands on his knees. "I'd watch myself—there are sailors about who wouldn't mind."

"Bloody bugger."

"Better. Less inviting." Finn straightened to have a look around. "Not that I look forward to closed-in dark spaces, but shall we return to the cavern? A couple of Mallory's men may still be alive." Finn shot him a wink. "And they'll talk—believe me."

Rafe nodded. "What say we find a patrolman about and have him blow his whistle? Get some blue coats to comb the place and— Christ."

Finn raised both brows. "Now what?

"We left Archie down there, defenseless."

∽ Chapter Thirty-four

Fanny pressed both hands to Mallory's chest and pushed. "Get off me."

He tried for another kiss. A swath of light from a passing streetlamp flashed inside the cabin. He was amused. He appeared to love every second of resistance she offered. The fast-moving carriage turned a corner and rocked them apart. "Lost your intrepid Yard man," he sneered.

Inching into a corner of the plush upholstered seat she ignored his remark and fastened the buttons on her coat. "Where are you taking me?"

He glanced outside. "Cavendish Square."

"Of course, the Royal Polytechnic Institution." Fanny chewed on her lower lip. "Scotland Yard knows full well you plan some sort of horrid mischief for the opening of the Exposition. I'd give it up if I were you—try for another day. Unless, of course, you can't resist the dramatics."

A cynical bark of laughter raked across his features,

which appeared ghostly pale and drained. Fanny blinked at the debilitated figure. "You are bad off, Mallory."

His head lolled with the rock and sway of the vehicle. "Indeed. I am not . . . well."

USING THE DEEP shadows of the cavern, Rafe signaled Finn to move forward by way of an adjacent alcove. Two of Mallory's guards walked ahead with Archie sandwiched in between, hands bound behind his back. Finn dropped into the nearby niche and nodded for Rafe to make his move.

He trotted up close, gun drawn. "Gentlemen."

Both men swung around to face him. "Detective Inspector Lewis, Scotland Yard. You are under arrest for an assortment of capital crimes. And I suspect more charges will be forthcoming. I will need you to turn over any weapons—"

Both guards raised their pistols.

"Tut-tut, now." Finn emerged from the shadows behind the men. "You really should listen to your betters."

Before the men could pivot, take aim, and fire, Finn took down a man from behind, and Rafe struck the other on the chin. A few well-placed blows and they had both culprits groaning on the ground.

Greatly relieved, Archie grinned. "You boys arrived in the nick of time."

While Finn untied Archie, Rafe confiscated weapons and searched pockets. Rafe looked about the passage. "Anyone see the jailor's keys?"

"I believe ye'll find the keys in there—across the way."

Rafe jerked up and ran toward the familiar voice. He passed a number of small chambers that looked very much like jail cells. Only one room remained closed. "Professor Minnow? Good God, you are a sight." Through a small pass-through opening in the door, Rafe could plainly see the man had been bashed about the head. "Are you all right?"

"I'd be feelin' a mite better with a pint in hand and a few chops in my belly," the big Scot groused.

Rafe nodded. "Hold on." He found a ring of keys and let the big man out of his cage. Minnow gave him a hug that lifted him off the ground and nearly crushed the air from his lungs. "Good to see you, Detective—is Fanny with ye?"

Rafe shook his head. "Everyone but Fanny, I'm afraid."

Minnow nodded. "Thought as much—dear girl. Ah, you'd be proud of her, Detective. And the wee laddie?"

"Delivered right to Scotland Yard's door."

" 'Twas Fanny's doin'. She made a bargain with Mallory. She's been playin' him for over a day now, but I dinna know how long she'll last."

The very idea of Fanny in that monster's hands was unthinkable. Until this moment he'd pushed the most fearful imaginings into the darkest corner of his mind. They were the kinds of thoughts a man could not let enter his head. They clouded his reasoning and interfered with his single-minded aim, which was to find her alive and take her home to Lochree.

With a nod toward Finn, Minnow raised the wild

hairs of both brows. "Well, now, if it isn't Mr. Curzon!"

Rafe shook his head. "Mr. Curzon actually turns out to be a Mr. Gunn."

"Long story." Finn passed a handgun over to Minnow. Archie and the professor helped them drag Mallory's guards into cells and lock them up. Clapping his hands, Rafe introduced Archie. "Professor Minnow, meet Archibald Bruce. Archie heads up the crime laboratory for the Yard."

The young director pumped Minnow's hand. "You're the inventor of the submersible! My word, you have a brilliant machine there, Professor Minnow."

"The *Horatio*'s here in London?"

Rafe grinned. "How do you think we got here? Might have taken us days to find the land route—our best bet was to find the old pirate's cove by taking the sub under the St. Katharine Docks."

Minnow stared and Rafe grinned. The large man's eyebrows never left their upward position. "The submariner's here? In this cavern?"

"Come along." Rafe escorted the professor down the passageway to the rickety stairs above the grotto. "Thar be your pride and joy, Captain Minnow." The slender shape of the *Horatio* lay placidly in the black, glistening water of the cove.

Rafe winked at the professor. "Why don't you and Archie take the sub out of here? Finn and I are going to make our way over to the Hall of Machines in the Polytechnic." Out of habit Rafe reached for his watch, but remembered that it was at the bottom of the Thames, south of Henley. "Blast. Anyone have the time?"

Finn retrieved his timepiece. "Not quite four. We have a few hours until the opening."

Minnow started down the stairs and turned back. "I believe Greyville-Nugent's entry is the first one up for demonstration. As ye well suspected days ago, Mallory's blokes have got a scheme up their sleeve. We've not much time, lads—do ye have something in mind?"

Rafe grinned with relief as he took stock of the men around him. This big-hearted bull of a Scot, Finn, and Archie; Melville, Zeno, Flynn—even the Yard dog. Every last one of them would lay down his life to help rescue Fanny and arrest Mallory. Rafe realized in that moment that *he* was the one with the formidable army on his side.

∽ Chapter Thirty-five

"What's happening to him?" Fanny stepped away from the tortured body thrashing about on the floor of the hall. Just seconds ago, Mallory was fine, signaling orders quietly to his men—calm, controlled, and fully in charge. Then quite suddenly his eyes rolled back in his head and he fell to the ground.

"Step aside, miss." The dwarf removed a kind of stubby wooden spoon from his pocket and thrust it between Mallory's clenched teeth. Foam drooled from the side of his mouth. "Havin' one of his fits." The small man cradled his master's head in his lap.

She nodded numbly. Her gaze ran up a wall to the barrel-vaulted ceiling and down again. The board of this year's competition had leased the Polytechnic's great hall and its fantastical Hall of Machines, which hailed back to the birth of the steam age. The original exhibit had been painstakingly re-created, including its most famous demonstration of all, the underwater diving bell.

Mallory's men had overpowered the guards inside

the exhibit. It was as though his men knew every niche and corner of the hall. Fanny bit her lip. Well planned, and well executed? She certainly hoped not. Earlier this evening, she had watched them bind and gag two kidnapped inventors. They packed the men inside the diving bell, replete with curtained windows, skylights, and ornate brass fittings. A crane at one end of the tank sputtered to life and lifted the bell high into the air. The elegant copper-clad underwater observation bell resembled a giant Christmas tree ornament hung above a great tank of water.

Fanny had never seen the apparatus, but she remembered Father talking about it. As a young man he had participated in the demonstration. Three volunteers would be placed inside the bell. The long, clawlike armature of the steam-driven crane would pick up and lower the diving bell into the water.

Fanny noted the walkway around the glass tank enclosure so visitors might watch passengers converse with one another and wave to onlookers. Absently, she backed up against a display platform and sat down. There were two men inside a diving bell that held three passengers. She could only assume everyone was accounted for but her. She tried not to speculate on Mallory's plans for the prestigious contest. A crane failure and they would all slowly suffocate from lack of oxygen. Or perhaps they planned a deliberate leak and drowning?

Still, if either of those scenarios were the case, why wasn't she bound and gagged and up there with the others? Fanny returned to the man writhing on the floor.

His thrashing about had eased, though he still appeared dazed and incoherent.

Several of his men approached her. All business, they were, except for the man in front, whose eyes leered. "We've come for the lady. We'll be wanting to bind her—" The gruff man's lip curled to reveal uneven teeth blackened by tobacco. Fanny shrank from the men looming over her.

"Leave her be." Mallory was up on his elbows. "I have other plans for Miss Greyville-Nugent."

The small but sturdy minion helped Mallory to his feet. "Tell the men to finish up quickly and make themselves scarce. They know their posts." He dusted off his coat. "Everything will commence on my signal, shortly after the Exposition opens."

Mallory escorted her upstairs, past a balcony viewing area, and through the Polytechnic's gymnasium. Inside a small room at the end of the exercise room, he sat in a chair behind a simple desk and placed his head in his hands. "I have discovered that your father's machine will be rolled into the hall after the opening remarks." He rubbed his temples. "I will ask you one last time, tell me the nature of the Greyville-Nugent entry."

Fanny's brows crashed together. "I swear I do not know it. Father wished to keep his latest invention a secret, a surprise of sorts, he said, until the unveiling." Fanny turned away from the infuriating man, who was most certainly mad. "If it's not a new thresher, you'll just have to think of some other way to grind me up."

Mallory exhaled impatiently. It was all too clear he was

uncomfortable with the extemporaneous quality of her demise. "Are you always like this? Provoking and infuriating?"

Now it was her turn to stare. "Are you always angry and vengeful?"

He rolled his head back onto his shoulders. "I'm tired." The sputtering gas lamp overhead threw the room into flickering light and shadow. "It is often quite impossible to think beyond the pain."

She was now quite sure Mallory's head injury had affected his brain irreparably. His eyes flashed red momentarily, then resolved into darker pools of despair. "Ah, Fanny. Pretend for the next few hours that I am not a monster."

RAFE TOOK THE broad steps of the Royal Polytechnic Institution two at a time. He was to enter the concourse from Regent Street while Finn and the professor came in through the square. Melville and a number of plainclothes operatives were already inside. At the entrance, banners trumpeted London's *Tenth Annual Industrial Exposition*. He followed the concourse past several guards and entered the Hall of Machines.

He was late. He and Finn had made the mistake of stopping by the safe house on Cavendish Square, across from the Polytechnic. They'd been delayed an interminable amount of time, interviewing distraught industrialists and inventor types. Two scions of industry had broken rank and left the premises last night—off to a pub or brothel—and the men had never returned.

There were three sapphire pins left to award. Two inventors and one industrialist suffragette was all Mallory needed. At the break of dawn, Rafe sent officers into the exposition hall. They had returned to report nothing out of order. Rafe rushed past stalls selling mementos and scientific toys and headed inside. Contest demonstrations were scheduled to begin on the hour.

The cavernous hall was already filled with spectators, there to behold all the miracles of the modern industrialized world. For once, Scotland Yard had managed to keep the case against Mallory out of the press, but it was a dangerous gambit. If any onlookers were seriously injured, they would pay a price for not informing the public.

He was greeted by a display of machinery in full, topsy-turvy spin. Mechanical arms pumped, pneumatic devices puffed up and down, and all of them whirred into action at once. Visitors ventured cautiously through the hall to stare in fascination as these great engines revolved and hissed and quivered.

He passed a theater where something called a physioscope magnified the human face to a gigantic size. A water tank made of glass panels stood at the end of the hall with a surface area, according to signage, of over seven hundred feet. Rafe squinted at the diving bell dangling above the pond. Pivoting slowly, he inspected the upper gallery, crowded with visitors waiting for the first demonstration.

Rafe spotted Finn moving through the crowd and recognized several men from the Yard stationed about.

Melville had planted himself halfway up a staircase that led to the upper viewing area.

The speaker, one of several gentleman seated on the dais, stood up and welcomed the public. "Ladies and gentlemen, we are gratified to be here today in the Royal Polytechnic's Hall of Machines. On July 18, 1837—fifty years ago this day—the Institute opened its doors to promote . . ."

Rafe wove a path over to the stairs and came up beside Melville. Neither man acknowledged the other, but continued to scan the hall. "Quite the spectacle," Rafe said.

Melville grunted. "Showmanship appears to be an integral part of the business of invention."

The speaker droned on: ". . . dedicated to the elevation of whatever may be found to be superior, in the scientific arts and manufactures, and to the display of these models of invention and other works of interest for public exhibition."

Rafe returned to the refurbished diving bell dangling from the crane arm. "I missed the diving bell as a lad—did it always begin in the rafters? I suppose passengers must have entered from the balcony above?"

Melville scratched an eyebrow. "If memory serves, the demonstration began lower, on a stage, where the volunteers would climb aboard . . ." Melville's eyes darted about nervously. "Good God, Rafe—you don't suppose—?"

"Hold on." Rafe nodded to the speaker.

". . . And without further delay, I have the honor to

present our first entry—just arrived this moment. Gentlemen, roll on the device."

A flat drayage cart was pushed onstage. The speaker adjusted his spectacles and read from a card. "From Greyville-Nugent Enterprises. Step back, gentlemen, this one is for the ladies." The brawny boys beside the cart rolled back a curtain. "Transform the drudgery of washday with an electric-powered washing machine."

A wave of titters and applause, oohs and ahs emanated from the crowd as men and women alike pushed forward to watch a demonstration. An attractive young lady stood beside the automatic laundering device and began to drop clothes into a large, rotating drum. "Saves time, labor, nerves, clothes, and strength."

A chortle of laughter drifted down from a viewing gallery above the dais. It started out as a giggle and ended in quite a loud belly laugh. "That's Fanny. I'd know her laugh anywhere." Rafe searched the crush of gawkers up on the balcony. And it was so like her—in the throes of an abduction and having a damn chuckle over her father's surprise household invention.

"Upstairs, Rafe—I shall collect Mr. Gunn and go after that crane operator." Melville stepped down and Rafe climbed to the upper tier. He needed to get to the opposite side of the balcony. The hall was long and narrow with a balcony that ran down each side and curved around the short ends. Rafe fought his way around the end loop and caught sight of both Fanny and Mallory.

She spied him. "Rafe!"

"Fanny!" Rafe shouted over the hubbub of the

onlookers. Mallory froze and looked directly at him. Rafe could not brandish a pistol in this assemblage lest he start a panic.

"Scotland Yard, clear the way please." He shoved a few disgruntled visitors aside and caught a break in the crowd. The clawlike arm held the diving bell suspended close to the balcony. Rafe leaped just as Mallory pushed Fanny onto the top of the bell—she grabbed hold of one of the crane's claws and Mallory jumped on beside her.

"Be careful, he has a gun!" Fanny called out to Rafe.

The crane arm began to move, carrying the giant diving bell and its two passsngers away from the balcony. "Hang on, Fanny." Something must be going on below— likely a struggle between Scotland Yard and Mallory's men operating the crane machinery.

Like a child's swing in a storm, the orb-shaped bell began to swing crazily from side to side. Rafe vaulted over glass viewing panels and onto the brass railing that wound around the hall. He felt like a Gypsy on a tightrope. Shutting out cries from the nervous assemblage, he walked the ledge, with one eye on the bell as it swung back toward him.

Mallory fired and hit an innocent bystander. Cries and screams erupted as the hysterical mob stepped over one another to get to the stairs. A few panicked onlookers leaped over the railings and into the tank of water below.

Rafe withdrew his gun, bracing himself as best he could on the glass panels and brass railing. He aimed, then lowered his weapon. Mallory had moved behind

Fanny, who squirmed and wriggled and—God love her—grabbed hold of the gun.

At that moment, the bell could not have been closer—Rafe leaped into the air and landed feetfirst on the curved edge of the diving bell. The entire mechanism groaned and shuddered. One of the claws snapped loose. Forced to let go of his gun, Rafe grasped onto a remaining arm to keep from falling.

The capsule swooshed away from the balcony, dangling from two mechanical prongs. Revolver in hand, Mallory prodded Fanny forward—to kill her or the both of them.

Rafe glared. "Pistols, Mallory? I was thinking something more—man to man?"

Mallory tipped his head to one side. The man's bloodshot eyes—the grin—were more than slightly deranged. "Spoken like a man without a gun, Detective."

A sudden shudder from the bell sent Rafe careening into Mallory. He reached for the hand with the weapon—and got hold of the revolver. "Let her go."

The crane rocked the bell with such force Fanny lost her balance. Mallory grinned. "As you wish, Detective." The monster let loose and Fanny plunged off the side. Rafe lunged to catch her but she slipped through his fingers.

Oddly enough, it was Mallory who caught her by the collar of her coat.

Whoosh! The bell swung well past the water tank. If he let go now, she would surely be killed or gravely injured. Rafe held his breath and crept closer. The ghoulish man with the jagged scar continued to hold on—barely—with one hand. With the other, he aimed his revolver at Rafe.

Rafe returned the cruel stab of Mallory's gaze with one of his own.

"Let me help—I'll give you a clear shot at me afterward."

Mallory's facial features contorted and his eyes rolled upward. The hand that held the revolver trembled. Rafe took a chance. He struck the weapon from Mallory's hand, and the gun flew into the air. Curious onlookers scattered as the pistol hit the floor below. Somewhere on the ground, Rafe knew there were Yard men waiting for a shot, and he meant to give it to them.

Rafe crawled around a trembling Mallory and reached for Fanny's arm. "Fanny, grab hold of me." She tried again and again, but each time her fingers didn't quite reach. Rafe prayed her coat would remain buttoned.

Mallory grunted, fighting unconsciousness. A stream of drool ran from one side of his mouth. The man's eyes were glazed, unfocused. Rafe inched farther down the side of the bell as the Utopian Society leader released a wretched cry.

Rafe caught hold of the same collar fisted in Mallory's hand. "I've got her."

Mallory's shaky grasp opened.

Inch by inch, Rafe lifted Fanny upward. "Rafe, save yourself," Fanny cried. "Harry needs a father."

Rafe braced a leg against one of the armatures and hauled Fanny up onto the bell. He pulled her into his arms. "Sorry, darling. He also needs a mother."

A terribly weakened Mallory struggled to his feet and pulled another gun from his coat pocket.

Rafe shoved Fanny behind him and shielded her with his body. "Take your shot."

Bleary, red-rimmed eyes blinked and tried to focus. The pop of a gunshot came from below, grazing the scarred man and twisting him sideways. A second bullet hit Mallory in the shoulder and pitched him forward. For a split second the man teetered on the edge of the diving bell, arms waving in the air. Rafe reached out, but it was too late. Mallory plunged over the side.

Rafe and Fanny both peered over the edge. The splayed body made a great splash in the tank and drifted below, leaving a trail of red.

The diving bell continued its thunderous swing from side to side—a sad, lopsided pendulum. Rafe eased Fanny back into his arms, and she held on tightly. She smiled at him. For once, they were both at a loss for words.

First the professor, then Finn called up to them. Rafe perused the activity below. "Have a heart and lower this thing, will you?"

He nudged her gently. "What of the others, Fanny— the two inventors?"

"Tied up inside the bell."

Rafe knew bell was airtight. "For how long?"

Fanny whispered her answer. "Hours."

It was almost certain the men were dead, yet Rafe still

leaned out from under one of the giant metal claws. "Get a move on down there!"

A belch of steam answered Rafe as the hefty machine chugged into service and lowered the dangling underwater contraption. They reached the tank surface and made a great whoosh of a wave as the bell glided to a stop on the surface of the pool.

Mallory shot up from the depths of the tank, wild-eyed and sputtering. In seconds, the Utopian Society leader was surrounded by Yard men with weapons drawn.

∾ Chapter Thirty-six

Rafe eyeballed Harland and shoved a good-sized toy boat under his manservant's arm. He opened the front door of his flat and poked his head out. "Excellent. Lovely weather—even an afternoon breeze. You and Harry shall do a bit of pond sailing and enjoy a shaved ice."

Harland gaped as though Rafe had asked him to take his son on a trip to the moon.

"Harry will enjoy sailing his boat about while I enjoy a briefing with our guest, Miss Greyville-Nugent." Rafe explained patiently. "Fanny and I will find a bench nearby and wave to you both on occasion."

Rafe smiled at Harry. "There, you won't be any trouble, will you?" He turned to stare rather pointedly at his man. "He's a four-and-a-half-year-old boy—what can go wrong?"

Wary eyes darted to Harry's eager face and back again. "Indeed, sir." After a brief pause, Harland reached down and took hold of a little hand.

"Lovely," Rafe replied, only a little smugly. "Be right with you both."

He raced down the hallway and knocked on the guest room door. "You decent?"

"Come in, Rafe." Fanny sat at a small writing desk turned into a vanity. "Though I suspect you'd just as soon have me not so decent?" She fastened a pin in her hair and smiled at him in the reflection of her looking glass.

Rafe stepped around the giant trunk of her things, which occupied nearly half the bedchamber. Fanny wore something frothy in a peachy rose color. The color of her blush. "I'm saving that astonishing indecent side of you for later." He kissed the nape of her neck. "About ready?"

Fanny turned around on her bench. The afternoon light haloed the mass of rich brown curls she had just piled neatly on her head. "Thank you for giving me time, yesterday, to recover." They had both slept and ate—and ate and slept—the day long. In the evening she had borrowed his copy of *Allan Quatermain*, retired early, and snoozed until late this morning.

"And you recovered beautifully." Rafe smiled. "An afternoon of fresh air and exercise shall also help restore you."

Their walk through Kensington Gardens was both amusing and invigorating. Harry wore a new outfit purchased at Harrods just that morning. "He was quite adamant about those pants with the silver buttons and the sailor jacket."

Fanny smiled. "Very smart, Harry. A gentleman should always dress for the occasion."

Rafe procured an empty bench near the sailing pond and settled Fanny beside him. "Detective Kennedy sent over a few questions. He wants a full briefing right away—if you're up to it. It seems the Yard is keen to know something about your captor."

"Mallory?" Her smile was sweet, yet strained. "Such an odd character, Rafe. I must admit he got under my skin somehow."

He steeled himself for the toughest question. He could not help but ask it first—get it out of the way. He swallowed. "Did he force himself upon you?"

"He did not." She moistened her lips. The familiar nervous habit of hers was oddly reassuring. "But . . . I would have done whatever it took to have Harry safely returned to you." She met his gaze shyly. "Would you have forgiven me?"

His heart beat wildly inside his chest—or were those rapid thumps hers? That was the way it had always been with them—as if they were one person at times. Her eyes remained locked on his. Rafe leaned close. "Fanny, you saved the life of my child. I would have forgiven you anything."

She looked unconvinced. He sighed. "It's plain that on some level, you and Mallory affected one another. His last act as a free man was to save you—he held on long enough for me to grab hold of you." Rafe hesitated. "It's just that—"

"Don't look at me that way, Rafe."

"I pray God you weren't stirred in some way by this monster. Villainous men are nearly always charismatic and attract a bevy of beautiful women, I've seen it on several of my cases—"

"Sh-h-h." Fanny placed a finger across his mouth. "And what about you? You were as brave as you were intrepid. I will say you had Mallory on the run. You should have seen the look on his face when they revealed the motor-driven washing machine in the hall. Father's very hush-hush surprise for me." Fanny chuckled softly. "I believe it was in that moment Mallory realized he was beaten. He might have stuck me in the bell—have done with me—but he waited, hoping for a grislier show."

How brave and lovely she was. Rafe could hardly take his eyes off her. "Much more likely you got to him."

"Do you know what will become of him, Rafe?"

"I believe they've taken Mallory to Bethlem Royal Hospital."

"Dear God, Bedlam? Poor, tragic soul. Though I suppose it's the right place for him."

"He'll stand trial if he's lucid." Rafe studied her. "Strange you should feel such compassion for the man who took your father's life."

Fanny outlined, briefly, some of Mallory's background. The tragic deaths of his family in the munitions factory, his wounding and discharge from the military.

Rafe stared at her. "And you believe him?"

"He is ill—of unsound mind—an injury to his brain." Fanny sighed. "This grand Industrial Era is not without its share of tragedy and sacrifice. I suspect he was telling the truth. The men under him likely had equally miserable stories, which gave them cause to enlist in his private army."

"The Utopian Society now resides in jail or has scattered to the four winds—disbanded for the time being." Rafe shook his head. "Hard to know if we got them all."

"I cannot tell you that Mallory's history and condition, pitiable as they were, had no effect on me." She leaned close, her mouth inches from his. "But I can tell you this." She brushed a kiss softly over his lips, enough to cause a pleasant tremor through his body. "I have loved you my entire life."

"I never knew you could be so publicly affectionate. Most stimulating of you, Fanny." He kissed the tip of her nose. "So, you have forgiven me?"

She returned his caress. "I forgave you days ago."

Rafe scooted to the shadowy side of the bench and pulled her with him. "There now—just so we don't get arrested for indecent . . . nuzzling."

Her low giggle built quickly into a musical laugh.

He smoothed a bit of loose curl on her temple. "When exactly was that—when you forgave me? I'm rather keen on knowing. Was it the first abduction? A splendid rescue as I recall—I pulled you out of the capsized furniture van."

"Yes, you were very gallant, I must admit." Fanny straightened his cravat. "But it wasn't that, I'm afraid."

"What about our escape from the mine?"

Her eyes rolled skyward. "Harrowing. But no."

"Our swim ashore, when the submersible sank?"

She shivered at the memory. "Ugh!"

Rafe exaggerated a frown. "I've exhausted nearly all of my best moments. I shall have to give up."

"O-o-o-h, and you were so close!" Fanny grinned. " 'Twas the night Harry had his nightmare. We said good night and you entered the nursery. But I did not return to my room. I eavesdropped outside the door." A rosy pink blush colored her cheeks—so achingly lovely Rafe swallowed.

"I believe it was when you armed yourselves with a cricket bat against the Nettlebed Troll. I knew then and there I wanted my children to have a troll slayer for a father. That's all there was to it." She smiled the Fanny smile, part grin and part—heaven.

"Mm-mm." He nuzzled the lovely blush on her cheek. "Had I known my strategy for night terrors would have such effect, I might have invited you down for a bit of goblin hunting and worm collecting years ago. You sure you weren't swayed by the lovemaking afterward?"

"Possibly." Fanny gazed out over the pond and waved to Harry. His sailboat was faring rather well in a race against another young man's toy vessel. The older boy had a long pole and began to prod his boat ahead of Harry's. "Rafe, that boy is cheating Harry." Fanny moved to stand.

Rafe held her arm.

Harland ripped the stick from the older lad's hand, broke it over his knee, and returned two shorter sticks to the scowling boy. Rafe grinned. "I believe Harland and Harry will get on just fine."

Fanny settled into the crook of his shoulder and toyed

with the buttons of his waistcoat. Her delicate fondling created a pleasant swell of arousal. Rafe was already anticipating an evening together behind closed doors. The flat closed up, Harry off in the land of Nod, Fanny in nothing but silky peach-colored underthings.

Even though their return to Edinburgh was inevitable, he hoped to have her to himself a few more days before traveling north. Fanny had a fierce affection for the hills and dales of Lochree, and no doubt friends and family beckoned. But he'd lived without her for so many years, he begrudged the notion of sharing her right now.

Rafe sat up, jostling her a bit. "I almost forgot." He reached in his coat pocket and retrieved a paper. "A wire for you forwarded from Scotland Yard."

Snugged up against him, Fanny opened the missive. "It's from Claire. She's returned to Edinburgh." Fanny quickly perused the rest of the message. "Seems the horrid news about Father finally reached her in Brussels."

"Intrepid of your cousin to contact you via Scotland Yard." Rafe did not bother to hide his sarcasm.

"I asked her to." Fanny nudged him with her elbow. "When we were on the run you spoke of a letter Claire had written from Italy. The one that gave you quite a knock, years ago."

"Yes, Fanny, I remember it well."

"There was something peculiar in the telling—it wasn't right—not from what I recall. Particularly the flirtation with the Duke of Grafton." Fanny sat up.

"I fully recall your chide on the road." Rafe grinned. "Wasn't he fourteen at the time?"

Fanny's brows merged as she drew her bottom lip under her teeth. "Our scheme seems awfully childish now, but it was never meant to be cruel. In the letter you described, things were stated much more seriously, including an implied announcement of promise."

He slumped back on the bench and shook his head. "I should have sold my father's watch and jumped on the fastest steamship to Italy, at the very least written an anguished letter pleading with you to break it off and declaring my love."

"I've a confession." Fanny angled toward him. "I borrowed a piece of your stationery in Nettlebed, to write Claire. And I must say you appear quite capable of writing love letters by the volume." A bit of pink flushed her cheeks.

"You were in my study?"

The guilty, sheepish grin gave her away.

"I see." His mouth twitched and his heart skittered about in his chest. "I don't suppose you had time to read them all?"

"Just one, from the top of one of the stacks." Fanny looked at him in a way that filled him with joy. "It was lovely, Rafe."

Rafe studied every nuance of her expression. "I'm so sorry, Fanny, for many things. Most of all I'm sorry for all the years we lost together."

Love poured from her eyes. Not the passionate attraction they both felt for each other but a love of deep affection. Fanny understood him better than any other human being on earth, just as he knew her brave heart and the kindness in her soul. Knowledge they had both lost for a time, but never again.

She breathed a sigh of relief and lifted her chin. "I believe the very best remedy, in a case like ours, is to get about the business of loving each other."

Rafe swept an arm around Fanny and tugged her close. "I look forward to a good amount of catching up."

"A few answers, as well." She grinned. "I mean to get to the bottom of this business with Claire, the moment we return to Edinburgh."

"And I shall interrogate Nigel separately. I've always suspected him of—fishy dealings." Rafe's eyes darted off into the near distance. "We shall see if their stories add up."

"The blame would appear to fall on one or the other." Fanny's harrumph sounded more like an impatient growl. "I'm surprised you haven't punched Nigel in the nose. It's something you are rather good at."

His laugh brushed the wispy hairs of her temple. "First off, as you may have noticed, I get enough violence in my life on a daily basis. Secondly, if it ever came to blows with that pathetic excuse for a man, the carnage would be brutal." Rafe brushed soft kisses over her cheek and paused close to her lips. "Thirdly—and I've saved the best for last."

Fanny tilted her head and parted her lips.

"He didn't get you." In the deep shade of the poplar trees, Rafe kissed her well and good.

*　　*　　*

FANNY PULLED UP the covers and tucked the sleeping child into bed. "Harry's had quite a long day. Shopping at Harrods, a long walk through Hyde Park, and a bit of pond sailing." She glanced at the tall, handsome figure in the door quietly regarding the scene in his bedchamber.

Rafe slipped off his cravat and collar. His shirt and waistcoat were already unbuttoned. A lovely, intimate energy moved between them. A glimpse, perhaps, into their future? Children to bed. Off to the privacy of their bedchamber. Everything about the picture was right—and sensual.

Relaxed against the door molding, one knee slightly bent, Rafe radiated masculine potency. "And how are you, my darling? Not too tired, I hope."

"What do you have in mind?" She rounded the poster bed and drew near. "A rousing game of Blind Man's Bluff?" Playfully she slipped a finger into his shirt opening.

"Did you say arousing?" He slipped an arm around her and pulled her close. Her body tingled all over—the erotic kind of shivers that caused her to have the most sensuous notions. Naughty, tantalizing thoughts ran through her mind, awakening sensitive female parts.

Her gaze lowered to his strong, firm mouth. "Kiss me," she said softly.

Rafe placed her arms around his neck. "It would be my pleasure." He planted his mouth on hers and kissed her with a tender passion that escalated into the most blissful assault on her mouth. Equally ravenous, she slipped her fingers into thick waves of chestnut hair and pulled him closer. She surrendered to every swirl of his tongue, every honeyed caress. Their tongues merged, slid, stroked a mating dance that left her wobbly-legged, with a hot need burning in her belly.

She opened his shirt to gain wider access to the warmth and strength of his powerful body. Her fingers traced rings around shades of purple, green, and yellow. A color for every day of their adventure. The hard muscles of his torso contracted from her touch. "Look at those bruises. Every color of the rainbow."

His emerald gaze sparkled. "I wonder, might this be a version of Thus Says Captain Savage? In which case I will have to insist you abide by article three of the First Geneva Convention." His whispered words brushed her cheek. "With regards to the aid and rehabilitation of the injured soldier, particular attention must be paid to the extremities . . ."

Fanny smothered a laugh and twirled a finger around his shirt button. "Yes, well, this variety of parlor game is called Lieutenant Cutthroat Takes Charge, and you are now under my command."

He kissed her temple. "Then you must order a vigorous skirmish in your bed."

Fanny slanted a sly look and took him by the hand—down the hallway and straight into her room. She tore off his shirt, pushed him onto the counterpane, and ravaged his chest. His smooth skin smelled of soap and her favorite scent of all—his own. The man brought out the wanton hussy in her. She licked his nipples and toyed with chest hair, and he answered with the deepest groan. The marvelous sound of a man lost in pleasure.

He untied his drawers and pressed back into the bed pillows, folding his arms behind his head. The muscles of his upper arms bulged in the most breathtaking way. Her gaze trailed over a hard chest that narrowed down to a flat abdomen and long masculine thighs. Adonis in recline, waving his angry sword.

Emerald eyes burned dark and hungry as he watched her boldly peruse his body. "I believe you like what you see."

She hardly recognized the throaty voice that answered him. "Very much." The singular importance of his gently spoken words, the intimacy of their discussion, caused her to catch her breath.

"Fanny . . . turn around, before I shred this pretty frock, and matching underthings, with my bare hands."

She was quite sure she blinked like an owl. A tingle ran from her breast tips to womb as he began to unbutton and unhook.

But oh, how slow he was!

"Whoever invented the hook and eye should be shot," he grumbled. She pushed his hands away and quickly shed every stitch. Everything but her stockings.

He kissed a bare shoulder and laid her back onto the cool sheets. "Allow me to roll them off." In the dim light of her room, she could just make out his smile. She trembled at the very thought of his touch. He rolled one stocking down, then the other. His fingers played down the sensitive inner flesh of each leg, but he did not enter her moist parts. He toyed close to the center of her pleasure, brushing lightly through curls. She thrust her hips upward and groaned.

Propped on her elbows, she met his dark, lusty gaze and brazenly opened to him.

"My little wanton, what a lovely shade of pink you are." He pressed gently into her moist petals—his soft strokes deepened their exploration, first one finger, then two. Her lower anatomy flooded with slippery invitation as his hand coaxed a slow build of arousal. She cried out from his pleasuring.

His raw, feral gaze moved to her bosom. "Touch yourself."

She took a deep breath and arched. Cupping her breasts, she rolled her nipples into hard points and thrust her hips up to greet his fingers as they swirled and danced over the center of her pleasure.

Seeing her breathless and flushed with color stimulated his own desire. He laid her back onto the bed pillows and cupped her buttocks. She elevated her hips and beckoned him to mount and breed with her. But he held back, fingers pressing deep. "You are so warm inside." Using two fingers, he pumped lightly, adding his thumb to the engorged nub, the focus of her mounting pleasure.

Rafe rolled onto his side and continued to slide his fingers across the spot that made her talk to him in breathless moans: "More. Oh yes. Don't stop!"

He grinned. "She also likes to be kissed."

"Oh, she prefers your lips, your . . ." He caressed the

hollow of her stomach and she shuddered with anticipation. Pressing his mouth against her inner thigh, he moved in.

"My beautiful goddess, salty and sweet." His tongue circled and laved languidly as he acquainted himself with every nerve ending. Her body writhed and arched against him as he suckled the engorged nub, stroking with his tongue, until the tingling and heaviness of her pelvis became unbearable. Such wicked arousal, shocking and yet oh so . . . heavenly. Fanny let go and her release broke in waves of exquisite pleasure.

Her eyes fluttered open. "How is it you always seem to know"—she tilted her head—"when I am close to satisfaction?"

He crawled on top of her and kissed a few tiny beads of sweat off her nose. "I listen carefully to every ooh and ah."

Rafe settled back in the pillows and reveled in her exploration of his body. Her fingers moved gently over the healing knife wound and the bullet scratch across his upper arm. She toyed gently with bruises on his torso and worked her way lower. "I look forward to pleasuring my wounded warrior." Her hand moved to his prick and she stroked gently.

He groaned. And she answered him, in a rather shocking way. She moved between his legs and gave the head a few licks, before peeking up at him and biting her lip. Christ, he was already close to bursting.

Then she did something with her tongue that drove him wild. She licked up from the base and over the tip—

and she did this several more times—until all he wanted was to bury himself deep and ride her until he came to pleasure inside her warm, tight sheath. Ah, but first . . .

Reluctantly Rafe lifted her up. "I believe it's time for the French letter." He grinned. "Did you not tease me about wanting to put one on?" He grabbed his trousers and scrounged in the pockets. "Aha!" Rolling onto his back, he removed the latex rubber goods from the paper packet. Fisting his erection, he showed her how to cover the tip. "Roll it down . . . slowly."

Fanny sat back and examined her handiwork. "No, it doesn't seem right." She rolled the condom back up and tossed it away. "I can't see any reason for this—I want nothing between us, Rafe. Just you and me."

He answered her with raised brow and a rather large smile. "Have it your way, Fan."

"Oh, that is good news." Fanny toyed with his chest hair. "As I'm a little sore, can we go slow?"

"Come here, you little minx, and straddle me. Then you control the penetration." His voice was harsh, breathless as she pressed down onto his cock. Rafe groaned as she slipped him into her moist, tight sheath. Fanny gyrated her hips—just as he'd shown her.

She rocked back and forth, rising to the point that his cock nearly left her, then pressed down again—deeper with every plunge. And there was something wonderfully erotic about her interest in his pleasure. She responded to his bestial groans by tossing her head back and answering with a moan. A beautiful naked nymph arched her back and rode him proudly with breasts swaying. He reached up and tweaked both nipples—just hard enough to make her hips buck and her body shudder.

Buried deep, Rafe answered her thrusts with a few long, slow strokes, and placed his thumb over her most sensitive area. "Yes, love?"

A flood of honeyed essence moistened her slippery sheath and he could not hold back any longer. With each thrust his arousal escalated until it was all about his pleasure . . . pure sensation . . . nothing but ecstasy . . . he plunged over the edge into heart-pounding, seed-exploding oblivion. "Dear God, Fanny." Dimly, he was aware she had reached a second climax with him.

She collapsed onto his chest and released a sigh of a woman well pleasured. Her skin glowed with color and glistened with perspiration. He tucked her into his arms, and held her until they both rested quietly. On the edge of sleep, Rafe whispered to her, "Let's skip the engagement this time and go straight to the vicar."

Chapter Thirty-seven

"Mother, may I present my son, Harrison Gabriel Lewis St. Aldwyn." Rafe kept his hand on the sturdy little shoulder beside him. "Harry, this is your grandmother, the Dowager Lady St. Aldwyn."

Harry made a deep, courtly bow, one that he and Rafe had practiced early this morning and was sure to please Mother.

The dowager smiled at Harry and raised her gaze to Rafe.

"And how was the travel north?"

Rafe marveled at how easy it was when one could speak directly to one's mother. "We arrived late last night, you were all abed. Harry and I saw Fanny to Lochree and then quietly tucked ourselves in here."

"Before I forget, Nigel Irvine is waiting in the vestibule—whatever for, I have no idea."

Rafe checked his new watch, a very extravagant gift from Fanny. "Prompt of him."

Mother tilted her chin and smiled. The first smile

he'd received in five years. "Why don't you run along, Rafe? I'll watch young Harry." His mother patted the seat beside her. "Shall we have some biscuits and tea?"

Rafe bit back a grimace. "He's a bit young for tea, Mother."

She never took her eyes off Harry as he climbed on the settee beside her. "What nonsense. One is never too young for a splash of tea in one's milk."

Rafe backed away. "I suppose . . . since you put it that way."

He found Nigel outside the great hall and ushered him into the trophy chamber. With its paneled walls lined with antlers and an ancient hearth at one end, Rafe found the room singularly primitive and cavelike. Fitting, under the circumstances.

"Thanks for making it up to Queensferry on such short notice."

"I look forward to seeing Fanny while I'm here. Terrible ordeal you two went through"—Nigel's gaze shifted—"by all reports."

"Your accusations didn't help the Edinburgh police."

"Now see here, how was I to know you didn't run off with her?"

"You won't be seeing her this afternoon, Nigel, because I'm going to marry Fanny this afternoon—if she'll have me." Rafe's smile was genuine, but strained.

Nigel ceased his inspection of mounted deer heads. "So it seems you've got the girl, Rafe. What could you possibly want with me?"

Rafe was nearly certain the man staggered a bit at the

news. "Some years ago, there were rumors. It seems the Irvines, in particular the Laird of Drum Castle, were in some financial difficulty, bordering on scandal." He sauntered closer. "Some sort of dodgy investment scheme, which your father went to a great deal of trouble to cover up. I wonder how much pressure might have been brought to bear on you to marry well."

The overbearing man edged up a thin smile. "The bane of some of our best of families, wouldn't you say, Rafe?"

"You and I have never really been close friends, have we, Nigel? Just those few months at university—at the end of the term, before graduation. I've had plenty of time, these last five years, to reconstruct that last spring together. A veritable obstacle course of bad luck, wot? Accusations of cheating, buried by academic work—off the team—and still, we did plenty of late-night drinking, did we not?"

A reddish flush of color rose from under Nigel's collar points. "We managed plenty of that."

Rafe pressed closer. "You orchestrated my introduction to Ceilia perfectly."

Throughout most of this recollection, Nigel had remained stoic, neither denying or acknowledging his speech. Now his eyes darted about, and he took a step back. "No one forced you to lie with her, Rafe."

Rafe nodded. "You're right, of course. And I paid for it, with all I hold dear in this world."

"What do you want me to say? Sorry, old chap? It was clear Fanny was infatuated, and I needed you out of the way. I cheated on McElroy's exam and steered the blame toward you. The letter was Claire's idea." Nigel exhaled loudly. "Does any of it really matter now, Rafe? You've clearly won in the end." The arrogant bastard donned his skimmer and tipped the brim. "You know as well as I— the rules of fair play do not apply in love and war."

"Nigel?" He turned back and Rafe struck him hard in the face. The large bloke landed flat on his back, blood dripping from a decidedly off-center nose. And there was a fluttering of eyelashes and a groan. Rafe leaned over the body. "Sorry, old chap. A little something I promised Fanny."

Rafe exited the trophy room and ran straight into Vertiline. "Have you seen Fanny?"

"She's down at the boathouse—looking for you, I suspect." Vertiline clasped his hands in hers. "Such a beautiful child, Raphael, and when will he get a mother?"

"As a matter of fact, I have the ring in my pocket. Cost me three years' savings."

"Oh dear, I do hope you managed at least a carat."

"I daresay if the lady agrees, she knows full well she is marrying a sometimes misguided, ne'er-do-well, second son of an earl."

Vertiline reached up and touched his cheek with her hand. "I think you've kept her waiting long enough, Raphael."

Summer was far from over; in fact, the balmy breeze encouraged Rafe to open his jacket and loosen his cravat. He took the shaded path and then cut across an expanse of lawn leading down to an inlet off the firth. A handsome new boathouse and a slip sat at the edge of the water.

Ambling along the grass, a familiar burly bearded chap headed uphill. "Detective Lewis! Ye never told me you were a St. Aldwyn. Yer great-grandfather fought alongside my great-grandfather Captain Minogue against old Boney himself."

"Good to see you, Professor." Rafe braced for the bear hug. "If you would excuse me—I'm on my way to meet Fanny, going to try and convince her to marry me." He walked away backward. "I understand you and she are discussing a business venture? You're staying on a few days—perhaps we can talk later?"

"Over a pint and dram." Minnow winked and backed uphill. "I believe she's waitin' for ye down by the water."

He found her walking beside the boathouse. "Hello, my darling."

Fanny whirled around to face him. "Harry needs a mother."

Taken aback, Rafe blinked. "Yes. I couldn't agree more. Apparently Harry feels the same way. He asked me over breakfast if I was going to marry you."

"Harry asked?"

"I told him I had made it rather difficult for us many years ago, but thought my chances were turning around on the matter." Rafe drew close, until there was little or no space between them. "Harry thought about that for quite some time, then dropped his spoon in his porridge. He does that when he's exasperated."

Fanny raised both brows. "And?"

"And he asked, 'Might she be swayed, possibly, if I asked her to marry you?'"

The loveliest twitch happened around the edges of her mouth. "How unfair of you to use a child to your advantage, even as hearsay."

"Shameless. But then, a man does what he must to win the love of his life." Rafe grinned. "And how is Cousin Claire?"

"I'm afraid her nose is a bit out of joint." Fanny rolled her eyes and rubbed a few reddened fingers. "And Nigel?"

"Writhing on the floor of the trophy room in a great deal of agony—I hope." Rafe reached out for her hand and kissed each swollen knuckle. "Might have to ice this one." He waggled her ring finger.

An impish smile lingered at the ends of her mouth. Fanny tilted her head up. "And why is that?"

"I took the liberty, directly after breakfast, of riding over to the vicarage. Turns out Mr. Shaw has a free afternoon."

Rafe pulled her into his arms. "Might you be willing to style yourself Francine Greyville-Nugent-Lewis, Lady St. Aldwyn?"

"My word, a triple-barreled surname and a title—well worth the wait." Fanny smiled, just before she kissed him.

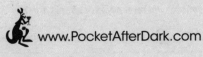

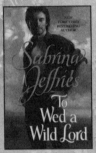